# SACRIFICE THE LIVING

—

MICHAEL ANDRE MCPHERSON

BOOK ONE OF *1000* SOULS
PECTOPAHBOOKS.COM

First Paperback Edition, January, 2014

(Originally released as *The Book of Bertrand*, 2011)
(Re-released as *Apocalypse Revolution*, 2012)

Copyright © 2011 by Michael Andre McPherson
All rights reserved.

Published by: Pectopah Productions Inc.
ISBN 13: 9780986864148
ISBN: 0986864145

All rights reserved. Without limiting the rights under copyright reserved above, no part of this publication may be reproduced, stored in or introduced into a retrieval system, or transmitted, in any form, or by any means (electronic, mechanical, photocopying, recording, or otherwise) without the prior written permission of both the copyright owner and the above publisher of this book.
This is a work of fiction. Names, characters, places, brands, media, and incidents are either the product of the author's imagination or are used fictitiously. The author acknowledges the trademarked status and trademark owners of various products referenced in this work of fiction, which have been used without permission. The publication/use of these trademarks is not authorized, associated with, or sponsored by the trademark owners.

# TABLE OF CONTENTS

For Paul and Bert,

The Dormant Heroes, waiting only to be called upon in times of need.

# PROLOGUE

It started out as the best month of his life, which is why he didn't notice the warning signs, the first tremors, of the collapse. College, as much fun as it had been, was winding down to the last exams of Bertrand's final year, and that was a relief. He and his housemates even threw a pulse-pumping party, rare for them because they were such a straight bunch: no drugs, not much booze, just four computer science geeks who usually spent Saturday night trading code, gaming, and competing to build the funniest app.

Better yet, Amy had gone on a second date and even gave him a long, deep kiss before she let herself into her apartment. The next Sunday afternoon she'd showed up unexpectedly at his house, and they played a wicked game of "Target Zombie." Azzim—Bertrand's best friend since they had shared a dorm room in first year—and his girlfriend, Cher, joined in, laughing and shouting as they made effective use of guns and grenade launchers. Bertrand could already picture life in a year: they'd all have good jobs, the student debt would be winding down, and maybe he and Amy would even be sharing an apartment. Of course, they'd have Azzim and Cher over to game together on Saturday nights. Best yet, no more studying. The future was just fantastic.

While Azzim's quirks complicated this vision, Bertrand tolerated them, understanding why his friend spouted dark conspiracy theories all the time and was suspicious of all government. When he was a little boy in Iran, Azzim lost his father in the failed Green Revolution, beaten to death in the street by the Basji. His mother had escaped the country with her children, but the trauma had left its marks on her son.

"Look at this," Azzim said one night, pointing to his laptop in the room they shared in their cramped townhouse.

Bertrand stepped around the pile of laundry he was gathering and looked over Azzim's shoulder at a fullscreen YouTube video. Several heavy artillery guns fired into a desert at night. Every few minutes an illumination round popped on the horizon, too far away to provide light near the camera. Men shouted and scrambled into 4x4 Toyota pickup trucks with machine guns mounted in the back, driving toward the battle.

"Where's this?" Bertrand wanted to show he cared, but there always seemed to be a revolution or a war somewhere in the world these days. What could he do?

"I'm pretty sure they're speaking Arabic," said Azzim. "But the poster didn't make any notes or anything, just stuck it up there." He clicked to another video. "This one says it's from Novosibirsk in Siberia."

A tank belched fumes as it rolled down a narrow street at night, bombed-out buildings lining either side, the camera's low-light capability producing only a grainy image. The tank came to an abrupt stop and its turret jerked to the right, as if in surprise, firing a dazzling round into a nearby building. As the muzzle flash faded, people on foot swarmed out of the ruins and charged the tank, even though its machine gun sprayed rounds. One man in a tattered, bloodstained parka seemed impervious to the bullets, or maybe just very lucky, because he got close enough to lob a Molotov cocktail. It splashed fire over the turret, dripping orange flames down to the treads.

Another attacker, his unshaven face gaunt and filthy, as if he'd spent many nights starving for meat and sleeping in dirt, noticed the videographer and turned toward the camera, his expression a snarl of hunger and anger. The view spun around, chasing a bobbing trail of smashed brick down a narrow path between destroyed buildings as the videographer fled. Seconds later, the video abruptly ended.

Bertrand didn't follow the news much, but he thought he'd know if there was a revolution in Russia. "I didn't see anything in the news. Did I miss a war or two?"

"That's what's so weird, dude." Azzim's Iranian accent and preference for American slang had earned him the nickname "Surfer Terrorist" in first year. "There is no war if you believe the old media." Azzim was much bigger on social media than Bertrand, keeping active accounts on everything from Twitter to Pinterest, always in touch with people from all over the world.

Bertrand shrugged, turning to pick up his laundry. "If it becomes a problem for America, I guess we'll hear about it."

Azzim caught his arm. "Dude, we're going to hear about it. It's coming to America."

Bertrand pulled free and escaped to the washing machine in the basement before Azzim could expound on what "it" was and why it caused him so much worry.

As he stuffed twice-worn socks and rumpled shirts into the washer, Bertrand found himself worrying just a bit. What if one of Azzim's conspiracy theories came true? Later that day, after reheating some pizza, he headed up to their room to ask about the tank video. Why were civilians daring to attack a tank? But Azzim was gone, and a few minutes later, Bertrand received a text from him stating that he planned to spend the evening researching at the library, so this might be a good evening to have Amy over. What a guy.

Amy. What a girl. She didn't care that Bertrand was a little overweight or that he had a name from the last century, one that had caused torment in high school. He didn't care that she also packed a few extra pounds, because she carried it so confidently, so flamboyantly. That night, they hung out on Bertrand's bed and went to second base, kissing and touching and gasping for over an hour. She kissed him some more after he walked her home, but she didn't invite him in, unready to cross that line. He was still elated. She wanted him as much as he wanted her. Life couldn't get better.

Except that more ominous news from Azzim hit closer to home. The next morning he showed Bertrand several articles on the Sun-Times website about a serial killer, the Chicago Ripper, who recently abandoned his fifth victim in a laneway of the Old Town district near St. Mike's Church.

"That's close to your parents', right?" Azzim looked up from the laptop for confirmation.

Bertrand frowned and nodded. "Yeah, we're a little west of Old Town, really."

For the first time since college began, Bertrand regretted going to his father's old alma mater of Rochester, over six hundred miles from home. He wanted to rush to his parents and protect them, even though he knew it was silly. He was their only child off at college. They were supposed to worry about him, not the other way around.

He skyped with his mother later that night while Azzim was out, embarrassed that he needed to reassure himself that she was okay. His mother didn't seem surprised to hear from him, even though it was only Thursday, and they usually skyped on Sundays. At first, they just talked about his upcoming triumphal return from college, and where he was applying for work, and which week would best suit him for a trip up to the lake house.

Finally, Bertrand summoned up the courage to ask about the murders. "What's all this about the Chicago Ripper? I hear the last stiff turned up in an alley near our house."

His mother assumed her teacher voice. "Young man, that 'stiff' was a person, a teenage boy whose parents must be in mourning now."

"Just be careful, Mom. You and Dad should get an alarm system, a monitored one. Things are getting weird."

His mother shook her head. "That's like living in an electronic cage. We moved into Old Town when it was a pretty rough neighborhood, long before you were born, and we're still here."

Bertrand chatted a bit more about school and his preparations to return home at the end of the year. As she said goodbye, she blew him a kiss. After looking over his shoulder to confirm that Azzim hadn't returned unnoticed, he blew one back, smiled, and logged off. He tweaked some code on a project before he crashed for the night. He slept well.

Bertrand's first clue that something had gone wrong—terribly, terribly wrong—was the silence of the townhouse. Friday at five o'clock usually meant loud music, beers clinking to toast the end of the week, and the steady machine-gun fire of first person shooters from the living room. Cher, Azzim's girlfriend, usually hung out on Fridays too, and she was kick-ass at GTA VI. Bertrand had invited Amy, but she couldn't make it because she had to hop a bus home to her parents in Saratoga Springs to attend some family get-together.

The silence of the house misled Bertrand into thinking his housemates were at the local pub, a new ritual now that they were all over twenty-one. As he dropped his pack on the floor in the hall, heading for the kitchen while checking his phone for a text from his housemates, he heard Azzim call his name.

"Bert, dude, wait."

Bertrand turned to their cramped living room and knew his life had irrevocably changed for the worse. Three of his housemates and a uniformed police officer rose from the couches and chairs, facing him, silent at first as if everyone were afraid, even the cop.

"Bertrand Allan?" The apology in the cop's eyes told Bertrand all he needed to know.

"Is my mom okay?"

Azzim spoke before the cop could reply. "Bert, they're gone. They're both gone, okay? I'm so sorry, dude."

Bertrand remembered asking if it was the Chicago Ripper, but the cop shook his head and calmly explained that it was just another car accident, one of the thousands that occur everyday. The rest of the evening was a fog. He remembered weeping on his bed, cradled between Cher and Azzim. He remembered them dropping him at Rochester Airport to catch a flight back to Chicago. Azzim had asked if there was anyone who could pick him up in Chicago, and Bertrand mentioned Stan Needleman, their reclusive neighbor from across the street, but he didn't know his number and didn't know if the man would care.

All the way home—to his real home, in Chicago—Bertrand replayed the conversation with his mother in his head, changing it to say all the things he would have if he'd only known it was to be their last. A few times he wondered how to pay for the funeral. He knew his parents had a will, but that could be months of paperwork, and it wasn't likely to amount to a lot of money. While his dad rarely shared much about the state of the family finances, he had admitted at Christmas that they took quite a fiscal beating during Black December's stock market disaster. The only person Bertrand could think of turning to for help was an aunt who lived out west, but she and Dad had never gotten along, and Bertrand had no idea where she lived. He was alone.

Bertrand planned to take a cab into the city, but to his surprise, Stan Needleman, the recluse, waited for him just outside the secure area. The old man had cleaned himself up, shaved even, and wore a grey suit right out of the 1980s.

"Your friend called me, told me your flight number." The man looked incredibly uncomfortable in his formal clothes. "So I figured I should at least get you home."

Needleman's words conjured a memory from a frightening day just after Bertrand had turned ten, when he rode too far from home on his new bike without his parents' permission. A car clipped his bicycle on a side street and roared away, leaving him frightened and bleeding but not seriously hurt. Needleman came puffing out of the local bar and scooped him up. He stank of beer and sweat, and he had said the same words: "I'll get you home." It was almost too much for the old man to carry a ten-year-old nearly a mile, but he refused to stop until he could place Bertrand into safety of his mother's embrace.

Needleman's car, a rusting Chevy that stank of cigarettes, was almost as old as Bertrand, but it was free, and Needleman was the perfect man to be riding with on such a grim journey. A recluse feels no need to make idle chit-chat.

"I got some money," he said, after parallel parking the car in front of his house. Like everyone else on the dense downtown street, he had no driveway. "I can loan you for the funeral expenses till you get on your feet. Your parents, they was good people, always good and polite to me, not like the other snots that moved in around here."

By that, Bertrand assumed he meant during the last twenty years as the neighborhood gentrified. He thanked Needleman, crossed the street to the little one-and-a-half-story house of his childhood, opened the front door, and stepped into silence.

He wandered into the kitchen first, opening the fridge door just as if he had returned for Thanksgiving or Easter. The lettuce was still crisp, and a couple of boneless chicken breasts were date-stamped as packed only three days ago. His mom and dad had planned a meal they would never eat.

To Bertrand's surprise, a six-pack of Samuel Adams was also in the fridge. He noticed that Dad had consumed a few beers at Easter, which was unusual for him. Bertrand now wondered just how stressed his dad had been about the markets and about his pension. Bertrand opened a beer, sat at the kitchen table, and contemplated his new life alone.

The next few days passed in a haze of condolences from his mom's co-faculty and his dad's friends at the office. Bertrand didn't know how he'd have managed it, but Needleman was there during all the visitations and funeral, the silent presence at his side. His six housemates drove out for the funeral, despite the fact that it was less than a week until the start of exams. He tried not to take it personally that Cher came but not Amy.

"She's got some family problems." Cher had a few classes with Amy. "Something about an aunt who was killed just yesterday."

Amy called Bertrand's cell the day after the funeral.

"I'm really sorry I wasn't there. My aunt was murdered, right here in Saratoga Springs. Like, this is the safest town. I just don't get why anyone would…" Her voice strangled off.

"It's okay, it's okay." Bertrand wanted to run to her, to protect her from whatever she feared. "Listen, we can talk when you get back. I've got a flight tomorrow."

"Sorry, Bert, but I'm not coming back. Dad says it's too dangerous."

"But you're almost finished." Bertrand didn't want to sound desperate, but she was a part of the future he had envisioned less than two weeks ago. She could help replace his lost family, help fill the empty house. "You don't want to waste all that work because of some nutbar in Saratoga."

"Dad knows stuff. It's dangerous everywhere now. Don't you see what's happening in the world? I have to go. Like, it's been really nice knowing you, and I really like you, but I have to trust my dad. Be careful."

"Wait." But the connection ended.

Later, after dinner, Bertrand found the website for the Saratogian and read the article about the murder of Amy's aunt. No wonder she was so freaked out. Someone had hung her aunt upside down from a playground climber and cut her throat.

Azzim, of course, had a conspiracy theory, which he shared the day Bertrand returned to Rochester, determined to finish college as his parents would have wanted. Azzim claimed thousands of murders were happening all over the country, but the police were hushing it up so that the public wouldn't panic.

"If I hadn't seen your parents in their coffins, dude, I would have wondered if their throats had been cut," he said that evening as they studied at the desks in their room.

"Sad thing is, frigging car accidents happen every day." Bertrand put his headphones on and turned up his tunes to block out his friend.

Azzim became more unhinged as exams progressed, sticking up grisly crime-scene photos of bloody corpses on the fridge and lecturing them all about not trusting the police. He stopped studying and just sat in front of his computer, delving deeper and deeper into his conspiracy. Bertrand took to studying at the library.

Bertrand returned to their house from his last exam, satisfied that he had done well enough to earn his degree, but the relief, the elation, the parties he had expected for this day a scant three weeks ago, had all vanished. His parents were gone. His girlfriend was gone, and his roommate, his best friend of four years of college, had taken a dive into the deep end of the crazy pool.

The crying, a woman crying, coming from his bedroom gave Bertrand sudden hope that Amy had changed her mind. He ran up the stairs, but it was Cher who sat weeping on Azzim's bed in their room. That side of the room was unexpectedly bare of any personal possessions. Azzim's posters of his favorite band and favorite game were ripped from the wall and hanging loose as if a windstorm had swept through the interior of the house. His closet door and drawers stood open and empty. He had left his furniture behind.

Cher looked up, quickly wiping her tears. "Sorry," she said. "Azzim left me here." She pulled a Kleenex from her pack and wiped her nose. "He totally lost it, Bert. He wanted me to run away to Canada with him, to live in the woods, but it was crazy. What would we eat? Like, he bought a cheap tent, but what do we know about living in the middle of nowhere? I couldn't go."

Bertrand slumped into the chair of his desk and booted up his laptop. "I don't think he wrote his finals. I mean, I didn't see him around the exams anyway."

Cher shook her head. "He didn't. Four years of studying and he gives it all up in the last month."

Bertrand's email opened and messages downloaded. Azzim had facebooked him, direct messaged him from Twitter, emailed him, and now his phone bleeped to let him know he had a new text. The messages were the same, a refrain of everything Azzim had been raving about for the last three weeks: "Dude. Trust me. Everything you know and love is coming to an end. Going off the grid. Run!"

Azzim didn't respond to any of Bertrand's replies, and by nightfall he knew that his best friend was gone forever, just like his parents, just like his girlfriend. As he packed to return to Chicago, it occurred to him that Azzim's message was not a prediction.

Everything Bertrand knew and loved had ended.

The only relief was that nothing else could go wrong.

# 1

# THE CHANGE

He knew he shouldn't be afraid to go home.

The elevated train squealed north out of Armitage Station, leaving Bertrand standing alone on the platform in the weak sodium-vapor lights. Discarded newspapers and fast food wrappers chased the train down the platform, and the occasional spark from the third rail marked its passage into the night, the clack of wheels on expansion joints fading. Bertrand watched the train until its lights were a distant, rocking speck, wondering why he wished he were still safely aboard, rumbling along with the other passengers toward Chicago's distant suburbs.

He knew he shouldn't be uneasy, even this late at night. He'd lived in this neighborhood all his life, his parents among the gentrifiers who had swept through in the eighties and nineties after the hippies had made Old Town a cool hangout. The yuppies, fed up with long commutes, came by the thousands back then and purchased houses that had been solidly built after the Great Chicago Fire. The young boomers had either elaborately renovated these narrow red-brick Victorian homes or replaced the less attractive ones with tall houses that made use of every square foot of property that city zoning would allow.

Bertrand's parents had arrived too late to find cheap real estate in Old Town, so they had grabbed a property farther west, a rare wooden house on a street that had been spared the Great Fire by a change in the wind. Bertrand's father had liked to say that they were in Upper Old Town, although they rarely heard the bells of St. Michael's over the city noise, even though it was less than a mile away.

Bertrand headed for the station stairs, wondering again why he was reluctant to descend into his neighborhood, why he didn't feel the relief of someone at the end of a long day. He should be hurrying along with a practiced step, at the brisk pace of a commuter who hardly needed to look where he was going. He had been doing this every workday for two months now, ever since he started this downtown job after graduation.

But Bertrand found himself pausing on his way down the stairs, as if out of breath. Something big was about to happen. His heart beat in fear. Or was it anticipation? He considered burying this bizarre unease by heading over to O'Malley's for chicken wings and beer and a game of darts—normal things—but his doctor would scold him.

*You're only twenty-one years old and you've got the heart and cholesterol of a fifty-year-old.* Doctor Sloane liked to wave his finger at Bertrand when he lectured. *You've got to lose at least twenty pounds, and for God's sake no chicken wings.*

Bertrand also knew what Sloane would say about the unease, the fear of some impending doom.

*It's only been three months since the accident. It's not surprising that you're anxious and worried these days. It's your body's way of trying to prepare for another disaster. Your subconscious just fears more bad news. I'll write you a prescription for Prozac.*

Bertrand never filled the prescription, preferring to dull the grief with work and beer.

He pushed out of the station, still trying to reason away this new premonition that something was about to go hugely wrong. He had a right to be anxious. He'd lived through tragedy and had no one to speak to other than a few old high school friends who would nod as if they understood while looking painfully uncomfortable. Bertrand preferred O'Malley's, a place he'd begun hanging around because no one there knew his history, so he could pretend there had been no tragedy in his life. The bartenders now knew him by name, but that was all.

Bertrand stopped outside the station, the day's heat still wafting from the asphalt, the stench of garbage from a nearby container reminding him that summer should be spent out of the city. Should he turn right and head for O'Malley's, or left and head for home and a plate of Lean Cuisine?

He turned left, walking to Bissell Street and the one-and-a-half story house that his parents had so meticulously renovated in anticipation of his birth. Tonight he would be good. He would lock the door, watch HBO and drink water. He would take a Sleep-Eze D and crash by midnight, then get up and start fresh.

But his feet dragged as he headed up the sidewalk, the sense of doom rising from his stomach to his heart, which beat faster now, reminding him that he'd failed to even start losing those twenty pounds. He'd almost reached home—the clapboard a pastel yellow, the gingerbread trim picked out in a pale green—when a smash of breaking glass from across the street brought him to a halt.

Was this the disaster? Had Needleman suffered some calamity?

His neighbor across the street also lived in a one-and-a-half story house, the only wooden structure that backed onto the 'L' train line. All the other houses on the west side stood shoulder to shoulder—three stories tall—like a nineteenth-century brick-and-glass wall against the noise of the trains. Needleman's place sat in stark contrast, a decaying shack sided with asphalt sheets. He had lived there for as long as Bertrand could remember. Developers and real estate agents circled around the house like sharks every few months, but the reclusive old man refused to budge. It was generally assumed that the day after Needleman died his house would go down in front of a bulldozer's blade.

Every light was on in Needleman's house, unusual for the stingy pensioner. Bertrand yanked his phone from his pocket, the fear rising to panic, but calling 911 made no sense. Would telling an operator that he heard a window breaking even prompt a response? He stepped past the parked cars and into the empty street, away from his home and closer to Needleman's, but halfway across he froze, the dread overwhelming. How could he even make it to the waist-high chain-link fence that fronted the property? He could hardly breathe.

Bertrand fell to his knees, his heart pounding, his panic climaxing. Was he having a heart attack? A panic attack? He tried to fight his broken respiration, to take calming breaths. *His chest hurt.* Was that a heart attack sign?

"Help," he said, but it was closer to a whisper than a cry. If only a car would come along the quiet side street now, they'd see him there, slumped in the middle of the road, wouldn't they? They'd call for help. Where was his phone? It had slipped from his grasp, but it had to be nearby.

A terrified shriek came from Needleman's house. That was it—Bertrand could call 911 now, but instead he found himself rising and stumbling forward, crossing the street and grabbing the gate of the fence, some heroic force welling up inside of him. Needleman might be smelly and crazy, but he'd been such a stand up dude after the accident. Bertrand had to help.

He lifted the latch of the gate, wondering what power had possessed him. From the moment of the scream, Bertrand's very soul had strengthened. His chest pain eased, his breathing calmed, and the anxiety faded. The gate swung open easily, and Bertrand rushed up the porch stairs to the screen door. He kicked at the aluminum panel on the bottom. "Mr. Needleman? It's Bertrand Allan from across the street. Are you okay?"

Stooped with some large burden, a figure rushed across the hall near the back of the narrow house. More breaking glass. That was enough. Bertrand yanked at the handle of the screen door and discovered it was open. He hurried in, heading straight down the hallway for the kitchen.

"Mr. Needleman. I'm here! Are you all right?"

Bertrand had a moment of doubt. What was he doing? Why hadn't he picked up his cell phone? Yet, he was ready to fight to save Needleman from whatever horror had prompted that scream, a concept that would be viewed as ridiculous by Bertrand's fellow call-center techs. Pudgy Bert fight? Azzim would've laughed.

But the kitchen was empty and the house was now silent. Had he imagined that figure with a suspiciously body-shaped burden? How could anyone move that quickly carrying the old man?

He tried to guess when Needleman had last cooked a meal, but the pile of pots in the sink, the food crusted and dried, gave no clue. The stove looked like it had last been clean during the First Gulf War. The table was strewn with dishes, as if Needleman rotated between chairs, abandoning each finished meal and moving to a clear place setting for the next, until he'd gone full circle.

"Mr. Needleman!"

Bertrand hurried back into the hall and went upstairs to the bedroom under the half-story eaves. The second floor was stifling in the heat, and it stank of sweat and mold. The bed sheets were gray and tossed aside, the dresser drawers standing open with clothes piled on them rather than folded in them. No one here. He headed back downstairs and into the living room.

A ratty La-Z-Boy chair, a sofa forty years out of date, and a thick cathode-ray tube TV were the only furniture, other than a standing ashtray full of cigarette butts by the recliner. A carpet that wasn't fit to piss on covered the floor, and the wallpaper was so tobacco-stained it was hard to determine the original pattern. Empty Budweiser cans littered the floor.

The room stank of old farts, beer, and tobacco. And something else. Something metallic and wet and fresh. It reminded Bertrand of a meat counter at the grocery store, but without the anti-bacterial cleansers. He stepped into the room, walking a circle around the La-Z-Boy but stopping when the carpet squished under his foot. It was wet beside the chair, a dark stain in the brown carpet, a dark red stain. Bertrand didn't have to stoop and smell to know it was blood.

"Mr. Needleman. Where are you? I'm here to help."

Bertrand fled the room, tracking a red footprint into the kitchen. Now he saw what he had missed the first time while overwhelmed by the domestic chaos: the glass of the back screen door was smashed. Then came the noise, a rumble and metallic screech announcing that another train approached on the 'L.' Bertrand rushed out and down the back steps, finding himself right under the train as it roared overhead on its elevated path. How did Needleman live with that noise? Bertrand's house was only just across the street, but it was so much quieter.

Bertrand waited until the train had passed and gave one last call, looking up and down the alley on the far side of the tracks for any sign of human movement. "Mr. Needleman," he shouted over the scrapping wheels of the receding train.

But the only sound now was a distant siren and the warm wind pushing through the trees. The dark lumps of garbage bins along the alley could hide any number of people, but Bertrand decided there wasn't anything to be gained by wandering in the weak light, looking for a potential murderer. He headed back through the house and into Bissell Street, where he found his cell still lying where he'd dropped it while panicking. The anxiety of that moment had totally vanished. He was ready to do battle, but he couldn't find the enemy. He dialed 911. There was blood.

# 2

# NEWS

The doorbell rang just as the microwave beeped to announce that the Lean Cuisine had finished warming. Bertrand opened the door to find two uniformed officers, one younger and trim with one hand raised, ready to again ring the doorbell. The other officer waited at the bottom of the stairs, his beer belly pushing over his belt, his eyes on his phone, and his fingers poised to text.

"Bertrand Allan?" said the younger officer. "You called in a 911 about your neighbor across the street."

"Yeah, but like, an hour ago. What took so long?"

The heavy cop—clearly close to retirement and fed up with dealing with the public—looked up from his phone. "Shut your yap if that's all you got to say."

The younger officer didn't exactly roll his eyes, but he looked like he wanted to.

"We're sorry for the delay." His expression was sincere. "The call volume tonight is unusual even for a hot night. Now, what makes you think Mr. Needleman was the victim of an assault? Did you witness an attack?"

What had he seen? Had he imagined the dark figure with the human-shaped burden? He'd just had a panic attack, after all, maybe even a mini-heart attack. He should go see his doctor tomorrow, but he felt just fine right now, better than ever.

"No." Bertrand didn't like admitting this fact. "But there's blood on the carpet in the living room and the glass in the back screen door is smashed."

The older officer looked up from his phone. "Well it's fricking obvious isn't it? The guy was probably stupidly drunk. He fell into the glass and cut himself and didn't even know it, and then went to sit and have a few more beers. Moron realizes he's bleeding and heads out for the hospital to get stitches and you waste my time with a 911."

"You've been over there?"

"Of course, sir," said the younger officer. "We even saw a bloody footprint going from the living room and out the back door of the kitchen. He clearly left there strong enough to walk. It couldn't have been a very serious injury."

"That was my footprint. That's how I found the blood. I stepped in it."

The officer drew a notebook from his chest pocket and flipped it open. "Are you a regular guest of Mr. Needleman's?" It was an accusation accompanied by a frown.

"What? No. I mean when I was a kid I used to go over there sometimes when he was working on something out back. He used to build little stools and stuff and sell them at garage sales, and sometimes he let me help. I haven't been over there since before college."

"So you really had no right to enter the residence." The young officer was all business now, no longer placating. The older officer looked up and put away the cell phone, studying Bertrand with new interest.

"Can I come in?" Big Belly officer walked up the stairs as he spoke and moved into Bertrand's personal space, which prompted Bertrand to step back as if he were giving an invitation. Before he knew it both cops had pushed past him, the younger one going into the living room and Big Belly heading for the kitchen.

"Hey, wait!" Bertrand followed the younger cop. "Excuse me! Officer ..."

"Gonsalves." The introduction sounded friendly, but Gonsalves surveyed the room with a trained eye. It wasn't that different from Needleman's in layout, but it was clean, the sofa only ten years old. The La-Z-Boy and the huge flat-screen TV that hung on one wall were new purchases, his graduation presents to himself.

"You don't think I had something to do with this?"

Gonsalves turned to Bertrand. "May I see your shoes please, the ones you wore while you were in Mr. Needleman's house."

The ones with Needleman's blood on them. Bertrand stooped into the front-hall closet. How had this gone so strange? Why were they treating him like a suspect instead of a concerned neighbor? He looked at the bottom of the Nikes as he handed them over, appalled that he'd forgotten the blood, that he'd put them away when he had burst into his front hall, already speaking to the 911 operator on his cell. One sole was brown and sticky. Before today, this might have turned Bertrand's stomach.

Gonsalves studied the shoes and leaned toward the stained one to sniff.

"That's blood alright. Bring them outside please."

Big Belly returned from the kitchen. "Dinner's in the microwave," was all he said before he started up the stairs. It wasn't clear to whom he was speaking.

Bertrand followed Gonsalves to his car, which was stopped in the middle of the street with the flashing lights quietly clicking away. Gonsalves produced a very large Ziploc and held it open for Bertrand. The order was obvious: hand over the shoes.

"Look here," Bertrand said while placing the shoes into the bag. "I was just trying to help. You should've heard that scream. It was, like ... It was a dying scream." But Bertrand knew that he had no true experience with death. He'd often imagined his parents' last moments, but he hadn't been with them, sitting in the backseat of the car. How would he know the sound of a dying scream?

Gonsalves made a note on the Ziploc with a Sharpie and placed it in the trunk of the car, slamming the lid. He again pulled out the notebook.

"Mr. Allan. Why don't you walk me through this? Start from coming home."

Bertrand left out his panic attack. That had nothing to do with Needleman's disappearance, did it? Unless one assumed that Bertrand had just totally lost it and started seeing and hearing things. But the blood was real. So maybe the scream was real, maybe the dark figure carrying the body was real. Each time Bertrand replayed that moment in his head, it seemed more and more like the figure had been carrying a body.

Big Belly officer returned in time for the end of the tale. "So let me get this straight: lights on, nobody's home, the screaming could be drunk teenagers on a patio three streets away, but you gotta waste my time because your drunken neighbor cut himself." He got into the passenger side of car, reaching over to start it before pulling out his cell to return to his texting.

Gonsalves flipped the notebook closed and removed his cap long enough to brush the sweat from his brow, his short black curls plastered to his forehead. "Look, I think you're a good guy, Mr. Allan, so I'm going to give you some advice, not as a police officer, but as one concerned citizen to another. The Ripper killed again this evening, so that's number eleven. This guy doesn't seem to care if his victims are old men or young women. You were right to call us." He glanced over at his partner, but the window was up and the car's air conditioning on full. "But you were wrong to go into his house. What if you did catch the Chicago Ripper in the act? It's not like I'm giving away any secrets if I tell you that the freak is brutal with a knife. I mean, don't you watch the news? You wouldn't have stood a chance."

Bertrand nodded, ashamed of his softness and his sweaty lethargy. "You're right, of course. It was just that I felt like superman for a minute there. I heard him scream and I felt stronger, ready to fight." His ears burned. What ridiculous nonsense.

But Gonsalves nodded. "I know what you mean. I've had those superhero moments myself in the last couple of weeks. Listen, between you and me, things are getting strange." He glanced at his partner again before he leaned in close to Bertrand. "Any other day we'd be bringing detectives in to speak to you. But they're all out on the Ripper case—top priority. And it's not just Chicago that's got this asshole. There are Ripper copycats in other cities, even up in Canada and over in Europe. There's talk that maybe there's a cult, a worldwide devil-worshipping cult. Buy a gun. Get an alarm system. We can't protect you anymore."

Gonsalves hurried around to the driver's side, giving Bertrand a last glance over the flashing lights before he got into the car. It was an embarrassed look, or maybe guilt. He certainly wasn't behaving with the detached professionalism that Bertrand had expected. Instead he sounded like Azzim at the end of finals, just before he disappeared.

Bertrand watched the car speed away with a short squawk of its siren. Where were they rushing off to now? Another nuisance call? He went inside to finally retrieve the Lean Cuisine from the microwave. The pitcher of filtered water in the fridge sat beside a cold can of Milwaukee. Bertrand intended to reach for the water, but his fingers closed around the beer. He popped it open just a little too easily as he headed for the living room, sat down in his La-Z-Boy and flicked on the TV.

"It's confirmed, Colin." The breathless blonde reporter spoke to a grave cable-TV news anchor via split screen. "This is already the third murder tonight, making this the fifteenth victim of the Chicago Ripper." Behind her, a stretcher with an occupied black body bag wheeled past, bound for a waiting ambulance. The scene was a confusion of flashing lights, police and firefighters tramping about the front lawn of a suburban house, and a crowd of curious onlookers held back at a safe distance.

"So it would seem his need to kill is growing exponentially." Colin—the mature anchor with hair that looked younger than his cheeks—said *exponentially* with just a hint of pride, as if he'd just mastered the word.

"Note to self," said Bertrand to the room as the photos of previous victims were splashed across the screen, people of all races and ages. "Tomorrow, buy a gun."

# 3

# DAY SHIFT

For the first time since he got the job after graduation, Bertrand didn't have to stand on the 'L' train as it rocked along its elevated path into downtown Chicago. Usually the suburbanites had claimed all the seats by the time the train arrived at Armitage, not that Bertrand cared, because he lived only four stops from the Loop. This morning he not only had a seat, but the one next to him was empty as well. He had never worked down town through a summer before, so he assumed that many of his fellow commuters had fled the city heat for a week, taking their kids to cabins by cool lakes.

Still, as he hurried down the steps, Bertrand did think it odd that the whole city seemed quieter than usual. Not that the noise of the train scrapping onward above his head on its way around the Loop was any quieter, but the bustle of traffic, both car and pedestrian, was subdued today, as if marking a day of mourning.

Bertrand hurried over to LaSalle, walking quickly because he'd slept late. If he skipped his coffee, he could be at his desk before Whitlock made his grumpy morning rounds of the cubicles. Bertrand reached the building on Monroe—a white monolith emanating solidity and permanence, towering over the corner—and joined a few stragglers heading for the elevators. Again, he was surprised that he didn't have to squeeze on board. If only things could be this spacious in the winter, when everyone packed into the metal boxes with heavy coats and colds and flu.

Any hope of avoiding Whitlock vanished as the gleaming elevator doors slide open. The man stood there as if waiting for Bertrand, checking the watch on his thick wrist, his normally tanned complexion a little redder than usual—a sure sign of stress. His muscles bulged below the short sleeves of his dress shirt, indicating that he hadn't missed his morning workout, which usually mellowed the man. His graying mustache was trimmed with military precision.

Bertrand tried to slip past him with an innocent nod, but Whitlock caught his arm. "Bert, thank god. We're down five people this morning. There's some kind of weird flu going around." He turned and led Bertrand through the rows of cubicles to their enclave near the north-facing windows. Bertrand had often looked at the gleaming office towers that blocked his view north. Would he be able to see the trees of his street if the view were unobstructed?

"Get in the queue," Whitlock said. "Start with the chats 'cause they're usually faster. Move onto the phones in between. We're backed up over half-an-hour. I have to go upstairs for a confab about employee absenteeism. As if I have time." He marched away before Bertrand could ask about the promised promotion to programmer. *Probably not the right time anyway*, he decided. Whitlock may have been willing to overlook Bertrand's tardiness, since the office was short-staffed, but the man angered easily, and he was clearly under pressure.

Bertrand logged on to his terminal and joined the queue, but the list of those waiting for tech support stunned him. "What the frig?"

"Bert, here dude. It's gonna be a long day." Jeff Aubert, holding two Styrofoam cups of coffee from the office's kitchen, kicked out the chair in the opposite cubicle, leaning his long frame over to place one of the cups on Bert's desk. "Thought you'd skip your coffee this morning." He placed his own down before he sat and pulled back his blond hair, binding it into a short ponytail with an elastic band. Jeff was only a year older than Bertrand, but cigarettes and booze had taken the youthful shine from his face. No one asked him for I.D. anymore when he visited a bar.

"You're a god." Bertrand popped open the plastic lid and took a sip, burning his tongue but still savoring the strong brew. "What's up? How many people skipped off?"

"I think half a dozen or so, but the problem isn't who skipped off here, it's who skipped off from the clients. There seems to be a lot of newbies doing the payroll this week, and they don't know a damn thing about Timetracks."

"Weird. Everybody's run away from the heat, I guess."

"Wasn't like this last summer." Jeff reached for his earphones and mic headset. "Should we do lunch?"

Chicken wings and beer. Bertrand's mouth watered at the thought.

"If Whitlock let's us."

He selected the first chat, a question about pulling payroll reports out of the database, completely basic stuff. He checked the client name—a big corporation, one that should have a deep pool of staff in accounting. Who was doing payroll there this morning? They should know how to do this. It was going to be a long morning.

———

Bertrand wondered if they'd get a seat fast enough at Flynn's to squeeze in a pint over lunch, but he needn't have worried. Only a few tables of the brewpub were occupied, and the young bartender—looking barely old enough to drink himself—just waved them in the direction of the line of booths by the window. "Wherever you want, gentlemen. Tracy'll be out in sec'." He continued hanging clean wine glasses above the bar, since there were no patrons on the stools awaiting his service. To the right of the bar, the high glass windows gave a view of gleaming stainless steel tanks so that patrons could see their suds under production, but the rest of the place was styled as an upscale Irish Pub.

"Okay, this is just too weird." Bertrand slipped into one side of a booth that could comfortably hold six. "Where the hell is everybody?"

Jeff leaned his tall frame back on the opposite seat, one arm resting on its back, the fingers of his other tapping the table. "This has been building for a while."

"What are you talking about? Building? You mean emptying."

"Yeah, maybe. You've been such a lunch time saint lately that you don't know: the restaurants have been hurting all around the Loop—especially the lunch crowd. We're not the only ones dealing with growing absenteeism." He held up two fingers to the bartender, who nodded and began pouring the pints.

"What'd you just order me?"

"A couple of Flynn's lagers. Don't worry, if you don't want one I'll drink both."

But Bertrand did want one, and he silently apologized to his waistline as he took the first cool sip, and he simply nodded when Jeff asked, "Chicken wings?"

"Speaking of totally weird," said Jeff after his first sip. "My neighbor went off the deep end last night. First it sounded like a party, loud music, that kind of thing. Then there's screaming like crazy, not fooling around screaming, or getting off screaming. I mean totally freaked out screaming. Horror movie screaming. It took me a couple of minutes to realize it was a guy screaming and not a girl."

Bertrand thought of the scream from Needleman's house. "So anybody call 911?"

"'Course." Jeff leaned forward now, both hands holding his pint, his expression embarrassed. "I mean, I guess I should've sooner, but I kept thinking someone else would call because the whole building must've been able to hear it, and it was above me, so I figured his next door neighbors would call."

"What happened?" Bertrand didn't like where this was going. It sounded too much like his own experience at Needleman's.

"Cops took nearly an hour to get there, and by that time the screaming had stopped. Me and a few others met them in the hall and they said they had no justification for entering the unit. Said since it was quiet and no one was answering the door that the party must be over. But one tough old lady—I don't know her name—she just pushed past the cops and tried the door. It wasn't locked. She shamed the cops into going in. Guess what?"

"Blood, but no body."

Jeff sat back in surprise. "Crap, how'd you know?"

"Same thing happened to me with my neighbor last night. Blood on the living room floor. No body, and as far as the cops were concerned, no crime."

"That's just what they told us. The old lady went straight in there, that's why the cops followed her. She said there were handcuffs on the four-poster bed, like four sets for kinky stuff lined with pink fur. She said there was blood on the pillow, a fair amount."

"What did the cops say?"

"Said it was bondage gone too far and the couple had gone to the hospital and would be back today. But the old lady said that she saw him ... crap, I can't remember his name either ... she saw him get home last night with an entourage, four hot chicks. She thought it was weird 'cause he's no lady's man—makes you look fit. Oh, sorry."

Bertrand took a sip of his pint before he spoke. "You know what? My neighbor, he's a recluse, and I know in my soul someone cut him last night. He's dead. I don't know where the body is, but he's toast. I think your neighbor's toast too."

"My thoughts." Jeff looked around the restaurant for a moment as if worried he might be overheard. "Do you think the Chicago Ripper is doing way more people than the police are letting on? I've heard talk of copycat killers."

Everyone sounded like Azzim these days. Bertrand wished he could contact his old roommate to tell him he was fast coming to the conclusion that maybe he should've listened to him, gone to Canada with him instead of getting a dumb job.

"One cop I talked to last night was a good guy," Bertrand said. "He told me there're copycats in other cities, maybe even a devil-worshipping cult. I mean, what are the odds of both of us losing neighbors last night? One guy can't have been running around that much, especially if he's getting rid of bodies. Besides, there were three confirmed Ripper murders last night, and that scumbag doesn't hide his bodies. What's really weird though is that your neighbor said hot girls, like a honey trap, like they were doing the killing. Doesn't fit my image of serial killers."

"Stranger and stranger. Ah, wings. Thanks, Tracy," he said to the waitress, who smiled before she turned away. Bertrand's eyes followed her tight bum in her black polyester pants for a moment, then caught Jeffery's sly smile. He grabbed a wing from the basket to cover his indiscretion.

"My doctor will be furious with me." Bertrand tore into the steaming wing, the Tabasco sauce making his eyes water.

"You still got that blood pressure thing going on?"

"And high cholesterol."

"Dude, you gotta get in shape. I eat anything I want and I'm still at the bottom of the body mass index."

"Go screw," said Bertrand "You're naturally skinny."

"I work out every night. Running, machines and I got a karate sensei who works us to death twice a week. Why don't you come out tonight? Might not hurt to be in better shape. If the Ripper comes after you, it'd be good if you could at least put up a fight."

"That's what guns are for."

"Think you can get a personal carry permit?"

Bertrand reached for another wing. "Is the karate tonight?"

"Nope, machines and running. Don't worry, Joyce is the coach on tonight and she's a trained pro. She'll set you up with a good program, and Bert, she's not hard on the eyes."

Bastard. Jeff had just found the one argument that would make him come out of his shell, get off his ass.

"I don't have any gym gear." Bertrand still held the chicken wing, ready to take another guilty bite.

"Dude, don't give me lame excuses. We'll buy you some stuff on the way and you can store it in the closet with all the other gear you own. Yeah, I thought so. Nada. You'd have to buy some shorts and good shoes anyway, because you can't run in those beat-up Reeboks you got on your feet right now. Don't worry your wallet 'cause there're great sales on everywhere this summer." Jeff leaned back and waved for another pint. "Eat without guilt. We're gonna work it off tonight at the gym."

Bertrand considered other excuses, like his possible heart attack on the street in front of Needleman's, but the truth was that he hadn't felt this strong since his teens. Last night's panic must have been a psychosomatic event—like Dr. Sloan had been talking about in his sermons on anxiety—his body just freaking out because his mind anticipated horrible things.

Besides, this Joyce woman sounded interesting, and Bertrand didn't want to die a virgin. Perhaps if he lost some weight and built some muscle he might finally get laid. Maybe even Tracy, the waitress with the amazing red curls and the freckles, would go out with him. He decided he was finally over Amy and ready to move on.

"Okay, I'll give it a try." Bertrand laughed before he bit into the wing, because he couldn't imagine being able to fight anyone, let alone the Chicago Ripper.

# 4

# MURDER

Bertrand stood on the scale, his ears burning with embarrassment. Joyce—the slim Amazon in bum-hugging shorts and a restraining tank top that ended far above her belly button—gave a low whistle. "Can't say as I'm surprised given the beer belly. You have to lose at least forty pounds." Her height was average, but she had cut muscles that spoke of machines and effort.

"My doctor said twenty." Bertrand stepped off the scale, wanting those glowing red numbers to vanish.

"Your doctor wants you to lose enough to live another twenty-five years. I'm going to put you on a program that'll turn you into a hot body within a year."

Bertrand couldn't restrain a snorted laugh. "I'm a call center tech. I don't think there ever was a 'hot body' under this flab." He pinched at one love handle for emphasis. There was nothing he could hide from this woman if she was going to be his personal trainer, and so there was no chance she would sleep with him, even in the dark. Somehow this thought helped him relax.

Joyce walked over to a pack hanging on the wall in the corner of the weight room. Machines—some of which Bertrand couldn't even determine a purpose for—sat empty over a large area, with only Jeff peddling on an exercise bike on the far side of the room, his iPod plugged into his head, his Kindle in one hand.

Joyce pulled a photo out of her bag and handed it to Bertrand.

"This is me four years ago. My life seemed empty and pointless. I had nothing to fight for and no reason to stick around. I was clinically depressed and my doctor had written a prescription for Prozac."

An angry woman looked out of the photo, clearly peeved with the photographer. Loose track pants barely contained wide hips. Her hair looked blonder than its current shade of light brown, maybe because she now wore it shorter, and that darkened the perceived color. The old Joyce's extra large sweatshirt bulked in the wrong places, and her face seemed an inflated version of the woman standing before Bertrand.

"Wow!" he said, looking from the photo to Joyce and back. "Wow! I mean, you look great. I can't believe this is—" He broke off in embarrassment. Since when did he openly complement a woman's figure, let alone imply that she had been fat in the past?

"You can't believe it's me." She snatched the photo and stuffed it back into her bag. "I keep that with me for the unbelievers like you, and whenever I don't feel like working out, I take a good long look at it to remind me why I'm here. Let's head for the track. I want to get your heart rate up before we start, so that you don't drop dead from a heart attack in the first set."

She'd jogged out the door and through the spacious lobby, heading for the open staircase to the second floor. Bertrand was winded before they even reached the narrow running track. It ran around the walls above the lap pool, leaving the center open for height above the water. A stiff wire mesh rose from the inner side of the track to the ceiling, marring the view of the swimmers, but it ensured fools couldn't try to jump the two stories from the track into the pool, probably missing and clipping the tile edge.

After the first lap, Bertrand stopped with one hand on his knee, gasping for breath and pressing a hand to his chest, but while his heart beat fast, it didn't race out of control like last night. There was no panic.

"Buddy." Joyce had already lapped him and stopped to walk beside him. "This is pathetic! Move your ass or I'll sic my Rottweiler on it. I don't care if you walk, limp or crawl, but don't you dare stop on my track."

Bertrand lurched into motion, but he failed to stifle a laugh.

"What?" Joyce turned and jogged backwards along the track, a don't-mess-with-me frown creasing her forehead.

"I didn't realize this was boot-camp fitness, Sergeant."

A smile cracked. "Call me captain and run for your life."

---

The showers were empty and so was the change room, but Bertrand still washed the sweat off his aching muscles and dressed hurriedly, careful not to look at the floor-to-ceiling mirror. One workout would not have made a difference.

Jeff had finished his workout and left earlier. "Can't keep a prospective ball and chain waiting," he'd said on his way out. It took Bertrand a moment to decipher that Jeff meant he had a date.

A date. It should be a normal event, but to Bertrand it was still exotic and foreign; Amy had been his only experience in college. He just wasn't bold enough for the ritual dance of mating, and while he experimented with the idea of asking Joyce out, he imagined lame excuses. Would she be bold enough to tell the truth? "Hey, I don't date fat guys," is what he guessed she would think. He would actually prefer that honesty. He finished dressing and pushed out of the club, his new pack slung over his shoulder.

Joyce was leaning against a concrete utility pole while studying a cell phone. She wore shorts a little longer than the ones she had on in the gym, as well as a sleeveless shirt, loose and buttoned-down because of the evening heat—or maybe to reveal a bit of cleavage. A large Rottweiler panted beside her, its tongue lolling out. Its red-rimmed eyes would have fit well on the Hound of the Baskervilles, and its impressive yellow teeth warned of a strong jaw designed for ripping and tearing.

Joyce looked up from the phone as the club door banged closed. "What's up?" she said, as if they'd arranged to meet. "Jeff said you live just a couple of streets over from me, so I figure if you're walking I'll keep you company."

Bertrand had actually planned to head for the 'L' station. Only two quick stops south and he'd be home, but he didn't dare admit that laziness to Joyce.

"Sure." Did he sound too eager? Did he sound like he had suddenly imagined he and Joyce naked in his bed? He started walking, his feet automatically aiming for the Diversey Station while his brain tried to come to grips with the fact that a woman actually wanted to hang out. The Rottweiler, however, walked between them without a sniff in Bertrand's direction, the dog's attitude showing all the warmth of an armored car guard on his way out of a bank.

Bertrand could see the station and gave it a last, wistful glance as Joyce turned them south on Sheffield, heading past the seventies-era high-rises that sat back from the road in the middle of their park-like lawns. Opposite, the red brick of St. George's Greek Orthodox Church rose in its nineteenth-century glory—the large addition desperately trying to match the flavor of the old church but still coming across as twenty-first century because of the parking lot beneath.

Bertrand fought to untie his tongue. Don't panic. They weren't on a date. There was no pressure. She probably just didn't want to walk home alone in the dark.

"So where do you live?" he asked.

"Bought a condo on Burling last year because I was fed up with the long commute. I sold my Dad's house out in Vernon Hills."

"Wow, Vernon Hills, that's way out, isn't it?"

"Half-way to friggin' Wisconsin, yes."

Why did she always seem angry with him? Did she like him? Bertrand had to restrain a snort at this absurd thought. But wait a minute, what had she said about her dad?

"You sold your dad's house? Is he—sorry, shouldn't ask."

"He's dead. Drunk driving when I was only eighteen and flipped his BMW." Joyce's eyes stared straight ahead and her voice held surprisingly little emotion.

"Wow, um, I'm so sorry."

"I was bummed at first, but he really wasn't a big part of my life. Aunt Rach pretty much raised me after Mom died of breast cancer. I was eight." She looked over, her eyebrows rising in challenge. Was she trying to shock him with her tragedies, scare him away with her baggage? Well, Bertrand could meet her head-on with this one.

"So I guess we're both orphans."

"Yeah, Jeff told me about your folks. Bummer. Like, I'm really sorry too." She sounded as if she meant it, and for a moment they met each other's gaze.

"No worries." But Bertrand wanted to seize her and tell her how hopelessly lost he was without them, how he drank and ate and watched mindless TV. How he went to work dreading coming home to the empty house that he just wouldn't sell despite the memories that haunted like ghosts. "You close to your Aunt Rach, then?"

"I was 'till she died two years ago. Breast cancer, same as Mom." Joyce glanced his way again. "I know. One trag' after another, but I'm good."

"So you're alone too. Like, no family."

"Yup." Joyce gave the dog a reassuring pat on its head. "My friends don't get what it's like to have no family left, to have Thanksgiving dinner by yourself."

"Spread out on the coffee table in front of the TV, with a full bottle of red," said Bertrand.

"So you do get it."

"Hey, maybe we should do Thanksgiving together this year. Catch a movie and make a reservation at some really nice restaurant." Bertrand caught his breath. What the hell? He'd just asked her out on a date. Since when did he have the balls to ask someone—especially someone he'd just met—out on a date, even if it was four months in the future?

Joyce gave a short laugh. "Who knows where we'll be in November?" She gave the dog another pat on the head, a quick one as if to check that he still walked between them. "But sure, Bert, I'm game for dinner on

Thanksgiving, although when guys ask me out it's usually a little closer in time, usually as soon as possible so that they can get in my shorts."

Bertrand marveled that he felt so comfortable with her despite the angry expression she wore half the time. "Well you can hardly blame them." His jaw dropped. He had never been that indiscreet without alcohol. "I mean all the work at the gym, it's really paid off. I mean—"

Joyce stared at him, the angry frown creasing her forehead.

Bertrand decided to just go for the truth. "There's no way I can gracefully get out of this, is there?"

"Nope."

"Well, you're hot so what else can I say? But don't worry, I'm not known for my hit and runs. I don't get laid much—at all." He pinched the fat through his dress shirt for emphasis.

Joyce snorted a laugh. "Okay, fair enough. Want to get a coffee, though? I'm not suggesting anything here, but it is kind of weird that you're the only other person I know who has already lost both parents. It's kind of cool to be completely free."

"Sure." But Bertrand wouldn't have referred to it as freedom. That was college, when he was living on campus away from home with no idea that he was squandering precious time with his parents. If he'd gone to University of Illinois instead of his dad's alma mater in Rochester, would they still be alive? Would they have spent that fateful day at home with him?

They walked in silence for a time, their route taking them through the campus of DePaul University, past the glass-and-brick athletic center, only a decade or so old and yet looking fragile compared with the gray squared-stone permanence of St. Vincent de Paul Church across the street.

"I like to go this way." Joyce turned them east, Bertrand nearly tripping over the dog when it was slow to turn with her. It growled.

"Sorry there puppy." Bertrand gave its head a pat but there was no friendly response.

"You'll have to forgive St. Mike. He thinks of you as competition. He's like that with all the guys I know, even Jeff."

Above them an 'L' train rushed along, quickly followed by another going in the opposite direction, the noise preventing further conversation. Soon they passed into a residential neighborhood like Bertrand's—narrow century properties set back only a body-length from the sidewalks. Occasionally the renovated old houses were interspersed with modern constructions that stood out and, to Bertrand's eye, didn't belong.

They walked without speaking, even now on the quiet street, and Bertrand enjoyed the peace, marveling that he'd found someone else who didn't have to fill every empty space with prattle.

Finally Joyce spoke. "So I was thinking we'd go to Starbucks over on Halstead. A friend on my works there and she may be on—"

A scream—a terrified scream—ripped from the nearest house.

Bertrand turned before he could think and slipped up the latch on the wrought-iron gate. He ran up the steps to the front door and rang the bell. The house was either new or had been so ruthlessly renovated that it might as well be. The doors were mostly glass, with stiff, sheer curtains for privacy. Joyce had followed, and now she leaned forward, hammering on the wood above the lock, making the doors rattle.

"Anyone in there?" she shouted. Every light in the house blazed.

A dark shadow flitted between one light source and the door. Bertrand drew in his breath sharply, because it reminded him so much of his experience the previous night at Needleman's.

"Stop right there!" He leapt the porch rail as he shouted, landing on the tiny lawn that sat between the sidewalk and a chest-high brick wall, which ran from the corner of this house to the clapboard house next door. The red brick had clearly been chosen to make the wall look old Chicago, but it was a modern construction for privacy. Bertrand stood in front of the wall, peering into the dark backyard, trying to decide if he'd lost his mind. He had no right to shout orders. He had no right to go running into someone's backyard in the dark, but he didn't want a repeat of Needleman's, to find nothing but blood and a mystery.

A low growl startled Bertrand. St. Mike stood beside him, his teeth bared.

"Grab him!" shouted Joyce from the porch. "Quick, grab his collar."

But it was too late. The dog tensed and sprang straight up, his nails scrapping the top of the wall for purchase as he crossed into the backyard.

"Shit!" Joyce leapt the rail and landed considerably lighter than Bertrand, but she continued in one fluid motion, taking three steps passed the bow window of the house to bring her to the wall, which she scaled with speed that would make an army sergeant proud.

"Joyce! Wait! The dog's on to someone! Don't go back there!"

But she was already in pursuit of St. Mike, who ran for the far side of the yard with quiet determination. He was going for a kill. Bertrand grabbed the wall and hauled his bulk up, scrabbling with his feet to climb the brick, rolling on his chest over the top and falling awkwardly onto his feet, scraping his back as he slipped down. He ran after Joyce but didn't have to go far: St. Mike had come up against a fence of pressure-treated wood that hid the back alley.

Bertrand could hear the hurried footfall of someone retreating on the other side of the fence, and St. Mike growled—again with bared teeth—but this time the fence, higher than Bertrand's head, was too high for the dog. Joyce and Bertrand exchanged a look of puzzlement and disbelief.

"What the ..." said Bertrand.

Joyce turned back to the house, where a sliding glass door opened up onto a spacious deck, populated with the various implements of summer living. "It's wide open," she said, as the heavy drapes flapped from within to wave out into the summer night. "We should go in."

Bertrand remembered his sense of doom before he'd entered Needleman's house. He didn't sense it tonight, but wisdom forced him to grab Joyce's elbow. "No. This might be a crime scene."

"And someone might be bleeding on the floor. You heard that scream."

"Then we should call 911 anyway."

Joyce shook her arm free of Bertrand's grasp. She yanked a cell phone from her pocket and hit a speed dial, holding the phone to her ear while she proceeded carefully up the stairs, her body turned sideways as if expecting attack.

"Hi, yes, we were passing this house on Webster, no I don't know the number, but we're just a block or so east of the 'L.' No, listen, we heard a scream coming from the house and my dog chased a burglar out of the backyard. I'm just going to look through the door ... No, I won't go into the house unless I see someone in trouble. Okay! I won't go into the house. Would you just send someone asap, already?"

Bertrand couldn't help himself. He had followed her lead up the stairs, his courage returning. "Okay, if we're going in, let's go in fast." But when he reached for the door, a thousand tiny reflections of light scattered on the polished wooden floor warned him that the sliding door wasn't open—it was smashed.

"Watch the glass." Bertrand put out an arm to warn Joyce back, but she pushed past him and through the billowing drapes. He followed her immediately, but once through the curtains, it was clear they were far too late to help.

The dining-room table, a modern effort that would have fit in an Ikea showroom, had been tipped on its side during the struggle, its matching chairs flung about the room. A chubby man, his hair thin and his goatee gray, lay sprawled near the far wall, the blood soaking his muscle shirt and boxer shorts. A squared chunk of his neck near the jugular, just a bit wider than a human mouth, had been cut right out with a very sharp knife.

"Can't save him," said Joyce, frozen where she'd stopped. She turned and pushed back out to the deck while Bertrand backed out cautiously, trying not to further disturb the crime scene.

He found Joyce sitting on the steps, St. Mike close to her side, her phone to her ear as she spoke to 911 to give them further details. Bertrand sat on the other side of St. Mike, petting the dog's back as if he needed comfort.

They were still there, an hour later, when the police arrived.

# 5

# NO NEWS OF MURDER

Ordered to wait by the first officer responding to their 911, Bertrand and Joyce sat at the patio table on the deck, unwilling voyeurs of the crime-scene processing. Where not occluded by the house, flashing lights from emergency vehicles did reach the backyard. Aside from that and the troubled voices inside, they could have been any couple enjoying a summer evening.

A man in a dark suit stepped out the patio doors, his thin gray hair failing to hide that he was soon to be bald. He carried a comfortable paunch of middle age, but it was a barrel-chested shape—maybe he used to lift weights but had given it up. His tie wasn't done all the way up in the heat, and he mopped the sweat from his brow with a handkerchief while a uniformed officer spoke in a low voice, reading from his notebook and pointing his pen at Bertrand. The plainclothes officer nodded and stepped forward.

"I'm Detective Sinclair. I'm sorry you had to see this, but the 911 operator warned you not to enter the premises." He stopped with his hands at his sides, but there was something so military in his stance that it made Bertrand wonder if the man were a first Iraq war vet. The age would be about right.

Bertrand stood. "All due respect, if we'd entered the premises faster we might have saved the guy's life."

"Or been murdered yourselves. Look, I don't want to debate you. I hear you've given your statements and I'll read those over later, but just a quick question: did you get any look at the murderer, even just height?"

Bertrand looked to Joyce, who now stood, holding firmly to St. Mike's leash as if the dog might bolt rather than sit there panting in the heat.

"He was already over the fence by the time I got back here." She pointed into the dark corner of the back yard beside the detached garage.

The chopping of a helicopter rose from subtle background to annoyance, causing them all to look up just as a bright searchlight switched on. The letters of a TV station on the side proved that it wasn't a police helicopter.

"Aw, damn, already?" Sinclair's shoulders sagged. "Look, folks, I'd consider it a favor if you didn't speak to the news. The last thing I need is to turn this into more of a circus than it already is."

A few days ago Bertrand might have quietly acquiesced, but this was the new Bertrand. "I'll keep my mouth shut if you answer just one question."

The detective's eyes hardened. "I'm not at liberty to answer questions about ongoing investigations, and if you feel uncooperative I can take you in for questioning for the night."

Bertrand held up his hands, palms out to signal surrender. "No, it's okay, I'm not going to ask about this case. I heard from another cop that Ripper murders are happening in other cities, but I've heard almost nothing on the news. So that's my question: are Ripper-style murders happening in other cities."

Sinclair's lips pressed into a tense line for a moment as he sized Bertrand up.

"Okay, I'll answer this one, but then you leave through the neighbor's yard and you don't talk to the news at all. You seem to be good at fence hopping." He pointed to the next yard over, the corner house on the street.

"We can do that," said Joyce.

"There have been Ripper murders all over the world, but in most cities they seem to have stopped. No reports of any in places like Paris or London for a month anyway. But why ask me? Google it."

"It's tough searching through the weird conspiracy shit. I thought you might have the inside track."

"If I did I couldn't share it with you. Now that's your question, Mr. Allan. Time to go."

The short fence to the neighbor's yard proved no effort even for Bertrand, although he had to help Joyce shove the dog over the fence, who seemed unwilling to jump without serious motivation.

The clapboard house was wider than Bertrand's narrow house and a full two stories—big by downtown standards. Bertrand glanced at the house as they hurried through to the street, wondering if this house, like his, had survived the Great Fire. A modern sliding glass door at the back opened onto a deck similar to the one they'd just left, and a man in a bathrobe stood safely inside the house, the door firmly shut. He held a shotgun, his wide face shockingly pale, even with three days of stubble.

"Stay away!" shouted the man.

"Just passing through." Bertrand tried to sound disarming, as if it were an everyday occurrence to have strangers run through your backyard while news choppers circled overhead.

The man responded to Bertrand's wave by stepping back a pace and leveling the shotgun.

"Let's get out of here," said Bertrand. Joyce only nodded her agreement as they scrambled over the low chain-link fence on the far side and into the street.

They walked to Joyce's condo in silence, one of four in a line of row houses—boxy, modern affairs that probably won awards for the architect in the eighties but now just looked dated.

"Hope you don't mind that I don't invite you in for a nightcap." Joyce didn't look back as she put the key in the lock.

"Yeah. Murder just spoils the mood, doesn't it?" Bertrand considered smacking his forehead. What had possessed him to say that?

Joyce turned back from her door, a smile teasing the corners of her lips but a frown moderating it. "You're a no bullshit guy, Bert. I like that. I'll see you at the gym."

She shut the door.

The first thing Bertrand did when he got home was turn on every light and search every corner of the little two bedroom house to ensure he was completely alone. He checked that all the doors and windows were locked before he booted his laptop, grabbed a beer from the fridge and turned on the TV to the local station, settling into his La-Z-Boy just as the eleven o'clock news rolled with all the dazzling graphics.

Absenteeism at city hall was the lead story, with the reporter interviewing people angry that they were unable to complete basic tasks, like getting building permits or paying taxes. A representative for the mayor's office stood just outside city hall, the street lights on and people hurrying by, some with looks back at the camera. His suit was impeccable and his tie a sharp red. "The mayor would like everyone to know that Chicago is still open for business. We have had some staffing issues over the summer due to the unexpected flu that's going around, but we're working late into the night to clear the backlog. We've extended our hours to include a special session between nine p.m and midnight, so if you were turned away today, please come down now and you'll find us open and ready to serve."

Bertrand put his beer down and opened his laptop. This was weird. Why not lead with the new Ripper murder? A quick check of the TV station's website, the same as the letters on the helicopter that had circled the crime scene, proved that there was no coverage there either—not a word, not even a headline promising more details to follow.

The next item on the news was the stock market's increasingly wild gyrations, but Bertrand was no longer paying attention. He searched "Ripper murders" and came up with results, but they were all a few days old and all from Chicago. He was able to find a reference to a serial slasher in New York, but those articles were also out of date. He was just about to give up when a result, 1000Souls.com, got his attention with a tag line that didn't seem to fit the search. It asked: *Has Your Soul Gotten Stronger?*

Bertrand clicked on it expecting to land on some cheap conspiracy theory blog, but instead he found a well produced website. They had started with a front-end framework, yes, but the developers obviously knew their way around a database, and the graphics of several overlapping circles indicated a professional designer. But what really caught Bertrand's attention was one line of text: "The Ripper murders are the reason you are stronger."

It went on to describe a new religion, one that believed there were only one thousand souls in existence, each soul spread between many humans. "Thus," said the author, "the one thousand became very diluted when the population of the earth exploded—each body containing only a tiny fragment of a soul. But for the first time in history, the process is reversing. Millions are dying, and each portion of the souls of those dying people flees to a living person. If you wonder why your soul feels more powerful, it's because it is more powerful. It is denser. The portion of your soul that you are a vessel for is greater than it has been for over two centuries."

"Okay this is crazy," said Bertrand to the room. He was about to close the tab when the next line galvanized his attention.

"Have you had a sudden panic attack recently?" the website's author asked. "Have you found yourself apprehensive for no reason, culminating into a surging heartbeat and unfocused terror, only to have it all end suddenly leaving you oddly better? These are the tell tale signs that someone whose body contains a portion of the same soul that your body contains has been murdered. When a person dies their soul portion should gently merge with the entire soul, a little bit entering each living human host. But in the case of a sudden and violent death, the soul-portion seeks only the nearest human vessel containing a portion of the same soul. This increases soul density rapidly. That is why there are physiological side effects.

"The Ripper murders are so numerous and violent that many soul-portions must flee to living hosts."

Bertrand sat back and shook his head. Just coincidence that this nutbar was describing a simple panic attack and ascribing ethereal causes. The guy even called himself by a plural: Erics, saying that he was only one of many host bodies for his soul, thus the plural. It didn't seem to bother him that the other host bodies weren't necessarily named Eric. "I use the plural as a symbol of the multiple bodies that contain my single soul."

Bertrand snorted and was about to click away, but his curiosity got the better of him, and he found himself typing into the "Contact Us" form. "How do you know there are one thousand souls and not one million?" He sent the message and closed his laptop.

The TV news was now dealing with the power outages caused by absenteeism at major power plants and whether this was an unannounced work-to-rule by the power workers union in advance of fall contract negotiations. Bertrand shut off the TV.

Why didn't the news cover this evening's Ripper murder? Why send a news chopper and vans full of reporters and camera guys but not report it?

Bertrand headed to his fridge for more beer but put the bottle back without opening it. He wanted answers. He wanted to prove to himself that the evening had not been some weird nightmare. There had been a crime scene, and Bertrand decided to go back and check it out, verify the police tape and the reality of a man's brutal murder in the absence of news coverage. He didn't have a gun, but there was a sheathed hunting knife in the basement, and Bertrand hurried to retrieve it. He slid it under his shirt and into the waistband of his jeans. Was he carrying a concealed weapon now? But Bertrand didn't care so much about the law—he had to go out tonight. He stood before his front door for a moment, summoning up his courage before he opened the door. Strange events had caused a strange reaction. He was afraid of the dark.

# 6

# SKULKING

B ertrand had planned to walk north on his street, but the neighborhood seemed far more alive than it had during the day. A couple kissed passionately under a street light about a stone's throw away, and Bertrand didn't want to disturb their tryst, so he turned south instead. But at the intersection with Armitage, a half-dozen rowdy teenagers threw beer bottles at passing cars and shouted obscenities. Surely someone would call 911, but in the meantime Bertrand knew they were out of control and to be avoided.

In fact, the whole city seemed to hum more than usual for a quiet summer night, and the traffic noise of fast engines, car horns, booming music and distant sirens all blended together. Distant shouts mingled, some just raucous, like those of the teenagers, but others sounded frightened, maybe even like distant screams.

Time to be invisible. Time to do the unexpected. Bertrand crossed to Needleman's house, surprised that someone had set a **FOR SALE** sign on the front lawn and replaced the screen door. Needleman had heirs? Bertrand couldn't recall Needleman having any visitors from friends or family. The front door proved to be unlocked, perhaps because the mysterious heirs didn't have the key and had correctly judged that there was nothing worth stealing. Bertrand crossed through the house quickly, relying on moonlight and his knowledge of the geography of his own house, the mirror of Needleman's, to guide his steps.

The back screen door had not been repaired, so Bertrand opened it slowly, careful not to dislodge the remaining shards of glass and announce his presence. To whom? Bertrand eased the door closed behind him and walked down the steps and stood under the 'L' tracks. The weak street light in the alley on the far side of the tracks did little to illuminate under the 'L,' thus leaving Bertrand in darkness. He was invisible. Now if he could just be silent.

He headed north, weaving a path around cars parked under the 'L', slipping briefly into the alley whenever his way was impeded by a fence, but returning to travel under the 'L' as soon as possible. A train roared overhead, allowing him to run, the slap of his running shoes buried by the noise of wind, steel wheels and electric motors. He slowed back to a stealthy walk after it passed. Only once, when a window clicked open in one of the houses that backed onto the 'L', did Bertrand wonder if he'd lost his mind. What if someone saw him skulking along like this? Would they think he was crazy or worse, a criminal?

But Bertrand felt safe under the tracks, off the main routes and invisible from prying eyes—dangerous eyes. He remembered the words of the young officer, Gonsalves: "We can't protect you anymore." If teenagers could drink beer in public and throw the bottles at passing cars with impunity, he was certainly correct. There was a breath of anarchy in the summer air.

When Bertrand reached Webster, he had to turn right to get back to the crime scene, and that meant he had to walk a short distance on the sidewalk like a normal person. He had walked only a few paces along Webster when he was presented with the first puzzle: the street was clear and open for traffic. Where were the police cars and the news vans? Okay, maybe the news people had moved on to more exciting crime scenes, but shouldn't there be at least one police car parked on the street, keeping an eye on the crime scene while it was processed?

But the street was empty, and the parked cars sat waiting for morning and their owners. No police cruiser lurked among them. It got stranger as he approached the house: it was dark. Where was the crime-scene tape? A square sign on the front lawn caught Bertrand's attention, and he hurried forward because he couldn't believe what he saw, until he was close enough that even in the weak streetlights he could read it: **FOR SALE**.

"What the—" Bertrand let his breath out in a gush. Just like Needleman's, only there couldn't have been time to alert the next of kin, contact a real estate agent and list the house, even if the police had somehow processed the crime scene in record time. Bertrand slowed to a stop in front of the house, but he didn't want to linger until someone came along and noticed his bizarre interest.

What about the back door?

Bertrand opened the latch of the gate and made his way to the brick wall, scaling it just as awkwardly as before, even though he didn't have to rush this time. He crept along to the backyard, staying close to the wall of the house to hide in its shadow. Was he out of his mind? What would someone think if they saw him, a fat computer nerd creeping along in the dark? Would they assume he was a thief or just plain high?

He peeked around the corner, expecting to see crime-scene tape and perhaps a bored police officer guarding the broken window, but the deck was empty. Only the two chairs that no longer tipped against the patio table—the ones he and Joyce had occupied—proved to him that he had been there just a couple of hours ago. He moved into the backyard proper, climbing the steps to the deck in disbelief. A new sliding glass door now sealed the back of the house.

Who had paid for that and how had they found a company willing to come out so quickly, so late at night? He tried to peer through the new window, but the heavy drapes were drawn and the house was dark. Was there still blood on the floor? He considered calling Detective Sinclair, considered asking him why the police were hiding the fact that this house was a crime scene. But what would the man say? *Can't talk about an on-going investigation.*

Bertrand went out of the yard the way he'd gone in, scrambling over the brick wall, but he just couldn't go home. He had to confirm that this hadn't all been a twisted nightmare. He didn't have Joyce's number, or he would have called her to ensure he hadn't lost his mind. But even if he did call her, what would he say? Do you remember that guy with the chunk of his throat cut out? His house is for sale—maybe it'll be a good deal after the blood is cleaned from the floor.

The neighbor's house presented an option, but he was unsure about ringing the doorbell of a man who had presented a shotgun earlier, for no apparent reason. Yet, the man had seemed more terrified than crazy. Perhaps he had seen the murderer. Had he already talked to the police?

Bertrand walked slowly up the front steps to the clapboard house, summoning the courage to press the button under an intercom speaker. Odd for a house to have one like this, and it looked brand-new.

"Who is it?" asked a male voice, a low voice that fit the big man in the bathrobe.

"Hi, my name is Bertrand Allan. You saw me go through your back-yard earlier this evening." Bertrand's ears burned with his embarrassment. What could this conversation possibly accomplish?

"I'm armed. You and your friends stay away. I know what you are and I'll shoot the first bastards who crosses my doorstep."

"Jesus Christ, dude." Bertrand backed up a step. "All I wanted to ask was when the cops left, 'cause it's totally weird that they're gone and there's nothing on the news. I mean, it's as if your neighbor's murder never happened." Bertrand backed down the stairs now. This had been a bad idea, and the sooner he got away from this nutbar, the better.

"Wait a second," the voice whispered over the intercom.

Nothing happened for a pregnant minute, and Bertrand backed far-ther away from the steps of the house. Finally the door opened, and the same unshaven man—the brown bathrobe wrapped around his wide waist—brandished a shotgun at Bertrand. "Say Jesus' name again."

Bertrand considered telling him where to go, but the gun riveted his attention. Fear can make people do crazy things, and this man looked terrified, his eyes wide, shifting left to right to check for threats in the street.

"Jesus Christ," Bertrand said. "Has the world gone mad?"

"Make the sign of the cross."

"Come on, dude. I just want to go home."

"Make the sign of the cross or I'll blow you away right now!"

There's no arguing with fear. Bertrand had to think to remember the routines of his childhood, before his parents had decided that church wasn't essential to his upbringing.

"In the name of the Father, Son and Holy Spirit. Look, can I go now. I'm really, really sorry I bothered you. I just thought maybe the police had said something to you."

The gun didn't waver but the man's face relaxed a bit.

"Like why they're covering up a murder."

"Yeah. Like that."

"You better come in."

"No." Bertrand stepped back, preparing to turn and run.

"You'll never make it home." The man raised the shotgun. "I'm your only chance. Get in here now before she comes around and kills us both."

"Who?"

"Rose. My neighbor, Rose. Now get in here, quick!" The man looked up and down the street in panic, as if a pack of wolves might come dashing along, hunting the unwary.

His fear was infectious. Bertrand looked up and down, but even though the street was empty, the sounds of the city seemed even more pronounced. Distant sirens, shouts and running feet. Was that a scream a few blocks away? Bertrand took a deep breath and hurried up the stairs into the man's house. Oddly, despite the gun and the craziness, it seemed safer than walking home in the dark.

# 7

# HAUNTING

Bertrand placed his hand to his stomach, hiding the bulge of the hunting knife in his shirt. Not that a knife would be much help against a crazy man with a shotgun, but it was the last option for Bertrand if things got violent.

The big man slammed the door, leaving them in darkness alleviated only by streetlight washing in through the living room windows, turning furniture into shadows.

"What's your name again?" The shotgun was leveled at Bertrand's chest.

"Dude, please put the gun down, okay. My name's Bertrand Allan, and I'm not the Chicago Ripper." Bertrand held up one hand—palm out in surrender—and hoped that the man wouldn't notice that his other hand was over his stomach.

"Chicago Ripper?" The man gave a derisive snort. "You believe that crap? This way, quick." He waved the gun down the hall. "We have to get into the shelter."

"No." Bertrand backed up a step into the living room, his heart really pounding now. He would have to fight. "No way. You're crazy."

"I'm trying to save your life. We're in danger every minute we're up here, but Rose doesn't know about the shelter. We've got to lock ourselves in until morning and then I swear by God I'll let you go."

Running feet on the sidewalk outside and a scream forced them both to turn to the bow window. A dark figure ran past, closely followed by several more.

"What the hell is going on?" Bertrand forgot about his knife as he stepped toward the window, pulling aside the sheer curtain to get a better look at the pursuit.

"I'll leave you to die if you don't come now."

The man backed down the hallway, opening a door. Pale light leaked up a set of stairs. Bertrand considered his options: run into the street to try and help someone who was being chased by thugs and was probably three blocks away by now, or follow the crazy man with the shotgun into his basement. There was no point in trying to run to the rescue tonight, because he could never catch those people, and even if he did, what could he do against several assailants, even with his knife? Besides, Bertrand craved information and this strange man knew something. "Okay, I'll go to the shelter or whatever, but stop pointing the gun at me, and at least tell me your name."

"Thomas, Thomas Nolan, and I'm sorry but you have to pass the human test before I trust you. Don't worry, it's nothing weird. You go first."

Bertrand headed down the stairs, finding a basement from the seventies lit only by a couple of nightlights, one plugged into a socket above a wet bar, another at the bottom of the stairs. The wood paneling, shag carpet and bar stools in front of the Formica counter all looked new, even though they must be forty years old. Someone had taken very good care of this house. The couch and an armchair were squared and small, designed for the healthier backsides of the twentieth century rather than the large behinds of the twenty-first century.

Nolan moved past Bertrand to a fridge against the wall behind the bar. He gave it a mighty shove and it rolled to one side, revealing more paneling from the seventies, but he placed the flat of his hand against the wood and simply slid it aside. A door that could rival a bank vault was hidden behind, except that it looked homemade, welded in the back of a shop or a garage and brush-painted gray. Nolan pushed on it—there was no handle—and the heavy door swung inward, allowing fluorescent light to spill out. Nolan waved the gun at Bertrand. "Get inside."

Bertrand found a room not much bigger than a walk-in closet. Narrow couches ran along each wall, and a small beer fridge sat between them at the far end, above it a very modern flat-screen was tuned to CNN, but the mute was on. Racked guns occupied every available space on the walls above the couches. There were shotguns, handguns and full-auto assault rifles. Uh oh. Maybe the guy was totally crazy.

"Help yourself to a beer and grab a seat."

Beer. God, he needed one, and if he was going to die he didn't have to worry about losing weight. Bertrand headed straight for the little fridge and found it full of Budweiser. He pulled two cold cans out and turned to find Nolan shoving the door closed with his shoulder—a door that looked about two feet thick. "What the hell is this place?"

"Bomb shelter. Three-foot thick concrete walls, built down here around the Cuban missile crisis by the guy who owned the house before me." Nolan pushed four heavy bolts—as thick as baseball bats—straight into a concrete wall. "I always thought it was funny, a good man-cave and all. Kept it a secret from everybody but Stan 'cause of the gun collection."

Nolan turned, putting his back to the door and drawing a heavy breath, the shotgun again pointing a Bertrand. "Have a drink. You can put mine down there." He nodded down at a little end table by the right side couch.

Bertrand popped open his beer and took a long drink, relishing in the freedom from guilt about his waistline. Today, he truly deserved alcohol.

Nolan watched him drink for a full ten seconds and sighed with relief.

"Thank God. You're human." He slumped down on the couch, resting the gun across his knees, reaching for his beer but still keeping a close eye on Bertrand, who took a seat on the opposite couch.

"Why the hell were you waving a shotgun at me?" Bertrand took a sip of his beer, sensing his own heart rate calming now that the gun wasn't pointed at his chest.

"You can't trust anyone." Nolan took a big gulp and wiped sweat from his brow.

Now that they were under the twin fluorescent bulbs, it was obvious that Nolan was in his late sixties, the stubble of his beard firmly gray, although his military cut hair was still salt-and-pepper on a thick head. His belly pushed at the draw strings of the bathrobe, barely allowing it to close.

Bertrand took a sip of his beer. "Who are you so afraid of, and what do you mean I'm human. Of course I'm human. What did you think I was, a space alien?"

Nolan finished his beer in one long series of gulps and crushed the can in his hand, tossing it aside into a garbage can at the end of his couch.

"A blood drinker." He heaved up his bulk and grabbed another beer from the fridge.

"What, like a vampire? You've got to be kidding me."

"Buddy, these stories about the Chicago Ripper, they're all bullshit to hide the fact that there are blood drinkers out there—not vampires, not like the movies—blood drinkers."

"Well what the frig is the difference?"

"These are real." Nolan slumped down on his couch and snapped open the beer. "They don't have fangs or weird shit like that. They use knives to open up your jugular, and they suck like crazy as you spew blood, until you've bled out."

"How do you know this?" Bertrand leaned forward, thinking about the blood on Needleman's living-room floor and the chunk cut out of the murdered man's neck.

"Stan's wife got snatched by this so-called Chicago Ripper two weeks ago, only there was three of them. We saw them grab her. Stan and I were having a beer right up there on my front porch, and we see Rose walking along the sidewalk on her way back from her bridge club. Suddenly a van just shoots up and the side door opens, and there's like three men in there, and they just grab her and haul her into the van and take off."

"Are you sure it was men. Could it have been three women dressed like men? It was dark wasn't it?" Bertrand was thinking about

Jeffery's neighbor, the geek who came home with four hot women and disappeared.

"They were men. The interior light of the van was on and I tell you they were men. The police said it was the Chicago Ripper—you ever hear of the news talking about the Chicago Rippers?"

"No. So are you saying they killed your neighbor—is that the Stan guy you were talking about—they killed his wife and then him?"

Nolan took a big drink. "Nope," he said, wiping foam from his mouth. "It was Rose who did Stan tonight."

"What the ...? How do you know?"

"I saw it, goddammit! I was right out back there." He pointed to the ceiling with the shotgun. "I was just coming out to put some burgers on the barbecue for a late-night snack, and I heard the glass break over at Stan's. You've seen that little fence between us, right? We're good neighbors, both did tours in 'Nam just a couple of years apart. So's I go over near the fence thinking I'm gonna catch a burglar on his way out with the TV. I had my Glock with me, so I figured I was ready. Then I hear Stan screaming, so I hop the fence and I'm going up the back steps and there she is, putting a knife to him as if she's a combat veteran—and I've seen combat. I heard you guys coming and split, but I tell you I haven't seen blood spray like that since 'Nam."

"Holy shit! What did the cops say?"

Nolan shook his head. "I don't talk to them no more. Don't you get it? They're in on it, man. Look what happened to Rose. Come on, think about it: Stan and I call the cops with this cockamamie story about his old lady being kidnapped and they took forty minutes to get here. They took our statements like it was a noise complaint and told us it was the M.O. of the Chicago Ripper. They didn't even blink when we said there were three of them. They were brushing us off over a frigging kidnapping! Just a quick 'We're sorry but it's unlikely we'll catch them and you'll never see your wife again' before they left. I tell you, if I were a cop and a couple of guys gave me such a bullshit story, I'd have turned their lives upside down. I'd have sworn the murderers were standing right in front of me putting on a good act with a stupid story, but instead they just left after half an hour. For Christ's sake, it took them longer than that to get here!"

"But they came tonight. I mean there was crime scene processing and all going on while Joyce and I were giving our statements. And we did have to give signed statements."

"Since when do the cops fix broken windows and put for sale signs up on crime scenes."

It was Bertrand's turn to take a long drink of his beer, finishing the can while he thought about the reluctance of the police to worry about Needleman or Jeff's neighbor, even with the bloodstains.

"It's just so crazy," Bertrand finally said. "I mean, why would they be in on it? What would the cops get for helping, well, these freaky blood drinkers you're talking about. Is this all some weird cult?"

Nolan heaved up and went over to the fridge to grab a beer for Bertrand. "I don't know what's going on, man. But I can tell you this: something is going on—something really big. And I know that you can't trust the cops, and you can't trust the government and you can't trust your neighbors."

"What can we do, though?"

Nolan passed him the beer. "We sit tight 'till morning. I don't know if they can come out in daylight and all, but all the crazy stuff so far is happening after dark. I came to get you only because I didn't want you cut right on my front doorstep. I don't go out after dark anymore. In fact, I'm not leaving this room till sun up and neither should you."

Bertrand thought about the trip back, about the chaos that was outside. Here he was safe and there was beer. He'd leave at dawn.

# 8

# NIGHT SHIFT

Warm sun spilled into the front hall when Nolan opened his front door, still in his bathrobe and still holding a shotgun, although it no longer pointed at Bertrand.

"I'm starting a blog about this, calling it 'My Undead Neighbor,'" Nolan said. "You should follow it, and maybe you can guest post about your neighbor. And listen, don't go out at night again, all right?"

Bertrand shook his head. "I can't promise that. They're out there at night. If we don't go out at night, how can we fight them?"

Nolan just shook his head and closed the door.

Bertrand walked through a very quiet city, the traffic very light even for early rush hour. After a quick shower and change of clothes at his house, he caught a train into town after a twenty-minute wait. There was no announcement to explain the delay, and when the train arrived there were many empty seats. How could Chicago Transit survive such a downturn in ridership?

Jeff joined him in the elevator, looking drawn and hung over. Oddly, they had the car to themselves.

"What happened to you last night," Bertrand asked as the elevator doors slid shut.

"Oh this woman could drink." Jeff hid his hands in his face for a moment and scrubbed at his cheeks as if he could massage away the hangover.

"Where'd you go?"

"Oh, just her place. She has a thing about not going out to clubs these days—likes to joke about vampire dancers hogging the floor and showing off. She keeps a well-stocked bar, though."

"Well, that makes her a cheap date, I guess."

"Yeah but I'm paying for it now. I have to quit this drinking-crap before it kills me and take up a safe hobby like sky diving."

The doors slid open on a quiet office.

"Where the heck is everyone?" Bertrand led the way out of the elevator and toward their nest of cubicles and, more importantly, the kitchen beyond.

"I don't smell coffee," said Jeff.

Whitlock was washing out the coffee pot when they turned the corner, his military bearing incongruous with his domestic task.

"Thank God. At least I still have three loyal employees." He began to fill the pot with water.

"Where the hell is everyone?" asked Bertrand.

"So far we pretty much are everyone. Only Destiny showed up for the New York shift and she doesn't drink coffee. She's out there now trying to manage calls for three. Get in the queue and give her a hand, for Christ's sake. I'll be your waitress and bring you coffee."

"Black for me." Jeff filled a large glass from the cupboard with water from the tap. He gulped it back while holding one hand against the side of his head in pain. "That'll have to do," he said before refilling the glass and heading out of the kitchen.

"Oh come on, John," said Bertrand. "Three of us can't manage the day's contact load. We've got to get somebody else in—a temp or someone."

Whitlock poured the water into the coffee maker. "I'm trying, but I'm not having much luck. This weird summer flu is affecting everything from the 'L' trains to the power stations. New York had blackout an hour ago, and they're blaming not enough staff at some nuke plant. Took out the whole eastern seaboard right up to Canada. Good news is that's made the contact volume a lot less, but I expect it to ramp up any minute as people on central time start sitting down at their desks, just like you should be right now."

"Okay, I'm going, I'm going."

Bertrand hurried to his cubicle. Jeff had just sat and now rummaged through a drawer until he pulled out a bottle of Advil and set it beside his keyboard. "Gonna be a long day," he said when he saw Bertrand's frown.

Destiny Kim sat two cubicles over, her straight black hair falling about her face as she punched at her keyboard, her voice hushed as she explained something to a client. She looked up for a moment and raised her eyebrows at Bertrand, the office sign that indicated a thick one on the other end of the phone connection.

Jeff popped a couple of pills into his mouth and took a quick drink of his water.

"By the way, remember my neighbor," he said. "The one I thought was murdered? Turns out he moved away. His unit's on the market, not that I think he'll get much for it with all the for sale signs I see around these days."

Bertrand sat heavily. This couldn't be happening, could it? This morning in the sun he'd nearly convinced himself that Thomas Nolan was a nutbar, but the evidence kept stacking up. Didn't Jeff see it too? "Wait a second," said Bertrand. "Your neighbor's dead."

Jeff, his headset on and one hand poised over the keyboard, met Bertrand's gaze. "I wondered what you'd think. The moving away is the story the police gave Kate, that busybody old lady who's his neighbor."

"Don't trust the police."

Jeff nodded and tapped his keyboard. "Timetracks help desk. How can I be of assistance?"

Bertrand was on his last call before lunch, his stomach rumbling. "That's right," he said. "Just like in the manual."

"Well don't I feel like a dunderhead." The woman on the other end of the connection sounded genuinely contrite. "I should've looked it up before I called, but this isn't my usual job, and since everyone wants their pay, I figured I'd better roll my sleeves up and get it done."

"That's admirable. Have you had a lot of vacancies at your work?'

"Way too many." The women's voice dropped to a whisper. "Frankly, I'm cashing my check, emptying my bank account and heading for the hills. Things are getting very strange and very bad. You wouldn't believe what's going on at night around here. I mean, this is Colorado Springs! It used to be such a safe place."

"What's going on?" Bertrand lowered his voice too, glancing around the office to see if anyone noticed that he'd strayed outside protocol.

"Fires, killings and worse. It seems every morning we wake up and someone else's house has burned down and the families are gone—dead in the fires I suppose, but they never seem to pull bodies out of the ruins, at least that's what my son-in-law says. He's in the fire department, and he says they won't even respond at night anymore, says there're mobs around these fires and the police won't back them up."

"That sounds worse than here."

"It'll spread there too," was the whispered reply. "It started in LA even though the TV news stopped covering it a couple of weeks ago. Get out of the Chicago now and hide until this blows over."

"What blows over?" Bertrand ignored the puzzled look from Jeff, who had removed his headset in anticipation of lunch and was now studying Bertrand.

"The plague."

The connection cut.

Jeff stood. "What was that all about?'

"Dude, we gotta talk."

"Great, let's do lunch at Flynn's. I need the hair of the dog."

But Whitlock hurried over before they could leave.

"I need you guys to work through lunch. I'll order Chinese for everybody."

"Not for me, you won't." Destiny popped up from her cubicle. "I want pizza, deep dish, true Chicago style with lots of meat."

"Okay, the Korean girl wants pizza. What do you guys want?"

"I'm from Chicago." She stuck out her tongue and ducked back down.

"I'll have chicken wings and beer," said Jeff.

"Come you guys. Don't bust my balls here. I'm working right alongside you, and a couple of people have promised to come in tonight to clear up anything that's left."

"Pizza's fine," said Bertrand.

Jeff rolled his eyes and nodded, reaching into his desk drawer for the bottle of Advil.

---

The sun had set by the time Bertrand logged off and put away his headset. Other employees had started to arrive, which was a good thing, because the contact backlog had grown over the last hour rather than tapering off as usual.

Jeff stood and stretched his tall frame, yawning as he twisted kinks out of his back. "Oh, and it's karate night with Sensei Stu. God I have to be better to myself."

"Malcolm doesn't look much better than you. Look at him. He should've just stayed home."

Malcolm had just stepped off the elevator and had to stop to hold onto a cubicle divider, looking as if he wanted to bend over and puke. His hair—dyed a flaming red—flew in all directions as if it'd been combed by a tornado. His short, ultra-slim figure looked more emaciated than usual. He got control of his stomach and headed their way.

"Dudes," he said, his voice flat and emotionless. "I can't believe I'm here."

"Buddy." Jeff gave him a heavy pat on the shoulder that almost knocked the young man into his chair. "You're a god for coming in this sick, but really, shouldn't you head back home? It's just a job."

"No, I got a habit I gotta support." He saw their looks. "What? I'm talking clubbing, not heroine."

Bertrand noted the incredibly anemic sheen to Malcolm's skin.

"Can I get you anything from the kitchen? I think there's some left-over pizza I can nuke."

"Oh god, don't mention food. No really, don't mention food." He pulled a garbage can close and bent over it, taking deep breaths.

Whitlock joined them, his arms crossed as he judged, watching Malcolm's battle with his stomach. "Okay, now I believe you," Whitlock finally said. "You're damnably sick. I'm calling you a cab—don't worry, on my dime. I'm the one that browbeat you into coming in. You gotta go home."

"Thanks. Really, I'm sorry but this flu, I hope none of you get it. I think I got it from this chick at Goth Knights. She's a freak let me tell you. Into really kinky games like you wouldn't believe. She's into—"

Whitlock put up one hand to signal stop. "Please, spare me, okay. I'm Christian and married. Do what you want as long as everybody agrees, but I don't want to hear about it. Bert, see that he gets a cab, would you? Get a receipt, Malcolm, and bring it in when you're healthy."

"Thanks." He shuddered. "Thanks so much."

Bertrand and Jeff walked with him to the elevator. When it began its drop, Malcolm had to put one hand on the side to steady.

"Sorry," he said as Bertrand and Jeff backed away.

"Are you gonna hurl?" asked Bertrand.

"I shouldn't ... wouldn't have come in if I'd known it was getting worse. I really need ... I don't know what I need."

"If it gets much worse, I'd go to emerg." Bertrand glanced at Jeff for agreement, but Jeff stared intently at Malcolm as if studying his inner brain with x-ray vision.

They flagged three cabs before one stopped. The first two slowed, saw Malcolm and sped away. The third driver didn't look happy, but when Malcolm pushed a fifty at him, he accepted it and drove off.

Bertrand and Jeff stood shoulder-to-shoulder, watching as the cab hurried away in the light traffic.

"May I never get what he has," said Bertrand.

"Ditto. Let's hit the gym. I get to introduce you to Stu tonight. He's gonna kill you."

———

Stuart Fisher didn't look intimidating when Bertrand first laid eyes on him. The man was short and stocky, but during the first *kata* his fluid moves spoke of grace and taut muscle. His hair was braided into tight rows, his skin a rich black and his accent from the Deep South.

"Come on," he shouted at Bertrand while they were doing crunches. "My grandmother can do better than that. Eleven, twelve. You got to fight to lift your chest into the air, not curl around that flab."

Fisher placed a foot on Bertrand's stomach, pressing down until he gasped while trying to lift his chest as instructed. "You didn't get here a moment too soon. Young man like you should have muscle there, not just guts."

The class continued, about forty people in all lining up in rows later to practice punches and kicks with aggressive shouts, something Bertrand had little energy for after all the calisthenics. But Fisher—Fish as everyone called him—was relentless, and even Jeffery and Joyce seemed surprised by his vehemence.

"Enough!" shouted Fish at the end, standing before the class like a disgruntled sergeant. "That was pathetic, a bunch of pussies waiting to be slaughtered. You got to fight like it's the end of the world. You got to fight like it's almost Judgment Day, when the dead shall walk among the living. Don't come here if you're just looking to get laid. Don't come here 'cause you want to lose few pounds. I only want people here who want to fight for their families and their lives." His voice had risen as he spoke, his eyes bulging from his head. He paused for a moment, studying all their faces and then shouted, his arms spread wide, "Doesn't anybody else see what's going on!"

He stomped out of the room, grabbing a bag near the door of the gym as he left his astonished class to dismiss themselves.

Eyebrows rose, and a few people chuckled as they headed for the change room, but Joyce looked Bertrand's way, and that proved to him that he wasn't the only one who didn't think Fish had gone off the deep end.

"Sorry, Bert." Jeff scooped up a towel from a bench and mopped sweat from his forehead. "He's usually a lot less intense—more fun. And I actually do come here to get laid."

Joyce joined them as the gym emptied. "You tell Jeff what happened last night?"

"Yeah, he did," said Jeff. "On the way here—totally weird—harsh. How you holding up?"

Joyce stretched her hands above her head, and Bertrand had to look away so as not to be caught looking at her breasts, even though they were restrained by a tight sports bra and a skin-hugging tank top.

"I'm fine," she said. "I didn't know the guy and blood doesn't scare me unless it's my own. But I don't think Fish has gone off the deep end. We saw a guy like ten seconds after he was murdered and there wasn't a peep about it on the news last night. That's a cover up. That's a conspiracy."

"Whoa." Jeff threw his towel over his shoulder, looking from Bertrand to Joyce as if making his mind up about something. "Okay, this is going to sound crazy, but has anyone else noticed that the city— our work—everything is starting to seem busier at night than during the day?"

"It does sound crazy," said Joyce. "But I was about ten feet from a murder-in-progress yesterday. That's crazy too. I tell you this: I'm keeping a close eye on people after dark. Some of them act like they're in some kind of secret club."

---

Joyce's use of the word 'secret' got Bertrand thinking and watching people closely over the next month. Why did all the night shift arrive after dark, looking flushed and excited? Why did they all want to work after dark at all? Thomas Nolan's claim that there were "blood drinkers" out there would only fit with this if they were afraid of the sun, like traditional vampires, but certainly no one at work had the Bela Lugosi look.

Malcolm in particular fascinated Bertrand.

"You've really recovered from that flu you had last month," Bertrand mentioned one evening as Malcolm sat, reaching for his headset and booting up his computer. There was a bit of blood on his collar and cheek, but Bertrand decided against telling the man he had cut himself shaving, although it did look fresh.

"Oh, I'm having fun these days." Malcolm cracked his skinny knuckles, getting ready to enter his password. "Remember that Goth chick I told you about? Oh, she keeps me very busy." He gave a wicked smile, and Destiny—rising from her desk to see him over the divider—gave him a sly grin.

"Not as busy as I'd keep you, big boy."

"Anytime, baby."

Malcolm tapped in his password, and Bertrand—close to Malcolm's chair while putting on a leather jacket—noted the keystrokes, recognizing the word even though he missed a couple of letters: Ripp3r.

Bertrand grabbed his pack from under his desk, his cheeks burning because Destiny's innuendo had caught his desire. She was petite and shapely, her skirt short and her blouse buttoned down, and Bertrand would definitely like to know more intimately what she meant by "busy." Joyce had been distant since the night of the murder, sticking strictly to their professional relationship and never available for coffee. Their only conversation involved topics like cardio and exercise machines, training schedules and goals.

"Well I'm off to hit the gym," Bertrand said. "I'll leave you two alone to discuss how busy you both want to be." He hurried for the elevator—still surprised with his newfound frankness in conversation. He also wondered why he had spied on Malcolm's disturbing choice of password.

Just before the elevator doors closed, Destiny and Malcolm exchanged a glance and both looked in Bertrand's direction. If Destiny weren't part of the day shift, Bertrand would have sworn she was in the secret club of night people.

Jeff caught up to him in the lobby.

"You're a changed dude, Bert. Look at you: pack over your shoulder, eager to get to the gym. Joyce tells me she's even got you jogging. Next thing you know she'll have you entering the marathon."

Bertrand pushed through the revolving door and waited for Jeff on the far side.

"I'll have to lose another twenty or so pounds before I think about something that crazy," he said when Jeff emerged.

"But you have lost weight." Jeff fell in step beside him as they headed for the 'L' station. Cabs arrived and departed in the chaos of after-dark rush hour, the headlights and taillights adding the confusion of hurrying people, some heading into the office towers for night shifts while others fought over cabs to go home, many apparently reluctant to take public transit.

Bertrand tried not to look too proud about his weight loss. After all, it would be a long time before he would approach Jeff's lean physic, and he'd never be that tall. "I've lost eleven glorious pounds. If I'm dehydrated, twelve."

Jeff slapped him on the back. "You the man. I know Fish is impressed. He told me the other day that you've got a natural talent for fighting—a focus and intensity. I was actually jealous."

"Dude." Bertrand couldn't restrain a good laugh. "That's nuts. I'm not even a yellow belt and you creamed me in the sparring match yesterday. I don't think you have much—"

A scream ripped through the street. A woman lunged out a cab and rushed across the sidewalk, turning to put her back to the window of Starbucks and stare back in horror, one hand over her mouth and a finger pointing back at the cab.

"What the frig?" Bertrand ran forward, his whole being demanding he save her from the terror in the cab. The back seat waited empty for the next passenger, but something about the driver's posture looked slumped and twisted—a heart attack?

Bertrand reached for the passenger-side front door but fell back when the door swung open too easily. Jeff caught him and pushed him back to vertical.

Bertrand and Jeff both bent to look across the front seat to the cab driver. Blood coated the man's shirt and trousers, and his head tipped back uncomfortably far. A large chunk of his neck under his right ear had been sliced out.

"Holy crap." Bertrand stood. "Right here in the street."

Jeff already had his cell phone out and was punching 911. They both stepped back from the cab, but a garbage bag stuck to Bertrand's shoe. He grabbed it to pull it off, lifting his leg in the process to reach it.

Jeff grabbed his arm. "Watch out! It's covered in blood."

That was why it was sticky. It was too late for Bertrand's right hand, the cab driver's blood smearing on his fingers. He succeeded pulling the bag off his shoe, but as it fluttered to the ground he noticed something strange.

"Look." Bertrand pointed at the bottom of the bag. "You know how people cut a bag to wear as an emergency rain coat? Someone's cut the bottom for a head and the sides for arms."

"Harsh." Jeff stepped back from the cab, looking from the bag to the driver. "Someone planned this and didn't want to get covered in his blood. Someone knew what they were doing, as if they'd done it before."

"Someone." But Bertrand was thinking about Malcolm, the blood on his collar was bad enough, but as he had typed in his password his finger nails had caught Bertrand's attention almost as much as the password. They were surprisingly dirty for a neat young man who liked clubbing, rims of brown outlining the shape of the nails and under the ends.

Jeff brought him back to the present. "Bert," he said, his voice emotionless in his shock, his eyes still on the taxi driver's bloody corpse. "I know a guy who sells guns. I think you should pay him a visit."

Bertrand nodded, his eyes going back to the blood. "Yeah. Long overdue. I need some way to defend myself."

# 9

## GOTH KNIGHTS

Bertrand had never been a big fan of swimming, not just because his bulk moved reluctantly through the water, but because he disliked chlorine. Joyce had overcome his reluctance by pointing out that the lap pool at the club was a saltwater pool, so only a fraction of the chlorine was required.

Every evening after his workout for a couple of weeks now, he had donned his swimsuit—a modest one with shorts-like legs that went almost to his knees—and splashed several laps with his imperfect front crawl, amazed that he had the energy for it at all after his workout or karate.

He reached the end of a lap this evening to see running shoes and shapely bare legs, causing him to stop and remove his fogged goggles. Joyce stood near the end of the lane, her black miniskirt incongruous with her footwear, her sleeveless green top lacy and alluring.

"Nice going, Bert. You know I've never seen anyone at this club work so hard and lose so much weight so fast."

Bertrand grabbed the ladder and heaved himself out of the water, not just a little proud. She'd noticed he'd lost weight! While he was not in the running to be an underwear model, he did love the sleeker feel as the water sloshed off his torso. He had even dared to look at himself in the mirror of the change room a few times, amazed that his belly and love handles could shrink so much in just a month.

Bertrand grabbed his towel from a hook on the tile wall and began to dry his hair.

"Well it's all thanks to you." He paused to shake water out of his right ear. "I wouldn't have known where to begin."

"Thanks, but you did all the work. I've watched guys come in here, bragging and over lifting, showing up four and five nights in a row, then twice a week—usually making excuses about pulled muscles—then once a month, then gone. No commitment. No guts. You have to be in this for the long haul."

"Well, like Fish says, I got to be ready for Judgment Day. Did Jeff tell you what we saw tonight?"

"Taxi driver murdered in broad daylight? Yeah, and I bet it won't be on the news."

They exchanged a knowing glance. Just like the man they'd found dead. A life extinguished without the world the wiser.

"So, Bert." Joyce avoided his eyes as she spoke, instead gazing at the far end of the empty pool room. "Like, I'm not asking you on date here, but I want to check out this club called Goth Knights." She finally looked at him to see how he was taking this invitation. "Thing is, I hear it's a bit of a rough crowd, so I don't want to go alone, but apparently some rock-star-like guy's going to make an appearance tonight. So I was wondering if you'd like to go."

"Go dancing?" Bertrand had danced in college, but only when it was absolutely necessary and only because he had hoped that if he gyrated with sufficient bravado his date would take his virginity.

"Yeah." Joyce's cheeks had noticeably reddened. "Yeah, we'll have to dance so that we don't stick out like tourists, but I'm not asking you to take ecstasy and get into the whole clubbing scene. So, you in?"

Bertrand didn't want to go, didn't want to head anywhere but his basement, where he'd moved his bed a month ago after putting bars on the windows and a steel door at the top of the stairs. He couldn't sleep at Nolan's every night. The guy was half-crazed and his conspiracy theories stretched over the top: even the president was a cult worshipper and a blood drinker. His blog, however, was racking up a fantastic number of hits. His theories had struck a chord with a large number of people.

But Goth Knights, that was the club Malcolm always talked about with fervent passion. Was it more than just a dance club?

"Sure," said Bertrand. "I don't get out much though, so I'll dance, but it won't be pretty."

Joyce barked a laugh. "I promise not to hold it against you. I'll wait out front."

---

The blood-red twisting neon spelled out goth knights, and the lineup down the sidewalk promised at least an hour's wait. Joyce paid the taxi driver, a Sikh judging by the turban, who accepted the generous tip and squealed the wheels of the cab in his haste to leave. The man had been reluctant to drive into this run-down industrial neighborhood, and it wasn't hard to see why: several buildings along the way—proud factories from the 1940s—were burnt-out shells now, their walls often surviving the conflagrations that consumed their innards, proving that they were true brick buildings built to last. The building with the club was a luckier version, having somehow avoided the flames of insurance fires long enough to become useful again, but the tall windows of the second floor were painted black, and the frantic light of the club leaked out only through scratches and gaps. The pounding music had no regard for the glass barrier, and Bertrand doubted the club could have survived the noise complaints in a more residential neighborhood.

"That looks hopeless." Bertrand pointed to the length of the line of waiting people. "I guess there aren't any other bars close to here?"

"Not if you're looking for chicken wings and beer." Joyce took his hand and led him across the street. "Let's give it a try anyway. A guy I used to train told me the other day that I could get in no problem. He said just go straight to the front of the line."

A doorman behind the velvet rope at the head of the line stood tall and bald, a heavy black trench coat emphasizing the bulk of his shoulders, multiple piercings on his eyebrows, nose and lip testifying that he had a high tolerance for pain. His expression indicated that he probably didn't mind dishing it out.

"Back of the line." He folded his hands back like a soldier at ease, but Joyce walked right up close.

"We haven't evolved," she said. "We're still monos. A friend told me that's a front-of-the-line pass."

The doorman looked down and bent close to Joyce's neck. The giggling crowd in the line fell silent. Bertrand grabbed Joyce's arm, getting ready to pull her away if the doorman moved to any of his pockets with his hands. Surely the man wouldn't cut her neck open right there in front of all the witnesses? But Bertrand was taking no chances. He should've asked the taxi to wait with the meter and engine running.

"Relax, dude." The doorman's left eye fixed on Bertrand even though his nose was still buried in Joyce's delicate neck. "I can tell she's telling the truth. Have fun and buy booze."

He unclipped the velvet rope, his nose still close to Joyce, shamelessly breathing in her fragrance one more time before he straightened and stepped aside, waving them through the door and up the stairs.

"Yum, yum!" called someone in the crowd, hoots and cheers rising to dim the music.

Joyce nodded her thanks and headed through the door and up the stairs, Bertrand hurrying to keep up and averting his eyes when he saw a flash of panties under the miniskirt.

"Joyce!" Bertrand had to shout to be heard over the music as they reached the second floor. Strobe lights dazzled him when they emerged into the rave hall, a large converted warehouse with heavy squared columns of timber supporting the ceiling. The walls were painted black, except where large mirrors reflected back the lights and the crowd, the lasers and disco balls filling in the dark when the strobes weren't pulsing with the music.

"Joyce!" Bertrand had to scream in her ear to be heard. "There's something very weird about this place. We shouldn't stay."

"I know." Joyce grabbed his shoulders and put her lips close to his ear. "But we need to know what's going on, and around here this is the center of things. My friend said they won't hurt us here 'cause they don't want any attention drawn to the club."

"Don't want any attention?" Bertrand waved at the crowd. "Look at these people!"

The dancers gyrated to heavy Goth music, an ominous voice ranting about the end of the world, electric base and pounding drums mixing with orchestrated voices that backed-up the male vocal. People were dressed in leather and fishnet stockings with shorts or simply black underwear, sometimes on the men as well as the women. Generous tattoos covered bare skin on backs and arms, on cleavage and torsos. Some men danced topless, and to Bertrand's shock, so was at least one woman.

"I'll get us a drink," shouted Joyce. "Just try and relax and keep an eye for this guy who's supposed to show up."

"Wait, I have no idea what he looks like."

"Apparently he stands out in a crowd."

Should he run after her and drag her out of here? But then who would look like the freak according to the cops: the dancers or the apparently abusive boyfriend trying to drag his girlfriend out of a club against her will? If he had known that they were coming here—if he had known the place existed—he would have refused to join her. But then she might have gone alone. Bertrand had never imagined a place like this whenever Malcolm had spoken of going to Goth Knights.

Bertrand leaned back against one of the squared beams, which would have fit just as well in a nineteenth century barn. He surveyed the crowd, trying not to look like he was ogling the women and disgusted with the men. All were thinner and cooler and more violent than him. These people looked like they were into pleasure and pain in the right doses, even extreme doses. Most looked unlikely to ever complicate their lives with children or mortgages, and Bertrand fought envy: he wanted a family to replace the one he had lost, yet he also craved the freedom of the dancers, the lack of care about the end of the world that the male vocal kept singing about in ominous tones.

Bertrand started to tap his foot to the music. If he didn't miss his parents so much, if he didn't want to fill their house—now his house—with laughing voices, would he be more like the dancers, pushing off procreative chains so that he could live only for his own gratification?

He swayed his hips now, his arms starting to pump with the beat. He was dancing, mimicking some of the moves around him, yes, but dancing. Somehow being alone—without Joyce opposite him as mating rituals demanded—he could dance just for the sake of it, just to pretend he wasn't lonely in life and didn't care.

He watched the other dancers, trying to pick up ideas for moves that he could replicate. Did he look ridiculous? Probably. He was still an overweight computer nerd, and while his shirt didn't have a pocket protector for pens, it had a pocket that could accommodate one. His blue jeans might have been cool a generation ago, but in this crowd it was all about leather—or as an alternative, black jeans with strategic rips to show off bare flesh were the preferred denim.

A tall man in leather shorts danced in perfect sync with his spike-haired girlfriend, both of them sporting metal for jewelry, in his case a spiked dog collar and handcuffs hanging from his hip. The man spoke in his partner's ear, neither of them breaking the rhythm of their dance. She looked over at Bertrand and he expected to see her laugh at his awkward moves, but instead she licked her lips and grabbed at her crotch, thrusting in his direction in time to the music.

Joyce weaved through the crowd with two bottles of beer, holding them far out and high up so as not to get wet if she were jostled and they spilled. Bertrand stopped dancing, his ears burning as she approached. Had she seen him dancing? He didn't mind looking ridiculous to strangers, but Joyce was a prospective mate, or at least perhaps a friend with benefits.

"Thanks," Bertrand shouted. He concentrated on Joyce and ignored the suggestive dance moves from the stranger. "Here's to being ready for Judgment Day."

Joyce saved her voice and just tipped back the bottle, taking a drink. She let her arms rise to shoulder height and her hips began to sway, forcing Bertrand to either stand there looking totally awkward or resume his dance. She must have noticed him from across the bar.

Don't wimp out now. Bertrand began the challenging half-dance that involves sipping beer and trying not to splash too much, which meant their dance became more energetic as the beer went down, until the bottles were empty and Bertrand sweated profusely from the effort.

One song transitioned into another with no gap, and though it was very similar to the previous song, Bertrand used the change to take Joyce's empty bottle from her hand.

"My round," he shouted before heading for the bar. Now that he had a beer in him he didn't mind giving an extra glance at a topless woman, dancing with her hands high in the air to show off her small-but-shapely breasts, a tattoo of three drops of blood dripping around one pert nipple.

People crowded near the bar, but oddly most of them faced out watching the dancers and not in toward the mirror and the gleaming bottles of hard liquor arranged in front of it like colorful art. Bertrand had no problem squeezing past the people to get his elbows up on the polished wood, a twenty held conspicuously in one hand in hopes of flagging a bartender's attention. Bertrand had assumed it would be a long wait, but a topless young man sitting on a stool just few paces farther along the bar stubbed out his cigarette and stood. The collar on his neck trailed a slim chain and must have been more for effect, because it looked fragile enough to snap under any strain. The opposite end was locked to a pulley on rod a full ten feet off the floor, running the length of the bar. This would allow the man to walk up and down the length of his workspace while giving the impression of captive servitude.

"What can I get you tonight?"

"Hey, how about a couple of Sam Adams." Bertrand pointed to the bottles with the Sam Adams logo, sitting in a glass-doored fridge, but his eyes strayed to the man's pierced nipple. He couldn't help himself. "Didn't that hurt?" Bertrand pointed at the nipple ring.

"Yeah, of course." He pulled out two bottles, popping off the lids in turn with an opener. "Stuff like that really hurt before I became a brid, but it's just one of those pains you have to live through until evolution. You coming up soon?"

"Not yet." Bertrand watched closely to see if he'd answered correctly. Joyce was right, this club was the center of something, perhaps a cult.

The bartender placed the beers on the counter and Bertrand slid the twenty over, waving away the change in his confusion as he tried to interpret their conversation.

"Hey, thanks." The bartender opened the till to deposit the twenty and retrieve his healthy tip. "When you do come up you're gonna love it. I mean, the change really hurts and at first you're just so sick, but wow!" He slammed the till and leaned on the bar so that he could get close to Bertrand. "It's way better than sex every time."

"Great." Bertrand picked up the bottles to hide his confusion. What were they talking about? "I can't wait." He fled back to Joyce but his unease had tripled. He leaned into Joyce, who was still swaying but slowed her dance to accept the beer.

"Do you know why someone would call themselves a brid?"

Joyce shook her head. "Who said that?"

"Bartender."

"Hot," said Joyce. "I'd like to work out with him sometime—just kidding. He's younger and way out of my league. I'll ask him about the brid thing when it's my round. Come on, let's dance again. Maybe the song is right. Maybe it is the end of the world. Might as well go out dancing."

Bertrand danced, letting the shame of his awkward moves wash away with the beer, allowing him turn and jump and swing his arms. Today he was alive and he loved life. His parents were a distant memory in this club, so out of the context of his regular routine. There were no reminders. The male vocals—backed up by a woman singing a middle-eastern influenced wail—sang about Armageddon. The song actually had understandable lyrics, and Bertrand began to sing along as he danced, his poor singing easily buried. *"Armageddon, Armageddon, dancing on the slopes of Armageddon."*

The pack of the crowd became denser as the dancers crushed their way, some disturbance on the far side of the room requiring more of the club's square footage, perhaps a fight.

A firm bottom rubbed against Bertrand's, prompting him to turn and look over his shoulder. The same spiky-haired woman who'd gestured obscenely at him before licked her lips. They were now hip-to-hip and she cupped his bum as they danced.

Bertrand tried to shift away while Joyce frowned at them. She bent over to retrieve her bag, which she'd left on the floor near the post where Bertrand had staked out his territory earlier. Was she jealous and getting ready to leave? Bertrand wasn't sure about that—Joyce was the one who'd made it clear this wasn't a date, and certainly he was doing the opposite of flirting with this strange woman.

"I need him," shouted the woman. "I need it bad and I can't wait."

Bertrand tried to move away. Was she talking to him?

An arm clamped around his chest and a hand grabbed first at his hair, pulling his head back, but when his hair proved to be too short to hold, the hand switched to his forehead. It was the boyfriend. With great strength, he held Bertrand close to his chest and tilted Bertrand's head back, exposing his neck.

"Fuck off!" Bertrand struggled in the grasp, but others in the crowd grabbed his hands while others shouted, "No, not here you assholes!"

A monster rose up in Bertrand's chest, a desire to fight. The enemy he had been looking for since Needleman's death had finally shown itself. Bertrand lunged and bucked against the grip, stomping on a foot, driving his elbow into a stomach, but there were too many of them.

The woman punched him in the stomach and then slipped a short, wicked knife from a hidden pocket of her shorts.

"Don't forget to leave some for me, Baby!" shouted the man who pinned Bertrand.

"Share!" shouted a man who now held Bertrand's right arm. Several around them now began to chant the same. "Share! Share! Share!"

"I will!" The woman stepped forward, the knife coming up to Bertrand's throat. She grabbed his shoulder to steady him as she aimed for his jugular.

Bertrand fought for his life, struggling and twisting, surprising those who held him even though it failed to break their grip. Where was Joyce? Did they have her too? Oddly, as the knife approached, Bertrand discovered he could bury his fear and channel it into anger. He'd never felt so strong, so capable of resisting to the very end of his life without surrendering. He continued his fight to the death.

A *snap* and a sharp pain—a vibrating shock—on Bertrand's shoulder broke his concentration on his struggle. The women with the knife collapsed on the floor, jerking spasmodically as if in an epileptic fit. There was another snapping noise, and a new shock radiated through Bertrand's back where it was in contact with the man who held him prisoner.

The room tipped away, and Bertrand couldn't free his arms to save himself from the fall. His head slammed the wood floor, dazing and confusing him, only the body underneath cushioning his fall and sparing him other injury.

People screamed and let go of him, which allowed him to turn and shove up to his hands and knees, fighting to regain control of his muscles. Why wasn't his body obeying commands? Why was it hard to breathe?

Joyce's shout penetrated the throbbing music. "Get up, Bert. Quick! We have to get out of here!"

A hand heaved under his arm, pulling and struggling to help him rise. He fought his spasmodic muscles into a semblance of control and staggered to his feet. Joyce held his arm and brandished a wicked-looking Taser at a circle of angry faces, several of the dancers now brandishing short knives and one man aimed a handgun.

Joyce kept turning them, hauling Bertrand around with her to threaten different parts of the crowd. "Stay back!" she shouted. "Stay back or I'll put forty-thousand volts through you!"

On the floor near them lay the man and the woman, both still writhing. When it looked like the woman might gain enough control over her muscles to crawl, Joyce lunged in, leaving Bertrand to stand on his own, and tasered the woman again with a snap of the weapon. The woman screamed and convulsed, the word "Bitch!" the only clear curse.

Joyce grabbed Bertrand's arm. "Crap, we're so doomed. I'm sorry, Bert."

Bertrand shouted more for the crowd that threatened them than to Joyce.

"Well we won't go down without one hell of a fight!" He felt a thrill—a relief. After months of loneliness and purposelessness, after months of sensing an enemy but not being able to bring it to battle, he could finally do something. He could take as many of these cultist sickos with him as possible. They might drink his blood in the end, but not without a price. He was free to fight.

He pulled away from Joyce's grasp and put his back to hers so that they faced opposite sides of the threatening circle of people. "I can stand!" he shouted to her, putting up his fists as Fish had taught him, one by his hip, the other extended to hold back his opponent. "You wouldn't have another of those Tasers, would you?"

"No. I'll do my best with this one."

"Try and cut a path through to the stairs. I've got your back."

The music shut down as if the power had failed, but the disco balls and the lasers proved this wasn't the case.

A loud voice called from the bar: "Wait!"

Several more voices took up the call, and the young bartender, trailing his broken chain from his collar, came rushing into the circle, brandishing a sawed-off shotgun, taking up a position with Bertrand and Joyce, his back to them and the gun threatening the crowd.

"The boss says wait!" He shouted. "Everybody just fucking chill. No evolutions in his club! Clear over there. Here he comes."

Several people looked where the bartender had gestured with the shotgun. Three big men in heavy black cloaks parted the crowd, shoving and pushing those who were slow to clear. No one argued or complained, and the people closer to the circle had enough warning to draw aside, creating a human-walled corridor.

The bodyguards took up positions on either side of the path they had cleared, staying back with the circle and not threatening the three in the center. A man walked between them, obviously the boss.

His height didn't exactly proclaim his authority, for he was a little on the short side, but he walked with an air of confidence—a man used to command. His stocky build spoke of tough old muscle, a life of hardship, but it was his face and his eyes that demanded unflinching attention.

His clothes were modern and black—not the garish apparel of many of the dancers—and they spoke of modesty and practicality. His cloak, however, was a total anachronism from the dark ages, a garment for drafty dwellings and bitter winters, with a hood hanging back that could be pulled up against the wind. His mustache also didn't fit the scene, a huge and rich handlebar, elaborately curled and waxed. Gaunt cheeks weathered by sun and wind framed his face, but his green eyes captivated Bertrand's attention. The man's left eye twitched involuntarily as he regarded them.

"Thank you, Nicholas," said the man, his accent rich, more French than anything else, but not quite. Was there a hint of Eastern Europe? "Return to your work."

The bartender nodded and put up the gun, hurrying away, his chain trailing like a tail. That left Bertrand and Joyce alone now, and they no longer stood back-to-back but shoulder-to-shoulder facing this new threat. The man clearly terrified the crowd, and Bertrand sensed that his and Joyce's fate rested with the boss's judgment.

"You're very brave to come in here. Did you come for pleasure or for understanding?"

Bertrand beat Joyce to the reply. "We came for information about the Chicago Ripper. We came to find out if there is a cult of murderers." He glanced at Joyce, who nodded her agreement. Bertrand had decided to go with the truth. This was the kind of man who would sniff out a lie and be angered by it.

"And what have you learned?"

"That this place is full of sickos and murderers, and that I should never come here again with anything less than an army." Bertrand knew he should be afraid, but the urge to fight hadn't left him. Here was the king of enemies, even though he had made no threatening gestures. Bertrand was sure of it, and he could barely restrain himself from snatching Joyce's Taser and charging despite the odds.

"They are disgusting, aren't they?" The man gestured at the crowd. "These men and women, they're not like you. They live for themselves and their own gratification. They would never make a sacrifice for the greater good. They would never risk their miserable lives." He pointed a gloved finger at Bertrand. "Not like you."

"But you're their boss." Joyce pointed the Taser in the man's direction.

"In my country I was always a man of God. I would have executed people like this just for their lewd attire, let alone their lascivious behaviors. But I must work with what I can to do God's work, and I doubt you are the kind of man who would be seduced by the rewards that have ensnared them."

Bertrand decided this wasn't the time to point out the man's chauvinism. Joyce was there too.

"God's work doesn't involve murder," Bertrand said instead.

"The life of Noah would tell us otherwise. Sometimes a scourge is required to cleanse the world of evil. It is time for you to go."

The man pointed at the woman, the dancer with the knife who had intended to cut open Bertrand's throat. A flick of his finger in the direction of the bar was enough command. Two big men from the entourage rushed in and grabbed her.

"No!" she screamed. "No. I'll never do it again, I swear!"

They dragged her, kicking and screaming.

The boss turned away without another word and followed his men.

"Okay, Bert. We better get out."

The crowd had opened up a path to the stairs, an invitation Joyce accepted immediately, lowering her Taser and pulling on Bertrand's arm. At the bottom, the door opened, held by the bouncer, who had one hand to his walkie-talkie earpiece, nodding as he received his instructions. He looked up and delivered his message.

"The boss says you're never to return, with an army or without."

Bertrand nodded and they fled into the night.

# 10

# GUNS AND HACKING

Bertrand stood in front of the North Chicago Gun Exchange, looking up and down the street as if he feared being observed entering the store. This little retail strip—far north of his own neighborhood—sat close to the parked cars of the street, the sidewalk narrow but with a roof that reached to the curb to keep the snows of winter at bay.

Bertrand's parents had been committed pacifists, and his grandparents had marched against the Vietnam War, so Bertrand had absolutely no experience with guns. He was surprised when Jeff had confessed to belonging to a gun club, but relieved that he had someone besides Nolan to turn to for advice on matters concerning self-defense. Nolan had suggested that Bertrand could borrow his tommy gun with the hundred-round drum, the type of weapon that Al Capone probably owned at some point in his career.

"You need to defend your home," Nolan had said. "As long as you're there between sunset and sunrise, you'll be safe if you have enough firepower."

But Bertrand didn't agree. He remembered what the woman from Colorado Springs had said about people being burned out of their homes. Bertrand's house was made of wood, and the bars on his basement windows couldn't hold back flames.

Jeff had a different outlook.

"You want a Glock," he had said. "Something that you can keep with you at all times, day and night. Think how useful that could've been at Goth Knights."

Jeff had absorbed Bertrand's tale about his near murder at Goth Knights with jaw dropping belief. He, Bertrand and Joyce had taken the unusual step of skipping their workout and driving there before dark in Jeff's Xterra SUV, but the door to the club had been replaced with a four-by-eight sheet of plywood, and a "Power of Sale" notice from a bank was stapled in the center.

They had spent a week trying to learn more, but the club had been owned by a numbered company that had leased the building. This window on the underworld had closed forever. Malcolm lamented its loss, unaware that Bertrand had been there for its last night of decadence. Neither Jeff nor Bertrand trusted Malcolm enough to share the details of that experience.

Jeff had promised that the gun store would be open on Saturday, and a neon open sign behind the bars in the windows proved him correct, but Bertrand found himself reluctant to take the next step, to open the door and admit that the world had changed forever. In the old world he had relied on the police and the government to protect him, with just a little dab of street sense required on his part.

Bertrand looked up and down the sidewalk again, noting that a sad little flower shop—its window displays oddly sparse but neat—sat next door, a sandwich board on the sidewalk stating that all the flowers were half-price until Monday.

The contrast between the shops had more to do with security than flower power versus fire power. The flower shop had no need for bars inside the glass display windows, and the gun shop also had heavy rolling metal doors, which Bertrand guessed came down each night to turn the shop into a fortress, impregnable at least to smash-and-grab thieves. Apparently the criminal types in the neighborhood had no use for flowers.

Bertrand at last opened the door to the gun shop, causing an electronic chime to alert the owner that his perimeter had been breached. A heavy man sat on a stool behind a counter at the back of the shop, his newspaper obscuring his face. The man didn't look up when he spoke. "Wondered when you'd find the balls to come in." He must have noticed Bertrand standing in front of his shop for so long.

"My balls are there when I need them."

The newspaper folded down; the man behind it had red cheeks, puffed from alcohol and food, his beard and mustache short and black, not so much trimmed as looking like he'd forgotten to shave for a week.

"No bullshit guy. Okay, let me guess: you've never owned a gun. Your parents are pinko-commies, and they've always told you that no one needs to own a gun, but now you want a gun."

Bertrand stopped in front of the display case under the glass countertop. Handguns of many types were arranged haphazardly, some missing as if recently purchased and not replaced. Above and behind the owner, racks of weapons rested vertically so as to allow maximum storage. The sidewalls of the shop displayed photos of hunters and fishermen—and a calendar with a buxom woman in a pink bikini washing a car with lots of foamy soap. "Yes, yes, yes and yes."

The owner took a sip of coffee from a huge plastic mug, capped to prevent spilling or wasting heat. "So what do your parents think of your newfound desire to own a self-defense device?"

"They're dead."

The owner put his coffee down and stood, holding out his hand to shake.

"Lake," he said. "Emile Lake. Sorry about your folks. You're hardly growed up. What happened? Was it recent?"

"Last May—car accident. I'm told it was probably quick."

"Right. Bummer, but at least they don't have to put up with all the crazy shit that's happening now."

"What do you mean?"

"Come on! I thought you were a no bullshit guy. What brings a yuppie like you into my shop looking for a gun? Do you know how many shirt-and-tie types—who probably all wanted total gun bans last year—have come flooding into my shop in the last month, all looking for a little self-defense? I have to rush order to keep me in handguns." He tapped the glass of the counter with a heavy finger to draw Bertrand's attention to the empty spots.

"Okay, I admit, totally weird shit's happening out there. I just wanted to know what you've heard, 'cause it's not in the news anymore."

"People are dying." Emile studied him in challenge, daring him to disagree. "Lots of people."

"And it's not on the news."

"Because the government's in on it."

Bertrand realized too late that he'd rolled his eyes, the sudden anger on Emile's face proving that he'd communicated disbelief.

"Come on!" Emile picked up his newspaper for evidence, turning it so that Bertrand could see. "What is this crap doing on the front page?" A photo-op showed men in suits—one recognizably the mayor—cutting a fat ribbon at a recently constructed school. Bertrand leaned in and read the caption, discovering that the other men were local congressional and senate incumbents.

"Since when," Emile said, "do three levels of government show up to open a school at night. What is this crap? What's a senator have to do with a kiddie school? And at night? No wonder there's hardly any kids in the shot: their parents are too smart to let them out after dark."

"They're not vampires," said Bertrand. "They're something else."

Emile folded the newspaper, calm now that he was believed. "Whatever they are, they're in on it."

"It's like some kind of cult." Bertrand looked back at the front window of the shop to see if anyone was about to enter and overhear his crazy talk. "They drink blood, but not like vampires. They use knives to open your throat."

Emile stared at him for ten seconds. "That's even crazier than my theories," he said at last. "But the Chicago Ripper was cutting people's throats open. You're right about that. I thought it was a plague."

"Rippers." Bertrand looked down at the guns, trying to figure out what would be comfortable in his hands. "There's more than one Chicago Ripper. I think there's dozens."

"Buddy, this isn't happening just in Chicago. I got a buddy in New Hampshire and he says it's happening there."

"I think it's happening in a lot of cities, but I tell you I've met these rippers—one tried to open my throat last week—and I was only saved by some kind of cult leader. They just called him the 'boss' and said something about no evolutions in his club."

Again Emile regarded him for a moment—judging. "I think it's a plague that they're trying to cover up," he said. His furrowed brow spoke otherwise, showing the concentration of a man sorting through a particularly challenging puzzle. "But you know, even though you talk weirder than a crackhead who sidelines in meth ... there is something to your ripper thing."

"All I know is that some kind of Judgment Day is coming. The east coast has had three black outs in the last two weeks. Before this summer, they'd had one in my entire life. At first they said it was because absenteeism had shut down a nuke plant. Now they don't even say why. It just happens."

Emile's fist pounded the counter. "Now that's what I'm talking about. All this absenteeism. People just aren't off sick, they're not coming back to work at all."

"Some of them are." Bertrand was thinking about Malcolm, but decided not to bring up that he only came in for the night shift these days. That kind of statement would bring them back around to vampires, and that wasn't the kind of nonsense he wanted to argue.

"Not enough men coming in to work to keep the lights on though." Emile noted Bertrand's gaze into the handgun display. "What's your pleasure?"

"A friend says I should get a Glock."

"Who's your friend?" Emile pulled a set of keys from his belt, held there on a retractable cable, and waddled toward the far end of the counter to open a sliding panel on his side.

"Jeff Aubert. I think you guys are in the same gun club."

"Jeff! Tall Jeff?" Emile held one hand in the air to indicate six feet. "Jeff with the Ruger Super Redhawk? Why didn't you say so? Now there's a guy who can shoot, and when that baby goes off it's deafening even with ears." He pulled a black handgun out and slapped it on the counter.

Bertrand picked it up with all the comfort of a librarian who has been handed a tarantula, moving it from one hand to the next while trying to figure out what a prospective buyer should be judging about the weapon.

It was Emile's turn to roll his eyes. He snatched the gun from Bertrand.

"First, it's not loaded, but you should never handle a gun without checking for yourself. Eject the mag here and inspect that it's empty. See? Pull back the slide here and check the breach to make sure it's clear. See?"

Emile's hand motions were fast and practiced, but Bertrand got the idea and repeated the maneuvers with only a few extra instructions from Emile.

"Okay. I'll take it," said Bertrand.

Emile took the gun back and studied Bertrand for the third time.

"You're not a cop." It was a statement rather than a question.

"No. Why?"

"Another thing that hasn't been in the news lately is that they passed a new gun law extending the cooling off period. You buy it now—pay for it I mean—and you'll have to wait six months before I can hand it over to you."

"But that's ridiculous. This is all going come to a head in less than six months. It's getting worse at an exponential rate."

"At a what rate? Never mind. Look, I'm not gonna sell you this gun." He slapped it down on the counter and slid it across to Bertrand. "I'm going to give it to you." He held up one meaty finger. "But I got two conditions: first is don't tell anyone, second is you gotta come down to my range in the basement every couple of days, starting today, and learn to shoot so that you don't blow your own fucking head off."

Bertrand nodded, because he shared the same concern for his head.

"Oh and third—" Emile's cheeks reddened and he didn't meet Bertrand's eyes. "Jeff's been talking around the club, says you guys are maybe going to form some kind of self-defense group, band together at nights and all."

"Really. He told you that?" Bertrand kept the surprise off his face. When did he ever say anything like that to Jeff?

Emile looked Bertrand in the eye.

"Yeah he did. My folks are way up north and my wife took the kids and split for New Hampshire last year, so I'm isolated in this shop. I can't get a handle on what's going on out there, and the papers are no fucking help. So when things fall apart and you guys band together to fight back, you come and get me out of here."

When things fall apart. In his soul, Bertrand had known for some time that this must all come to a head, that there would be a day of reckoning when civilization could no longer function. But part of him wanted to cling to the old world—the safe world where the greatest danger to his life came in the form of chicken wings and beer. He longed for the days when he worried about whether he'd live into his seventies. Now he worried about whether he'd live through the next night.

"We'll keep you posted."

Temptation beckoned in the form of Malcolm's computer. Bertrand had switched to an eight a.m. start so that he could leave at four. Despite this schedule change, the shorter days would eventually compress to the point where he would have to go out while it was still dark, either on his way to work or on his way home. That was Chicago's winter.

Bertrand had been thinking about his own prediction to Emile: that this would all reach a crisis in less than six months, a prediction he'd made two weeks ago. The office had achieved a new normal that could not be sustained: the evening staff grew each day, the call load shifting to a peak near midnight, and only a skeleton crew managed the day.

Destiny was their anchor: sarcastic, witty and preferring to make sexually suggestive comments rather than talk about work or news. She seemed to enjoy shocking Bertrand or making him blush.

Whitlock looked more harried each day as he tried to find daytime temps to fill in when needed, and rumors said that his workouts in the club downstairs had taken on a new ferocity. Jeff spent every lunch with Bertrand at Flynn's, where they compared notes on the latest weird events and discussed theories, which usually revolved around a widespread Satanic cult, although Emile's plague theory still lingered, for the chaos did seem to spread like an epidemic.

Each morning for a couple of weeks, the news opened with reports about another house fire, the occupants all lost, sometimes murder-suicide the suspected cause, but then even those reports ended. Jeff, Joyce and Bertrand had all come across fire trucks and hoses encircling the burnt shell of some home—on different days and in different neighborhoods—but like the Ripper murders, the news media stopped covering these unpleasant events.

Bertrand sat at Malcolm's chair and booted his terminal, planning a little surfing before everyone else arrived, and it wouldn't be wise to do it from his own terminal, since his browsing history would be available if Whitlock wanted to check up on him.

The Chicago Police Department's website had changed a lot since Bertrand had written a paper about it back in high school for a civics class. Back then, he'd been able to see the images of every Chicago police officer ever murdered in the line of duty, and the focus of his paper had been about how many of those deaths had occurred during prohibition, numbering in the hundreds per year. The new website stuck with recent history, only listing all murder stats for the last few years, comparing them year-over-year to show a drop in violent crime.

Bertrand clicked on the murder rate but instead of a PDF of pie charts and bar graphs downloading, it popped up with a 404 error. The page was missing? He tooled around the site while puzzling this glitch. Why were the murder stats missing? Was it negligence or had someone intentionally pulled them off. This called for a little hack.

Bertrand began by looking for weakness in the site, but it was all new and well built, not like the old site from the nineties that had all kinds of backdoors into the server. He would need help with this one, so he went to some of his favorite bulletin boards, ones the F.B.I probably looked for unsuccessfully. You had to know a guy, and things changed almost daily, but Bertrand was one of the guys.

He didn't hack for greed or mischief, but for education and entertainment, so he had access to a number of servers, and he'd been careful to keep that a secret from the owners, slipping in and out without notice just for fun. It didn't take long to find out that someone had already been into the Chicago P.D. server, and they'd made notes that Bertrand understood. So he carefully breached one of his previously hacked servers and carried on from there, intending to destroy the logs when he was done, so that if anyone detected his hack they'd reach a dead end at this server when they tried to trace him.

The notes from his fellow hacker were great. Bang! He was in. Now where to look for the crime stats? Perhaps they were still there, just not exactly where they were supposed to be, maybe someone moved them to prevent deletion. A quick search proved the theory correct. There was a file of crime stats, just in a different directory that prevented the public from seeing it on the website. There would be no need to hack through the firewall, because someone had left them there to be found. Perhaps the police weren't all in lock-step cooperation on this issue. Maybe there were good cops out there too.

Bertrand burned the statistics onto a USB stick—proud that he was in and out of their system in less than ten minutes. He was about to destroy the server logs for his hacked server so that he couldn't be traced, when he heard the elevator ping, announcing that someone, maybe Whitlock, was arriving on their floor.

Bertrand quickly logged off of Malcolm's computer and headed for his own cubicle. He pulled on his headset and got in the queue, opening up a chat while selecting a call, dual-tasking to clear a minor backlog. Later he tried to call Nolan to tell him that maybe his government conspiracy theories weren't so crazy, but the man didn't answer his phone. Was he down in his bomb shelter?

Bertrand went back to work, but he was distracted from his job several times by the USB stick that waited in his bag. Why had these stats been pulled from the public server, and why hadn't they been destroyed if they were so dangerous?

Tonight, he would check them out. Someone had wanted them hidden, and Bertrand couldn't wait to see why.

# 11

# LAST WARNING FROM
# THOMAS NOLAN

B ertrand had planned to leave work early so that he could get home well before dark, but the call volume kept him late. He was just about to log off when he received an e-mail from Erics—plural—the guy who claimed on his website that there were only one thousand souls and that the seven billion people on the planet shared only a small portion of each soul among many bodies.

Bertrand had to scroll down through the e-mail to remember that he'd asked this guy how he knew it was a thousand souls and not a million.

"We have performed many complicated calculations and personality assessments in order to determine that there are approximately one thousand souls. There is a margin of error that could mean there are slightly more or less, but it is close enough to one thousand souls that I use this as a teaching point. People need round numbers. Why don't you take the test and determine which soul you possess a portion of? I suspect you have a strong soul or you wouldn't have contacted me. Has it gotten denser in the last few months? Do you feel bolder?"

This gave Bertrand pause. How many times in the last few months had he surprised himself with bold statements, the kind that were getting him a reputation as a no-bullshit guy? Why did he always want to fight? Like the time at Goth Knights when he'd had to repress the desire to attack "the boss" against all odds. Only common sense and Joyce's wisdom had prevented him from taking on the man in his own lair.

"I'll take the test," Bertrand wrote back. "Just not today. Must get indoors before dark."

Jeff had agreed to work late and was still in the queue, guiding someone through the software with his eyes rolling to the ceiling. He feigned stabbing himself through the heart with a pen. Bert raised one hand and high-fived him on his way out, thankful that he was done for another day.

But as he rolled north on the train, a restlessness took him, the thought of his basement with the bars on the windows unappealing, even though he'd moved the flat screen down there and turned the wet bar into a mini-kitchen by bringing out an old hot plate that his parents had stored away years ago. It was his night of rest from the gym, Joyce insisting that he take at least two nights off each week to allow his muscles to heal and grow. No exercise machines and no karate tonight.

As the 'L' train rocked its way north, Bertrand tried Nolan again on his cell. It would be more fun to open those crime stats with a friend who was on the same page, but still Nolan didn't answer. Where the hell was the guy? Sunset was less than a couple of hours away, and Nolan would never go out after dark.

Bertrand hurried down the stairs from Armitage station, but on his way to his home, the loneliness took hold. He didn't want to go into that empty house and be reminded that his parents were gone. At Nolan's he could pretend that he still had parents somewhere not far away, and although the guy was a bit scary with his paranoia, he was one of the few people who didn't take Bertrand's multiple ripper theory—the cult theory—with a grain of salt.

So Bertrand walked right past his little clapboard house and headed for Webster Avenue. It wasn't dark yet, so he decided the open sidewalk was safe, but it wasn't the Sheffield neighborhood he remembered. People hurried along the sidewalks and cars raced through the streets, litter chasing. Since when did his neighborhood have so much litter? Where were the Madvacs and the street sweepers? Where were the cops that usually laid the odd speed trap to remind drivers to slow down?

But the people fascinated Bertrand the most. Their hurry wasn't that of commuters rushing to pick up kids from daycare or get dinner. Instead people looked over their shoulders to ensure they weren't being followed. They avoided eye contact with Bertrand. Some ran, even though they were burdened with bags or high heels or too much weight. These weren't fitness freaks like Joyce and Jeff. These people hurried to beat a deadline far grimmer than any boss could hand out. They were fighting the sunset.

Bertrand stopped in front of Nolan's house, the gray clapboard well-maintained, the house far larger than Bertrand's but still humble compared to the monster homes far out in the suburbs. Thomas Nolan was a bit crazy when it came to his fear of the dark, and Bertrand worried that he had caught some of that craziness, that paranoia. But the house next door still had a **FOR SALE** sign on the lawn, the one put there by the cops.

A car with two men in it sat not far down the street past the **FOR SALE** sign, looking for all the world as if they were on a stakeout. Bertrand turned away from Nolan's house, his heart rate picking up. Was Nolan right after all? Was the government after him for knowing they were in on the Chicago Ripper murders? Had Nolan's blog got him in trouble?

Bertrand wanted to challenge—to do something—so he headed straight for the car. It was still daylight, and he was a law-abiding citizen if you discounted the Glock he had tucked under his jacket near the small of his back. But the car pulled out as he approached, the driver hurrying away, but not before Bertrand got a good look at him. He had only met that man once before—on the night he and Joyce had discovered Stan's blood-soaked body. The car's driver was the investigating detective: Somebody Sinclair. Maybe Michael Sinclair?

What was he doing here on stakeout and who was the other cop with him? Did they have a clue about the neighbor's murderer? Were they hanging out because they finally believed Nolan's ravings that it was the supposedly dead wife who cut the guy's throat? Were they waiting to see if she returned? Why didn't they want Bertrand to see them?

He turned back to Nolan's house and climbed the four stairs to the porch, pondering these puzzles. The doorbell chimed when he rang, but there was no angry voice over the intercom demanding his name as usual. Bertrand tried again a few more times, and finally used his cell to try phoning Nolan, but the phone rang on. Bertrand could even hear the ring through the front door.

What the hell? Nolan was never out after dark, and while not yet sunset, he had a stated preference for getting home a couple of hours early. Bertrand walked back down the stairs to the sidewalk, glancing up and down the street to see if there were any witnesses, but all was quiet, like the hush before the storm.

The red brick wall proved far less of a challenge for Bertrand than it had on that summer night when he'd been forced to chase Joyce and her dog into the neighbor's backyard. The workouts had paid off, slimming Bertrand's waist and strengthening his muscles, but he still had a little stubborn belly. Yet, he had never been so fit, felt so strong.

He literally hopped the little chain-link fence from dead neighbor's yard to Nolan's yard. All was quiet at the back of the house, and Bertrand's hope that he would find Nolan frying a few burgers on his barbecue ended—it was covered and cold to touch. Bertrand peeked in the window and noticed something unusual: the two-by-four that Nolan usually used as extra security to prevent the screen door from opening lay on the floor by the window, the unfinished yellow of the two-by-four a garish contrast to the finished wood floor.

Nolan must be out. But another thought struck Bertrand as he turned away from the sliding door: why would Nolan leave by the back door when he could leave the extra protection of the two-by-four in place and leave by the front. This made no sense. Wait a minute. Nolan's sliding door had been from the eighties or nineties, something that didn't have the modern triple-pane glass of these very new sliding doors.

Bertrand's heart raced now, not for fear for himself but his friend. He rushed over to the barbecue and threw up the vinyl rain cover, finding utensils hanging from the side shelf. He snatched up the spatula and turned to the door, shoving it between the lock and the door jam. It took several tries to get it beyond the latch, but then it was easy to shove down and unlock the door. Bertrand damaged the door frame in the process, but he now feared Nolan was beyond caring about such earthly concerns. The door opened easily, something that could never have worked if Nolan's two-by-four were in place in the track, blocking the door's slide.

The vertical blinds parted, and Bertrand stopped to listen in the gloom.

"Thomas? It's me, Bertrand Allan."

Not a sound except for the blinds clacking together behind him as they settled back into place. The house was empty.

Bertrand decided against turning on lights, just in case that cop circled the block and was watching this house rather than that of the murdered neighbor. He headed for the basement door, hoping to find it bolted, hoping that Nolan was asleep in the basement in his bomb shelter, but the door swung at a touch. It had been left open a crack. Downstairs, the evening sun filtered through the orange curtains on the two high windows, providing plenty of light to show that all that seventies furniture was undisturbed. The fridge behind the wet bar was in place too, but it slid aside easily and so did the wooden panel in the wall. A firm shove on the vault door proved it was unlocked. It swung in noiselessly on its well-oiled hinges. The gunroom—the refuge—was vacant.

Where the hell was the conspiracy blogger?

Back upstairs to check the front door. Locked, but the bolt wasn't shot, indicating a departure by someone with a key. Maybe he had gone out and just forgotten about the two-by-four at the back window? But something literally didn't smell right, a scent of bad meat. Bertrand walked back into the dining room, sniffing as he studied the room, but then he noticed the painting. It was not art by most standards—a simple still life of a bowl of fruit, perhaps painted by a friend or relative—but it was big, easily three feet by three. The painting was no longer centered on the wall beyond the dining-room table. It had been moved so far to the right that the hole for the old nail showed starkly in the center of the wall, even in this low light.

Bertrand walked around the table slowly, approaching the painting with caution, lest he disturb some precious clue that must be preserved for a forensics team. The floor was perfectly clean, though. He retrieved a pen from his pocket and used it to lift the corner of the painting from the wall so that he could look beneath.

Thomas had not died without a fight. A shotgun blast had sprayed pellets into the wall in a pattern about the diameter of a tennis ball. The painting had been moved to hide this evidence of violence.

"Fuck!" Bertrand released the painting and turned away, punching at the air in his anger. "Assholes!"

He headed back into the kitchen, grabbing the counter near the sink and breathing deeply, trying to convince himself that this wasn't proof of murder, but then the dining-room carpet caught his eye. It wasn't centered under the table anymore. He lifted a corner, not getting far when the carpet stuck, forcing him to give it a strong yank at whatever glued it. The brown proved that this was the source of the slight scent of rot. The blood stain blended well with the wooden floor, barely visible in the waning light, but on the carpet it was an obvious brown circle. The carpet had been moved to hide Thomas's blood. They hadn't even bothered to clean it up.

"Bastards!"

Bertrand shoved open the sliding door and drew deep lungfuls of cool air. They'd murdered Thomas Nolan and covered it up—this sick cult of rippers. Rage such as he had never known welled up from the pit of Bertrand's stomach. He had to fight not to draw the Glock and fire randomly around the neighborhood in frustration. Where were they?

He ran back through the house and out the front door, slamming it behind him, and rushed down the stairs and out into the middle of Webster. Where was that cop—that so-called detective who was more concerned about the news media than the victims? The street was dead. Hardly a car moved anywhere near here, as if the whole city held its breath in anticipation of the night. The sun hung low, turning high cirrus clouds a delicate pink, a beautiful sunset that Bertrand might have enjoyed with his parents at the lake house in other years. But now the sunset promised danger and menace, a bloody sky and not a peaceful sight. An 'L' train crossed over the street in the distance, for a moment occluding the sun and startling Bertrand into motion.

He patted his back where the Glock rested in its inside-the-belt holster, his extra weight helping to hide it. Bertrand set off at a fast pace, not for home, but in search of an enemy he could kill. Rage had taken hold of him, and it needed to be satiated. Let them come for him, these rippers. He was ready to fight.

# 12

# BATTLE AT ST. MICHAEL'S

For an hour, Bertrand had the streets of Chicago remarkably to himself. Car traffic, even on major streets, trickled along, nothing like the gridlock that would have been normal even this late into the evening. Pedestrian traffic was even less, leaving Bertrand feeling as if he traveled in a post-apocalyptic world. Only the windows proved that he wasn't alone, but usually drapes were drawn and voices were few. No laughter carried into the dusk.

At full night, a man walked out of a house just ahead of Bertrand, prompting him to reach back and lift his jacket and shirt, going for the Glock, but the man simply turned up his collar against the autumn chill and headed away, walking in the same direction but faster. Soon other people walked under the streetlights here and there, most ignoring Bertrand although one or two nodded a greeting as they passed.

Bertrand's rage subsided as his confusion grew. These were just normal people going about their evening. They weren't rippers, and they certainly weren't vampires.

He had talked to Nolan two nights ago, a short conversation about food, about how grocery store shelves were increasingly empty, as if the supply chain had broken down, even though the news media didn't seem to notice. All the conspiracy bloggers had many theories, most of them echoing Nolan's government conspiracy theories.

So sometime yesterday, someone had murdered Nolan. Was it something to do with his blog? Bertrand couldn't imagine that they'd ever have got him to leave his vault at night, so had someone murdered him during the day? If that were the case, the theory that the rippers only operated at night was out the window. But then why were so many people working nights instead of days?

Teenage laughter behind caught his attention, because young rogue males are unpredictable even without a cult of rippers. Bertrand glanced over his shoulder. Three young men—probably not old enough to drink and barely shaving—followed about half a block behind. The good news was that none of them carried beer bottles, so perhaps they were sober, although their excessive giggles hinted at drug use.

Fish, Bertrand's karate sensei, had taught him that confrontation should be a last resort, and as much as Bertrand wanted to fight now, he wanted to fight an enemy of civilization, like the so-called "boss," rather than exuberant teens. Besides, they weren't threatening him, so he turned south, heading toward St. Michael's Church.

More laughter, mean laughter, forced Bertrand to again glance over his shoulder.

They had turned to follow.

As if the world hadn't become crazy enough, now he had to deal with the mundane problem of bored teenagers looking for someone to harass. Okay, it could simply be a coincidence, and it certainly had nothing to do with Nolan's death. Bertrand forced himself to take several deep breaths to calm his rage. Had he always been this person?

He intentionally slowed his pace, projecting ignorance of their possible attention. When teenage males are looking for trouble, the biggest mistake is to show fear. He could run, of course, but that would set off a pack mentality, and he would be playing the part of a well-fed deer. Best to just relax and not change his direction.

Now Bertrand was in the Old Town neighborhood, proven by the fact that he could hear St. Michael's bells chiming eight o'clock. The church was Bertrand's destination, and the high spire on the left side rose above the houses to guide the way. His parents had taken him there a few times when he was a child as part of his religious tolerance education. They'd also visited several Protestant churches, a mosque and a synagogue, but Bertrand had been awed by the ornate grandeur of St. Michael's, of the gold and the statues, of the stained glass and the high columns that swept up to the ceiling.

His parents had taught him that St. Michael's was a symbol of Chicago's diversity, built by German immigrants before the Great Fire. Its sandstone brick walls survived when the conflagration swept through Old Town, consuming everything else in its path, and its parishioners rebuilt the interior in just a couple of years, extending the bell tower to well over 250 feet, making it the highest landmark in Chicago in its early days.

When young Bertrand had suggested that it was a miracle that the church had survived the Great Fire, his atheist parents had assured him that it was simply a testament to the faith of the Germans who had saved and restored their church, making it the anchor of their neighborhood. It was a monument to community, they had assured their little boy.

But to Bertrand the story of St. Michael had been as captivating as the church. It awed him that anyone, even an archangel, would agree to go down and fight Satan mano-a-mano, to risk all to defeat evil. Even as late as high school, when particularly troubled with teenage angst, Bertrand had often visited the cobbled yard in front of St. Michael's to stare at the life-sized white statue on its pedestal facing the church. The Archangel stood with his left hand over his heart and his right hand casually holding a sword with the point down. His left foot was planted on the head of a figure, presumably Satan, and his right foot on the vanquished one's back. It took Bertrand a few years before he realized that the statue was also a war memorial. The inscription read: "St. Michael Archangel assist us in our battles against the evils of the day."

The teenagers laughed, approaching casually as if they had always intended to come this way, yet heading straight for Bertrand and St. Michael's statue.

"Assist me now," Bertrand whispered up to the statue before turning to climb the steps to the church, the gothic architecture and columns and statues still amazing him. How many laborers and artisans had struggled to create this masterpiece?

The heavy door swung open, granting Bertrand sanctuary and peace. He proceeded down the aisle, his neck tipped back, as if he were still six, so that he could stare at the blue and gold vaulted ceiling in awe. He headed for the altar, wondering what they called the elaborate structure behind, rising like the facade of an elaborate cathedral, as complicated and delicate as any church Bertrand could image. The cupola rose high above the altar, gold and white, with symbols that were a mystery of the religion to Bertrand. Why was that heart impaled by a sword? What did that mean? On the stained glass, a woman received a blessing from a saint or an angel. Was that the Virgin Mary, and who blessed her—Angel Gabriel?

Bertrand had reached the front row pew and was about to take a seat, when the great door of the church banged shut. Teenage giggles proved that they had followed him into the church.

A taunting voice called out. "He thinks he's safe here, that we're old movie vampires."

Vampires? Bertrand turned to face them. The three approached up the aisle, white kids trying to look like gangstas, their baseball caps sideways and their jeans hanging low, their baggy jackets hanging open to reveal T-shirts and gold chains. Bertrand had grown up in the city and knew that real gangstas wouldn't waste their time harassing someone who didn't owe them money. There was stuff to do, and there was no benefit in dealing with the heat that came with a beaten or dead taxpayer. These kids were wanna-bees who didn't even know what that life involved.

The Glock hung in that little holster still pressed into his spine. Should he draw it now? Why? They hadn't made any specific threats.

"Long way from the suburbs, boys. Shouldn't you be running home?"

"Yo, I burned my home and fed on my parents!" shouted the teenager in the center, taller than his friends, his body gangly and yet to fill in to match his height.

Still Bertrand resisted the temptation of the Glock. He couldn't just start shooting people because he was angry or because they were rude. But why had one talked about vampires? Bertrand struggled with his desire to lash out. Instead, he stepped into the altar area, where the public could only go for readings or their weddings by invitation of the priest.

The kid spoke of feeding on his parents, but he was in a church. Bertrand walked to a pole with a shining crucifix at the top. He had a vague memory from his childhood of an altar boy carrying this at the head of a procession on a Sunday, and Bertrand had begged his parents to allow him to train for that job. They had taken him to a Quaker service the next week instead.

He hefted the pole of the crucifix and it lifted out of its base. A little kid could carry this? It was pretty heavy. Bertrand could finally lead a procession if one happened by, but he again turned to face the teenagers. "If that's true, that you murdered your parents, you're going to Hell."

The teenagers laughed, looking to one another for support.

"Fuck you," said the leader. "You have to die to go to Hell, and we're brids. We've evolved. We'll never die."

Brids? Evolution? These kids talked just like the dancers at Goth Knights. This was a cult. Bertrand's heart rate didn't speed up so much as become more pronounced, pounding in his chest with a heavy rhythmic thump. For the first time in his life, he knew he was going to fight, not a school-yard fight but a fight to the death. Still, he had to give this kid one last chance.

"Everyone dies." Bertrand stepped toward them, the crucifix held high like a talisman against evil. "I'll die. You'll die. Everyone."

"That can't save you." But the teen looked uncertain. "It's not like the horror movies, you shit head. We're not afraid of crosses. We've got the bugs. We're symbiots. Just 'cause the sun'll fry the bugs doesn't mean we're scared of a lump of metal."

They couldn't go out in the sun? Bertrand tried to process this information, hoping to cram it into his cult theory and failing. He decided to put all that aside for later, because now was the time for struggle.

"Then come and touch it." Bertrand tipped the crucifix slowly forward until it was only head height off the floor, but to ease the strain he slid his hands closer to the middle of the pole, the center of gravity.

"You dumb shit." The teenager stepped forward, pulling out a switchblade from his baggy jeans and snapping it open. "I'll touch it, no problem, and then when you get it too late that a cross ain't no weapon, I'm going to cut your throat open."

Bertrand tensed, focusing all his energy and concentration into the crucifix. He remembered all of Fish's lessons, breathing to calm, channeling his energy. All the power had to come out through that crucifix. The kid stepped forward, trying to swagger and just looking afraid. Now that he was close Bertrand could see the peach fuzz, but oddly no acne. The boy stretched his arm high, glanced back to make sure his friends watched, and placed his hand firmly over the body of Christ, his fingers closing around the image's throat.

"See." The kid met Bertrand's stare. "Fucking harmless lump of metal."

Bertrand unleashed the power with his loudest karate scream, pivoting the pole of the crucifix on his right hand so that the figure of Christ swung up into the air and the lower end of the pole drove between the teen's legs.

"Ah, FUCK!"

Apparently they could feel pain. The teen fell and writhed on the ground. One of his friends charged forward with a knife, but Bertrand now held his weapon like a pole vaulter. He charged, slamming the friend in the chest with the base of the pole, driving him back off his feet as a gush of wind escaped the kid's lungs.

The third teen pulled a handgun, and Bertrand backed up as if distance could help. He should drop the crucifix and grab for his Glock, but there was no time and he panicked, freezing with the crucifix held in front as if it could ward off bullets.

"Shoot him in the gut. Save the blood!" shouted the leader from the floor as he struggled to rise.

A gunshot slammed Bertrand's ears, echoing from the walls and the vaulted ceiling as the teen with the gun dropped to the floor. A hole in the center of his T-shirt oozed red.

Where had that come from? Bertrand looked left and right until he saw the shooter approaching, causing him to freeze again, not with fear this time but shock. A priest approached, his black cassock pushed forward by a middle-aged belly. He had a rifle presented, and as he approached he aimed it for the fallen leader.

"No! No! No!" shouted the leader, but the priest pulled the trigger and the teen's head jerked back, a hole appearing in his forehead, blood splattering behind on the floor.

The last teen, the one Bertrand had spiked in the chest, rose and ran for the back of the church. The priest took steady aim and fired, hitting the teen in the back and causing him to spill forward onto his face, the momentum from his run sliding the boy several feet along the polished stone floor after he had died.

The priest turned to face Bertrand, but his eyes went to the crucifix above Bertrand's head. "Forgive me, Father, for I have sinned."

He knelt and laid the rifle aside before crossing himself to pray.

# 13

# END OF DAYS

After five minutes, the crucifix grew very heavy in Bertrand's hands. How did those little altar boys manage this thing every Sunday? Bertrand didn't want to disturb the priest's prayer, since the man was probably—hopefully—going through an emotional trauma after committing a cardinal sin three times in less than a minute. Bertrand stepped backward as quietly as he could and placed the long pole of the crucifix back in its holder so that it stood once again on the right side of the altar near the pulpit.

He watched the priest for another few minutes, letting his own heart rate slow. The man was not old, but he was definitely over forty. His dark curls were thick and natural, salted with gray, but his face was very clean-shaven and his skin tone whispered of the Mediterranean or Central America, somewhere exotic and more temperate than cold Chicago.

Bertrand didn't want to hurry the man, but three bodies lay in the aisle, and unlike the vampires of the movies, they weren't getting up. Just when Bertrand had decided to at least pull them away to the side, the priest crossed himself and stood.

"I'll need your help to get rid of the bodies." The priest's accent hinted at Spain or Latin America.

"Father, shouldn't we be calling the cops? I mean, if you are really a priest you'll be a great witness."

"I'm sorry." The priest extended his hand. "I really am a priest, and I'm the new pastor of this parish. I'm Father Pablo Alvarez. I apologize for my abruptness, but you saw what they were, and so it is too dangerous to trust with the police."

Bertrand shook Alvarez's hand. "Okay, I just gotta ask: do you always wander around your church with a rifle?"

Alvarez picked up the rifle and hung it over his shoulder on a well-worn sling. That was Bertrand's first clue that this was a very old weapon.

"One of my parishioners gave it to me after saving my life. Please, we need to get rid of the bodies. Sometimes my sheep flee here at night, and I must guard them against these devils. That's why I carry a gun now." Alvarez stepped forward and placed a hand on Bertrand's shoulder, meeting his eyes. "We are at the end of days here, but I can't hide and pray. I watched people do that in Nicaragua when the Sandinistas or the Contras were coming, and it is not helpful. God helps those who helps themselves. Hurry, grab this boy's feet. Later I will pray for his damned soul."

———

Moving a body was more difficult than Bertrand ever imagined. It was heavy, there were no convenient handholds and it had a tendency to shift its weight in unpredictable ways. But Father Alvarez proved he was still strong, and there was a toughness to the priest that spoke of deprivation and hardship endured, the kind of life middle-class Americans hadn't known since the dirty thirties.

They shoved the bodies into a closet in the basement, and then they mopped up the blood with janitorial mops, cleaning up the stairs and finally back to the altar. All the while, Alvarez kept the gun slung over his shoulder, and the comfort with which he wore it didn't fit with the typical training for a priest.

Afterward Alvarez insisted Bertrand come back into the rectory. "You cannot go out at night without great reason. It is far too dangerous."

He led Bertrand to a small kitchen, one that looked as if it had last been renovated in the seventies, and installed him at a Formica-topped table. Alvarez had said very little so far. When he put the gun aside in the corner, it was again a movement too familiar, too practiced.

"You've used a gun before—a lot," said Bertrand.

Alvarez nodded as he ran water into a kettle, but he didn't look back at Bertrand.

"I was with the Contras in Nicaragua."

Bertrand tried to remember who they were and when they had existed, but Central American history had never been part of his studies.

Alvarez snapped on the gas stove and turned to Bertrand. "That was before you were born. We were guerillas and we fought the Sandinistas."

"Wow, I mean, I don't know who the Sandinistas were either, but you must've been young."

"I was sixteen and very foolish. There was no need for that fight, and I watched many die. Later I turned my back on the wars of men and sought God's forgiveness."

"But now you're again killing men."

Alvarez turned and opened a cupboard, reaching up for mugs and a box of tea.

"Those were not men. They're devils—blood drinkers—vampires."

"Murderers, yes, I'm sure of that, but supernatural vampires? One kid put his hand right over the crucifix and he didn't bat an eye, much less look afraid."

"One needs faith to fear the symbols of faith." Alvarez dropped tea bags into the cups. "But even then, these are not the vampires of legend. They are very real."

"But those kids, how can you be so sure they were vampires. I saw the knives—no doubt they were going to cut me, but that makes them rippers just like the Chicago Ripper. It doesn't make them vampires." But even as he said this, Bertrand remembered the teenager saying he couldn't go out in the sun or "the bugs'll fry." What else had he said? Something about feeding on his parents.

"My flock comes to me with their fears and confessions. One man begged forgiveness for murdering people and drinking their blood. He said he had to because he was starving. He said he'd become a vampire."

"Okay but—"

"Wait. After he received his absolution, he left the confessional. I realized too late what was happening when I heard him shout to God, 'Father, into your hands I commend my spirit.' I rushed from the confessional but it was too late. He shot himself through the heart."

"Okay so he was nuts—"

"I've known him for years, and I can assure you that he was a man of God and very sane and practical. He worked on our fundraising and was preparing to join the lay clergy. You must open your eyes to what is going on around you."

The kettle whistled.

The two men sat in silence with their tea. Bertrand kept replaying Nolan's theories about blood drinkers, trying to rectify it with the teenager's hints about feeding and fear of the sun. "They're not horror movie vampires," Bertrand said after his last sip of bitter tea.

"No. There are far more of them than in the movies."

---

Just after sunrise, Father Alvarez brought his rusting Jeep Cherokee around to a side door of the church, one on the laneway and discreet. They shoved the teens into it—Bertrand sweating despite the cold—and Alvarez drove them to a golf course on Lake Michigan. He had brought shovels, and they dug a shallow grave in the beach sand. Once it was deep enough, they dumped the bodies out the back of the Jeep and covered them up.

Farther up the beach, a hand was sticking out of the sand. Bertrand pointed to it. "Did you do that?"

Alvarez shook his head. "No. One of my parishioners, a jogger, discovered that they were burying thousands all along this shore. Another says that bodies are in parks everywhere, hardly buried, and others are in the graveyards. One man who works in a graveyard told me that a fresh grave may contain as many as ten bodies—no coffins, of course. The police don't go to these places anymore. They don't investigate murder. No one comes to the beach. You must be very careful who you talk to."

Bertrand rode with him back to the church but elected to walk from there to his home. He needed time alone, and walking quickly in the cool air, the collar of his leather jacket turned up, helped clear his brain. He needed a shower and he needed to think. Should he call in sick? He hadn't even had a chance to look at the hacked crime statistics.

As he passed a Chicago Tribune box, he noted a screaming headline about the accelerating housing crash, the second in less than a decade. At another time, Bertrand might have kicked himself for not selling his parents' home sooner to get the maximum value, but Father Alvarez's words just kept coming back to him: "We are at the end of days." Real estate prices probably didn't matter.

The shower was hot and Bertrand spent a long time washing off the guilt. Were those three kids really going to kill him? Should Father Alvarez have just threatened them with the gun, driven them away? But the teen with the gun, he was going to shoot, and the leader had ordered a shot in Bertrand's belly. Don't waste the blood. By the end of his shower, Bertrand had no doubt that Father Alvarez had been right to kill.

The bathroom light failed just as he turned off the water, and it didn't take long to determine that the power failure was at least street wide. Gathering clouds promised rain and made the interior of the house gray and dull. Bertrand and the city had become used to these frequent blackouts, but the mayor's excuse that it was related to adding "green energy" to the mix of power supplies was getting thin.

McDonald's seemed like a good bet for a late breakfast, because the enterprising manager at the franchise closest to Bertrand had brought in a trailer-mounted generator—a big one—that continued to power his restaurant through these power interruptions. Bertrand was on his way there when his cell rang.

"Bert." Jeff's voice was hushed, anxious. "Don't come into work. There're cops everywhere and they've got a thing for you."

"What?" Could they have found out about the murders in the church? Did someone see them dumping the bodies?

"Yeah. Someone hacked in the Chicago P.D. website from Malcolm's computer, but it was at eighty-thirty yesterday morning. Bert, dude, everybody knows that Malcolm doesn't work during the day and you started early. Where are you anyway?"

"I was planning to call in sick today."

In the background a barista shouted, "Order up on a double latte."

"Jeff?"

"You're not really sick though, are you? Like, Malcolm sick?"

"No, no. I just had a bad night is all. I thought I'd head over to Ronnie's for an Egg McMuffin and hang out at my place for a bit."

"Don't go home. I don't like the way the cops around the office are talking. They didn't even want to let me out for a Starbucks run, but Whitlock shouted them down by pointing out that I got to work late yesterday morning. He even showed them a note in my file. Bastard wrote me up for that, even though I told him about the power killing the 'L' for half an hour. I can't afford to lose this job."

"Yeah, well I'm beginning to think I might quit."

"Aw, no. It'll be miserable around here without you. Who's gonna teach me programming? I can't handle these support calls forever."

"Jeff, dude, if the power keeps failing at this rate, no one's gonna be programming, but I think that's the least of our problems."

"I gotta run, but we really need to talk. I don't think this cult theory of ours is gonna fly. Some very weird shit's going on. Much weirder than a cult if you can believe that."

"Meet me at the gym after you're done work. We may need to get out of Dodge for a bit or something. The city's falling apart."

The barista called out another order in the background of Jeff's phone.

"That's me," he called. "Right, we'll talk, but like I said, don't go home."

---

The McDonald's was packed, many coming here like Bertrand for a late breakfast because of the power failure. The reputation of this outlet having a generator must have spread far beyond their little neighborhood.

The lights on a building across the street came on while Bertrand waited in line, so he checked his cell and found he now had a signal. He quickly checked his e-mail before the power again failed: one from the Erics nut reminding him to take the survey to determine where he fit among the thousand souls. Another from Whitlock demanding he come into work or face unspecified "disciplinary action." Of course he couldn't threaten to fire Bertrand, because there were no replacements. A text from Joyce came through while he was still trying to think of an answer for Whitlock.

"Need to talk asap. Where r u?"

"Breakfast. U?"

"Fired. Company folding. Emptying bank account. Selling mutual funds."

Bertrand moved forward in line as he absorbed this news. Did she know something he didn't? Emptying bank account? What did she plan to do with the money? What should she do with the money? Father Alvarez's warning about the end of days gave Bertrand an idea.

"Buy food. Lots."

"Next on list. Gym?"

Shouting at the front of the line distracted Bertrand for a moment before he replied. "6pm."

"C u."

A stir in the crowd of the restaurant warned Bertrand that something was wrong. People from all the lines turned to look at the front of Bertrand's line, making him step to one side so that he could determine the cause of the disturbance.

A leather jacket and a big bum in old blue jeans were all Bertrand could see of the man at the front of the line, but he could hear the shouting.

"I want a fucking Big Mac. That's what this restaurant is all about ain't it! Big Macs. I don't care if it's breakfast. I don't want an Egg McMuffin. I want a Big, Big Mac."

The cashier was plump and young and flustered. Her reply was inaudible this far back in the line, but it clearly wasn't what Leather Jacket guy wanted to hear, because he reached across the counter, showing way more plumber's butt than anyone could want to see, and grabbed her by her polyester uniform. "I won't take no for an answer!"

"Let go! You'll rip my top! Let go!"

Bertrand moved before he'd even decided to, running between the lines and up to the front. The desire to fight—to do something after all the stress—took over. He kneed Leather Jacket hard in the tailbone, not really a karate move, but he was improvising on an exposed weakness.

Air gushed from Leather Jacket's lungs because of the pain, and he released the cashier so that he could turn to face Bertrand, who by this time discovered that the Glock had magically appeared in his hand.

He pointed it at Leather Jacket's ruddy face and bloodshot eyes, holding the weapon with one hand as Emile had taught him and supporting the gun hand with his free hand. Leather Jacket looked hungover and terrified.

To Bertrand's surprise—too everyone's surprise—the big man burst into tears.

"Please," he said, backing along the counter. "I don't want to die. Please, I know I'm being crazy but I didn't get any sleep last night. The screams, so much frigging screaming and there's blood all over the sidewalk down the street but there's no bodies." The man drew a shuddering breath. "What if they come for me tonight? I just want a Big Mac."

The manager approached from the back of the kitchen, tall and bristling, his skin a dark shade of black, his belly slim and proving he didn't feed on the McDonald's menu more than he should. "I've called the police," he shouted.

Bertrand lowered the Glock. "It's okay, it's okay. I wasn't gonna shoot the guy." He turned back to Leather Jacket. "Look, dude, you gotta stay with some friends tonight and you should arm yourself. Keep the lights off so they don't know you're home. If there's a house in your neighborhood that's got a for sale sign in front, just break in and then bar the door—put a new lock on it—whatever. But for Chrissakes, lie low. Don't call the police and don't go out until sunrise."

"Who are you?" asked the manager, placing one hand protectively around his young cashier, whose cheeks were still wet with tears of fright. "What makes you say this?"

"I'm nobody special." Bertrand looked around to see anxious faces focusing on him with a desperate intensity. These people knew something was wrong but didn't know what to do about it.

"You need to organize," Bertrand called to the whole room. "The cops can't or won't protect you anymore. There are roving gangs going around killing people at night, and the only way to protect yourselves is to arm yourselves and band together. If you live alone, you're in very grave danger, because it's loners they're going after right now."

"But how do you know this?" asked the manager, although Bertrand got the sense that the man completely believed him.

"Because I have eyes to see with and ears to hear with, just like this guy." Bertrand used his free hand to point at Leather Jacket and then stuffed the Glock back into its holster in the small of his back. "He heard screams last night. He saw blood this morning. How many of you have had similar experiences?"

Hands went up and shouts came in reply.

"Then you don't need me to tell you that there is an undeclared war going on here. You can call your congressman if you like, but if they could do anything about it—or if they weren't involved—it would be all over today's paper."

More shouts and more questions. Leather Jacket slumped against the counter, still sobbing. "But I don't know anybody," he said. "My folks are in Georgia and they don't answer the phone no more. My buddies' up north are gone and the cabin's burnt out. I don't know where to go."

"You can stay with me," shouted a man farther back.

"I'm getting out of town. Today," shouted a middle-aged woman.

The crowded pushed in, many trying to get a look at Bertrand. Many calling questions and some loudly exchanging stories and rumors.

"Back in lines," shouted the manager, his powerful voice rising over all. He curled a finger at Bertrand, inviting him beyond the counter and into the inner sanctum of McDonald's. "You better come back here before there's a riot. I'll set you up. And you," he pointed to Leather Jacket, who had composed himself although he still looked frightened and exhausted. "You just take a seat and I'll bring you a Big Mac in half-an-hour, and we'll get you set up with someone to stay with tonight. Just jump over the counter." The last was to Bertrand.

He clambered over the counter with as much dignity as he could manage.

"What do you want to eat, sir?" asked the young cashier, her cheeks red and her eyes puffy.

"Oh, anything. Big Mac—no—I mean Egg McMuffin, whatever."

She laughed in relief, almost a cry at the same time, and turned to the receiving trays.

"Bring it to the office, Alison." The manager took Bertrand's arm and guided him past the grills, the shouts still coming from the crowd in the restaurant.

"Wait a second." Bertrand pulled to a halt in front of the office door. "I gotta get out of here, okay? Forget about breakfast. Is that the way out over there?"

"Wait, wait, wait. I didn't call the cops if that's what you're worried about. I sure as hell didn't need you to tell me you can't trust those assholes anymore. I just need to talk to you for a minute, and breakfast is on the house. Please, take a seat."

Bertrand entered the little office and warily took a seat, deeply regretting waving the Glock around. He had wanted to avoid attention, not become the center of it.

The manager took a seat in a creaking leather chair behind his corporate-issue desk. "I started closing by sunset a couple of weeks ago. The place would be full after dark and no one was eating, then suddenly they'd all go—flash mobbing maybe, I don't know. But they'd all come back a few hours later and they'd all be pumped. And not just kids—not just teens, there'd be old folks hanging out with them too, but as energetic as twenty-year-olds. We found a body in the bathroom one night, throat cut deep on one side."

"What did the cops do?"

The man leaned back in his chair. "What do you think they did? They came, carted off the body and left us to clean up the blood. They didn't even dust for fingerprints, but they did tell me it was the M.O. of the Chicago Ripper."

"There are hundreds of Chicago Rippers out there, and there are New York Rippers and L.A. Rippers and London and Beijing and Mumbai. We're just not hearing about them anymore, and bloggers who do talk about them are being shut down or hunted down. I know I sound like a complete nut, but they take over the media and the police first."

"You need to talk to people, let them know what's going on."

"Everybody knows what's going on."

The manager leaned forward, clasping his hands on his desk. "But you're convincing. You need to spread the word. Until today I was too afraid people would think I was crazy, but I hear you and I believe. We need to organize for more than just for one night, we need to build our own army, a resistance."

A tentative knock spared Bertrand a reply.

Alison opened the door after the manager's invitation, bearing Bertrand's breakfast in a bag. "I didn't know whether it was for here or to go."

Bertrand stood, reaching for the bag with one hand and his wallet for another. "To go is great. How much?"

"I told you, on the house." The manager stood. "You fight for my staff, you get free food. Just one thing, promise me you'll come back and talk to folks. I'm going to spread the word quiet-like. How about tomorrow afternoon, say around four?"

"What do you want from me?"

The manager held out his hand. "I'm Martin, Martin Morley, and I want you to say the same stuff you said in there today."

"I'll see what I can do."

"Folks need you. They need someone who'll just tell it like it is."

"Okay, tomorrow afternoon around four. But if I see a cop, I'll just book."

"There'll be no cops."

---

Bertrand didn't obey Jeff's warning not to go home, but he was very careful about it. He went to Needleman's first, slipping from the alley, crossing under the 'L' and up the stairs through the back door. An animal, probably a raccoon, had visited the house and opened the fridge door to pull out rotting food. Judging by the stench and the state of the contents, this had happened quite some time ago.

One hand held over the face and the other up to guide in the gloom brought Bertrand safely to the living-room window. No cops out front, at least not a marked cruiser, and he couldn't see any suspicious men hanging out in other cars.

He slipped across the street, resisting the urge to run for fear of drawing attention to himself. He unlocked the door and hurried to close it and lock it behind him. The power went up and he quickly checked his phone for messages and discovered one from Whitlock and several from a Detective Costa.

In and out as fast as possible. He went straight for the basement and closed his Mac laptop, unplugging the power cord and hurrying back upstairs. Just as he was reaching for the knob on the backdoor, his cell phone went off like the alarm klaxon on a World War Two submarine, a ring tone that Bertrand had set for his boss. It startled him so much that he nearly dropped the computer.

He checked the call display anyway as he answered, but sure enough it was Whitlock's office number.

"Bertrand Allan?"

"Hi John, look I'm really sorry but I'm really sick. I just can't come in today."

"Are you changing?"

Oh, oh. That wasn't Whitlock. Bertrand nearly hung up, but then he remembered when Malcolm was desperately sick back in July—before the taxi driver was murdered.

"I'm sick. I'm really, really sick. I can't keep normal food down, and I just can't come out of the basement and into the light, not today."

"So you're one of them now?"

"Yes, I guess so. I didn't know it would happen so fast. Who is this?"

"Detective Alfred Costa. I'll give you a free pass today, but I want you in my office tonight to answer a few questions about the hacking. If you're one of them now I guess it's not such a big deal, but I want to chat just the same."

"Of course. Where's your office." Bertrand repeated key parts of the address back as if he were diligently writing them down.

"Ten tonight should be okay," Costa said. "But remember, I'm off limits, officially in the Daylight Brigade, so get your dinner somewhere else."

"Yes, of course."

Off limits? Dinner? Daylight Brigade? Bertrand stared at his iPhone for a moment as if he could find the answers in the menu. He slipped it into his pocket and headed out the back door, crossing the little yard he'd played in as a child, and opened the pedestrian door to the detached garage. He hardly ever used his Volkswagen GTI since he lived downtown, but now he needed mobility. He needed to go grocery shopping, and he feared if he didn't go soon there would be no food left on the shelves. Once they were empty, Bertrand was certain that they would never be replenished. He wasn't sure that it was the end of days, but in his soul he knew that it would soon be the end of civilization.

# 14

## FEEDING FRENZY

The doorbell woke Bertrand. He sat up in panic, struggling to remember the day of the week, the hour of the day. The light through his west facing basement windows could only be afternoon light, and the slant of the rays through the dust suggested mid to late afternoon.

Right, he'd skipped work and gone shopping, driving from one grocery store to another to buy any canned or preserved food he could find. The fruit and vegetable bins sat empty except for a few stacks of apples. Oddly, there were no line-ups to buy the remaining food. Why were people not out grocery shopping? Surely people during their regular shopping must've noticed the depleting supplies, which would usually provoke panic buying, like stocking up on water and batteries in advance of a hurricane.

Bertrand had also emptied his bank account and called about his mutual funds, ordering his adviser to sell them and convert them to cash. The adviser had begged him not to, pointing out that even though the stock market had recently plunged, it was still fractionally up from last year. If Bertrand would just wait, his advisor was sure the market would rush back up to those stratospheric highs from which it had fallen. Bertrand didn't care. He wanted the money now. He also considered putting his house up for sale, but so many houses were for sale in Chicago—indeed across the country—that there were simply no buyers. Housing prices had plummeted to levels that made stories of the 2008 crash sound like a minor blip in the market.

The doorbell chimed. That was what had woken him. Jeff would be pissed that he had ignored the warning and returned home, but after the conversation with Detective Costa, Bertrand wasn't as worried about the police for today—until now. He threw off his bedclothes and rushed to the window. There was no hope of seeing the front door, but maybe he could see if a police cruiser was parked in front.

"Bert! Are you there?" It was Destiny's voice.

What the hell was she doing here? She should be in the office, answering phones.

"Please, Bert. I'm really scared! If you're there can you let me in?"

Bertrand reached up and slid back the little window. "I'll be right there."

He scrambled through the basement, finding his jeans and yanking them on in haste. He snatched up a dress shirt from the back of a chair and hurried up the stairs, buttoning it on the way.

"Hey," he said upon opening the door, but before he could say more, Destiny threw herself at him, hugging him and weeping as if she'd just found a long-lost lover.

"Oh, thank God you're here. I'm so scared."

Bertrand awkwardly patted her back and tried not to feel her breasts pressing against his torso, fought not to be aroused by the scent of her, the curves of her body. But his protective instincts went full throttle as she buried her face in his chest and wept. He looked past her into the street, but there was no one else around so he pulled her into the house and slammed the door.

"We've got to be careful," he said when she had calmed down enough that he could push her away without being rude. "Come into the kitchen and I'll make you some tea."

"You got anything stronger?"

"Beer?"

"That'll be good."

He took her hand and led her down the narrow hall, feeling like a boyfriend rather than a coworker. What would Joyce say? It wasn't like they were dating or anything, yet he felt a special connection to Joyce that he didn't share with Destiny. But Destiny was attractive, and she had come to mind more than a few times when he was involved with himself late at night. She slipped her jacket off, revealing a blouse unbuttoned deep into her cleavage, a gossamer covering more suited to summer than Chicago's fall.

"Take a seat." Bertrand averted his eyes as he spoke, but didn't fail to note that she didn't appear to be wearing a bra.

Bertrand had renovated the kitchen a month after his parents had died, a desperate attempt to make the house his own and to bury the past. He had donated the nineties countertop and cupboards to Habitat for Humanity and replaced them with a granite countertop and expensive white cupboards. The floor was now stone tile, which he had discovered was very cold in early morning once summer ended. The table of the breakfast nook was the same granite as the counter, and the bench seats with it were red leather and overstuffed, making that corner look closer to a fifties diner. Destiny slipped onto one bench while Bertrand opened the stainless steel fridge door and pulled out a couple of Sam Adams beers.

"What happened?" He twisted each open, tossing the caps into the garbage can under the sink and handing one to Destiny.

"It was Malcolm. He's totally a freak." She took a gulp of the beer to calm her breathing and her tears. "He invited me back to his place this morning. I worked a double yesterday, stayed till midnight and Malcolm went home early cause the call volume dropped off. That's when he asked me over."

"So ... like ... he assaulted you?" Bertrand knew he wasn't the right person for this conversation. He didn't know anything about sexual assault counseling. It wasn't her fault. She at least needed to be told that, but what else?

"No. I mean it was weirder than that." Her eyes stayed with the beer bottle, and she began to peel the label from the brown glass. Her embarrassment made Bertrand's ears burn in sympathy.

"You don't have to tell me what happened." Did he sound panicked?

"I want to. I want you to understand what a sick bastard he is. To think I liked him." She finished peeling the label and proceeded to fold it in half and half again as if involved in origami. "You see, I went there because I wanted to get with him. Everybody thinks I'm some delicate little virgin, you know."

"I don't." What did he just say? "I mean, the way you talk and all it's obvious that you're not frigid or anything like that. I mean, oh forget it. I can't dig my way out of this one."

Destiny laughed and met his eyes for the first time since she had sat down.

"It's okay. I have been around the block once or twice, but I admit I talk sluttier than I act. Everybody thinks that 'cause I'm a tiny Asian I should giggle behind my hand and wear school-girl uniform kilts and be all modest. That's why I talk dirty, 'cause it shocks mundanes like you. But Malcolm's so cute and funky, and I really did want to bone him—that's why I went back to his place."

Bertrand was surprised she was alive, given his suspicions about Malcolm.

"He was interested in something else," Bertrand said.

Destiny nodded and took a big gulp of her beer, summoning up her courage to retell the story. "He's kinky, and I kinda thought that was attractive. I was looking for adventure, so when he wanted me to tie him up I thought it was all cool. I'd be in complete control and nothing could go wrong."

Bertrand's ears flamed and pressure in his jeans filled him with dread. What if she asked for another beer? She would see his erection and think he, too, was a sick pervert. He wasn't into bondage, but Destiny talking frankly about sex while sitting there looking so pretty and vulnerable in her low-buttoned blouse had an effect. Bertrand fought to restrain his lust.

"But something did go wrong." Bertrand hid his interest with another sip of beer.

"He couldn't get it up. He's just lying there, spread eagle on the bed." Destiny studied her beer again, not quite as embarrassed as Bertrand. "I was doing everything, you know, to get him excited, and I know some good tricks, but he was just totally Mr. Flaccid."

Bertrand was relieved and the pressure in his jeans thankfully subsided. He had feared a pornographic story with Destiny in a prominent position. "Okay, I don't think Malcolm's well. In fact I think he's even sicker than you know."

"I'm not finished." She gave him a quick glare and looked back down to her beer. "I'm naked and doing everything and I'm getting pretty pissed with him. So he asks—like—begs me to cut my finger and drip some blood into his mouth. I really wanted some action by this time so I decide to one up him. I'm not afraid of a little blood or a little pain, so I cut my wrist."

"Crap! Destiny!"

"Just a bit." She held up her right arm and pulled down her sleeve to show off a Band-Aid. "See, not like a suicide cut to my wrists, but just a little nick on the vein. I put it to his mouth and he went crazy, I mean sucking like crazy. And then he is going, I mean totally up in the air and I'm thinking it's sick but at least I'll get some action and then before I can do anything, boom! He blows—"

"Stop! Yes, I get it." Bertrand hands were up, palms out in surrender in his futile panic to prevent the graphic image from generating.

"All over the place."

"Yes, like, spare me. Please. I get the idea. He's a really lousy lay and he's twisted."

Now she met Bertrand's eyes. "Sorry. I just wanted you to understand how sick he is. Anyway, he wanted more and said the action would last longer, but I got my clothes on and got the heck out of there. But just before I left I untied one of his hands, and he shouts after me while he's still untying the other that he's not done with me. The perv wants to do it again! I'm afraid to go back to work 'cause I don't want to see him tonight. I should never have tried to sleep with someone from the office."

Bertrand finished his beer, appalled at how quickly he had consumed it, his head buzzing from the quick blast of alcohol on an empty stomach. Even so, he stood and grabbed two more from the fridge. "You can go back to work easily enough." He reclaimed the seat opposite her, sliding a beer across the table. "Just do like I do and tell Whitlock that you won't work late. Malcolm never comes in before sunset."

"Yeah, but don't you think it's totally weird. I mean, he likes to suck blood—really likes it, and he never comes into work during the day. I mean—" She looked up from her beer, her expression far more embarrassed than when graphically describing her attempt at sex with Malcolm. "I know this sounds totally freaky, but do you think he's a vampire?"

"Did he have fangs or anything like that?" Bertrand leaned forward, hungry for information that would confirm or deny the growing dread.

"No." Destiny also looked disappointed. "No fangs. No weirdness other than just Malcolm weirdness.

"What the heck is going on?"

Destiny started to peel the label of the second bottle. "Did you find anything when you hacked?"

Should he admit to the hacking? Bertrand caught himself looking at the bare skin between her breasts—definitely no bra. His cheeks flamed and he fought his eyes up to her face, thankfully getting there before she looked up from the beer label.

"Yeah. Crime stats—totally crap, crime stats. Want to see?"

"Absolutely."

"They're in the basement. It's safer down there anyway."

He grabbed his beer and led her down the stairs where his computer waited on his old desk from high school, some of the mementos of those years still push-pinned to the cork board above it: ribbons from the debating team and the computer club. A photo of Bertrand graduating taken by his dad.

"You sleep down here?"

Bertrand's bed was shoved up against the old couch so that there would still be a maneuvering area in the cramped little room.

"It's safer down here at night. They can't get in when I've got that door at the top of the stairs locked, and I keep the blinds drawn and the lights really low if the power's up."

"Weird." Destiny plunked down in the chair in front of Bertrand's desk, moving the wireless mouse to wake the laptop.

"Let me show you weird."

He put his beer down far from the computer and stood beside her, leaning over to take control of the mouse and see the screen. Her scent— a subtle perfume—filled his nostrils and forced him to acknowledge his proximity. Don't look down now. He would be looking right down her cleavage. He carefully kept his eyes on the computer screen, finding the icon for the USB stick and opening up the Chicago P.D.'s crime stats. The pie charts and bar graphs all splashed across the window, and Destiny sat forward to study them.

Bertrand turned away and went to the window, stretching up on his toes to look through the bars to the sun, which was just above the peak of Needleman's house, closer to the horizon than Bertrand had thought. Destiny would have to spend the night with him. His breath shortened at the thought of lending her a T-shirt for pajamas, of sleeping on the couch so close to her. But what about his appointment with the detective? If he didn't show, would the police come here—or worse, the rippers? They'd better get to Thomas's bunker and they could sleep on the couches. They'd still be very close together.

"Are these graphs right?" Destiny studied the computer with hungry intensity.

"Who knows? But if they were crap, why did they pull them off the public site and hide them?"

He turned from the sun and again looked over her at the screen. Eleven murders in May, twenty-six in June, over two hundred in July, over a thousand in August and then nothing. Either there were zero murders or the stats had never been loaded and just defaulted to zero.

"Check out the missing persons though. That's the really scary part." Bertrand took control of the mouse and clicked over to another set of graphs. These bars also rose exponentially: over one thousand reported missing in May, and by August, over fifty thousand reported missing. Again, September showed zero.

"What the—"

"That's what I said." Bertrand picked up his beer and fought not to gulp the whole thing down. Was Needleman included in those numbers?

"What is going on?" Destiny sat back and stared at the computer, and Bertrand took a seat on the edge of the bed.

"There's a cult, I think—a blood cult. What's really weird is that so many people in the government, even the cops, are in on it."

"No." Destiny shook her head but kept staring at the crime stats. "If Malcolm was just in some kind of cult, then why won't he come into work during the day? Why have so many people switched to night shift? And I don't mean just from our office."

Bertrand let the silence hang as he faced the impossible that Father Alvarez and those teenagers had forced him to face. There were murderers out there who wanted to drink blood, and there were more of them every day, and like vampires, they couldn't go out in daylight. What had that detective said? *Get your dinner somewhere else.* And something about the Daylight Brigade.

"What's weird is there are people who can come out in the daylight who help them—like cops and stuff," he finally said. "I just can't figure out—I mean, vampires? But they use knives, they're not afraid of crosses or stuff like that. I doubt garlic helps. This is all something else. Something real." He thought of those teenagers last night, about their limp bodies sliding down into the sandpit at the beach. These kids didn't need a stake through the heart—bullets had worked just fine. Bertrand still feared that Father Alvarez was crazy and that they were just violent teenagers. But those kids had talked about being "brids."

"Bert, can I stay with you tonight?" Destiny turned in the swivel chair to face him. "I don't want to go into work, and my gran went to visit her sister in the country. I just don't want to spend the night alone in my apartment."

"Sure. I mean, if you want to spend the night with your folks too that's okay."

Did he overdo the nonchalance? His heart beat faster at the thought of sharing a room with her, but his conscience wanted him to hold out for Joyce, to make his first time really special and not just some lay.

"My folks moved way out west. I could never drive there before dark." She stood and finished her beer. "I have to get some stuff from my place. I'll be back before sunset." She turned and hurried up the narrow stairs, but Bertrand rushed after her and caught her by the elbow in the kitchen.

"Wait. I'll go with you, because we're not spending the night here—not with the cops looking at me for the hacking."

"We can't stay at my apartment." She shrugged back into her short jacket. "That building is full of freaks at the best of times."

"I got a place." Bertrand headed for the hall closet for his jacket. "It's very secure."

"I'll meet you back here, Bert." She opened the door. "I have to shop for some woman things so I don't want you with me. I promise I'll be back before sunset. Where's your safe place?"

"Not far. You sure you don't want me to come with you?"

"Definitely. I'll see you around seven."

"Make it six-thirty. We want to be safe and locked down very early." She had already slammed the door.

———

Bertrand stood on his front porch in the gathering dusk. Where the hell was she? The city had fallen into that twilight lull—something that Bertrand now came to expect, that moment of waiting for the world to wake. How much longer should he give her before making a run for Nolan's bunker? Needleman's house across the street looked more forlorn than ever, even the **FOR SALE** sign tipping as gravity began to get the upper hand.

What if she didn't get here until after sunset? Could they go to ground here and make it through the night? Bertrand pulled his iPhone from his pocket and checked the detective's contact number and dialed it. Maybe he could buy another night.

"Homicide, Sinclair."

"Oh, I'm sorry, I've got the wrong number. I was looking for a Detective Costa about a computer hacking case." Bertrand tried to sound innocent and casual, but he was spooked. Sinclair was the detective he and Joyce had met the night that Nolan's neighbor had been murdered.

"Detective Costa will be in later tonight. Can I leave him a message—ah—Mr. Allan?"

Damn call display. It didn't sound like his name meant anything to Sinclair, and who knows how many murders the man had investigated in the last three months. *Okay, sound relaxed.*

"I have an appointment for ten p.m., but I was hoping to push it later or maybe until tomorrow."

"Tell you what, he'll be here in about half-an-hour. Just call back and you can tell him yourself."

"Thank you."

Bertrand gave it a full hour and was about to give up on Destiny—it was true night now—when a motorcycle roared down the street and squealed to a stop in front of Needleman's. Bertrand backed against his front door, getting ready to run inside and lock it. One hand went under his jacket behind his back and closed around the Glock, but he didn't draw it yet.

It wasn't until the rider was getting off the bike that he recognized Destiny's lithe frame, now clad in tight black leather. She pulled off the helmet and shook out her glossy hair.

"It took you long enough." Bertrand made no attempt to hide his anger. "We've got to get the hell out of here."

She hurried up the stairs, a pack thrown over her shoulder, one hand holding her helmet. "Gotta pee." She stretched up on tiptoes to kiss Bertrand's cheek. "You're my hero for waiting."

She rushed through the door, Bertrand trailing behind.

"Well make it fast," he shouted as she pounded up the stairs to the house's only bathroom.

Bertrand closed the front door but didn't bother locking it, since they were about to leave. He would take her across the street to Needleman's place and from there out underneath the 'L' to the alley. He considered taking his car, but he didn't want it parked anywhere near Nolan's place. A smart cop with a good computer database could link him to the neighbor's house, and it wouldn't be too hard to guess that he was somewhere near the murdered guy's place. And the motorcycle just attracted too much attention, although the thought of riding behind Destiny was alluring. No, they would practically be calling every ripper from miles around with that flashy bike. He would take them up the alley where people usually feared to tread after dark. Rippers were more of a problem now, and he had his Glock to deal with muggers.

At least he could get ready. He put on his camping pack stuffed full of canned food, his computer and lots of extra clothes. He wandered into the living room, taking one last look at the house of his childhood, his teen years, his last years with his parents—finally, his lonely season. He would come back if he could, even if only to visit the empty shell of family life, but he knew he could no longer live here.

His cell rang. He checked the call display, saw Jeff's number and answered it. "Hey, dude. Guess what? Destiny's here."

"Bert, thank God. You've got to—"

The phone went dead just as all the streetlights went dark, and the light in the kitchen flicked off. He checked the display and discovered that the signal was gone. The power failure always flatlined the cell phones. Why hadn't he kept his parents' landline? If Jeff was at work, he could try him there. They might still have power in the Loop. "Destiny, are you okay? We've gotta move."

"It's too late," she called from above. "We should just stay here for the night. I don't want to go outside again in the dark."

"No friggin' way." Bertrand stomped up the stairs, his pack slowing him down. "The police could be coming for me. We need somewhere really secure that they don't know about."

"Where is this place anyway?"

"It's a bunker." Bertrand stopped in front of the bathroom door. He couldn't just go in, damn it. "Come on. I'll show you."

"I don't want to go."

Wait a minute. Her voice didn't come from the bathroom. It came from his parents' bedroom. "What are you doing in there? That's my parents' room."

Bertrand hurried down the hall, wondering if he could drag her to his car. He stopped in the doorway though, because she was stretched out on the bed in the dark. Enough moonlight came through the window to sculpt naked skin. Bertrand's breath drew in sharply and his heart raced. Why now? Finally a woman had the hots for him, and not only was she lying in his dead parents' bed, but their very lives were in danger.

"Not here and not now." He stayed in the doorway, his imagination filling in what the shadows hid—the darkness between her legs, the color of her nipples. His erection rushed up in seconds, demanding attention.

"Come on, Bert. No one knows we're here." She rose up on one elbow and held out her other hand. "I've been so scared, but around you I feel so safe. Let's just forget everything for one night and have some fun."

He wanted to. My God he wanted to, but every fiber of his being knew this was wrong, knew this wasn't the time, place or person. He didn't want to lose his virginity to someone who looked upon sex as nothing more than recreation.

"No way. I'm going back downstairs. I'll give you two minutes to get dressed and come with me. Maybe later, when I think we're safe." But somehow he didn't think so. She was pushing too hard, and it felt all wrong. Besides, he doubted he could perform to her expectations, and he doubted she would be patient with his lack of skill.

"Oh come on. It's not like I want to tie you down or anything weird." She stood—completely shameless—although with only weak light coming through the window, she was a silhouette of hips and arms and shoulder-length hair. She stepped forward and grabbed a fistful of his jacket. "I've got condoms if that's what you're worried about."

"I'm worried about having my throat slit open by a ripper."

She yanked fiercely on his jacket just as someone hit his head from behind. He tripped forward and fell heavily, barely getting his hands out to block his fall. His forehead hit the wood floor, causing as explosion of pain.

"Get his arm, quick," shouted Destiny.

Bertrand fought for control of his muscles, but it was too late. The snick of a handcuff on his right wrist suggested that the police had caught up to him with Destiny's help. But she was naked. Would she do that for the cops?

"No!" Bertrand managed to shout as he struggled against hands and arms that lifted and shoved him up onto his parents' bed. Someone pulled at his free arm, yanking it over to the other bedpost. He fought to pull it back, but the male shadow overhead punched him in the eye, making him gasp and convulse with the new pain. The click of cuffs made everyone settle down: Bertrand because now he couldn't use his hands, his abductors because they knew there was no longer any rush. Bertrand was theirs for the taking.

# 15

# END OF AN ERA

Bertrand's pack pushed up his back, which made his hands stretch taunt on the handcuffs, the metal biting into his wrists. The bedposts of his parents' bed were cheap and old. Could he break one with a mighty heave? All he needed was to get his hand back to his Glock and he could shoot.

"Nice work, babe."

Bertrand froze in his surprise. He knew that voice. "Malcolm?"

The monster of rage rose in Bertrand's chest—a monster that wanted to fight, that felt safer fighting. "You lying slut!"

"I mostly told you the truth." She stood at the end of the bed, shameless in her nudity or perhaps knowing that with only moonlight for illumination, Bertrand couldn't see much. Malcolm stood beside her, one arm around her slim waist. He leaned over and kissed her passionately.

"You lied!" Bertrand shouted. "You lied about everything."

"I just pretended it was a month ago, when Malcolm and I first hooked up. The only thing I changed was that we did go for a second round."

Malcolm giggled. "And a third and fourth and fifth the next night."

"Why the hell didn't you two just carry on your fornicating ways and leave me the hell out."

"Oh Bert, because you're such a trouble maker." Malcolm left Destiny and walked around the corner of the bed, pulling something out of his pocket in the process. A snick and a glint of light off the metal warned Bertrand that it was a switchblade.

"All I want is to be left alone."

"No you don't." Malcolm stood over him. "People who want to be left alone don't go to Goth Knights. You complete idiot. What the fuck were you doing there? And crime stats? People who want to be left alone don't go hacking crime stats to show that there have been a lot of murders. We can't have you loading that up onto the Internet, even if only conspiracy scum will think its true. That's why the order came down right from the boss himself. You were designated fodder. No evolution."

Stall for time. Focus your strength. He would have one chance to break that bedpost before they figured out what he was trying to do and Malcolm got to business with the knife.

"What's evolution all about?"

Destiny climbed onto the bed from the end, moving up over Bertrand's legs. "Nice try, Bert, but we've got business to take care of."

"Shall we do him together?" Malcolm knelt on the bed at Bertrand's side. The knife was cool against Bertrand's neck.

"Definitely. I've always wondered how long it would work while you were drinking." Destiny started to undo Bertrand's belt.

He was going to die. He was very afraid, but that fear transferred to bitter anger. How could she betray him like this? How could she help a sick ripper like Malcolm? He would not go quietly. He would not let her defile him.

Bertrand brought his knees up and bucked her off the bed, the knife cutting into his throat in the process. He yanked with all his might on his right hand, the one farthest from Malcolm, ignoring the pain of the steel cuff.

Destiny flailed at the air and fell off to the window side of the room, farthest from the door. "Bastard!" she screamed as she hit the floor. "I was just trying to give you a good time on your way out."

"Oh, I smell blood," said Malcolm. "Hurry, baby. I can't wait. I'm so hungry."

Destiny, her naked figure framed by the moonlit window, ran around to Malcolm and received something from him. A clink of metal on metal warned Bertrand that they had more handcuffs.

Fight. Fight to the bitter end. He twisted his feet this way and that, trying to prevent her from securing his legs. He pulled his neck as far from the pain of Malcolm's knife as possible.

Destiny had just gotten a cuff around his left ankle when a dark shape charged into the room, leapt onto the bed and smashed into Destiny. Growling, barking and screaming came from the floor by the window as Destiny struggled with the dog. Malcolm suddenly convulsed, and the knife jerked away from Bertrand's neck and stabbed into the pillow. Malcolm fell to the floor in a seizure while a figure stood over him, shoving a weapon against him. Another electronic snap sounded, reminding Bertrand of Joyce's Taser. Joyce!

Destiny screamed repeatedly as she shook off the dog and lunged for the knife in the pillow. "Call off your dog! Or I'll slice open his throat."

She reached for the knife.

"No, no, NO!" Jeff's shout was a warning but Destiny didn't heed it. She stood as the dog lunged.

"I'll kill him!" she screamed, raising the knife above Bertrand's chest.

A gunshot exploded, deafening Bertrand. The muzzle flash highlighted all for a split second as if a bolt of lightning had struck the house, a freeze-frame of naked Destiny clutching her stomach before darkness returned, made worse by dazzled eyes. Bertrand heard Destiny stumble back against the wall, and the dog barked in confusion, turning away from her even as she slipped to the floor.

"Shit!" shouted Joyce. "Where'd he go?"

A flashlight clicked on, illuminating Joyce beside the bed, looking at the empty floor where Malcolm had fallen, her Taser poised to shock.

"He must be under the bed!" shouted Jeff. "Back up!" The flashlight he held blinded Bertrand for a moment. "Shit, he's bleeding."

Joyce rushed onto the bed and pressed her hand against Bertrand's neck. "Grab St. Mike. I don't want him licking her blood."

121

But the dog held back from Destiny, a low growl coming from its throat.

The flashlight moved over near the dog, proving Jeff had complied.

Silence after the chaos, except for a slurping and sucking sound.

Jeff's flashlight illuminated Destiny's naked body, clasped in Malcolm's arms, the bloody knife in his hands and his lips locked to her neck—drinking her blood.

"Stop that!" shouted Jeff, aiming a handgun.

Malcolm looked up, blood coating his face and chest, his eyes bright in the light of the flashlight, his expression euphoric—totally high. "You shot her. I'm just making sure she doesn't go to waste."

He returned to his feeding, leaving Bertrand and Jeff and Joyce looking at one another in helpless horror. Finally Joyce leaned over the edge of the bed and zapped him with the Taser, again making him convulse and fall off Destiny's body.

"He said stop that, you perverted scum."

———

Joyce kept pressure on Bertrand's wound while Jeff prompted Malcolm, with the aid of a huge revolver, to unlock the handcuffs. Jeff restrained Malcolm on the bed while Joyce helped Bertrand down to the kitchen.

"Can you hold your neck?" Joyce asked after they had reached the kitchen.

Bertrand pressed his hand to the cut, and that touch informed him that—despite the pain—it wasn't deep. His heart rate slowed. "It's okay, I think. There are candles and matches on top of the fridge. The first-aid kit is in the top right cupboard."

Joyce turned on the kitchen tap and let it run while she lit a fat candle and set it in the middle of the table. In short order she'd bandaged Bertrand's cut, got them beers from the fridge and put out a bowl of water for St. Mike. Jeff came to join them, taking a seat opposite them in the booth.

"She's way dead." He twisted open his beer. "And it wasn't my shot that killed her. I hit her low down and to the left, about here."

Jeff pressed into his torso on the left just above his belt. "I mean, if untreated that would've killed her 'cause I'm sure she lost some muscle and intestine, but Malcolm opened her neck right at the jugular and she bled out in less than a minute." He took a long drink.

Bertrand wrapped both hands around his bottle and squeezed to hide the trembling. That had been so close. He had given himself up for dead and was having trouble controlling the thrill of being alive. The beer tasted so good. "How did you guys know they were coming after me?"

"Loose lips," said Jeff. "Malcolm had just come in when Destiny called his line. I took the call, because I didn't know he was just climbing the stairs after a power failure, but something about her voice made me suspicious. She sounded guilty—excited, I don't know. Just not her. I hung around and listened to Malcolm's end of the conversation, and it wasn't hard to tell he had murder in mind, and I sure as hell wasn't going to call the cops after today."

He paused for a sip of his beer. "But Malcolm messed up. He wrote down an address on a company pad, and after he left I did that rub-a-pencil-over-the-next-sheet-of-paper thing." He mimicked turning a pencil close to horizontal and rubbing it over paper. "It didn't work as well as I had hoped, but I saw your street name."

"He texted me just before the power failed," said Joyce. "I just couldn't get here any faster because I was out buying groceries, what I could find anyway. I hurried this way as soon as I got the message."

"I saw her running up the street with St. Mike on my way here," said Jeff. "So I picked her up and I drove as fast as I could. Your buddies had left the front door wide open in their rush to kill you."

"Why was that crazy bitch naked?" Joyce's tone was an accusation.

"Honey trap." Bertrand's ears burned with the memory of the sex he had hoped to have with Destiny in the bunker. His thoughts didn't make him guilty, did they? It wasn't like he and Joyce had made any kind of connection, and their only date had been to Goth Knights.

"And you fell for it?" Joyce's tone was angry now.

"I did not! You see me with any clothes off? Fuck, I still had my backpack on. No." He took a sip of his beer, the embarrassment replaced with defensive anger. "She came around with this sob story about Malcolm being a sex perv and said she wanted to spend the night with me 'cause she was afraid. I said fine, but not here because the cops are looking for me over the hacking."

"Yeah," Jeff said. "What about that?"

"Let him finish."

Bertrand nodded to Joyce and carried on. "She said she had to get some stuff and promised to get back before dark, but it was full night, way after sunset. At the time, I just thought she was clueless, but I guess she was stalling for Malcolm."

"She was naked," prompted Joyce.

"When she got here she just ran up to use the bathroom—another delay tactic—and then she capped that off with the ultimate delay. I go up to find out what's taking so goddamn long and there she is, stretched out on my parents' bed."

"Creepy," said Jeff.

"Totally killed the mood for me. Not that I was in the mood." Bertrand glanced over to see how Joyce was taking the tale. "I wanted to get out pronto and told her to get dressed or I'd leave her here. That's when Malcolm hit me. He said they were sent by the boss to kill me, that I was fodder."

"We should get out of here." Joyce started to push against Bertrand to get him to slide out of the booth, but Jeff held up his beer.

"Wait, wait, kids. If this is the same boss as Goth Knights, we've got a bit of time. He's assuming that Malcolm's chowing down right now. Besides, we've got us a prisoner upstairs, and I think it's time to ask him a few choice questions. But Bert, your hack. What got them all stirred up like that bee hive my cousin once poked with a stick?"

Bertrand told them about the crime stats.

"Holy crap," said Jeff. "Well maybe that explains why the grocery stores are running out of food—no one left to stock the shelves or drive the trucks."

"Or buy the food. No wonder I haven't been fighting lineups." Joyce shoved against Bertrand with more determination this time. "We've got to talk to this guy. I need to know what these creeps are, whether they're really vampires."

Bertrand held up one finger to beg her patience. "Wait, wait. Here's what I know. They drink blood all right, but they're not like movie vampires. They aren't afraid of crosses and religion and stuff. They don't turn into bats and shit, and you sure as hell don't need a wooden stake to kill them."

He told them about the teens at St. Mike's.

"Dude, you're right in the thick of all this, aren't you?" Jeff stood now.

"We all are." Bertrand stood and Joyce grabbed the candle and led the way upstairs. St. Mike stood to go with them, his nails clacking on the kitchen tile floor, but Joyce put the lead on him and looped it on the rail at the bottom of the stairs. The dog whined once, then sat in resignation.

"Well, well." Malcolm still looked buzzed. "The murderers return to the scene of the crime."

"You killed her." Jeff stood at the end of the bed, arms crossed in judgment. "Not me. I could've taken her to a hospital and they could've saved her, even with a gut shot like that. You cut her throat."

"You wouldn't want to take her to a hospital at night." Malcolm twisted briefly against the handcuffs. "They'd take her in all right, but later they'd tell you she'd died on the operating table. We own the hospitals too."

"Who the hell is we?" Bertrand kept is eyes on Malcolm's face, refusing to let them wander over to Destiny's naked and twisted figure, still crumpled in the corner near the window.

"I don't feel like talking."

"What happens when the sun rises?"

Silence.

"Okay." Bertrand looked first at Joyce and then at Jeff. "We can go now. I know a good place to spend the rest of the—"

"No! Wait! You can't leave me here. I have to be in the basement before dawn, in a room with no windows or the windows painted black."

"Why?" asked Bertrand. "We'll move you to the basement before dawn if you spill your guts. Why can't you go out in the sunlight?"

"Cause the bugs'll die. There's a wavelength in full spectrum light that kills them."

Bertrand had so many questions he didn't know where to start. While he was still deciding, Joyce took over the inquisition. "What are bugs?" she asked.

"You guys really don't know?" Malcolm looked to each of them in turn. "Wow, you all seemed so with it that I thought you'd already found out."

"The bugs, buddy," said Joyce. "What are they?"

"They're what make us brids—you know—hybrids. Symbiots. Fuck, you guys don't know anything. That's what this is all about. I got them from that Goth chick I told you about. Do you remember I talked about her, how she tied me down to a bed, pretty much like you've got me now only with no clothes."

"Spare us your sex life," said Joyce. "What about the bugs."

"Oh, biology was never my strongest subject, but they're single-cell sized organisms and they're just so great. They heal whatever ails you, can even stitch together cuts and stuff."

Bertrand struggled to understand. "So they're like an infection?"

"Yes and no. I mean an infection kills you doesn't it? Or makes you sick like with the flu or something? But these things make you better."

"How did you get these bugs?" asked Joyce.

"Like I said, the Goth chick gave them to me. She cut her own wrist—not deep you understand—and put it to my mouth. I drank it because I just thought it was some totally weird Goth foreplay. I was naked after all. But then she gets up and says, 'have a nice ride' and leaves. Can you believe that? She left me alone and tied up, and that's definitely against the rules. She even ignored my safe word."

"How totally tragic." Jeff's sarcasm was lost on Malcolm, who still rambled like a man on coke, unable to stop his tongue and totally engrossed in himself.

"Yes, I thought it was until the change hit me. The bugs take over your stomach first, and to keep you from panicking or doing anything crazy, they secrete some drug that is just so much better than anything I've ever taken. It's just totally, sparklingly *yum!*"

"So she didn't drink your blood?" asked Joyce.

"No, no, no. They need the Night Brigade and she had a quota to keep. Everyone is supposed to evolve at least one person a night. I was hers for that night. I mean it took a full day for the change to finish, and I got really sick for a while because I was hungry and I tried to eat, but the bugs throw it back up. They want hemoglobin or whatever it is in the blood. You have to drink blood, and they pass on the nourishment to you, and best of all, they reward you with another hit of that drug. Oh my God, it's good."

It bothered Bertrand that Malcolm dared to name God. "But you're killing people when you drink their blood."

"I do feel badly about that, but if I'm not doing it, then someone else will. I mean, there are thousands of us brids in Chicago. It's not my fault if I'm evolved and regular people aren't."

"You're not evolved." said Bertrand. "You're frigging parasites. You're totally dependant on us. You aren't better. You're sick."

"I'm just peachy right now. But don't worry, we won't always have to kill to feed. We just have to get you guys organized and start you donating blood. I mean, we've had the technology to preserve blood in a drinkable form for years, but the boss didn't know about it until recently. Now that he knows it, we can change the order of things. I can tell you guys don't want to evolve, and you won't have to. You'll just have to get used to donating blood every month. It'll be like being drafted."

"My grandparents marched against the draft even though they were too old for it." Bertrand resisted the urge to strike Malcolm. It was cowardly to hit a helpless man.

Joyce—perhaps sensing Bertrand's rage, stepped closer to Malcolm. "Who is this boss?"

"He calls himself Vlad the Scourge but everyone knows he's Vlad the Impaler—not like the phony Count Dracula and all, but the real Prince Vlad who fought—like—the Turks or somebody way back in the dark ages."

"Bullshit," said Jeff, but his doubt showed in his frown.

"No really—like, I hear you guys met him so you know. Isn't he just totally *old*, and I don't mean like gray-haired old. I mean he doesn't talk like us or act like us and he's just so freaking ancient somehow. The bugs keep you alive if you have them long enough. They can repair your organs, pretty major cuts and eventually they even replace all the cells in your heart. It's like they all link together and become your heart, and they reproduce really fast. Vlad's probably all bugs by now, except maybe his skin and tongue and eyes, anything that sees a lot of light."

"If the bugs die in sunlight," Bertrand said, "then why don't you just go out in the day and purge yourself of them right away."

"Cause I don't feel like dying of a massive stroke." Malcolm looked from Joyce to Bertrand. "Don't you guys get it? There're millions of them in your blood, your organs, everywhere in your body. If they die, they come loose and totally clog up your veins and arteries. No more blood to the brain and massive stroke. Oh, and if you've had them a long time they've replaced the cells in—like—every organ of your body. Your heart, liver, stomach, they'd all just fall apart if the cells died. I mean, literally just crumble right inside you. Instant death."

Jeff broke the silence that followed Malcolm's tale. "I'd walk outside at first light or I'd eat my Ruger."

"Some people do that." Malcolm was totally unaware of the horror he had generated. "They can't handle having to drink and all. Vlad says it's because they weren't well chosen, that we have to find people who have a will to survive even if it means killing other people."

"Serial killers." Bertrand took deep breaths to calm. Sensei Fish would chide him for allowing emotions to cloud his judgment and impair his fighting edge.

"Yes." Malcolm was still oblivious to their judgment. "I guess serial killers would make good brids. I mean they're totally free when it comes to other people's pain."

"God you're evil," said Jeff. "We should just leave him here guys, let the sun purge the bugs right out of him."

"Hey wait, no! You guys promised me. That's why I'm talking, and you know there's still a lot more I could tell."

"Then tell," Joyce said. "Tell us everything."

"Not tonight. I don't trust him." Malcolm nodded in the direction of Jeff. "You put me in a basement and keep me safe through the day, and I'll tell you more tomorrow night."

"No way." Jeff sliced the air with one hand for emphasis. "You tell us everything now or—"

"Answer one more thing tonight and I'll put you in my basement," said Bertrand. "There're no windows in the furnace room."

"Depends on the question."

"Hey, you don't have a choice unless you want to greet the sunrise from the middle of my street. Why do some people, cops, Destiny—people like that—why do they help you?"

"Vlad set it all up. They're people who were given the choice: evolve now or evolve later and live in luxury. Vlad says they're special, because they're willing to wait and work for their reward. He has whole squads of people who are trained to find and turn recruits for the Daylight Brigade. They hold everything together for us during the day, but they're a hard personality type to find. There's never enough of them. The boss'll be totally pissed that you guys killed Destiny."

"You killed her." Jeff raised his revolver and pointed it at Malcolm. "I shot her, yes, but she'd still be alive if you hadn't put a knife to her throat and bled her out. How would your boss feel about that? I'm sure we could get word to him via the Internet."

"Please no!" Malcolm shouted. "He'd impale me for that. No, I'm not kidding. He'd put me on a spike and let me die a slow death. We watched it at Soldier Field one night, all of us summoned to see what happens to traitors and people who break his laws."

Ten seconds of absolute silence followed until finally Joyce broke it with a low whistle. "Wow," she said. "You guys can fill a football stadium and no one hears about it?"

"You've no idea how powerful we've become. We're all over the world. Vlad says he's going to be a scourge on humanity for environmental crimes and corporate crimes and—oh I don't what else. But I heard him say that you humans are sinners and you need to be culled, and we're going to do it and you are all going to be our servants."

"You're slaves," said Bertrand.

"I mean the end of this era and the start of a new world order—one where you humans aren't at the top of the food chain."

# 16

# GATHERING DISCIPLES

Bertrand kept his word over Jeff's objections, releasing Malcolm from the four-poster bed and ushering him down to the furnace room. They handcuffed him to the gas line.

"You'll come back tonight for me, won't you?" Malcolm's buzz appeared to have worn off. "I'll need to eat eventually, or the bugs, they release some other drug, one that makes you very, very hungry."

Jeff slammed the door to the little room. "Bastard. If he thinks I'll let him—"

A flash of red light swept through the living room. Joyce—already at the top of the basement stairs—hurried to the front room, and Bertrand and Jeff hurried up the stairs to follow. They found Joyce standing to one side of the window, careful to ensure that her profile couldn't be caught by a flashlight.

"Cops." She put a finger to her lips. "Just one car," she whispered. "And they don't look like they're in a hurry. Just sitting inside." She ran to the hallway and freed up St. Mike's leash.

"Crap, this way, quick!" Bertrand led them through his kitchen and out the backdoor. He looked left and right, but the tiny backyard was empty. They hurried across and into his garage, but his Volkswagen GTI gave a double squeak as he pressed the key.

"Sh-h-h-h!" hissed Joyce.

"Get in." Bertrand didn't waste time blaming technology. Why was she always angry with him? He hurried to the end of the garage and reached up to pull the handle that would disengage the electric garage door opener. It was quieter this way, even if the power had been on. Bertrand had cursed sometimes in winter that his detached garage exited into an alley that was rarely plowed clear of snow, but today it meant they could leave without the police seeing them pull away. He slid up the garage door and hurried into the car. They were gone in moments.

"Where to?" asked Joyce from the backseat, the big dog panting beside her.

"I know a place, but I want to make sure we aren't followed first." He turned from the alley onto Armitage and headed away from his street, under the 'L' tracks and over toward DePaul University campus.

"Does anyone smell smoke?" Jeff rolled down his window and sniffed. The acrid scent of burning wood and plastic filled the car. "There's a house on fire somewhere."

"There!" Joyce pointed between them.

Ahead and on their right, flames licked out of the upper-floor windows, and smoke leaked from under the eaves and out through the roof vents.

"No fire trucks, but people." Bertrand slowed the GTI and shut off the headlights, driving only by the daybeam lights. "What are they doing?"

"I'm putting your parking break on a bit to turn off the day beam lights." Jeff pulled up the handle a notch or two making the dim head lights go out. The silver car would be difficult to see now, and Bertrand coasted to a stop a baseball throw short of the house and the cars that were skewed across the street in front.

A crowd of at least thirty people had gathered around the house, some clumped near a side door and others near the front. The Victorian-era dwelling was of solid brick, but the bow windows were smashed, and as Bertrand watched in horror, someone from the crowd lit a Molotov cocktail and threw it into the house, its flames augmenting the fire that had already claimed furniture and carpet.

Bertrand opened his door, but before he could reach back for his Glock, Jeff grabbed his arm and stopped him from leaving the vehicle.

"This isn't the time, Bert. Look."

A figure climbed out a second-floor window onto the porch roof, a man judging by the size and shape. He ran along the roof and jumped to the ground where the fewest people waited. He rose up to run but it was hopeless. The crowd rushed him, and even from the GTI they could hear his screams.

"I'll kill them." The monster had risen in Bertrand's soul, bringing with it the desire to fight, to be safe through battle. He wanted to shoot into the crowd, to drive them away from their victim, to rescue the man or at least ease his end.

Joyce grabbed his shoulders and pinned him into his seat from behind. "Not now, Bert. There will be a time when I'll fight them right beside you, but I won't let you throw you life away for someone who's already dead."

The rage burned even though Bertrand knew she was right.

"Time to go. Just drive," Jeff said.

Bertrand took a deep breath, watching as several dark figures detached and drifted away from the scrum around the man's body. Fire now owned the house, the upper windows the exit for roaring flames that pushed black clouds into the night, obscuring the stars while warm air caused the half-moon to shimmer.

Jeff and Joyce were right, but it didn't satisfy Bertrand to run away. It didn't feed his desire to do something about the nightmare. He put the car in reverse.

"Live to fight another day." Joyce patted his shoulder. "I promise we will fight."

They drove aimlessly for the rest of the night, arriving at three other fires, always lured there by the flames, always arriving too late to help.

Sirens greeted the sunrise, fire trucks emerging from their halls and rolling through the streets to douse the flames of hundreds of house fires, some of which had already burned low, while others had spread to neighboring houses. Only concrete and brick had prevented another Great Chicago Fire.

The power came back on just before dawn, the streetlights powering up only to switch off even before the sun crested the rooftops. Bertrand weaved through cluttered streets on their way to Joyce's condo. Cars had been abandoned during the night without regard for proper parking etiquette. That their doors were left open indicated their owners had departed in a panic.

Joyce and Bertrand made breakfast—greasy eggs and toast but no bacon, because it wasn't available at the grocery stores. Jeff took care of the coffee. St. Mike munched at a bowl of dog food before curling up to sleep on the living-room couch.

"We need to warn people." Bertrand pushed away his empty plate. Should they do dishes? Would they ever come back to Joyce's house?

"We need some sleep." But Jeffery stood and poured more coffee into his mug from the carafe. "If they're sleeping during the day, then we'll have to be up at night too."

"We're gonna have to push hard for a few days." Bertrand added more sugar to his coffee. To hell with his waistline and his diet—he'd be lucky to be alive tomorrow. "Every person we get the word out to today is one more person who can help spread the word tomorrow. They've got to the ISPs, so Twitter and Facebook are going to be heavily edited if not just shut down. We need to get to people we trust as quickly as possible."

"I trust Whitlock." Jeff leaned back against the counter.

"Good. But don't go into work, just in case. It may take a while for them to figure out about Malcolm and Destiny, but I don't want you getting arrested. Get Whitlock to meet you somewhere public, and make sure that he's alone before you talk to him. Do it all by phone if you can."

"What about you?" Joyce said. "Where are you going today?"

"To get guns. I got a buddy who is already aware."

"I'll come with you." Joyce stood, her hands on her hips as if daring Bertrand to say no.

"Great. Anybody got a pen?"

Joyce tossed him a pad and pen from the counter near her landline.

"Thanks, we'll meet you at this address by sunset if we don't talk to you sooner." He scribbled down the address and passed it to Jeff, who frowned at the piece of paper.

"But this is just a little ways away from here. Why not just meet here?"

Joyce glanced at the paper. "Hey, I know that address. Isn't that where that guy was murdered?"

"It's next door. I was buddies with the owner until he bought it. The rippers got him for sure. I thought he was a bit of a conspiracy nut because he believed the government was in on it and all."

"He was right, after all. But why here, then?" Joyce grabbed her coat from the back of her chair, a pink ski jacket that emphasized her hips and slimmed her waist.

"Cause he has a bunker in the basement that's very well hidden, and it's built to survive nuclear war. Better yet, he's got guns. Lots of guns. Best, he's got a for sale sign on his front lawn, put there by ripper-sympathetic cops. They assume the guy's house is empty, so I doubt anybody will bother burning it."

"Okay." Jeff shrugged into his thigh-length coat, a hi-tech, expensive affair designed for rugged outdoors travel, and while not camouflage, it was a dark green. Bertrand looked from one to the other.

"We should get you a new coat," he said to Joyce. "One that's hard to see in the dark." He shrugged into his leather jacket.

Jeff forestalled Joyce's response. "Let's cruise by your place and see if the cops are still there. If not I'll grab my car."

"And if they are?" asked Joyce.

"I'll grab someone else's."

---

The Chicago North Gun Exchange looked as if it had been through a riot. Shards of glass clung to the frames of the windows, but most of the crystal coated the sidewalk in front. Yellow police tape warned the curious to stay away, but no patrol car lurked in front and no uniformed officer waited at the door.

"Sorry, Bert." Joyce actually touched him, squeezing his arm, which gave him a thrill despite the tragedy. "It looks like they got to your buddy.

"They pick off the loners." Bertrand ducked under the police tape and walked through the open front door.

"Bert, we shouldn't be in here. The last thing we need is to be arrested now." But she ducked under the tape all the same and followed him into the shop.

The row of gun racks at the back sat empty, and the display cases were smashed, their guns also gone.

Bertrand turned in a full circle. "Was it rippers or cops? I don't see any blood."

A woman appeared in the doorway, her gray hair shorn short.

"It was cops. They came for his guns." Petite, but seemingly tough and fearless, she stepped into the shop. She wore an apron and green gardening gloves, and in one hand she held a set of clippers. "Who are you and what do you want with Emile?"

"I'm Bertrand Allan. Emile was giving me some gun lessons, and I promised him that when things fell apart I'd come and get him." But he had failed Emile, waited too long, and now the big man who had patiently taught him to shoot was dead.

"Don't look so sad." A wry smile curled one side of her mouth. "Emile's not one to wait around to die. I'm Helen. You folks better come next door so that we can decide what to do. After last night, I doubt even my shop is safe."

"You're from next door," Joyce said. "The flower shop."

"Smart girl. That's right. Follow me, now. This is no time for gawking." She turned and ducked under the police tape, leading them to her shop.

An electronic bell chimed as they entered the store, but that was the only nod to the twenty-first century. The flower display cases—mostly empty but for a few roses—would have fit nicely into a shop from the nineteenth century, the wood frames stained and polished, and the cash register looked too big to be useful, reminding Bertrand of one he'd seen in a small-town museum that had rescued knickknacks of their heritage.

"Emile. We've got company, the good kind."

A curtain behind the counter parted and Emile appeared—a sawed-off double-barreled shotgun in one hand. He actually looked as if he might have shaved in the last three days, but his eyes were bloodshot.

"Bert. Good man. I wondered if they'd got you during the last week. Where've you been?"

"Waiting too long. Things really fell apart last night, didn't they? It's like the rippers aren't worried about flying under the radar anymore. What the hell happened to your shop?"

Emile rested the gun on the counter and practically growled.

"Daylight raid by the cops, but lucky thing I got a buddy from my gun club on the inside who tipped me off to get the hell out, otherwise I think I'd have spent the night in jail for some bullshit paperwork infraction."

"I think that would be a death sentence."

Helen lifted a section of the wooden counter and walked over to Emile's side to open the till. "You bet it would've been. I bet no one is in any prison now. They've either been cut or turned into one of them vampires."

"The rippers." Bertrand wanted to separate the real from the supernatural. No one should think that garlic or crosses or refusing to offer invitations to enter a home would keep them safe. "We have to go, and I was hoping you'd come with us."

Helen slipped off her gloves and had begun to empty the register. "Yup, that's what we were figuring. We were just having a little debate about where to go."

"Come with us," Joyce said. "Bert's got a place we can hide in tonight."

"And after that?" asked Emile.

Helen beat Bertrand to a reply. "After that, my good man, we will see what the day brings." She walked over to a display case and opened it, removing the last four roses. "Couldn't get any more flowers anyway." She retrieved the shears and snipped the flowers short, carefully removing the thorns. "None of my suppliers answer their phones or e-mail anymore." She handed one to each of them. "My last customers." She removed her apron and slipped into a crinkled leather jacket that hung down to her knees, placing the rose through a buttonhole. "I'm really going to miss this place, but we've got work to do."

Her expression was more of one going on a short trip than abandoning her livelihood, her lower lip firm. She took the flower from Bertrand's hand and threaded it through a buttonhole on the pocket of his jacket.

"Lead on." She gave Bertrand's chest a firm pat.

———

Father Alvarez shook his head at Bertrand's invitation. He stood in front of St. Michael's, all the big doors open wide to accept people who hurried into the church with blankets and sleeping bags. Some carried rifles. Joyce and the others had split up to clean out the grocery stores of anything left on the shelves, all promising to meet at Thomas Nolan's house.

"I don't need to go with you," said Father Alvarez. "Christians from all over Chicago have been invited to spend the night. This church is now a true sanctuary, and it's open to anyone who fears for their lives. We even have Muslim, Hindus and Jews who will share our home tonight, just as the synagogues and mosques and temples all over Chicago will harbor local Christians tonight."

"But you're sitting ducks." Bertrand stood by the statue of St. Michael. "The rippers know you're here and they'll come for you."

"Not tonight, I think. Have you watched the news? They still wish to present the illusion of status quo, that everything is normal and the power failures are simply a side effect of adding wind and solar power to the electrical grid, a problem they promise will soon be solved. It is one thing to burn down a home, but another to burn down a prominent land mark." He waved up to the tower of the church.

"Your call. But I think people need to hunker down out of sight. Fortresses can be encircled and besieged. We need to be hidden and to strike out like a guerrilla army—like the Contras."

Pain flashed across Father Alvarez's face, and he heaved a deep sigh.

"This is a terrible type of war that you don't understand. You have no idea the horror that comes with being a guerrilla fighter."

"No, I don't. That's why I need you."

Father Alvarez looked up at the statue, silent for so long that Bertrand wondered if the man was in prayer.

"Tomorrow we will speak more on this," he finally said. "But tonight I must prepare this sanctuary, even if I make it into a fortress to protect my flock. Come by the rectory at noon and we will consider what we can do against this scourge."

———

The scent of frying steaks greeted Bertrand as he slid open the back door of Thomas Nolan's house. The carpet under the dining-room table—the one that had hidden Nolan's blood—was gone, and the wood floor had been scrubbed clean.

Bertrand's salivary glands went into overdrive at the smell of the cooking, and he headed straight for the kitchen with his burden of bags of groceries. Helen was once again in an apron, but this time she had a spatula in one hand rather than pruning shears.

"There you are." She turned back to the stove, where thick steaks sizzled in two iron frying pans, but Bertrand thought he caught a look of relief. "Should be cooking these on the barbecue outside, but I was overruled by that fat tyrant downstairs. He's worried about attracting attention. Set the table would you?" She leaned over from the stove to shout through the open basement door. "He's finally here. Come up for dinner."

Joyce was the first to pound up the stairs, taking them two at a time. "Where the hell have you been? It's almost sunset."

"My car's full of groceries, and I stopped at a McDonald's this afternoon to—"

"You've eaten already?" asked Helen.

"No. It was business. I'm scheduled to speak there tomorrow. The manager's a believer and he wants to help get the word out."

"What makes this house so special again?" Jeff climbed the stairs with less haste than Joyce.

"Did you find the bomb shelter?"

"No," came Emile's voice from the basement. "And we looked in every fucking closet and cubby hole down here."

"It's behind the fridge back in the wet bar. There's a panel that slides back."

Jeff raised his eyebrows. "I missed that." He turned and went back down the stairs.

Bertrand opened a cupboard and found a stack of plates.

"You keep me posted from now on, Bert." Joyce gave him one angry frown before grabbing stack of glasses. "Think of me as a coordinator. We all have to know what's going on."

"Fair enough. I was just trying to keep my cell phone use to a minimum because the battery's nearly toast and I don't have the charger."

"Yours is an iPhone, right? I'll lend you mine. Plug it in before dinner, because who knows if we'll have any power over night."

"Great." But Bertrand sensed something else, something more seriously wrong than him not calling in. "Is everything okay?"

For the first time since he'd met her, Joyce looked vulnerable. "Bert, St. Mike's gone." Her expression was neutral, but Bertrand sensed that it was an effort to hide her sense of loss, of pain.

"What?"

"I went by my condo and there was police tape across the front door. No cops, just crime-scene tape. I snuck in the back way through my neighbor's yard, going through my back door. My home was totally tossed, and my dog is dead. The fuckers shot him, probably because he went for them."

Bertrand wanted to hold her close, but he worried that she would consider it too familiar. "I'm so sorry, Joyce. He was a good dog. He saved my life."

Joyce nodded, her lips pressed to a tight white line as she continued to place glasses around the table with sharp, angry movements.

Jeff and Emile emerged from the basement just as Bertrand and Joyce finished setting the table.

"Smells great." Jeff leaned over the frying pan, but Helen shoved him away.

"You'll get it soon enough. Sit your butt down."

They all sat, Emile handing out cold beers from the fridge while Joyce uncorked a bottle of red wine. "Last of my favorites—South African. I rescued it from my place before I left. Somehow I don't think I'll be able to find it for a while."

Bertrand had a sip, letting the flavor settle on his tongue before swallowing. But it wasn't the wine that caught his attention, it was the clatter of dishes, the passing of bowls of mashed potatoes and vegetables, the sense of family around the table—something he hadn't experienced since his parents had so abruptly vanished from his life.

They ate in the gathering dusk, keeping the curtains open to the backyard for light, but leaving the electricity alone. No need to advertise that the house was occupied. For a time, it was all about filling stomachs, the most essential of needs.

But the peace couldn't last. Bertrand had hardly finished his steak when the doorbell chimed and someone pounded on the front door. For a moment everyone froze, exchanging glances and frowns or quietly putting down knives and forks.

Bertrand eased back his chair and tiptoed through the dark living room and into the front hall, others following. He put his eye to the peephole, hardly daring to breath for fear the caller would sense his presence.

Outside in the twilight, a man in a dark suit and two uniformed police officers stood on the front porch. It took Bertrand a moment to place the plainclothes detective until he remembered the murder next door. It was Detective Sinclair of the Chicago P.D. Maybe they were just canvassing the neighborhood about the neighbor's murder. Maybe they didn't suspect that anyone was home.

The detective raised his fist and again pounded on the door.

"Bertrand Allan! It's Detective Sinclair. Please open up now. There's a warrant out for your arrest for the murder of Stanley J. Needleman and Destiny Kim."

Bertrand reached behind his back and drew his Glock.

# 17

# A FUGITIVE

E mile grabbed Bertrand's gun hand. "I know this guy," he whispered. "And he's not an asshole."

Bertrand met Emile's gaze, but it was too dark to read the man's expression.

Should he run for the backyard? He could get out through the alley unless other officers waited there. He could run for the basement and lock himself in, but he just couldn't leave the others to their fate. Perhaps they could all tiptoe down before the police smashed in the door, but they'd be cornered if the cops proved better at finding the bomb shelter than Emile and Jeff.

Helen suddenly pushed forward.

"What the hell do you want with an old lady!" she shouted. "I've got a shotgun and my daddy taught me how to hunt, so you better have a good reason to be on my property at night."

Jeff tiptoed toward the basement.

"Ma'am, there's no tactical team here. It's just us. We mean you no harm, or Mr. Allan, but we need to talk to him before someone else figures out where he's hiding. He needs our help. We're not here to arrest him."

"Don't draw your guns when I open this door," called Helen. "Or this'll be the gunfight at the O.K. Corral."

Emile produced an obscenely big revolver that had been hiding under his loose sweatshirt. He nodded to Helen and she pulled back the bolt and unlatched the door. She stepped back as the door opened, and Bertrand slipped behind it.

"Thank you." Sinclair and the two uniformed officers crowded into the front hall. "Didn't want to be out there any longer than necessary." He closed the door and locked it. The shorter of the two uniformed cops turned on a small Maglite and aimed it at Emile's face.

Bertrand raised his Glock. "Turn that off," he said. "You want to get us all killed? The rippers will be out soon and we're in hiding here."

"He's right." Sinclair put his hand on the Maglite and pushed it to the floor. "We have to keep it dark, but don't I know you?" he asked of Emile.

"Yeah, you were gonna bust my shop on some bullshit paperwork charge, but then you proved you were a good guy by giving me a couple of days to round up some serial numbers that you guys already had anyway."

"Chicago North Gun Exchange. I remember. I hear they really cleaned you out yesterday."

Jeff turned the corner from the kitchen, his Ruger in hand but not aimed.

Helen put out one hand to warn him back. "Okay kids. Before this becomes a Mexican standoff, I think we need to get out of the dark and into the basement. There's blackout curtains there, so we can put on a light and everybody can lay their cards on the table. But first Mr. Detective Sinclair. Are you working for the rippers or are you on the side of humans."

"The rippers? You mean the vampires? No. We're not working for them. We're on the run from them. Just like you."

———

The power failed just after they got to the basement, but Helen had already placed candles on the wet bar and the seventies-era end tables at either side of the couch. Jeff had brought extra chairs from the dining room and Emile had passed around beers.

"We've met before," said Bertrand to one of the uniformed cops. "I think you're the cop who told me to buy a gun. Gonsalves isn't it?"

Gonsalves smiled and took off his cap, revealing thick curly hair. "Yeah, I remember you because that was when I first started wondering if my partner was bent. You can just call me Simon. And you are—"

"This is the man we're looking for." Sinclair sat in the armchair, his belly sticking out enough that he could rest his beer on it. He was lucky enough to still have a head full of graying hair, but it was thin. "You're Bertrand Allan. For a while you were my number one for the ripper murder next door."

"Me?"

"You were first at the crime scene. Your neighbor had disappeared, and a couple of weeks later I'm canvassing my victim's neighbors and you walk by. Seemed like a lot of coincidences."

"He talked to me," said Gonsalves, "but I told him you didn't fit the type, that you were really worried about your neighbor, that you'd known him since you were a kid."

Emile shifted his big bottom on a skinny dining-room chair. "So what the hell's going on at the Chicago P.D. these days that has them working for the rippers?" He pointed with the bottom of his beer bottle. "And don't you try to deny it."

Sinclair gave a heavy sigh. "I won't, but some of us are good cops and we resisted the scum as long as we could, but over the last month, cops who didn't go with everything have been disappeared. I played along, and when Simon and Julia came to me I advised them to do the same."

The other uniform, an Asian woman who had refused beer but accepted a glass of wine, had taken a seat on the couch next to Joyce. "We joined the Daylight Brigade," Julia said. "I signed a contract stating that I would take any and all orders from my captain regardless of whether I thought they violated people's rights. He told me we needed to step on the constitution a bit in order to save the city from a crime wave of serial killers."

"We all had to sign their damn contract," Sinclair said. "At first I didn't even think it was a big deal, but there are layers and layers. Some cops started only coming in for night shift and others got really cagey. By last month I knew it was bad, and the only cops left that I trust my back to are Gonsalves and Chen here."

Emile twisted open another beer, well on his way to drunk. "So why are you after Bert?"

"I'm not," Sinclair said. "But the rippers ups are. Were you people out at all today? Didn't you see all the house fires that happened last night?"

"We noticed," said Bertrand.

"Right, then I don't have to tell you we crossed some kind of line last night. They don't care if people see what's going on now except on the news—that they're still careful about. We jumped ship in the middle of the night because we didn't feel like being disappeared ourselves. What we heard coming over the radio was good cops calling for help and night cops answering, and then nothing more from the good cops. We drove to one scene where some good officers were trying to stop a mob from burning a house. When we got there we saw night cops arresting the good cops and leaving the crowd to burn and murder. We had to just watch from up the street. Nothing we could do."

Joyce stood, and Bertrand knew her well enough now to know she was angry just by the stiffness of her movements as she walked to the wet bar to pour more wine. "Why couldn't you do anything," she said. "You're cops for fuck's sake." She turned from the bar to accuse Sinclair, sloshing red wine onto the floor. Bertrand jumped up and mopped the spill with a paper towel from a dispenser under the upper cupboards.

"By the time we knew what was going on," said Sinclair, "they owned the department. I don't know why daytime cops are going with them, but I can tell you that every one of them was an asshole or a creep long before this all began. It's like they seek out guys like that to join their side."

Bertrand threw the paper towel in a wastebasket. "So what brought you here looking for me?"

"We've been driving around all day trying to figure out what to do." Sinclair paused for a sip of his beer before he went on. "I've been on the force for twenty-five years, and suddenly, I'm afraid of cops. When we heard them talking about you on the radio, saw the news reports—"

"There are news reports?" Bertrand had never aspired to fame and was even less comfortable with infamy.

"Oh yeah. Something about you really concerns them. Their higher-ups tried to kill you, I hear, but I guess that didn't go so well."

"Rumors of my death are greatly exaggerated."

"Funny. But as the three of us drove around I heard over the radio that you have a hidey-hole somewhere near your home, and they're doing a house-to-house search on your block, checking the basements, but I'd seen you up here, and I figured a smart man would hide in a dead man's house. So we tried next door, but that was a dead end. Dust says nobody's using that crib. From the backyard, Chen smelled cooking from over here, and everybody knows that a for sale sign means dead people, so someone, not the owner, was home. We figured we'd give it a try."

"Crap, I wonder how they knew I had a hide out?" Bertrand said.

"Oh that was easy. Your buddy Malcolm King told them."

"That son-of-a-bitch!" said Jeff. "I knew we should've killed him!"

"You should've," said Gonsalves. "He's all over the news, weeping about how you're in a sex cult that likes to cut people's throats and drink their blood, how he only escaped because some cops stopped by to check on a noise complaint about screaming."

"I will kill him." Bertrand wanted to fight, but there was no enemy to engage. "I'll drag his sorry ass into the sun and watch him fry."

"They're painting you with their brush," said Sinclair. "That's why I'm here. You've got them convinced that you're going to stir up some kind of trouble."

Bertrand reclaimed his chair and his beer and took a gulp. "I am. Starting tomorrow at four p.m. at McDonald's, I intend to make a lot of trouble."

"All right," shouted Emile, only to be shushed by Helen. "What? Oh right, low profile. I just can't help it. I can't wait to fight."

"You'll get a lot of fighting in the next few days, I think." Sinclair didn't look excited about the prospect. In fact he looked very weary. "I suspect that we'll all be in it up to our necks."

# 18

# WORD AT MCDONALD'S

B ertrand opened his eyes, but it was still so dark in the basement that only lumps on the floor indicated the location of his sleeping companions. Helen and Julia Chen, the uniformed cop, had been given the honor of the couches in the bomb shelter, and Emile snored away on the rec-room couch, leaving the rest of them to find space on the carpet, using blankets and comforters from Nolan's linen closet to soften their rest.

What was happening out there? The fridge in the wet bar hummed away, indicating that even though the lights were out, the power was back on. Bertrand rose quietly, retrieved his Glock from the end table and padded up the stairs. He listened carefully at the steel door before he slid back the bolt and crept into the kitchen.

A peek beyond the living-room drapes proved that the first blush of pre-dawn, a faint purple, teased the horizon and played tricks with the eyes. Was it really less black or was it false dawn? How long could the rippers stay out at night?

Bertrand crept up to Nolan's office and booted the dead man's Mac. Nolan had given him the password—tommYgun—so it was no problem to get online. Bertrand first checked his Facebook account, but like last week, none of his friends from university had posted any updates. They had all vanished, either because they couldn't get online or because they were dead. Not for the last time he wished they'd paid attention to Azzim's ravings.

He went to Twitter next, and a different world spoke to him through a shallow code. If you knew anything about the rippers it was easy to decipher.

*Had some tasty that put up a fight, big guy but down all the same.*
*Get ur #share?*
*Two times.*
*#Glutton.*

Another back and forth caught Bertrand's attention.

*Fodder is getting smarter. Waiting for us in basement with firepower.*
*#Bugs saving me.*
*Hit?*
*Leg.*
*By tomorrow full heal if u r new. If old, already fixed.*
*Newbie.*
*By tomorrow.*

So Malcolm hadn't lied: the bugs could fix them. Bertrand googled bugs but only the standard Wikipedia entries came back—nothing unusual. He tried hybrids and got electric cars; he tried vampires and got only Count Dracula references—all the websites related to modern vampires had vanished. Nolan's blog had vanished.

He checked his e-mail and found one from Erics of the 1000 Souls religion. The subject line read, "They came for you." Bertrand opened it.

"I believe you are a very strong soul, and I am confident you are still alive, otherwise I would not have seen your picture in the news. You have yet to take my test to determine your soul, but I have extrapolated based on your actions, and I believe you are the 'Dormant Hero,' a very special soul. This soul is shared by people who lead ordinary lives until presented with extraordinary challenges, when they rise up to fight. It may be that you will be called upon to lead the resistance against the rippers, unless someone else with a portion of this soul has already taken on that burden. Have you begun to gather disciples? Have you begun to speak before crowds? I have an extensive network of followers, people who believe in both in 1000 Souls and the vampires, the rippers as you name them. If I am correct in my deliberations, you are the first person with the Dormant Hero soul to step forward to meet this crisis. You must contact me so that I can aid you."

Bertrand's fingers paused over the keyboard. Could he trust this guy? All he knew about him was that he had a decent website and a new-age religion, yet he had followers, and Bertrand needed followers. He couldn't just Twitter or Facebook or rely on any other social media sites. He needed another avenue to reach large numbers of people.

"Today I speak at McDonald's at four p.m." He added the address. "Only tell followers that you trust—true believers."

Bertrand again deliberated for a time before he sent the e-mail.

He'd either just made a big mistake or cunning move, but he wouldn't have to wait long to find out. In eleven hours he would know the truth about Erics of the 1000 Souls.

⸻

The large yellow generator behind the restaurant—one big enough to be built into a trailer—roared at full throttle, a white noise the drowned out the chatter of the crowds that pushed toward the front entrance of McDonald's.

"Wow." Jeff patted Bertrand's shoulder. "You the only speaker here today?"

"As far as I know. Dude, there must be hundreds."

The restaurant was packed, but still people pressed close, gathering in large groups around the front and side doors, even around the drive-through window. The rear door of the restaurant opened and Alison—the same young cashier Bertrand had helped—now waved them inside. "Quick," she said. "Mr. Morley is worried they'll riot if you don't speak soon. My dad's speaking now, but most of them say they came to hear you. I don't know how they all heard."

Morley hurried back when he saw them but gave Gonsalves and Chen in their uniforms a suspicious stare. "I thought you said no cops. Who invited them?"

"I did," said Bertrand. "I trust them. Not all the police have been turned by the rippers."

Morley gave a curt nod, but frowned at the uniformed officers nonetheless. "You better come up to the front," he said to Bertrand. "Who is this Erics friend of yours? I thought there'd be about thirty people here—people I trust. I can't guarantee your safety with all these people. One creep with a gun and you're a dead man."

"We don't live in a safe world anymore."

Morley snorted. "We never did."

Yelling came from the front of the kitchen. "You got to gather into fortresses to protect yourselves," shouted a man who stood on the counter facing the crowd. He was thick and balding, but he had the big shoulders and arms of a man who'd grown through his prime years doing heavy labor. "You need weapons to combat the vampires."

Bertrand had planned to let the man speak for longer, but he couldn't let that go. "They're not vampires!" he shouted.

The man on the countertop turned, revealing a wide face and sharp blue eyes. "You're Bertrand Allan? I'm Alison's dad, Barry St. John. Come on up. I'm just the warm-up." He held out one hand.

The moment of truth. Only once in his life had Bertrand ever spoken before a large crowd, and that was to give a speech to convince people to vote for him for student council president—a hopeless task, since he wasn't one of the cool kids. Why he had tilted at that windmill he had never been able to say, except perhaps that a girl whose attentions he had craved had told him it was a great idea.

That day he had trembled before the crowd, and he hadn't believed his own speech that claimed he could do more for the school than his oh-so-popular opponent.

But today he believed what he had to tell people. He knew he could offer them more than meaningless slogans with no real promises or solutions. Was Erics right after all? Had he really changed in the last few months because others were dying—others with a portion of the same soul? Had his soul gotten denser?

Bertrand accepted Barry's helping hand and climbed onto the counter, expecting the man to continue speaking for a time, but he jumped down on the kitchen side of the restaurant, leaving Bertrand alone.

"Are you the Dormant Hero?" shouted someone. Others called out similar questions, forcing Bertrand to hold out his hands to quiet the crowd.

What should he say? For a moment, the panic of stage fright started to well up, but Emile's gruff voice intruded. "Just tell them the truth, Bert. They're ready to hear it." He stood beside Alison's dad, looking up at Bertrand, ready to support him.

"I'm Bertrand Allan, and I'm here to tell you that we all need to be heroes now." He took a breath and waited to hear shouts of derision or disbelief, but the crowd waited in desperate silence. His confidence began to build.

"We are on the cusp of the greatest tragedy of humanity, but don't be fooled by talk of vampires. These rippers do drink blood, yeah, but they're not like the vampires of horror movies. They don't fear crucifixes or religious objects. Holy water won't hurt them. They don't need an invitation to enter your home and garlic doesn't faze them a bit."

"But they do drink blood?" shouted someone, a question more than a statement.

"Yes. Like the Chicago Rippers, they will cut your throat with a knife and they will drink your blood, but they have a disease, a plague that they spread by intentionally infecting people. They force some to drink their blood, and that spreads the parasites into the body."

"Why would they do that?"

"Because they're building an army and they intend to take over the world. They want to reengineer society so that people are slaves, forced to donate blood to an elite of rippers. They will allow only those to live who are cattle for them, to provide them with food, the rest they will sacrifice on the alter of their gluttony." He paused to give the crowd a moment to absorb, the he spoke with careful enunciation. "They are evil. We must kill them all."

The crowd cheered their agreement, but as they settled one voice called in disbelief. "This has got to be bullshit." But the crowd grumbled and turned to accuse the shouter rather than to challenge Bertrand.

"If you think I'm full of it then take a walk tonight after sunset," shouted Bertrand. "Unless you're in league with them, part of their Daylight Brigade, you'll be bleeding to death in a few minutes. I've spoken with a ripper face-to-face, and but for these two people," he said, pointing to Jeff and Joyce, who stood at the far end of the counter but on the kitchen side, "I would be a dead man. A woman I trusted came for me in daylight, holding me up until after dark when her ripper friend could come around."

"I thought you said they weren't vampires."

Bertrand fought to be patient, reminding himself that everything he said would have sounded ridiculous even a few months ago. "They're not like vampires because the rippers are very real and superstitions won't protect you. They only have two things in common with vampires: they need our blood for food and the sun will kill them. You all know in your hearts what's going on out there or you wouldn't be here, and now is the time of your greatest peril, because the rippers still control the media and the government, the police and maybe even the military. The news will tell you they are working through a crisis, but they'll always be vague about what exactly that crisis is all about."

Alison's dad, Barry St. John, pounded the countertop to get Bertrand's attention. "But what do we do?"

"We need to go on the offensive." Bertrand looked up from Barry and back to the crowd. "Right now. We have a great advantage here: daylight. Mr. St. John here was right when he said that you need to arm yourselves and fortify your homes, but we can't just sit and wait for them to come for us at night. At the rate they're recruiting and murdering, they'll outnumber humans by Thanksgiving. We need to start thinning their numbers. Right now! If you have a neighbor or a coworker who never comes out during the day, then you need to go into their houses and search their basements and drag them out into the light. Today! Right now!"

"Commit murder!" shouted that same dissenter.

The crowd roiled, an angry mutter, but it was again directed at the dissenter, not Bertrand.

Bertrand held up his arms to quiet them before he continued. "Anyone who is human can volunteer to come out into the sun and bask in its glory. Anyone who is a ripper is a serial killer who must drink blood to survive. I'm not advocating murder. I'm simply saying that the sun can prove right now who is innocent and who is guilty of multiple murders. Right now!"

"All right!" shouted Emile, startling Bertrand.

But the crowd loved it, joining him to shout and cheer. If the dissenter had any further comments, he was too afraid to shout them or simply couldn't be heard over the crowd. Someone began chanting, "Right now! Right now! Right now!"

The crowd took up the call, and Bertrand let it roll for a full minute, his heart soaring, until he decided it had nearly run its course. He held out his hands to again order silence. "We are at a dangerous moment in history, one that could tip either way, so we gotta act quickly and smartly. You need to organize into militias—defense committees—that can travel together doing basement-to-basement searches. We haven't the strength yet to clean out the police stations or the state house or city hall, so we have to do onto them as they've been doing onto us: we start by going after their loners. When we've made our streets safe, we go after their bosses. This is our time to act! Right now!"

Cheers followed by the chant of "Right now!" shook the restaurant, but even over this noise, the sirens penetrated the crowd's awareness. It fell silent as several police cruisers approached, screaming to a halt with flashing lights. Police officers leapt from their cars and ran toward McDonald's, several with guns drawn. Two managed to clear a path into the restaurant.

"Bertrand Allan," shouted one. "You are under arrest for the murder of Destiny Kim and Stanley Needleman."

The room fell into a hush. Just the moment Bertrand needed. He repressed the urge to run, because he wanted to fight, and these were his enemies. "How many people here think I murdered our fellow humans?"

"Shut up and put your hands on your head." The two officers had managed to push halfway up the restaurant, but the crowd became increasingly incompliant, forcing the police to push and shove to get farther.

Sinclair climbed awkwardly up onto the counter and held up his badge. "This man," he said, pointing to Bertrand, "did not commit murder. But if these traitors to the Chicago P.D. take him into custody they will cut his throat today. He'll be their victim."

"Are you going to let them take him?" shouted Barry St. John.

"No!" shouted many, followed by someone calling, "Right now!"

The crowd took up the chant, and a hostile circle surrounded the two officers.

"Don't kill them!" shouted Bertrand. "Maybe they don't know what's going on!"

But the chant grew in volume, forcing the police to back up, guns now aimed at the people nearest them to hold them back. Outside, the chant had been picked up by those who'd been listening at the front and side doors and the drive-through window. A police car began to rock, and shouted orders were ignored. A gunshot snapped and someone screamed.

The crowd exploded, swirling around the police cars and besieging the cops. More gunfire made the crowd surge away in panic, but suddenly a flaming bottle hit a cruiser, splashing burning liquid across the hood. There were more gunshots, and one of the cops fell, pulled back to a good cruiser by his fellows. A third cruiser tipped up, lifted by dozens of hands, as much as a shield as an act of defiance. The cruiser teetered on its side for several seconds before rolling onto its roof, smashing the flashing lights.

"Right now!" shouted several people, and more gunfire cracked.

"Holy crap," shouted Bertrand, jumping from the counter and running toward the front door. They mustn't engage the police. That was a futile effort.

But Joyce outran him and turned in to put her back to the door and a hand out to order a stop. "No way, Bert. This is way out of your hands now. We have to get out of here."

The police succeeded in piling into a cruiser, two of them sitting in the trunk and firing indiscriminately back at the crowd even as their car sped away. A window beside Joyce shattered, and they all dropped to the ground.

Bertrand knew fear like he had never known before, but not for himself. He scrambled forward through the shards that now littered the floor.

"Joyce! Joyce!" *Don't let her be dead!* His whole being screamed it—prayed it. *Please don't let her be dead.*

Joyce looked up, her cheek bloody. "We have to get you out of here," she said. "Now!"

Bertrand didn't argue.

# 19

# SANCTUARY OF ST. MICHAEL'S

They ran for the back of the restaurant, Morley waving them in but stopping Gonsalves and Chen at the back door. "You can't go out dressed like cops. That crowd will tear you apart after what your buddies did."

"They're not my buddies," shouted Gonsalves, looking like he wanted to draw his own gun.

But Morley stood tall and firm. "Doesn't matter. You need to get out of those uniforms now and into one of mine. Follow me, quick." He led the two into his office while Bertrand and the others considered their options.

"My place is up north," said Barry, his bald head shiny from the sweat generated by heat of what, until moments ago, had been an overcrowded restaurant.

"We need to go somewhere closer," said Joyce. "This is a bullshit charge but there's no way Bertrand will get a chance to defend himself if he gets picked up. We need a sanctuary where we can't be cornered. I don't trust the house we were in last night because it's too easy to connect to you."

Bertrand hit on the word sanctuary. "St. Mike's. It's close by and the pastor there is a friend and a believer. There's also lots of people sheltering there overnight these days, people who don't have to be told what's going on, and some of them have guns."

Screams and shouts from the front of the restaurant and the street proved that the riot had taken on a new and desperate phase, and more sirens announced that reinforcements were speeding their way.

"We have to move." Joyce looked enviously at Jeff's Ruger. "And I have to get a gun, dammit. Why didn't I grab one from that house when I had the chance."

"Love that Super Redhawk," said Emile, referring to Jeff's Ruger. "A little big, though. Here's something you can handle until I get you a few gun lessons," he added to Joyce.

He pulled a .45 Colt from under his sweatshirt. "You didn't know you were coming to a gunfight?" He handed it to Joyce with his left hand. In his right he already held a .357 Magnum, one of the guns he'd been able to save before his shop had been raided. "She's right though, Bert. We have to move before this place is surrounded and the crowd's dispersed with full-autos. Don't think they won't use them. They don't have to worry about TV news or courts."

Bertrand nodded. "We'll wait for the others to change, and we'll all go together."

Emile looked like he was about to argue, but Gonsalves' and Chen's arrival in McDonald's uniforms made him laugh instead. "Don't we all look so ready for business. I'll have a Big Mac, large fries—"

Gonsalves looked like he was preparing an acid response, but Sinclair beat him to it. "Forget it. We're all going to St. Mike's to regroup," he said to the late arrivals. "We'll leave the cars because they'll have cordoned off the neighborhood. So it's into the back alleys. Everybody ready?"

Bertrand nodded and Sinclair kicked open the back door. They ran through chaos.

---

Father Alvarez didn't look surprised to see Bertrand.

"I'm glad you've returned." He warmly shook Bertrand's hand. "Some of my parishioners heard you speak at McDonald's and have told me of the police firing on the crowd. Come." He led them through the paneled corridors of the rectory and into a meeting room, one with a heavy table and comfortable chairs around it. "Please," he waved to the chairs. "Martha will bring us some tea, and please, you can put your weapons away. My people will give us plenty of warning if we need it." A large wooden crucifix dominated one of the paneled walls, and a portrait of the pope faced it from the opposite side of the room.

Bertrand's cheeks burned as he stowed his Glock in the holster in the small of his back. He had brought a drawn gun into a church—mind you, Father Alvarez had killed three teenagers right in front of the altar.

They all sat and introductions were made for the benefit for Father Alvarez and Barry St. John. He was the only one Bertrand didn't know, but then he hardly knew Emile or Helen or the cops.

Barry took a seat by his daughter Alison, right across from Bertrand. "I don't see how we can stay in the city anymore. It's too late tonight to risk it, but I think we should make a run for the country first thing in the morning. It's harder for rippers to gather in numbers out there."

"I'm not leaving everyone in Chicago to die." Bertrand looked around to see if anyone else agreed. "There's a war going on here and half the population doesn't know about it."

"Word is spreading quickly though." Father Alvarez had taken a seat at the head of the table. "My people continue to spread the word every day, but we have a population problem at this church now. So many come here for sanctuary each night that we are overcrowded. It concerns me that there may come a night when we have to turn people away. Where will they go?"

"Canada." Barry leaned forward, his hands clasped together. "I'm building a fortress up there, far from the cities where this plague is the worst, and I'm moving my family up there soon, but we're going to need numbers to protect the place. It's got farm fields around it, solar panels and windmills and even a hydro-generator."

"No." Bertrand stood, too restless to stay in one place, and began to pace as he spoke. "Fortresses are targets and by moving there you're giving up on all the humans everywhere else. What we need is to do exactly what you've done." He pointed to Father Alvarez. "We need to organize people into defensive positions at night, yes, but during the day we have to go on the offensive." Bertrand stopped at the far end of the table and turned to face everyone. "Don't you see? We have the advantage because we fight both day and night. They desperately need their Daylight Brigade to protect them during the day, but if we can get the word out, if more people revolt like they did today at McDonald's, then the Daylight Brigade will be exposed. Once they lose control it'll be easy to get the rippers simply by pulling them out into the sunlight."

"ALL RIGHT!" Emile's shout startled several of the others. "What? I just like that kinda talk. I never thought of it that way, but Bert's right, we can beat them easy."

"It won't be easy," said Joyce. "Basement-to-basement searches are going to be dangerous and time consuming, and first we have to take care of this Daylight Brigade."

"But it's doable." Emile looked around for others for confirmation. "We can beat these guys."

"We can." Bertrand continued his pace down the opposite side of the table, behind all the chairs. "But first we need to save lives. I think their whole plan—and it's clearly been well thought out—has been designed around numbers. Think about it: who did they turn first? Government, media and cops, maybe the army too, who knows? This gives them control of the message, gives them the ability to convince everyone that it's all okay. I drives me crazy that I missed the early warnings, like when you told me to buy a gun last July." He pointed to Gonsalves. "But I just couldn't believe that blood drinking murderers were walking around at night, much less that the government, the media, and cops were covering for them. It's like I had to go through the stages of grief only now it's the stages of belief. First I was in denial, then I was into bargaining—like maybe this would all go away if I ignored it."

"What stage are you at now?" Joyce, looked over her shoulder and up at him as he passed behind her chair.

"I'm angry. People are going to die tonight all over Chicago. Hell, all over the world maybe, and we can't save them. But that's what I mean: numbers. Their boss, who calls himself Vlad the Scourge, is trying to flip things around by making more people rippers than not. Their plan is to take over so irrevocably that we can't use the day to our advantage because there simply aren't enough of us."

"Okay," said Barry. "I get that, but don't you think we need to organize fall-back positions? I tell you, the place I've got is just perfect."

"Please." Father Alvarez waved Bertrand to a chair on his right before turning back to Barry. "Tell us of your fortress."

Barry looked up and down the table. "I'm a contractor and my specialty is student residences."

So that explained the hardened muscles and the weathered skin. This man was used to life outdoors and around heavy equipment. Bert could easily imagine the hardhat over the bald head.

"A year ago I got a contract to build a residence for a little college up in Canada. I guess I must've figured out about the vampires before the rest of you, 'cause I was having trouble getting crew, and I didn't like what the guys I did get were telling me. Most of them would only come up if they could bring their families.

"So I said sure, but then I noticed that no one seemed to give a shit about the job. I couldn't get inspectors to come out and look at the site. I couldn't get college officials at all during the day, and at night they were too busy to attend site meetings. No one cared. That was my big clue that this went way up the ladder."

"But you kept going?" Bertrand tried not to sound accusing, but he wished Barry had done something, had at least shouted the bad news from a street corner. How many people might still be alive if they'd known what was happening?

"I changed the project." Barry looked left and right to see if anyone understood his boldness. "I moved the building a mile west over an abandoned mine. It's a single twenty-story building, but I've sealed in the windows of the bottom two floors, leaving only gun slits. It's like a giant medieval fortress."

"Why the hell build it over a mine?" asked Joyce. "Isn't that dangerous?"

"Oh, no." Barry laughed and shook his head. "This is Canadian Shield granite we're talking about, some of the oldest and stablest rock in the world. But the mine is the great thing: it's got an underground river running through a cavern down there, and I've already got one generator running, and I'm ordering two more as backups. The solar panels look nice and all, but in the middle of a Canadian winter I'm going to need something other than that."

"You've given up on the world," said Bertrand. "You think civilization is going to totally collapse and you've run for the hills."

A silent moment passed through the room as everyone digested the possibility that Barry was right and their world was ending.

"Buddy." Barry spoke gently, like a man explaining to his child that Granddad wouldn't be coming for any more visits. "Society already has collapsed—even faster than I thought. You think I'd have let my daughter keep working at McDonald's if I knew she was in so much danger? When my wife got a hold of me around midnight last night and told me half the city was on fire—" His hands clenched, the knuckles whitening. "I kicked myself for the idiot I was not to get them up there sooner. I drove all night and through the morning to get here, and the only reason we're not on the road right now is that we can't make it up there before dark, and I haven't slept in thirty hours, but I tell you first light tomorrow—after I get whatever supplies I can—we're on our way out. I'm inviting you all to come with me. I could use some believers who've got guns."

Again, Barry had stunned everyone into silence.

Father Alvarez finally broke the moment. "Everyone must decide for themselves what is right. Of course I will be staying with my people, and I invite you all to spend at least tonight among us. Volunteers are at work in the kitchen downstairs right now to prepare an evening meal for after mass. We worship every day now, just before sunset to prepare our souls for the night."

Barry shook his head and put his arm around his daughter. "I'll be with my family tonight."

"You'll be isolated," said Bertrand. Couldn't the man see that they had to all band together now?

"I've got a bunker that I built under my house last summer. It's impregnable and it has secret tunnels that lead to exits away from the house. In fact, they could burn the house down on top of us and we could walk into the sun tomorrow. I'd invite you guys to join me, but I've already got four families coming to join us, including my son's family, who are on the road from Nevada right now."

Bertrand turned to Father Alvarez. "We'll take you up on your offer. We could use a safe harbor for tonight, and I need to make a plan." Bertrand looked to Jeff and Joyce for confirmation, and Jeff nodded.

"We do," Jeff said. "You're the leader of a movement after today."

———

Bertrand tired to doze in the pew, tried to pretend that he was asleep so that he wouldn't disturb the other nighttime residents of the church, but he was too afraid to sleep. He didn't fear for his own life, for he agreed with Alvarez that—for now at least—the church was too important a symbol in Chicago for the rippers to risk its destruction, but he did fear for those he could not save tonight.

How many were being attacked right now? How many quotas were attained as rippers converted humans into more rippers? How many murders would that mean for the future? He turned onto his back and stared up into the darkness, the candlelight of the church failing to illuminate the delicate gold and blue of the ceiling. How many people had knives at their throats right now, just as Malcolm's knife had been at Bertrand's throat?

He couldn't let it go. He had to act. Right now. Wasn't that what the crowd had been chanting? Isn't that what he believed? *Right now.* Bertrand shifted quietly to sitting, noting that Joyce and Jeff slept deeply, Joyce closest to Bertrand and Jeff farther along the pew. Emile, one pew up, wasn't snoring for a change.

Bertrand stood and headed down the aisle, tiptoeing carefully past bundled sleepers on row after row of pews, many of them with sleeping bags and pillows and foam mats to soften their rest. Father Alvarez had run the heating at full blast while the power was on, but it had failed shortly after dark, so now the cool fall night seeped into the church. Bertrand's lined leather jacket had helped keep him warm, but it stopped at his waist, leaving his legs cool—aggravating his insomnia.

Bertrand reached the front door of the church only to find Father Alvarez sitting in a chair, his rifle across his knees and a bible in his hand. It wasn't the same old rifle as before, but a modern M-16 as far as Bertrand could determine. Another man dozed on the opposite side of the door, a shotgun on his lap. A candelabra on a low table beside Alvarez provided sufficient light for reading, and he turned a page in study, but an incautious shuffle from Bertrand caused him to look up.

"I am sorry not to be able to offer you better accommodation." Alvarez closed his bible and sat back in the chair. Bertrand tried to picture this middle-aged man as a young Contra in Nicaragua: smooth the face, dress him in green uniform, make him skinny and imagine him walking through a tropical forest with that rifle over his shoulder. He could just build the picture, but not the intent to kill. This was a man of God.

"You've been really great. You saved my life and all at least once." Bertrand's heart rate increased. He wanted to hurry out the door and into the night. "But I'm called to work."

"What work do you refer to?" Alvarez stood and slung the rifle over his shoulder, putting his back to the door.

"There are people out there who will die tonight, but I might be able to save someone."

"If you go out these doors—if that is what you propose to do—it could very well be your death of which you speak."

"You believe in God, Father, so you gotta believe that I'm part of the plan. I can't stay in here. I need to fight."

"I will not let you go out alone."

A bump and a curse in the dark caused Bertrand to turn. The large bulk of Emile shuffled down the aisle, coming to stand by Bertrand.

"He won't be going out alone, Padre." Emile turned to Bert. "I can't sleep anyway, so if you're going to pick a fight, I'll go with you."

Bertrand actually didn't want Emile to go along, fearful that the big man would slow him down, but it was already crazy to be going outside at night. To refuse an offer of assistance would give Alvarez more of a reason to dissuade him from leaving the church.

"Okay. You're in, but you better keep up."

"Where would you go and what would you do?" Father Alvarez crossed his arms and continued to block the way.

"I'm going to find someone whose house is besieged by rippers, and I'm going to save them." Bertrand stared defiantly at Alvarez.

But Alvarez was not so easily cowed. "How would you save them?"

Emile drew his .357 and held it up, barrel aimed for the ceiling. "With guns."

Alvarez studied them closely, and Bertrand could sense an internal debate.

"If we can save one person tonight, isn't that God's work?" asked Bertrand.

Father Alvarez nodded. "But I will come with you."

"But Father—"

Alvarez gave a short angry shake of his head and held up one finger in instruction.

"I was a Contra, a guerilla soldier. You have no idea what you need to do or how you need to attack. You will let me come with you, or I will not let you go without a very loud argument, one that will bring the rest of your friends here to talk sense into your head."

"All right. But promise me you'll take care and not get yourself blown away."

Father Alvarez smiled. "How could I make such a promise when I have just agreed to go to at your side to war?

# 20

# RIGHT NOW

Father Alvarez could move very quickly for a man in his late forties. He led them to a side door of the church and they slipped out, Alvarez warning the volunteer guard to lock it behind them and not let them in until sunrise, to prove they were not infected. Bertrand chose their destination: Oz Park, named for *The Wizard of Oz*, because author Frank Baum had lived nearby at the turn of the twentieth century. The rectangle of green sat flat in the middle of their dense residential neighborhood, but it had baseball fields and playgrounds. Statues of Dorothy, the Scare Crow, the Cowardly Lion and the Tin Man dotted the park, but Bertrand wanted it for the baseball fields—big open spaces that would allow him a clear sightline to approaching threats, even in the dark.

Far to the south, the office towers of the Loop blazed with light, proving that the power outage was restricted to outer neighborhoods. If it weren't for the light of the moon, Bertrand's sortie would have failed, as he had underestimated just how black night was without streetlights. When a heavy cloud blocked the moon, the three had to halt for fear of running into unseen objects like utility poles or garbage containers, leaving Bertrand with a new understanding of dark.

Emile caught up to them at the edge of the park, gasping for breath even though their jog had been slow. "What are we looking for?"

"Be quiet. We're here to listen."

The three stood in the center of a baseball field, back-to-back and silent.

The murmur of a city in agony floated through the park. At first it seemed like the innocuous hum of traffic, but attention to individual sounds proved otherwise. A car sped out of control and crashed, it's occupant—or perhaps people near it—screaming hysterically. Distant gunfire cracked, followed by panicked shouts. Running feet, maybe several, came from the east side of the park—not joggers, but people running in a life-and-death race.

The same sounds repeated, sometimes nearer and sometimes farther. People were being hunted and murdered. Now they just had to choose whom to save.

"Over there," whispered Emile, pointing to the east. "There's a house just at the edge of the park that's in trouble. Hear it?"

Teenage voices sang and taunted, and a young woman's voice shouted defiance.

The superhero inside Bertrand begged to attack.

"Let's go." He ran in the direction of the shouts, intending to charge straight out of the park, across the street and into the rippers. But before he reached the edge of the lawns, Alvarez caught up with him and grabbed his arm, yanking him to a halt near the statue of the Scarecrow, who looked rather roughed up, as if the monkeys had made a pluck or two at his metal stuffing.

"Two minutes of reconnaissance and preparation can save many lives," said Alvarez, moving to block Bertrand's path.

Emile puffed up, wheezing and out of breath. "He's right, Bert. Going in there shooting may feel good, but let's not just spray and pray."

Alvarez gave a curt nod to Emile and turned back to Bertrand. "First we decide where to rally if it goes badly."

Bertrand took a deep breath to calm his frustration at the delay. "How about by him." He pointed his Glock at the Scarecrow.

"Good," said Alvarez. "The Scarecrow will be our rallying point, our fall-back position in success or failure. Now, we approach slowly, spread out so that all three of us cannot be taken out in a single burst of machine gun fire or from a single grenade. Do you understand this? The different vantage points will also help us locate enemies who may be behind cover. Are you ready?"

"Bummer that I don't have my walkies," Emile said. "Next time."

"We will watch one another for hand signals," said Alvarez. "Now we can go."

They spread out, putting several car lengths between them, with Bertrand on the point as they moved toward the edge of the park. The power failure worked in their favor now, for the teenagers attacking the house were lighting Molotov cocktails, which placed them in the light while leaving Bertrand's little squad in the dark.

The house itself might once have been ordinary, for it was brick painted white, semi-detached and very old, occupying the corner lot of the street that dead-ended at the park, but someone had made some odd adjustments. The ground floor windows had been bricked in—the cinder block used by an amateur in haste oozed mortar, now dried and solid. The front door had an extra door of solid iron bars, roughly installed without regard for appearance. The bars of this door were clearly designed to protect the front door from a battering ram like the kind police might use. The second floor windows were smashed, little more than black openings making the house appear to have two square eyes over a mouth blocked shut.

Three teenage males danced to music in front of the fire, more of a war dance than a mating dance with lots of whoops and aggressive gestures. Two waved Molotov cocktails back of forth, creating flaming torches that couldn't last.

"Watch this you little bitch!" shouted one. He tossed the Molotov at a car parked in the street. The flame splashed across the hood, setting the car's paint on fire but doing little other damage.

Bertrand wanted to charge. The new light was a danger. Could the teens now see him approaching across the grass, or were their eyes sufficiently dazzled? How close did he have to be to shoot accurately, and how could he tell that they really were rippers, besides the fact that they were out after dark? Bertrand became very aware of his heart rate, a heavy pounding. He looked left to Father Alvarez.

The priest's black cassock, his black hair and olive complexion made him almost invisible in the dark, but Bertrand knew where to look, and the man was much closer to him than the teens. Alvarez put his fist in the air and stopped.

What did that mean? Bertrand stopped too and put his right fist in the air to communicate the signal to Emile, in case he couldn't see the priest. Maybe Emile knew what this meant, for he stopped his advance as well. Bertrand looked back to Alvarez, who had begun to moved away on a path that would circle down the street, not bringing him any closer.

"See that you little cock tease!" shouted one of the teens on the sidewalk not far from the burning car. "We can burn you and your bum-boy out of there if you don't come down now. I'm getting tired of all this shit."

A young woman—her blonde hair and pale face turned a shade of orange by the fire—appeared at the second floor window, a crossbow in her hands. A tall young man joined her with another one, and both aimed at the speaker.

"Fuck you Wormason!" she shouted.

The two crossbows fired together, one bolt skipping off the concrete and the other zipping into the teen's leg. Both aggressors vanished from the window, anticipating retribution.

The teen screamed in rage and grabbed at the bolt in his leg.

"You little whore! You think the bugs can't fix this?" He yanked the crossbow bolt from his leg, provoking another scream and curse.

A wave from Alvarez caught Bertrand's attention.

The priest carefully pointed two fingers at his eyes and then at the back of the house. This one Bertrand knew from the movies. What did Alvarez want him to see? Shadows moved near the back of the house, and Bertrand understood. There were people in the back yard.

"That's it you bitch," shouted the teen, jumping around as if he'd stubbed his toe rather than taken a crossbow bolt to his thigh. "I was gonna bring you up, give you the bugs so that you could be one of us. Only Terrance up there was gonna be fodder tonight, but not now." His voice dripped contempt on the name Terrance. "Now I'm gonna do you both. You hear that? I'm gonna burn you out and I'm gonna drink your blood!"

His friends shouted encouragement and turned up the heavy metal music, the pounding drums and screeching voices speaking about Satan without understanding evil. One teen brought their spokesman another bottle with a rag, and he lit it.

*Now.* They had to act now before the house was set ablaze. Bertrand couldn't wait any longer. He pointed ferociously at Alvarez, forcing every bit of rage he had into his command in hopes that the priest would both understand and obey without question. His finger chopped from Alvarez to the shadows at the back of the house. *Those are your targets*, was his unspoken command. Bertrand looked to his right and saw that he already had Emile's attention. He pointed at him and then swept his hand in a circle, followed by a sweeping motion past the burning car, the flames dying as the paint was consumed. *Go around the car and shoot from there.*

Bertrand put his Glock into the air and then punched forward. *Charge!*

He ran at the teens even as the leader stepped onto the postage stamp of a front lawn and prepared to throw the Molotov cocktail high at the gaping window. Bertrand skidded to a halt less than two car lengths away, steadied his aim and fired. The teen dropped and the cocktail broke on the front walk, the flames leaping harmlessly into the air. The other two teens turned at the gunshot, producing handguns and ineffectually aiming them sideways. They both fired several shots at Bertrand, who turned to present the smallest target, amazed at his calm despite the fear, despite the fact that he had nearly pissed himself. He was exhilarated to be fighting, to be doing something. Emile had always warned him against the dumb Hollywood thing of turning your weapon sideways, since there were sights on the gun for a reason: *You might as well spit at them for all you'll hit.*

Perhaps this helped with Bertrand's fear, for instead of ducking he aimed carefully and squeezed the trigger. A second boy dropped, and the third, seeing his friend go down, ran for the shelter of the burning car.

But Emile had already circled to the far side, his movement hidden by the flames and Bertrand's attention galvanizing shooting. Even before Emile could shoot, however, a crossbow bolt hit the teen in the back, dropping him in a sliding sprawl on his face along the sidewalk.

Gunshots from the back suggested that Alvarez was being liberal with his interpretation of the Fifth Commandment. Bertrand was about to run that way to help when two men—not teenagers but middle-aged men, balding and pudgy—rounded the corner, one with a sawed-off shotgun presented and another with a handgun held properly.

Bertrand froze for a moment in his panic. Were they humans or rippers? Should he shoot? The shotgun's muzzle flashed. It no longer mattered which side they were on because they were firing on him. Bertrand pulled the trigger, taking the man with the handgun in the chest and dropping him to the ground. The shotgun bearer didn't have time to pump before Emile's shot blew through the man's skull.

His heart pounded so hard in his chest that Bertrand feared a heart attack, and he took deep breaths as if he had been running the whole way here, even though their last charge had been a very short sprint. Emile appeared on the sidewalk past the end of the burning car, his .357 aimed at the teen with the crossbow bolt in his back. He writhed and reached back, fighting to yank the bolt free.

"Don't shoot him yet!" yelled Bertrand, putting one hand out to warn Emile. "We want a prisoner. Don't move, dude!"

A movement by the lead teenager—the one Bertrand had shot first—snagged Bertrand's peripheral vision. He turned even as the teen, still on the ground by the burning fluid, raised a handgun. A rifle cracked and the teen collapsed and didn't move. Father Alvarez stood at the corner of the house, the rifle still aiming at the lump on the ground. It cracked twice more, bullets tearing through the corpse.

"I'd say he's dead this time," Emile said. "And if you don't want to die in about two seconds, kid, you won't move either or I'll turn you over to Father Death there."

"Please, I can't die." He spread out his hands, staying face down in the dying light of the flames that burned low—both on the car's hood and the front walk—as they consumed their fuel. "If I die I'll go straight to Hell."

Father Alvarez walked up and knelt close by him. "Not if you repent your sins." He made the sign of the cross. "I can still save you before you die."

# 21

# INTERROGATION

The young woman appeared at the window, her crossbow presented and her tall friend aiming over her shoulder in case he was called upon to shoot.

"Whatssup?" she called to Bertrand. "You guys want to come in? I could use the extra guns tonight 'cause the city's really going to rat shit. Lost my base and my partner house last night."

"You can't let us in." Bertrand walked onto the lawn and looked up to the window. "We could just be competition for these guys for all you know. Only in the sunlight can you be sure we're not rippers."

She nodded. "Rippers—like vampires—got it. Fair enough, but you should go to ground till sunrise. I don't want you attracting anymore attention this way." She tossed a key to the grass at Bertrand's feet. "That's for the garage behind my house. I fixed it up as a fall back position, so you'll find it's pretty defensible—bars on the windows, that kinda stuff."

"Thanks." He picked up the key and turned to Emile. "Lets bring that one with us for a chat."

"Hey dude," called the woman. "You better pass some lead through my math teacher's head there and that other creep. I've seen these pricks come back from some really bad wounds, and don't use the fat guy's cannon. Use your Glock."

Emile looked up at her in adoration. "Who the fuck are you?" he asked.

But she and her boyfriend had disappeared.

"She's right, of course," Emile said to Bertrand. "My .357 is loud."

Bertrand nodded. They were already dead. It was not a sin to shoot someone to keep them dead. He went to each corpse in turn—ones that hadn't already died from head wounds—and 'passed some lead' through their skulls.

"Let's go to ground," he said.

Father Alvarez led the way, his rosary dangling from his left hand, which held the barrel of his rifle, leveled and ready to shoot as he headed for the alley behind the house.

The garage proved to be everything she'd promised. It was modern, built of concrete blocks although the roof was a wood-frame construction with asphalt shingles. That could burn. The windows were barred, but the glass was still intact, and Bertrand was glad of that when they got inside, because the pre-dawn chill had settled in, warning of Chicago's approaching bitter winter.

Once inside they found the garage to be even more of a bunker than Bertrand had thought. The garage door looked normal from the outside, but from the inside more of the amateur bricklayer's work was evident. A head-high concrete block wall had been hastily constructed on the inside of the rolling door, again with little regard for neat mortar. If anyone succeeded in prying up or smashing through the garage door, they would simply find the new wall.

"She built this as a trap," Emile said as he looked at the wall. "The rippers would pry up the garage door thinking they were about to find a bunch of hopeless dweebs, and instead they'd find this wall and a couple of people firing crossbows over the top. She's just great! Give these kids some firearms and training, and I'll give you back a couple of captains."

Father Alvarez had more immediate concerns. He went to a bench of tools at the back and searched in the gloom by the light of a match. First he found a candle and lit it. Then he pulled a coil of rope from the wall and turned to their prisoner. "Please get in the chair."

The teen trembled with fear or cold. "What are you gonna do?" He was freckles and clear skin, pushing twenty with sandy hair cut into a faux-hawk. A tattoo of a snake rose up from his shoulder and licked under his ear—all the toughness and gangsta attitude had evaporated.

"You are sick." Father Alvarez pointed to the chair. "I will hear your confession."

"I don't wanna die. Please Father. I'm not Catholic. I don't need no confession. Can't you just let me go?"

"Get in the chair." Bertrand pointed his Glock at the teen's head. "Or I put you down right now."

He sat and Alvarez secured him, hands behind his back, ropes around his chest. Emile closed the pedestrian door of the garage, shaking at the bars someone had screwed over its window. "Not pretty but good and strong," he said.

"You have to cover the windows before sunrise." The ripper looked as if he might weep. "Otherwise I'll die."

"You already are dead." Bertrand found a large plastic paint pail—the five-gallon size—and pulled it over in front of the prisoner so the he could sit facing him. "What's your name?"

"Ted. Ted Walcott. Please don't kill me."

"I'm not going to kill you, Ted. But you need to tell me everything. Start with why you chose to attack this house tonight—why here?"

Ted looked left at Emile, who had taken a seat on another paint pail, but found an unsympathetic expression. He looked right to Father Alvarez, who had pulled up an old wooden chair splattered with paint, and found pity, which didn't seem to make him feel any better. He again faced Bertrand.

"Harrison, Steve Harrison—the guy she hit first with her crossbow— he had a thing for her, see? I mean like she's hot but she never puts out, and she was a grade above in our high school but then she got into college and we didn't, so I guess her nose turned up even more. Then the boss said we each had to evolve someone every night, make a quota you know, and Harrison thought of her. Like that wasn't really the rules, 'cause we're supposed to find people who can adapt to the change—you know, people who want to live forever no matter what you gotta do."

"Murderers." Bertrand resisted the urge to immediately shoot Ted.

"No, no, it's not like that." Ted leaned back in the chair, apparently sensing Bertrand's anger. "See like it's just for a little while that we have to, you know, take people out to survive. But when things get reorganized, when the new world order gets going, we won't have to kill anybody anymore because you guys will be in camps and stuff and will be donating blood, right? So we get this blood like at a blood bank and nobody has to die."

"You'll put us in camps!"

"No! I mean yes but it'll be for your own protection. Some guys don't adapt well see, even after the evolution. They go rogue and don't join with the rest of us brids, but just go hunting alone all the time—so see, it would be good for you guys to be in the camps. We can take care of you and all."

"It'd be better for us if you stopped making people into rippers."

"Rippers? You mean brids? We're not rippers."

Emile leaned in, looking like he wanted to hit Ted. "The fuck you aren't. What were you gonna do to that little girl tonight and her friend?"

"Hey dude that little girl is a freak, man. Harrison and some buds caught her parents in the alley like a month ago and fed on them. I mean, I know it's wrong and all but you gotta feed the bugs or it's just torture. So we figure she'll want to join and all, but Harrison says we gotta give her a few weeks so that she's not too pissed at him for doing her mom and dad."

"No shit," said Emile.

"Okay, I know, I know that it probably really sucks to lose your folks. I got evolved by my mom so I don't really know what it's like, but we figured a bit of time, and we even told other brids to stay off this street, that it was our turf, but we left her alone."

"So you killed everyone else on the street instead." Bertrand fought to keep the wrath from his face. Here was a sociopathic enemy.

Ted looked left and right to see how Emile and Alvarez were taking this story, but still found no sympathy. He nodded.

"That was the idea, but she's some kind of psycho general or something because the bitch, I mean, Bobs—that's her name, well, it's Roberta I think but everybody calls her Bobs—she like organizes the whole street, I mean the whole freaking neighborhood into forts. Most people used to hide out at the community center in the park, and it was like fucking Fort Knox, like they keep people on the roof with crossbows and a few guns and they got a generator at night for lights so nobody can get near there, and she set up houses like hers that are all bricked up, and they sort of act like outlying forts. It was so messed up that word came down from like the top, from the boss himself, and he says just leave this area alone for a while. Says pockets of resistance like this will be mopped up later and doesn't want to draw attention to them and all."

"So why are you here tonight?"

"So you guys didn't hear?" Ted couldn't keep the sly expression off his face, the pride. "Wow, they kept it off the news? The boss sent his, like, top general to take out the community center last night. He came with hundreds of brids with a grenade launcher and everything. The fodder, they put up a hell of a fight and Bobs was running around the roof. I tried to tell this general guy that she was the one organizing them and shit, but he wouldn't believe me. Said a nineteen-year-old girl didn't know crap, you know. I saw her a couple of times shooting down with that crossbow, but they had hardly any guns. The cops are our buds, right, and they've been rounding up guns for months to make sure we're good and all."

Ted suddenly seemed to be aware that the three men looked at him with a mix of horror and anger.

"Yeah, well, I guess it was kinda sad for like the families with kids and all. But Bobs was really smart at the end and even the boss's general was surprised. She let us break into the gym and a bunch of the guys ahead of me got really fucked up when all these gasoline bombs dropped from the ceiling onto their heads right in the middle of the gym. Like, she set people on fire!"

"I'm in love," said Emile. "This girl is fantastic."

"Yeah well a lot of my buds got totally like burned and messed up—just totally harsh. But I guess it was good for the fodder because they all bailed out the far side of the building while we were trying to figure out what the fuck had happened. Then the boss's general calls and says 'Go! Go! Go!' 'cause they're all getting away, but it's too late. Nobody wanted to go any farther into the building 'cause there might have been more booby traps, see, and by the time we get around the building they've all got out of the park and into the neighborhood, and that's when we find out that they've been preparing all these little forts see? So now we gotta pick them off one at a time, and they're really hard to break, and it was like nearly sunrise."

"My heart bleeds for you." Bertrand tried to configure what he'd seen tonight with what he'd just heard. Had she already set up the kind of organizations he wanted to set up? Was the burned-out shell across the street the "partner" house she spoke of? Were they choosing houses so that they could support each other through the night with cross fire?

"It's tough though, see." Ted looked shaky and thin. "When you get hungry the bugs are pretty harsh. They make you really hungry, not like missing one meal or so but just starving and starving. I'm so hungry." He looked around for mercy. "Maybe one of you guys could like do me a favor and give me a hit, you know? Just a little slice on your wrist and let me suck just a bit of blood. You'd be safe and all because it's outbound you know. There's no bugs in saliva so it's like AIDS, has to be blood into blood—or into your stomach really."

"My son." Father Alvarez leaned forward, the rosary clasped in his hands. "To feed you would be a sin."

"All due respect and all Father, but no way. Where does it say in the bible that you can't drink somebody's blood—I mean if it's all consensual and they don't get bled out?"

"To covet another man's possessions is a sin, and what possession could be more precious than one's own blood?"

"Please! I haven't tasted in a couple of days, and I'm so friggin' hungry. Just a little lick?"

"How often do you need to eat?" asked Bertrand.

"Well," Ted looked embarrassed now. "A good way to start your day, see? I mean a balanced diet is like every night. It used to be easy but people are starting to figure it out. They don't go out at night anymore, and you have to get them out of their houses and that can be tricky."

"Holy shit." Emile sat back, the .357 resting on his knees. "This kid murders once a night. This is a catastrophe."

Bertrand stood and walked over to the window in the pedestrian door. The first blush of purple edged the eastern horizon. He turned to face Ted. "Will the glass protect you from the sun? I heard it has to be full-spectrum light."

"Dude, I don't know. I just stay the hell away. I tried to go to the window the first morning after Mom evolved me. They say everyone does, but my eyeballs just felt like they were melting and my head spilt with the worst headache of my life, so I went back to my room and hid under the bed all day. Next night I had the basement like totally ready, you know, windows boarded up and taped up so that we could party all day. Mom had already moved in with her boyfriend."

Bertrand sat in front of him. "You need to pray, okay? I figure you've got about half an hour."

Ted's eyes went wide and tears started. "No, please don't do this to me. I'm too young to die. Please."

"Terrance and Bobs in that house are also too young to die, but you were gonna do for them tonight, and we can't let you go or you'll kill, what, three hundred? Four hundred in just the next year? You're a mass murderer."

The tears were in full flood now and his head bowed into his lap. "You don't understand. The only way I can stay out of hell is to live. I mean I'm really sorry about all those people—especially Vicky, that's my girlfriend—was my girlfriend."

Father Alvarez looked up sharply. "Repentance is essential. Was she the first person you killed?"

Ted met the priest's steady gaze. "I didn't plan it, see. After I got evolved I talked to Harrison 'cause he was already up—looking for a few pointers on how to feed and all—and he just suggested I get with Vicky like always, but that while we were doing it I should just prick her neck and suck a little bit of her blood, so I kept—like—a box cutter handy and did just what he said, just a quick little stab." He stopped. "Is this like a confession? Don't I have say some mumbo jumbo or something first?"

Alvarez shook his head. "Just tell me what happened. Tell me about your remorse."

Ted nodded. "She freaked when I cut her, but I held her and really apologized and said it was a kink that Harrison told me about, about sucking a little bit of blood vampire-like while we were getting off, so she went with it for a while because she's game for fun and all, but once the blood got to my stomach the bugs gave me the blowback—totally, totally awesome bang for the buck. At first she just thought I was being a rock-star lover, but I couldn't get enough blood fast enough and I still had the box cutter in my hand...." Ted's voice trailed away, and for a moment they all sat in silence. "I am going to Hell, aren't I?"

Bertrand and Emile looked to Father Alvarez to answer that question.

"I believe you are already in hell and that only repentance can set you free. Let us pray together for the soul of Vicky and all the others you have murdered. Do you know the Lord's Prayer? I'll lead us."

He stood over Ted, putting one hand on his head—crushing down the faux-hawk— and holding the rosary in his other hand. Bertrand stumbled along with them through the prayer, remembering bits because one Sunday School teacher had drilled it into him for weeks until his parents decided that the class was too fundamentalist and pulled him out.

Over the next half-hour, Alvarez spoke several more prayers in succession, one about Mary, something else about contrition and back to the Lord's Prayer, the rosary beads moving through his fingers to help him keep count. Bertrand sat and watched, mesmerized by the rhythm. It was like meditation, only with words to numb the mind. He'd never thought of it that way before, just viewing the beads as some sort of pagan device.

Father Alvarez stopped, kissed the crucifix and hung the rosary around his neck. "Do you repent the murders you have committed?" He placed both hands on Ted's head.

"I do." The tears started again. "I really do, especially Vicky. I never meant to do her, you know. I loved her. We talked about kids and everything."

"Then I absolve you from your sins in the name of the Father, the Son and the Holy Spirit." He made the sign of the cross over the teen.

Ted looked up. "Father, I told you I'm not even Catholic."

"God will know his own. Go in peace."

Ted turned to Bertrand. "Dude, Mister, please. I can see you're their leader and we're like the same age aren't we?"

"I'm a bit older," said Bertrand. "I'm finished college."

"But close enough, man. We've both got our whole lives ahead of us. Please, please cover the window. My eyes are burning already. Please don't kill me."

"I'm not killing you." Bertrand stood and walked over to the window as he spoke. "Your mom killed you the night she made you drink infected blood. There was no turning back from that moment, and no hope but to kill yourself."

"Maybe I could drink animal blood or something?"

"Can you?"

Ted shook his head and stared into his lap and closed his eyes. "I don't know. No one does so I guess maybe not, or maybe it's not as good or something."

"If you could drink a cow's blood then maybe we could do something for you, but you and your friends have put us in the middle of a war."

The sun was above the horizon now, and the first orange rays breached the glass to shine on Ted. The four men waited in silence.

"My eyes are burning." Ted took deep breaths, his eyes now squeezed shut. "I hope you're right, Father. I hope I'm forgiven, man. Aw fuck this hurts!"

Ted rocked back and forth, swearing and cursing.

Father Alvarez looked over at Bertrand. "I think you should open the door," he said.

"No!" shouted Ted. "I think I can hold on if I just don't open my eyes."

Bertrand opened the door and stood aside to allow sunlight to flood the garage.

Ted convulsed, blood hemorrhaging out of his nose. The chair rattled on the floor and would have tipped but Alvarez caught it, turning Ted to face the sun. The convulsions lasted for nearly a minute. Finally Ted threw his head back with one last gasp, his eyes going to the rafters of the garage before his head slumped forward, only the ropes around his chest preventing him from falling from the chair.

They'd stared at him for a full minute, Bertrand wondering if this would be added to his murder charges. Finally Emile broke their silence.

"That is just too freaky."

They laid him out in the backyard of Bobs' house, careful not to touch his blood.

# 22

# WORLD FALLS APART

**B**obs and Terrance were already on the front lawn inspecting the bodies of the rippers with crossbows at the ready. She barely reached his shoulder in height, and yet there was something deferential about his posture that made it obvious to Bertrand that she was in charge. Despite being blonde and petite, there was something coiled in her stance, like a puma ready to charge. She looked up when Bertrand came around the corner with his Glock ready but pointed at the ground.

"Whatsup," she said. "That was some nice work last night, especially sending the fat guy around the car to flank them. You guys are good."

Emile heard this but it just made him laugh. "Wow, you are one hell of a pistol little lady. We heard from the kid about the community center night before last. Sounds like you did some good work yourself."

If she took pride in the compliment, it didn't show, because she still looked left and right, checking bodies and assessing the surroundings before she let her crossbow point to the grass. Terrance, gangly and still pimpled despite being near the end of his teens, stayed a step behind her as she turned to Bertrand.

"So what's your story?" she asked. "Like, what brought you out hunting in the middle of the night?"

"Just as you said—hunting." Bertrand put his Glock in his holster. "We're with the crowd at St. Mike's, but I couldn't sleep, so I decided to go out and see if we could save anyone from the rippers."

"I like that you call them rippers. Hey, St. Mike's?" Her eyes went wide. "Was that Father Alvarez with you? He helped me bury Mom and Dad. He didn't buy it, did he?"

"He's saying a prayer over Ted's body out back. You know him, then?"

"My folks were regulars at St. Mike's until Wormison and his buddies offed them." She turned and walked over to the body of Harrison and kicked it hard in the gut and carefully and deliberately spat on his corpse. She turned back to Bertrand.

"I promised my Mom and Dad in my prayers that I would do that. I doubt it would make Mom feel any better in heaven, but Dad would sure be happy."

She showed no emotion, reporting this to Bertrand as if commenting on the price of gas or the chance for rain. Was she in shock? Was she too numb to grieve? Bertrand decided that she needed help that he was unqualified to give. Maybe that flower shop lady, Helen, could talk to her and draw out something other than clipped reports.

"We're heading back to St. Mike's," said Bertrand. "And there's a whole community there set up for defense."

She snorted, throwing Bertrand for a complete loop. "Defense?" she said. "St. Mike's is about as defendable as a goldfish bowl, unless you want to brick in those stained glass windows. Otherwise a few rocks and a Molotov cocktail or two on those nice wooden pews and everybody'll be outside in the middle of the night, or dying of smoke inhalation. Besides, now that I've lost the community center, St. Mike's'll be a magnet for action in the next couple of weeks. Its only good will be for luring vampires in and blowing it up once they're inside."

Emile started laughing, unable to contain himself, shaking his head in disbelief. "My God, you're something. And you're absolutely right."

"Well there's a lot of people there who are depending on us," said Bertrand. "So we're headed back."

Father Alvarez came around the corner, wiping dirt from his hands, his M-16 slung over his shoulder. When he saw Bobs he smiled. "Roberta, I didn't recognize you last night, but when Ted mentioned your named I guessed it was you. I'm glad to see you well."

"I'd be dead or worse if it wasn't for you, Father." She looked at Bertrand for a moment, sizing him up, judging him. "This guy tells me you got a bunch of hold-outs at the church, but I gotta tell you, Father, it'll be a tough go to defend that place in the long run."

Father Alvarez spread his hands. "I do what I can and the rest is up to God."

Bobs nodded, looking from Bertrand to Alvarez. She was about to make a decision, and Bertrand didn't speak because he wanted her to make her own choice, decide her own future. It wasn't like he could promise her a safer world.

"You know what? I think Terry and I will join you guys at the church, but I'm gonna bring my people from the community center, and Father, I'm going to organize the defense. I got us out of that community center without losing one person."

"From what I have heard so far," said Alvarez, "it was truly a miracle."

She shook her head. "Just had to see what was coming and plan for it. I can do something with that bell tower on the church, but a sniper or two won't be enough. We're gonna need some concrete barriers and a bulldozer."

———

The story came out in bits and pieces over breakfast. Her father had been with the National Guard in Desert Storm, but after Bobs was born, he'd become an investment adviser. Her mother sold insurance, but Bobs had taken after her father in politics and interest so much that her mother had always joked that Bobs was the son her husband had always wanted.

She had completed her first year in history but hadn't returned to DePaul after her parents had died.

"I was gonna flunk out anyway," she said between forkfuls of scrambled eggs in the basement of St. Mike's. "The professors are all commie wimps who'd rather talk about socioeconomic history than battles and bombs."

Ever since seeing the movie *Enemy at the Gates*, she'd been fascinated by the battle of Stalingrad. "If only Hitler had listen to von Manstein and let the 6th army break out right at the beginning when they were first encircled, the whole history of the world would be different."

"Then it's a good thing he didn't listen." Helen fussed around their table in the basement of the church, pouring more coffee and making sure everyone had enough to eat.

"What?" Bobs looked up with a frown. "Oh yeah. I just hate it when a battle is lost that could've been won. Take the church here: you guys are just hiding in it at night, but what you really need to do is go out during the day on search-and-destroy missions. We have to make the whole neighborhood a no-go for the rippers."

She had taken to Bertrand's name for them because, as she said, "Vampires can be sexy. There's nothing sexy about these assholes."

Joyce on the other hand was furious with Bertrand. "How could you go out there without me and Jeff? We were worried sick when we woke up and found you guys gone."

Explanations about insomnia and a desire to do something didn't wash.

"Next time you frigging wake me. I thought we were a team, the three of us." She gestured in Jeff's direction, and Bertrand remembered that without them he would've been Malcolm's dinner.

Helen, the flower shop lady, joined them at the table with a plate of eggs for herself. "You and Emile should get some sleep somewhere safe. That was good work you did last night, but an internet hero needs to be ready for every night."

"Internet hero?"

Jeff sat across from Bertrand with an iPad. "Yup." He turned it to Bertrand, who hadn't finished his toast. "That was how we first figured out where you were and that you were alive. As soon as the power came on this morning this went totally viral."

A grainy image—a video camera working at the edge of its ability to resolve an image in low light—showed Harrison and Ted and their other associate threatening Bobs and Terry with the Molotov cocktails. The cocktail that Harrison broke across the hood of the car provided the light for the shoot out, and the camera zoomed in on Bertrand ordering the attack while the rippers were still unaware of the threat.

"Who shot this?" asked Bertrand.

Bobs stood to watch over his shoulder. "Hey, that's gotta be from my neighbor across the street's house, Mr. Guillard. I thought he bought it a couple of nights ago, but it looks like he's hiding out in the one house on the street nobody's going to look for him, because it's a burnt shell. Smart. I wonder where he's hanging during the day, 'cause it's gotta be somewhere with power."

"So this is up on YouTube?" asked Bertrand.

"Oh yeah." Jeff slid back the tablet to his side of the table. "That's not all. Someone from that Erics crowd videotaped you at McDonald's yesterday too, and they put that all over the place. Both vids have had millions of hits. This thing is being shared all over the world by the supporters of your maybe-crazy friends, the Erics."

"He's bigger than I thought. I just figured he had a couple of dozen followers, nothing like what we saw yesterday." Bertrand reached for the tablet. "Gimme that. I need to check my e-mail."

Helen pushed the tablet back at Jeff. "Later my internet sensation," she said to Bertrand. "You and Emile and these two kids need to get some sleep."

Weariness suddenly did take hold, but Bertrand knew that the church would not be peaceful today, and he wanted security after last night's danger. He wanted a bunker.

"She's right. I'm going back to Nolan's to recharge my batteries."

Joyce nodded. "Fine. We'll come with you and keep watch for the cops. After yesterday you're going to attract a lot of heat."

———

Hushed voices were still loud enough to wake Bertrand. They spoke with excitement, horror and amazement. Bertrand wanted to curl down in the sleeping bag but he opened his eyes, trying to understand why people had entered his house. It wasn't his parents' voices. These were strangers to him, until he recognized Joyce. Bertrand's dangerous new world rapidly replaced the safe world of only a few months ago, and he sat up quickly to determine where he had gone to ground.

A snore from the couch parallel to his and only a few feet away helped his memory. He and Emile were in the bomb shelter at Nolan's, but they had left the big door open a crack, since it was daytime and several others were out in there doing—what? Bertrand rose quietly, careful not to disturb Emile, and groped at the end table near his feet until he found his Glock, then pulled the big vault door open as little as possible. He squeezed through and into the basement, but it was empty and dim, the light from the high windows suggesting late afternoon. He strapped on the gun.

The voices floated down the basement stairs from the dining room above.

Several people looked up when the basement door creaked as Bertrand reached the main floor. Jeff sat at the big dining-room table with his laptop—several people gathered around him, including Joyce sitting close on his right. The detective, Mike Sinclair, and his fellow ex-cops, Simon Gonsalves and Julia Chen, were on his left.

"Bert, you gotta see this." Joyce stood to make room for him, her jaw now clamped shut, a sign Bertrand had learned was the closest she ever came to intense emotion.

"What?"

"The end of the world." Jeff turned the laptop toward him but kept one hand on the track pad.

A video showed a nighttime riot in front of Buckingham palace. Crowds climbed the fence and the gate, some continuing to attack even after being shot; riot police were totally overwhelmed and beaten down. Another video showed a couple captured after a foot chase—still in England judging by all the cars with the drivers' seat on the left, skewed and abandoned on the streets. Several rippers pinned the couple down, one man wielding a long hunting knife with the proficiency of practice, cutting neatly into the jugular and clamping his mouth over the flow, quickly trading places with others to give them a taste.

"So it's happening there too." Bertrand sat back, his eyes turning to the polished wood of the tabletop rather than watching the couple die, but their screams still reached his ears from half a world away.

"Not just there." Jeff took them to websites of the *Hindustan Times* in India, where English-language articles spoke of a new plague that had swept the country, leaving bloodless corpses in the streets. An editorial begged people to donate blood to help with the epidemic, but Jeff switched to anti-government websites that showed what was really going on: a bulldozer shoved a massive pile of bodies into a crater-like landfill, the guerrilla videographer climbing up into a tree to give the viewers a sense of the depth of the hole.

"There's got to be ten thousand bodies there." Bertrand couldn't believe the scale of what he was seeing. He'd known it was national, and thanks to Azzim he had guessed it was international, but this was beyond his worst nightmare.

"I've been at this all day." Jeff clicked through graphic images from website to website. "It always starts the way it started here: they go for the government, the cops and the media first. They get them on board and keep things going as long as possible, as if everything's cool, but the bloggers and the tweeps start to get the word out. But the government and the ISPs shut them down, so for a few weeks everything seems like it's getting back to normal. Then the social media gets more insistent and it becomes like a game of whack-a-mole. People put the word out, the ISP pulls them down, but the same video footage or whatever keeps popping up elsewhere. That's when the governments begin the power shutdown's—to totally hammer down communication. But I think the rippers maybe need the power too, so they let it come up every now and then, but as far as I can tell, certainly in the middle-east and Africa, it eventually goes down and stays down."

"What's going on in Africa?" asked Bertrand.

"Same as everywhere, but it's become a hole for information. I can't find an updated website that's anything less than two weeks old. China's harder to figure, but there's a few rogue images like you saw from England. No need to show you 'cause it's more of the same."

The basement door creaked open and Emile stood at the top of the stairs rubbing sleep from his eyes and yawning, looking for all the world like a giant little boy waking from a nap. "Sounds like the world truly has gone to Hell this time." He turned to the fridge in the kitchen. "Anyone else need a beer?"

We deal with disaster in different ways, thought Bertrand.

Jeff spoke up first. "What the hell. I'll have one. Bert?"

"Sure. I have a feeling I won't being seeing my doctor again for a while, so I don't have to worry about a lecture anyway."

Sinclair got up and walked over to look out the sliding glass doors into Nolan's little backyard. He still wore the rumpled suit he'd been wearing the night he knocked on the front door to announce that Bertrand was wanted for murder.

"Is there anywhere in the world you don't think this is going down," he asked without looking back. It was a plea.

"Nowhere." Jeff opened his beer and leaned back from the laptop. "I mean I can't read anything other than English, but the videos that people upload speak for themselves. We're pretty fucked."

"But one guy couldn't do all this then." Bertrand also sat back trying to find a vent for his frustration. "If they really do have to infect people by getting them to drink infected blood, then it can't be happening all over the world at once unless there are thousands of rippers acting in concert."

"I think there must be," said Jeff. "There're weird Twitter posts that are clearly about killing people and drinking blood, but I can't find any-thing like, well, a command structure. Like someone giving orders."

"Well keep looking. I'm going upstairs to check my e-mail and see what Erics has to say."

He headed for Nolan's office with his beer, relishing the cold fluid even though it was on an empty stomach. He sat at the solid desk, pondering Thomas Nolan's life while the man's twenty-first century Mac booted. How could a man who had seen so clearly what was going on have been so oblivious to the implications? What kind of man could think a bunker could protect him from the disaster that only he saw happening? Perhaps the same man who didn't bother to change the seventies decor in the basement even as he adopted modern tech.

To Bertrand's amazement, he still received spam, but most of it went straight to the junk folder, so it wasn't hard to find several e-mails from Erics.

"Even though you have refused to take my survey to determine your soul, it is now clear to me that you possess part of the Dormant Hero soul. I have searched for others vessels of your soul, and they are emerging all over the world, but here in America yours is the densest. This density is abnormal and it is critical to fight the coming scourge of ages.

"You must understand that a Ruthless General has risen. This is not an evil soul by intent, but by nature. It does what must be done, regardless of who must die and who must live. He has gathered others and has taken upon himself an evil task: to drastically cull the human population. That is why he has chosen this time of year to enact his plan. Food will be a weapon."

Bertrand sat back and shook his head in disbelief. It was so obvious, why hadn't he realized it before? "Jeff!" Bertrand ran up the cellar stairs. "What about the harvest? Are farmers harvesting their crops?" When did farmers harvest anyway? Should it all be in by now: wheat, corn—certainly fruits and vegetables?

Jeff looked as startled as Bertrand felt. "Hell, I don't know."

"They aren't." Sinclair turned from the window. "Even if they are, it'll rot in the silos or whatever. Think about it: why are grocery store shelves empty? At first I figured it was just a trucking problem, but if so why aren't farmers' markets open and raking it in? Why is no one stepping up to make a killing from this huge shortage of food? Because they can't."

"Maybe they are in smaller towns?" But even Bertrand didn't believe his hope.

Sinclair shook his head. "I went to Moscow and St. Petersburg back in the nineties. The reason people could get cheap fruit and veggies even as the old Soviet thing fell apart was farmers from as far south as Uzbekistan would take a train all the way north, carrying bags of tomatoes or whatever as luggage and selling it from street kiosks. And it was damn cheap. Farmers are smart. There're thousands upon thousands of farms just a few hours drive from Chicago, and here we're scraping the bottom of the barrel for food. Those eggs we had this morning were taken from an urban farm where the owners have been disappeared. As the numbers grow at St. Mike's, we can expect more canned food and less fresh food."

"We have to bring this to a resolution before the winter," said Bertrand. "We have to hunt down this guy, this Vlad the Scourge, and put him down like you would a mad dog."

Sinclair sat and for a moment put his head in his hands. He wiped his face to clear his weariness and looked up. "You know, maybe I will have one of those beers, Emile. We'll be short of those soon too." He accepted the beer, opened it and met Bertrand's gaze. "Bert, you've got to keep getting the word out, but it's too late to save the world. All we can do now is salvage what we can and rebuild. Even if every ripper in existence spontaneously disappeared tomorrow, it's still going to be a very bad winter for humans."

Two contrasting figures came up the back steps to the deck. Martin Morley, the tall and fit manager of the McDonald's where Bertrand had spoken, and Barry St. John, the shorter, barrel-chested contractor. Both had heavy coats on, perhaps warmer than the chilly fall day called for, but good for concealing weapons. The former flower shop owner, Helen, came up the stairs behind them, a cigarette dangling from her lips. Alison St. John was beside her. All of them wore backpacks.

Jeff reached the window first, sliding it open. "What the hell? I thought you guys were all heading up to Canada."

"We were." Barry marched straight in, noted the beer in Emile's hand and headed for the fridge.

Martin slipped the pack off his shoulders. "There're police road-blocks on all the highways and they're turning everyone back into the city, 'for their own safety.' Lying scum. On most of the side streets they've got buses and trucks and cars all piled up together, and not from no goddamn accidents. They've been put there to block the way. They're building a wall around Chicago to keep people from getting out. Thank God I sent the wife and kids up to our cabin in Wisconsin last week."

Barry opened his beer. "I never figured it would all fall apart so suddenly." He took a drink, not making eye contact with his daughter as she and Helen moved into the living room and deposited their packs. "I should've got Alison out a month ago. What was I waiting for?"

"Who would think it would all mess up in less than a week?" said Helen. "Give yourself a break."

Martin took off his pack. "St. Mike's is crammed. We hoped we could stay here for the night until we figured out what to do."

"Of course," said Bertrand. "You can stay as long as you want." The house would be crowded. They couldn't all fit in the basement anymore, but they also had enough people for sentries—not that Bertrand planned to stay safe.

But Helen was studying Bertrand, her head cocked at an angle as if she were listening to a voice. "You're planning to go raiding again, aren't you boy."

Emile shouted, "Right now!" He laughed and drank.

"Actually I was going to wait until after sunset."

Several people spoke up in alarm, but Joyce cut through all of them.

"Not without me. In fact, I won't let you the hell out of this house unless you promise to listen to me. Emile told me that Father Alvarez saved your guys' butts last night, that you would have charged straight at them and never known that there were five rippers at the back of the house."

Bertrand looked to Emile, who shrugged without guilt. "It's true. You'd have made a mess of it if Alvarez hadn't made you stop and think."

He wanted to argue, wanted to point out how well it all worked out, but Bertrand had to admit that he had just wanted to recklessly charge into the fight until Alvarez took control. "Fair enough." He turned to Joyce. "You can lead us if you think you can do better."

Joyce didn't look pleased or triumphant. She just nodded and said, "As a matter of fact I think I can." She looked around the room. "Whoever wants to go should get something to eat and then go pick up some weapons and ammunition from this guy's bunker in the basement. We'll leave just after sunset."

# 23

# MASSACRE AT ST. MIKE'S

They wore dark clothing. They wore soft sneakers. They had Emile's walkie talkies with ear pieces so that they could keep in touch. They carried a lot of weapons. Emile had opened up his secret stash of guns in the basement of Helen's Flowers.

The first night they were careful, they found a house besieged not far from DePaul University. Over a dozen rippers were in front preparing to burn it when they arrived. Joyce split her people into two groups: one led by Bertrand with Jeff, Emile, Martin and Barry and another with her and the former cops. Helen stayed with Alison in the bunker.

Joyce attacked the rippers at the back of the house first, and when those at the front turned to respond, Bertrand attacked. It was a rout, and even though the house burned, a family with a young son was saved. During the day, Bertrand and several others fortified a house across the street under Barry's direction, stealing concrete blocks and mortar mix from an abandoned Home Depot so that they could seal all the ground-floor windows. Bertrand intended to use Bobs' tactic of mutually supporting forts. They gave it to the family to use, and that night the father joined Joyce's Raiders. Emile had given them that name with a laugh.

The next night they weren't so lucky, arriving at a house too late, the second floor already in flames and rippers inside feeding on a husband and wife. Bertrand had charged in at the screams, and the fight had been short and sharp, but not without value. Before the woman had died, she had pointed to a closet and called, "save my son." Bertrand, his stomach pressed to the floor in an effort to stay under the smoke and heat, found a saucer-eyed boy, who lay on Bertrand's back while he crawled from the house. They took the child to St. Mike's, and he was placed in a new orphanage that Helen now oversaw in the basement.

The next night, they ambushed two different parties of rippers. A total power failure for the day apparently made it difficult for the rippers to get out the word of these ambushes. This time Joyce hit the jackpot: many people had taken refuge in both houses, so her ranks swelled. By now no one had any doubt who should lead them into a fight. Whitlock came to join them, bringing his marine training and his teenage sons. Fish, the karate sensei, joined them and they found a safe house for his wife and two young sons. His nineteen-year-old daughter joined the Raiders. Many others heard about them and flocked to their protection. The sunsets, oddly, were magnificently orange and red, even when there were no clouds to catch the dying rays.

Bobs visited them once, demanding Bertrand get online more when the power was up. "Who knows when we'll lose this tool to spread the word, and you're the god since you went viral."

Bert was forced to spare time to record messages warning about Vlad and the rippers, which Terry uploaded whenever the power was up. But each time the young man left, he would say, "This might be your last message. If it weren't for the fact that California is all rippers, the Internet would be gone. Don't know how much longer they'll let it stay up."

Bobs loved what Joyce was doing and assembled her own little army with her followers from the community center and volunteers from St. Mike's. They went on house-to-house daylight raids, clearing basements of rippers and scavenging canned food for the church.

Within a week—between Joyce's Raiders and Bobs' Army—they had cleared Old Town of rippers. The power went back up for two days, but it was no reward. Twitter and Facebook suddenly came alive, and it was all about the "terrorists" who were attacking at night, led by the maniacal Bertrand Allan, deemed by the news media as the greatest evil since Osama bin Laden. The rippers were being warned that they were hunted.

By the end of the second week, they could patrol for miles at night and come across no rippers. Whole streets in Old Town were fortified, but they had no news from the outside world other than what the ripper-controlled media fed them. Bertrand's greatest fear was the army. November approached, but no one was prepared to give much thanks other than for being alive.

It turned out it wasn't the army they needed to worry about. It was the Chicago P.D. who came to attack.

———

Dinner/breakfast at four p.m. was Bertrand's favorite time of day. They all crowded around the dining-room table—extended into the living room now with the aid of some pilfered folding tables—and ate as if they were a very big family. The food was usually simple, although Emile had successfully brought down a few Canada Geese that were late on their way south. People chatted, laughed and exchanged gossip, and Bertrand basked in the sense of family, something that had been absent from his life since the house he shared during college.

But tonight, Emile's cell phone broke the silence and startled everyone, its ring tone the Ride of the Valkyries. It was the ring tone he had chosen for Bobs.

"Yeah, whatsup?" Emile at first seemed happy to receive the call, but as Bobs relayed her news his eyebrows went up in surprise. "Okay, just keep it locked down and don't let the bastards in. We'll round up who we can and try to get there before sunset."

He slapped the phone closed. "The cops have surrounded St. Mike's and are using bullhorns, telling everyone to come out. They say the people in the church are breaking some new anti-assembly law the state passed last month, one that totally violates the frigging constitution."

Joyce said what Bertrand was already thinking. "But it's only a couple of hours to sunset. Why would they order them out now unless—"

"They're planning a massacre." Bertrand had never been so sure of anything in his life. "Before Father Alvarez can get organized to defend St. Mike's for the night, they intend to isolate them and hand them all over to the rippers. We can't let that happen."

"No shit," said Jeff, exhaling smoke. Helen had got him hooked on cigarettes again.

"Okay." Joyce turned to Jeff. "Can you pull up a Google map of the area around the church? Alison, Helen, you guys head out right now and call everybody up. Be sure to get others spreading the word. We're going to need more people than we've ever taken on a raid before."

Joyce moved to sit in front of Jeff's computer, studying the map. Bertrand resisted the urge to run out the door and steal the first car he could find to drive to the fight.

"Okay," she said finally. "We're going to need trucks, big ones. We come at the from three fronts in the dark."

"No," said Bertrand. "The rippers will be there by then."

Joyce shook her head. "Bert, we can't just charge in there without guns or people anyway, and it'll be a couple of hours before we can organize all that, so it'll have to be after dark anyway. Think about it: they aren't planning to arrest these people, they're planning to feed on them. Remember what Malcolm said, about you being designated fodder? This congregation has been designated fodder, and the only good news for them is that it means none of them will be made into rippers."

"But if we wait too long—"

"Give that hellion some credit. She can hold them off for a couple of hours. My guess is that those daytime cops don't mind doing what their masters tell them, but I bet none of them will stick their necks out while waiting for the rippers to come out after sunset. They'll just keep them pinned up in there. We're the ace in the hole! I bet they think we're all at the church. They don't know that we're in the clear."

Bertrand stood and pulled out his cell phone. "But we need numbers if we're really going to make this work. We're going up against trained men and women, not disorganized rippers."

"Who are you calling?" asked Joyce.

"Erics e-mailed me the other day to say that he can make hundreds available to us at a moments notice. He sure as hell did at McDonald's. Let's see what he can do tonight."

"Wait a sec there, Bert," said Emile. "Can we trust all those people not to give us away to the pigs? Oh, sorry guys, present company excepted, but trusting a couple of hundred strangers?"

"I'm only trusting one," said Bertrand. "So far, he's proved to be pretty clued-in despite his wacky religion."

———

Bertrand hadn't expected a Skype chat, but Erics had already sent an e-mail wanting to be listed as a Skype contact, and for the first time, he and Bertrand met electronically face-to-face. Erics turned out to be old, very old. His accent was distinctly Jamaican, his hair and beard long and white. It wouldn't have surprised Bertrand if the man had appeared wearing biblical robes, but instead he wore a three-piece suit that a Wall Street banker would have been comfortable wearing in the 1980s, except that it was a purple pinstripe.

"Hello Mr. Allan," he said. "I have great need to speak with you. My followers in Chicago warn me that a great disaster is planned for tonight."

"Are we talking about the same thing? Are we talking about St. Mike's?"

"Verily, we are. Good. You will go to their rescue, no doubt?"

"That's the plan, but we need more people."

"Marvelous. If I had any doubt that you possess a big portion of the Dormant Hero soul, that doubt would be vanquished, but I was already convinced." He leaned forward, holding a carved walking stick in his hands for support even though he was sitting. "But now is our first great task, and I am ready. I have prepared squads for you, people who have heard my words and yours and are prepared to follow, even at great risk."

"What sort of people?" Bertrand couldn't keep the suspicion out of his voice. Leading a crackpot mob of religious fanatics could only result in a blood bath.

"Good people. You must remember that I have made it my life's work to catalogue and recognize the 1000 Souls. For this task I have prepared companies, three of them, each numbering near one-hundred people, and each company has roughly equal numbers of battle worthy souls: there are Fighting Souls, Courageous Souls and Selfless Souls, and even a few Ruthless Souls. I'll include a few Ralliers too. They are sometimes the most important, for when the battle is failing they will rally your troops to one last great effort that can win the day."

Bertrand wanted to believe, craved to believe, but he feared a dozen or so hopeless sheep would show up rather than the hundreds promised. "How can you be so sure?"

"My friend. I have been preparing for this since my own soul became mysteriously more dense over a year ago. When all of my followers experienced this to one degree or other, I understood the truth. Where were these soul portions coming from but other people, and why were the absorptions so obvious to the new hosts except because of violent death?"

Bertrand considered his options. "Do they have guns?"

———

Bertrand fought with the five-ton truck's gearshift, grinding the gears a few times before he was able to get the truck to roll forward. They'd found it parked along with three others at a public storage locker, a for rent $19.99 sign painted on each truck. Emile had liberated the keys by smashing into the office, waving at the dead surveillance camera. For once, a power failure had worked in their favor, and Bertrand wondered if the office's alarm system came back on when the streetlights popped back to life an hour later. A beautiful sunset painted high cirrus clouds pink and orange and finally red.

"You sure you can drive this?" Joyce belted herself into the passenger seat, her Uzi machine pistol on her knees. Emile had given her one quick lesson and four spare mags two weeks ago, but since then they'd lucked out into a house filled with boxes of ammo. Who had collected it and where that person went was a mystery.

"Well it's not exactly my GTI, but I'll do my best."

Bertrand had gotten a shotgun from Emile's stash to go along with his Glock.

"Nice choice, Bert," Emile had said, pumping the slide and checking the breach. "This is a Winchester 1200 defender. I don't know who sawed the barrel short and put on the pistol grip instead of the stock, but it makes it a good close-quarters-combat weapon, but it only takes five rounds cut short like this—still really good for up close and personal with bank security guards." He gave a smile. "I'm pretty confident it was never used in the commission of a felony, but I wasn't totally sure, which is why it ended up in the hot inventory."

"Why is the power up tonight?" Bertrand asked as he turned onto Sheffield to head back toward Old Town.

"Isn't it obvious? They need it for the streetlights, so that if people make a break for it from St. Mike's like they did that night at the community center, they won't be hidden by the dark. Clouds are moving in now." Joyce leaned to the side to look up through her window. "We may see some rain before long."

Bertrand changed gears, gaining speed although he occasionally had to weave around abandoned cars.

"You'll have to teach me how to drive a shift," said Joyce. "I don't like being a passenger."

"Think of me as your chauffeur. So you need to talk to Bobs anymore or do you think we're all good?"

Joyce checked her phone. "No texts. Bobs said she'd text if anything important changed. I'd love to know what that little psychopath thinks is important and what's not, but at this point we're going have to take it on faith. You think she has a brain?"

"Everybody agrees that she was the savior at community center, and the rippers must think she's important if they pulled out all the stops like this. They must be after her."

"But do they even know she's there? They could be after you."

"They know we're around somewhere. Maybe they're taking out the church just in case. Maybe they're after Father Alvarez, although you could hardly see him in that YouTube video, what with him going around back and all. Maybe the rippers are just starting to get really hungry."

"Here, Here! This is Eugene."

"Oh shoot, yeah." Bertrand heaved over on the big steering wheel, but they were going a bit fast for the corner and the truck bumped up the sidewalk and back down.

"Okay, wait, wait. Stop here." Joyce lowered her chin to speak into a walkie mic that she had clipped to her jacket. "Emile, you there?"

"Go for me." Emile's voice came through the walkie earpiece that Bertrand had in his ear.

"Let us know when you're in position and we'll go. Jeff?"

"Slight complication." The sound of arguing voices in the background caused Bertrand and Joyce to exchange a worried glance.

"What's going on?" asked Joyce.

"Mike is walking up the goddamn street. He wants to talk to the cops."

"What? How does he expect to get through all the rippers?"

"His badge."

"Shit, shit, shit!" Joyce looked like she wanted to punch the dashboard. "He's going to totally blow the element of surprise."

Bertrand ground the truck into gear. "Should I go?"

"No! Wait. We don't even know if the Erics people are here." She keyed the walkie mic again. "Everybody just hold on. I'm going to call Bobs."

Joyce pulled out her cell again and hit a speed dial. "Bobs? Joyce. Listen, our cop friend, Detective Sinclair, is walking up the street to try and talk to the cops. Don't shoot him as he comes through the rippers okay? What? Because he's got plainclothes cop written all over him: ten-year-old suit, dark overcoat, bald head, pot belly, okay? Tell your buddies not to shoot him."

"What if we're all wrong about him?" Bertrand drummed on the steering wheel with his fingers. He wanted to drive in and fight right now. His heart pounded in his chest, and the excitement was his new drug, that feeling of stress relief, of doing something to fight all that was going wrong. "What if he's bent too but he was spying on us all this time."

"He didn't come across that way to me, and he's shot a lot of rippers in the last two weeks. I'd say he's living in denial. He just doesn't want to admit that so many cops have gone over to the other side, are taking orders from bloody murderers."

"We should just push in now and fight."

"We will, but I just want to give him a second to see if they'll talk to him. Any delay gets us another minute closer to sunrise."

"But they were there in daylight."

"It's not the cops, it's the rippers I'm worried about. Bobs said the police line is pretty thin, which makes me think they're running short on daytime people. But behind the police line is a huge crowd—got to be rippers—mostly in front of the church. They must have planned this, because they're not from around here and they assembled pretty fast. They're waiting for an orgy of murder, otherwise they'd all be off getting their nightly feed somewhere safer."

Bertrand gunned the engine. He didn't want the air brakes locking just when they were ready to go. He flipped on the wipers to remove a light drizzle. "Hey, look!"

A man with a white armband came hurrying down the street. He ducked under the running lights and hurried up to Bertrand's side, waving and pointing to attract Bertrand's attention to the white band, which had the number 1000 scrawled across it with bold marker. When Bertrand nodded, the man grabbed a hold of the mirror and stepped up on the running board so that they could talk.

He was young—that was Bertrand's first thought as he rolled down the drizzle-coated window—shaving yes, voting maybe, legal drinking age ... no. Blue eyes, eager and excited, met Bertrand's.

"The 1000 live on," said the young man as his greeting. "I'm Murray—the captain soul. Are you Mr. Allan?"

"Yes, but dude, I thought there would be a hundred of you here."

"Closer to a hundred and fifty, but there are rippers everywhere so I've been keeping them in the basements and undercover. Don't worry, they're assembling in the laneways now, and I've been texted by B and C company captains. They're moving out behind your other trucks now. You scatter the rippers and deal with the cops, and we'll come in shooting. Do all your people have armbands?"

Bertrand held up his right arm to show off the white bandage he'd wrapped around it. Joyce had scrawled the number 1000 on it for him earlier, her minimal perfume teasing Bertrand's nostrils. He had averted his eyes so that she wouldn't think he was looking down her top while she wrote the number.

"Great." Murray jumped down and raised one fist in the air. "The 1000 live on! They can't kill our souls." He ran up the street and into an alley.

"Crap," said Bertrand.

"Are they going to be any good?" Joyce checked her phone for messages.

"They're going to be great because they think they're all immortal. I just hope they aren't too reckless."

"I'm calling Bobs. She must have someone in the church tower who can tell us what the hell is going on." Joyce focused on the phone. "Hi, yeah, so can you see what's going on? We're all ready here. Okay great."

Joyce looked over at Bertrand, relating what she was hearing over the phone. "The rippers let Mike through, he's right in front of the church holding up his badge. Okay, they're taking him into custody with a couple of swat-type guys. Right, that makes sense. Good. They're walking him to the command motor home in the northwest parking lot. No wait, they've stopped."

The dull crack of a gunshot reached Bertrand's ears.

"NO! Fuck! They just gut shot him and they're handing him to the crowd! GO! GO! GO! Everybody go!"

Bertrand popped the clutch as if it was his GTI and nearly stalled the truck, but after a few bumps and burps it rolled down the street, gaining speed fast. Parked cars and houses blurred past, the wet street reflecting the lights and making it obvious where the crowd waited.

"Not too fast, Bert." Joyce leaned forward so that she could look into the passenger side mirror. "Wait for a second so they can get in behind us. I think I see them."

Bertrand desperately wanted to charge to Sinclair's rescue, but he knew Joyce was right, so he geared down and applied the breaks, checking his side view mirror at the same time. The red light from the break lights illuminated dozens of people rushing into the street behind the truck.

"Here we go, Bert." Joyce checked her seat belt. "Whatever you do, remember to be ruthless and don't stop. They're multiple murderers and they're planning the massacre of hundreds of families, so you can't worry if a few of them end up as bugs on the radiator grill."

He had agreed with Joyce's plan of attack, but the reality of it dawned on him now. He'd have to repress years of driving instincts that demanded he not crush pedestrians.

"Right." He looked over, suddenly afraid for her. "Take care, right. I'd really be sorry if you weren't around."

Joyce turned her attention to Bertrand for a moment, her cheeks slightly red in the dashboard lights. "Likewise." Her cheeks got redder. "I mean about you. I'd really miss you, so just don't get shot."

Hundreds of human shapes hung out on the street ahead as if waiting for a rock concert to begin. A quick check of the mirror proved that the Erics people now ran in two lines behind the coasting truck.

Several faces in the crowd—made paler by the headlights—turned Bertrand's way.

"Now!" shouted Joyce into her walkie and to Bertrand. "Everyone give it all you got, now!"

Bertrand changed gears and flattened the accelerator. The truck's diesel engine roared as they rushed the crowd. Too late, the rippers realized that Bertrand had no intention of stopping, and at the last second panic ensued as they trampled one another to get off the street. One man waited too long, his wild eyes bright in the headlights—a true Mohawk and garish jewelry proclaiming him a counter-culture rebel. He disappeared below the hood, and the truck didn't even bump.

A skirmish in the parking lot on Bertrand's left caught his attention—rippers fighting at one another for a piece of a victim, unaware of the new threat. "There!" he shouted, turning into the parking lot. Faces now turned their way as the headlights yanked their attention. They looked so normal, some even surprised, others angry.

"Don't you dare stop, Bert. Mike's dead. You go for that command bus! You stick to the plan."

Bertrand wanted to stop, to get out shouting and clear them away from Sinclair, but she was right. He screamed in rage and frustration as they passed close to the frenzy. More rippers got in the way, but Bertrand repressed the urge to swerve and plowed right through, several bodies slamming off the grill of the truck, and judging by a bump, at least one fell underneath. Machine gun fire rattled out, and Bertrand heard it through his earpiece and through his unaided ear in a weird stereo. Someone with an open walkie mic was already shooting.

"Here we go!" Bertrand shouted, slamming on the brakes too late. The tires locked and slid on the wet pavement, and the truck carried on without stopping. One officer opened the door of the mobile command center, saw them coming and ducked back inside, slamming the door as if it could protect him from the truck. Bertrand burst out laughing at the absurdity, at his fear and the cop's, at how they were about to affect each other's lives so dramatically even though they'd never met.

The truck smashed into the command mobile home, glass shattering and metal rending, the five-ton pushing the mobile unit several feet farther into the parking lot. The seat belt strap snagged Bertrand's shoulder and the air bag exploded into his face. He lurched out of the air bag and looked over at Joyce, who gave him one wild glance and reached for her seat belt.

"Remember they're murders!" shouted Joyce at Bertrand and into her walkie. "Go! Go! Go!"

She jumped from her side of the truck and Bertrand jumped from his, the Winchester in his hand. He pumped a round into the chamber before smashing a small window in the command center— a window higher than his head—with the barrel of his gun. He tossed in a tear gas canister, one from Emile's 'hot' supply under Helen's flowers.

Gunshots, three round bursts, came from the other side of their five-ton.

"Joyce!" he shouted, forgetting the walkie. He turned.

The rippers came at them, some shooting wildly and others just running. Bertrand pulled the trigger, the pistol grip slamming his hand and the barrel leaping into the air, causing him to pump a new round into the chamber, just like it had during his practice shots. He fired again at the hopeless onslaught. If the Erics people didn't attack now he would die, but not without a fight.

Shooting—a lot of it—erupted from the street where Bertrand had cut a path through the rippers. The crowd of rippers slowed, several looking back to see what was going on now. They could see what Bertrand could: muzzle flashes lit up the square like bolts of lightning. Murray and his company had used the confusion and the path cut by the truck to charge into the rippers.

"It all has to be close quarters or we'll kill one another," Joyce had said when they were planning. "You have to see who you're shooting. Like Emile always says, it can't just be spray and pray."

Well, this was close. Elation, fear and relief, they all washed through Bertrand, freeing him from convention, from years of early childhood learning that had conditioned him to never kill. He pulled the trigger and a college-aged student with a bloody mouth and a red knife fell. Bertrand pumped the gun and ran forward a few steps to the back of the truck, checking his white arm band to make sure it was obvious. He prayed that one of Erics' guys wouldn't shoot him by mistake. He fired at a middle-aged man who could have been out taking his dog for a walk in this neighborhood if he didn't look so crazed and angry.

Bertrand was supercharged. He was invincible. He was a hero.

Muzzle flashes came from the church's bell tower and from near the roof—snipers that Bobs or Father Alvarez had somehow placed in the upper windows. Had they broken any of the stained glass in order to shoot? Did it matter?

Cops dropped their riot shields and ran, not making any attempt now to pretend they had more authority than the mob. Some of the cops even turned on their fellows with knives, bringing them down to drink blood. Bertrand put his shotgun to one rogue cop, 'passing lead,' as Bobs would call it, through the riot helmet and the brain. The cop underneath him had clamped a hand against his own throat, staunching the wound, but Bertrand could see it hadn't cut a major artery, because there wasn't enough blood spewing.

Bertrand bent over and shouted, "Do you really want to be with them? Your buddy just tried to cut your throat!"

Wild eyes met Bertrand's, the cop taking shallow, frightened breaths. He shook his head.

"Then stay down until this is over!" he shouted, as he frantically fed more rounds into the shotgun.

"Bert! Over here!"

Joyce had moved from the back of the truck, like Bertrand seeking out and shooting anyone who came near her, but now she turned. Bertrand ran to join her and look in the same direction, back toward the mobile command center. A heavyset man kicked at the windshield from inside the vehicle, unable to open the door because of the damage caused by the five-ton. He jumped out with more agility than Bertrand had expected, given the man's weight, but when he turned their way, the explanation became obvious. Blood coated his puffy cheeks, and a knife flashed in one hand. He had a uniform on, a white shirt with military embellishments and dress pants.

"Ripper!" shouted Bertrand.

The man shouted back—an incoherent roar—and charged. He took the hits to his chest from both the shotgun and the machine pistol, yet still he came at them, forcing Joyce and Bertrand to skip back several steps. Bertrand pumped the shotgun and fired another round, taking the officer in the face and blowing brains out the back of his skull.

The man's momentum carried him until he fell flat onto his face in between them, both stepping aside and tracking him down to the ground with their weapons.

"What the fuck?" said Joyce, panting for breath. "That was totally superhuman. I didn't see any of the others take hits like that and keep moving. Quick, let's finish off that command post."

They ran to the windshield of the mobile command center, but tear gas had turned the inside of the vehicle into a gray cloud. No one emerged coughing, in fact no one sounded like they were reacting to the tear gas at all. It was as silent inside as a tomb.

"Can't go in there now," shouted Bertrand, the excitement still coursing through him. He turned back to the parking lot and the street, but the crowd of rippers had vanished, leaving behind dark lumps on the pavement, some of which crawled or cried, giving the pavement a rippling look, as if a restless sea. People with white armbands now patrolled the corpses and occasionally discharged a firearm at point-blank to end one of the rippers forever.

"Sir, please!" shouted the cop that Bertrand had saved. He still lay on the ground, wisely not rising to attract the attentions of the Erics patrols. "Can I surrender to you? I'm begging you. I've a wife and kids." Clearly he saw that no one was taking prisoners.

Bertrand wanted to move deeper into the parking lot and the street to kill more of the rippers who had so torn apart his world, but he forced his breathing to calm, his heartbeat to slow. He must think clearly.

"Help me with this guy," he said to Joyce. "A ripper cop cut him, but I think we can save him."

"Should we?"

"For Mike Sinclair. I'll save him in memory of Mike."

# 24

# THE HERO

The chant—more like a repetitive shout—that greeted Bertrand at the entrance to the church at sunrise was deafening. Crowds jammed the pews and the side-aisles, leaving only the main aisle free for Bertrand's passage to the front of the church.

"Bertrand! Bertrand!"

He turned to the others, not wanting to enter the church. "What the fuck? I didn't save them. I was just one guy. If they should be shouting for anyone it should be for Joyce, who planned it, or Erics, who gave us the numbers to make it work, or hey, what about Mike Sinclair, who died trying to save them single-handed without firing a shot?"

Father Alvarez stood with him on the steps, his cassock disturbed by a cold wind that promised to bring more than drizzle. "You must understand," he said. "Roberta told many about how you were the only one brave enough to go hunting in the dark for rippers, about how you saved her even when she was surrounded."

He took Bertrand's hand in both of his, enveloping it. "People were very afraid last night. Many gave themselves up to God and even some of those who were not Catholic begged for confession, but the hope that spread throughout the church was that you would come. Many watched your videos exhorting people to fight, watched the video of your rescue of Roberta and Terry. Many in the church were rescued by your Raiders. Many prayed that you would have the strength, and here you are, their hero."

It was Jeff, however, who convinced Bertrand to go in. "Dude," he said as he climbed the steps to stand before Bertrand. Jeff had blood on his face from a scrape on his forehead, his jacket had stuffing protruding from under his right arm due to a near miss by a bullet.

"Timetracks, how can I make your day easier?" said Bertrand, repeating their usual call script.

Jeff began to laugh, weariness falling aside, and to Bertrand's surprise—maybe to Jeff's too—they embraced, pounding each other on the back.

"Oh dude," said Bertrand when they stood awkwardly apart. "I so thought we were toast that time. I guess all those years playing Call of Duty weren't a total waste."

They both laughed, because the video game had done nothing to prepare them for real combat. Bertrand had to suppress memories that flashed before him, the startled face of the first man he ran down with the truck; shooting the ripper cop several times to kill him; finding Mike Sinclair's body and listening to his last words as he bled out: "Had to try. Sorry—failed. Glad you're here. Like to see sunrise." The only other person Bertrand had seen who had looked so pale was the first ripper victim he and Joyce had found three months ago.

Mike Sinclair's body now lay beside the statue of St. Michael, the weak sun ensuring that he wasn't infected with the parasites. He would not be a ripper.

"Bert," said Jeff when their laughter had chopped short, perhaps because Bertrand had looked back at Mike's body. "You gotta go in. They were promised a hero last night and they got more than they know how to thank. Even the Erics people can't stop talking about you, and some of them are in the church too."

"But I'm not the only hero here."

"No, but your face warning people in McDonald's is the face that went viral; you're the face that people have watched over the last couple of weeks urging them to fight, and right now they need the simplicity of a hero. Go in. Give them a short speech like you did in McDonald's, or like you do in those vids that Terry's always posting, and then lets have a drink to celebrate the living and remember the dead." It was Jeff's turn to look down the stairs and back to Mike's bloodied body.

"We've got a lot of work to do." Bertrand shook his head.

"Then that's what you tell them."

Father Alvarez led Bertrand up the aisle, Joyce and Jeff not far behind. At the front of the church Bobs and Terry waited like a groom and his best man, but Bobs wore a sweat-stained white T-shirt and had an AR-15 slung over her shoulder. The church, despite the cold outside, was quite hot, the huge crowds now making up for the boiler's stops and starts caused by the power fluctuations.

"Thanks for coming and bringing an army," Bobs shouted so that Bertrand could hear her over the crowd. Bertrand resisted the urge to pat her on the head. Could this little elfin waif really be so violent? Father Alvarez had said that it was Bobs who had organized and led the snipers, and when Bertrand had attacked, Bobs had led her little army in a sortie out of the church to join the slaughter and help rout the rippers. Bobs yelled something else, and Bertrand bent his ear close to her lips so that she could repeat it.

"Talk them down. Then we got to get raiding. A lot of them must've gone into basements in our hood to beat the sun." She waved to the pulpit.

Bertrand climbed the stairs more afraid than he had been all night. What to say? There must be a thousand people, chanting as if he were a rock star. Yet a calmness rose up, a strength that he'd have thought impossible even just yesterday. It was almost as if a little voice had whispered, "You're the rock star."

He raised both fists, arms out from his sides at forty-five degree angles.

They cheered. A roaring cheer that only an amplified microphone could silence, but still Bertrand had to shout into it to be heard.

"Last night!" More cheering. "Last night we took back Old Town!"

The crowd screamed, and Bertrand took a moment to take in the sea of faces, all races, all ages, all hopeful.

"But our work has just begun. The rippers are everywhere."

That settled the crowd a bit, because that was not news to cheer.

"The rippers are in Washington, in Springfield, in our own city hall." He put out his hands again to quell the shouts of agreement, the anger at the government. "It is time to take back our city, our state and our country."

The crowd exploded in cheers, but Bertrand again held out his hands to quiet.

"This will not be an easy task, but it is the task that our generation has been called upon to perform. Some ... some will lament that we see these evil days, but I say thank God that we can take on this task and spare our children from this burden. I say thank God that we have been entrusted with so important a mission, so important a war that in generations to come they will look back on this day and wish they had been here in this church at this moment, will hope that they would have been brave enough and strong enough to do what we must now do. They will call us a great generation!"

Again the cheers were deafening, and Bertrand remembered Bobs' words: *Talk them down.*

"But now we are here, and the road ahead will not be an easy one. It is a dangerous road, one that will bring disasters as well as triumphs, that will bring tears and pain as well as joy and victory. We must travel this road now, and I promise you that we will lose friends and family members on this journey, but we will save millions. Our blood will be spilled, but not to feed the rippers!"

The crowd still cheered.

"Today," said Bertrand. "Today we must work and fight so that tonight we will not fear. Today we continue the struggle, and when you are downhearted and hungry and tired and afraid, remember this day.

Remember that we were victorious. We saved this church. We saved the people of Old Town, and we will save our city, our state and our country."

The crowd again roared—even louder.

"So today we must begin. I know you're all tired, but now we must act. Old Town now has many rippers hiding in basements because they can't bear the light. Today we must drag them out into the light!"

More cheers proved that he didn't know how to calm them.

"Today we must insure that the corrupt government of our city can't send police to arrest us and hand us over to the rippers like they did with Detective Mike Sinclair!"

Bertrand couldn't help himself. He couldn't think of anything to say that was calming, that would really allow them to go to work. A movement caught his peripheral vision, and he turned to see Father Alvarez moving to the stairs of the pulpit. Bertrand seized the chance, hurrying down the stairs and waving Alvarez up.

"Now," said Alvarez, his manner calm and practiced, the pulpit his home. "Now we must give thanks for the miracle of last night, for our rescue. In the name of the Father, and the son and the holy spirit."

Bertrand stood beside Joyce, his hands clasped together and his head bowed, but rather than prayer his thoughts were with Joyce. Would she ever consider standing at an altar with him for a happier purpose? Would she marry him? For last night, as she'd leapt from her side of the truck, he knew he wanted not to just get laid, but to be with her, to have children with her. Out of the corner of his eye he watched her pray, memorizing every curve, the blood smudged on her cheek, every imperfection that made her beautiful—that made her Joyce.

———

Father Alvarez ushered them into his meeting room, the carpets a deep red, the carved crucifix large and gaunt. Even as they sat, Helen arrived with food and assistants, younger boys and girls eager to help but too young to carry guns. Bertrand's stomach growled as the plates of scrambled eggs hit the tables, the children dispensing knives and forks, glasses for water and mugs for coffee.

"The eggs are powdered." Helen slapped a spoonful on Bertrand's plate. "But I guess we should be happy that we've at least got that."

Father Alvarez sat at the head of the table, Bertrand to his right. Several other church leaders had wanted to join this meeting, but Alvarez had conspicuously cut them out, promising a later meeting.

"This is a meeting about war, not God's work," he had said to one gray haired gentleman before closing the door.

Bertrand found it interesting who Alvarez did allow to this meeting.

Whitlock was there, looking as military trim as always. He'd served with Jeff's company, and being ex-marine had performed very well, but he didn't look comfortable. Was it because few people here were military? Was it because he wasn't Catholic?

Bobs sat to Father Alvarez's left, but her friend Terry wasn't there.

"Got him doing other things," was all Bobs said as she sat to eat.

Barry St. John and Martin Morley sat side-by-side at the far end of the table, a contrast of different ethnic origins and body types, and yet the two men seemed cut from the same practical cloth, and they shared their own stories of the night's battle as they ate.

Emile was here, but whether it was because he'd been the leader of the third company or because Helen wanted him there for breakfast, Bertrand didn't know. Simon Gonsalves and Julia Chen were there, perhaps because Alvarez wanted honest police represented as a tribute to Mike Sinclair's sacrifice.

The chatter over breakfast was unlike anything Bertrand had ever heard before the rippers, but it was what he had become used to during the last two weeks of going out with Joyce's Raiders.

"One guy took three bullets—"

"I took one out with a headshot and that worked right away—dropped like a stone."

"I guess the parasites can't rebuild brain cells."

"Then Emile came around the corner of the truck—"

"So this Erics guy says something about the 1000 live on and gives us this weird fist-in-the-air salute."

That last comment caught Bertrand's attention. Where were representatives of the Erics companies? Surely they were the real saviors of last night, providing over three hundred fighters. Where was that company leader Bertrand had met? Murray, that was his name. Why hadn't Alvarez invited Murray to this meeting?

For their part, Jeff and Joyce had elected to skip the meeting and talk with the Raiders to find out who had done well, who had died and who could be trusted as a lieutenant.

Father Alvarez insisted on leading grace before the meal and a thanksgiving prayer after. Bertrand was happy that he got the sign of the cross correct the second time, watching the priest out of the corner of his eye to make sure.

"Once again," Alvarez said when he'd finished his prayer. "I thank you all for the miracle of last night, but as Bertrand said, we must forego sleep today to ensure we're ready for tonight."

Helen sat and lit a cigarette while he was speaking. Alvarez raised his eyebrows but didn't comment. She blew a smoke ring into the air and spoke before anyone else had a chance. "You also need to think about how you're going to feed all these people. There's a lot of volunteers down there in the basement willing to cook, but the grocery store shelves are empty, and from what I saw last night, I don't think that's going to change anytime soon. What's odd is that over the last few weeks, I've noticed the grocery store shelves had been emptying over night. I wonder why the hell the rippers are taking food?"

"We'll go farther with our house-to-house searches later in the week." Bobs looked as if she'd had a full night's sleep. Her blonde hair was combed straight, her cheeks clean and she'd changed from the T-shirt into a white blouse. She could have gone to college today and no one would have guessed that she had been in a battle.

Helen nodded and blew another smoke ring high into the air, perhaps as an attempt to minimize the secondhand smoke. "That's a good idea, but you'll need to remember we've got a whole winter ahead. There should be a lot of canned food out there somewhere."

"We'll search for rippers and food." Bobs leaned forward and clasped her hands together, looking eager to get to work. "But first we need to clear out each basement within a mile of the church, purge the rippers that got away from our neighborhood before dark. By tonight we need to block the roads and laneways in a ring around us with buses and concrete barriers and whatever, so that the police can't get cars or urban assault vehicles or anything else down here. Rippers can't fly like frigging vampires, and I bet they hate walking just as much as the rest of us."

Bertrand looked to Whitlock, the only one with actual military training. "What do you think, John?"

Whitlock looked into his mug and then looked up at Bobs. "I think you should put her in charge. It's all really good."

Whitlock had witnessed Bobs lead over a hundred from the church into the fight, and earlier he had spoken to Bertrand of her with awe. "As cool under fire as any marine I've ever seen," he had said.

Father Alvarez nodded his agreement. "Roberta has certainly earned the loyalty of many, but let's not speak about leaders or command structure today. We have too much to do." He stood, his hands still on the table as he regarded each in their turn while he spoke. "I propose that we divide up the neighborhood and begin the house-to-house search immediately. I have older church members in the basement with a large city map now: they are too old for fighting but are eager to help by coordinating our efforts. Break yourselves into groups of three or four people—that's all you need for a basement—and select a route, making sure you tell our volunteers."

"Except for Barry," said Bobs, looking up at the priest.

"Ah, yes. Mr. St. John, I believe you are in construction. If we might have a word, we have a task for you."

Bertrand looked across at Whitlock—his old boss—to see how he felt about being bossed around by a priest and his barely twenty-year-old sidekick, but Whitlock was nodding his agreement. Religion and old hierarchies had vanished out of necessity.

"Right," said Bertrand. "I'm going with Jeff, Joyce, and I'm going right now. Only ten hours till sunset."

Everyone stood.

---

It was Joyce's turn to go into the basement first, but it was Bertrand's house.

"Come on," Bertrand said. "I know every nook and cranny. It only makes sense for me to go first."

Joyce nodded her grudging consent and stepped aside. Tear gas didn't work on the rippers the way it worked on humans, or they would simply toss one of Emile's canisters into the basement and wait to see if anyone came out. Bertrand headed down the stairs, his shotgun leading the way as he searched for targets, although because the windows hadn't been covered, he thought it unlikely.

He fought to desire to lie down on his bed for just a minute, even in its rumpled state. How long ago had he moved it down here thinking that he could be safe with bars on the windows? Three months? It seemed a lifetime ago.

The furnace room was his destination, the last place they'd seen his former fellow employee, Malcolm. The door stood open a crack, the first clue that there were no rippers inside. Still, Bertrand pulled the door open and stepped back quickly, the shotgun aimed into the dark. The power had been off since midday, but enough light leaked through the west-facing windows of Bertrand's basement that it was easy to see that the little room was empty, that the handcuffs and Malcolm were long gone.

But there was something new, very new. It was a letter taped to the gas pipe where Malcolm had been handcuffed. Bertrand's name had been inscribed on the envelope by a penman so masterful that it bordered on calligraphy, and the 'mister' was spelled out in full: **Mister Bertrand Allan.**

"What the fuck?" said Joyce.

Bertrand tore into the envelope to find a crisp sheet of quality paper with more of the same great penmanship. It was dated November 10th—yesterday.

"Dear Mr. Allan," Bertrand read aloud for Joyce and Jeff. "I salute your victories and applaud your desire to ally yourself with the Church. You have proven the most worthy adversary I have encountered since arriving on this new continent, and it is refreshing to meet a man who will sacrifice all for the most holy members of the Church. In my time we valued men like you. It is my hope that we should meet before long, for I would talk with you. Alas, I know that if we were to meet face-to-face you would make every effort to end my life—as you should. So that we may talk without fear of attack, I have arranged for a Skype account. Please feel free to call me tonight, or any other night. My preference is three a.m., but I will have someone at my computer in case you prefer another appointment. I will arrange for the power to be on all night."

Jeff had walked over to glance out the windows into the street—his height allowing him an easy view out the ground level windows—but he turned sharply at the last statement. "He will arrange for the power to be on. He can do that? He has that much control of power stations, the grid, the government?"

Jeff's phone trilled, causing him to raise his eyebrows in surprise. "I guess the power's back on. Hello ... hello can you hear me. Yeah, no, I've got a bad signal. Wait, wait, I'll get out of the basement." He headed up the stairs, switching on the basement lights on his way up and proving that the power had indeed come back on.

Bertrand stared at the letter, trying not to show how disheartened he was by this letter. Remember you're tired, he thought. You're very, very tired. He didn't want to read out the signature, but Joyce was already reading it over his shoulder.

"Vlad the Scourge," she said. "Oh my God, this guy is a complete nutcase."

"One with a lot of followers. One thing I still don't get, if this is happening all over the world—and sure looks like that—how could this guy be doing it all. He wrote this letter sometime before dawn this morning.

He was right in this room unless he sent someone else to deliver it, but he sure as hell couldn't have been far away, so I gotta wonder, how can he be the mastermind? I mean someone's got to be spearheading this thing in England, France, hell the whole continent of Africa or Asia, Australia. The world's a big place."

"Maybe it was well planned." Joyce closed the door to the furnace room just as the forced-air gas heating kicked on. "Maybe he recruited people a bit at a time, building up numbers until he was ready and then sent them out into the world to do ... whatever it is they're doing. Spreading the disease? The scourge?"

Bertrand folded the letter and stuffed it into his inner jacket pocket. "It's getting late. We should clear up this street and head back to the church."

"Not tonight," called Jeff. "I talked to Emile earlier and he says it's completely packed. Bobs and he and a bunch of others are setting up in blockhouses, one at each corner of the compass from the church. Barry and some other construction types have been hard at work today, bull-dozing most of a couple of streets, apparently to create fields of fire and lines of sight."

"Wow." Joyce shook her head in amazement. "I mean, what can you say but wow. And the police didn't even bother to come around?"

"After last night I wonder how many daytime cops there are." Bertrand led the way out of the basement. "I just keep thinking about that command center."

After the tear gas had cleared out of the mobile unit, Bertrand had backed up the five-ton so that they could open the door. Joyce had gone in first and found bodies in uniform and plainclothes, policemen and woman who had been at work when Bertrand rammed the command center, but none of them looked as if they had died from the accident. There were gashes and hurts that could be attributed to the crash, but each corpse had had their throats cut, and all had clearly been bled out. It was the scene of a massacre by a powerful ripper.

"That police chief," Joyce had said. "The one Bertrand and I had so much trouble putting down. He did this rather than let them fall into our hands."

Jeff's voice brought Bertrand back to the present and dispelled the memory of the corpses. "Hey Bert, there's still beer in your fridge, and it's actually pretty cold—here." Jeff passed them both brown bottles.

They sat in the red booth in Bertrand's kitchen, Joyce's elbow just touching Bertrand's on the table. He found himself very aware of that touch, and wondered if she was oblivious or aware of his passion.

"To a moment of sanity." Jeff raised his bottle. "Now if only we had some chicken wings it would feel like old times."

Bertrand relished the cold fluid flowing down his throat, but he knew it would only make him sleepier. "Seems like a hundred years ago, doesn't it? If you told me last summer when I started at Timetracks that you I would be packing heat and doing house-to-house searches up the street for vampires, I'd have told you that you were smoking too much weed."

"If you'd told me all these houses would be empty," said Joyce, "I'd have told you that was impossible. How many do you think have died? We haven't come across a single living soul, ripper or human, all day."

Bertrand had wondered about that ever since he and Father Alvarez had dumped the teens' bodies. "I'm hoping that a lot of people did like Barry was planning to do, headed for the hills."

"But Barry's still here." Jeff pointed the top of his beer bottle at Bertrand.

"Only because he couldn't get out and then found out the border to Canada has been closed. There're a lot of places people could have gone, like Martin's family who got out early and are hiding at their cabin in Wisconsin." But the hand sticking out of the shallow grave on the beach flashed through Bertrand's memory. "But I admit it's got to be in the thousands. I could write a program to figure it out, but I'd have to know how many rippers we started with and when."

"The first Chicago Ripper murder I remember was right after Christmas last year," said Joyce. "That's when I bought my Taser."

"How many rippers did we start with?" Bertrand's question was rhetorical. "Vampires have been with us in legend for centuries, but they're supposed to be lone stalkers, so I guess the big question is what changed?"

"Red-eye jet schedules?" Jeff took a sip of his beer while he pondered. "Hell, for all we know it could be sunspots."

"Remember that guy, the one in the garage that we interrogated." Bertrand's ears burned self-consciously. He was still uncomfortable with being an 'interrogator.' It made him think of waterboarding.

"Yeah, the one who tried to kill Bobs," said Jeff. "The one you guys fried with the sun."

"What struck me was that he said we'd *want* to go into camps controlled by rippers, to protect us from rogue rippers. He said some of them don't adapt well to being rippers, that they prefer to hunt alone and don't take orders from ... whoever ... this Vlad guy I guess."

Jeff's phone chimed. "Sorry guys, it's Emile again. Hi yeah? Hang on." He looked up. "He's inviting us to spend the night in his blockhouse, says they've got the ground-floor windows bricked in, a new steel door taken from Home Depot, the works. Alvarez says they need every person they can to man these outlying forts. There's a bunch of them. You in?"

Bertrand shook his head. "I'm going to stay in Nolan's bunker again tonight. I've kinda turned his computer into mine, loaded my e-mail settings and stuff. I think I'm going to talk to this Vlad the Scourge tonight, and I want to get in touch with Erics."

"You shouldn't stay alone. Is the regular crowd staying there?" Joyce looked as exhausted as Bertrand felt, in fact Bertrand had wondered if she had been nodding off over her beer, for she looked as if she'd just been shaken awake.

Jeff shook his head. "Emile says that everyone's going to stay in these blockhouses to cover the church. Helen's going to be feeding the crowd there tonight." Jeff looked from Bertrand to Joyce. "Why don't you guys take a night off? You both look totally bagged." He turned back to his phone. "Hey Emile, I'm going to join you guys. I've still got my Ruger, but have you got any rifles I could use? Great. No, don't worry about Joyce and Bertrand, don't want to say over the phone, but they're good. See you in a bit."

He stood and pulled a couple of beers out of the fridge and slipped them into his coat pockets. "For the road," he said with a grin.

"Why don't you come with us?" asked Joyce.

Bertrand's heart sank just a little. The idea of spending a night alone with Joyce produced a rapid succession of erotic images, but there was no danger of an unwanted erection right now. He was just too tired. He did, however, fear that Joyce's concern was that she didn't want to be alone with him—didn't want him to make a pass at her. Well fine, he wouldn't. He needed her as a friend and a comrade-in-arms more than as a lover, but still, it irked that she wasn't interested in him. Had she guessed he'd fallen in love?

Jeff retrieved his open beer from the table but didn't sit. "Thanks for invite. But I left my laptop back at the church with Father Alvarez, and if the power really is up, I want to do some surfing to see if I can find out when this all began and see if we can guess where it's going."

"Listen." Bertrand stood now, also going for the fridge and the last four beers, handing two to Joyce for her pockets and pocketing the others. "You call us from Emile's before sunset so that we know you're good, and vice versa. Cool?"

Jeff presented his fist and they knocked knuckles. "Get some sleep before you talk to Mr. Anti-Christ."

No one laughed.

# 25

# NIGHT AT THE BOMB SHELTER

D inner was romantic but the food was basic. Bertrand had boiled
some pasta in Nolan's kitchen and found a jar of prepared spaghetti sauce—a meat and herb combination that wasn't bad for processed
food. Joyce found some apples in the bottom of a pantry cupboard, and
two of them were still okay, so she sliced them for desert. It was odd being in the house alone, but it was also a relief not to be jostling elbows
for the first time in a two weeks. The sunset out the back window was a
spectacular red, and they both commented that it was the most beautiful they had ever witnessed.

They did have a bottle of red wine, and they ate by candlelight even
though the power was still on, keeping the house dark just in case the
rippers, or just a rogue ripper, happened to pass down the street. Who
knows how many from last night were roving their neighborhood, starving because the promised massacre at the church had been reversed?

They talked trivialities, inanities about their former lives, things
that would have been important a few months ago but had been buried
by recent events. Joyce spoke again of being raised by her aunt, then,

before turning sixteen, losing her to the same disease that had taken her mother.

"My dad wasn't a bad guy, but after Mom died he really didn't pay me much attention. He never got married again, but he was always on the make, whether it was selling a house or bedding the owner if she was hot. He loved divorce cases, you know when people were selling the house to split the assets. He got laid a lot with angry divorcees."

"And he told you this?" Bertrand poured more wine for her and then him. He wasn't trying to get her drunk and doubted that alcohol would change her mind about love. She was still all bristles and points.

"Oh no. We never talked much. Aunt Rach told me about him. I guess maybe she shouldn't have, but when she was on the morphine near the end a lot slipped out that probably shouldn't have. Dad pretty much never came to see her when she was sick, so I imagine that didn't go over well for her either."

"Bummer. But I thought you said your dad was dead too?"

"One too many drinks and his car finished him." She had a gulp of wine and returned to her pasta as if it was the most important thing in the world.

"Oh, right, I remember. I'm really sorry." Bertrand cursed inwardly that he'd brought up her unhappy childhood. What had he been thinking? Must be the booze— his head did have the haze of a good drunk after a few beers on an empty stomach.

"I'm not so much." Joyce twirled spaghetti onto her spoon, still turning long after it was ready for eating. "He always poked fun at me because of my weight, and it got worse after Aunt Rach died. He'd say things like: how's my little porker today?" She shoved the pasta into her mouth.

"What a bastard."

Joyce finished chewing before she replied. "He was, and not just to me. I don't remember what he was like with Mom, but he was a creep to me. I used to just eat more to get back at him, and I knew it was self-destructive and all. I just felt like I had no reason to exist, no challenge, and that went on for a year or so after he died. But then I was stuffing my face in the cafeteria at college one day as the cheerleaders went by, and I thought, fuck it. I'm as hot as they are, and now that Dad's gone I can just let it out. I signed up for my first fitness class the same evening and I've never looked back."

"Well you sure are hot now." Son-of-a-bitch. It must be the booze. Why the hell else would he say that out loud? She'd think he was making a pass at her. Bertrand braced for that angry glare, but Joyce actually smiled, meeting his gaze while she chewed another mouthful.

"You've done really well over the last few months, Bert. Even before the rippers, you must've lost twenty pounds, but I'd say you've lost another twenty just in the last month."

Bertrand's ears burned, but he straightened his shoulders, the alcohol inspiring him to puff out his chest. "I've been forced into a less sedentary job with lighter meals, but the hours suck."

They both laughed, but it quickly trailed off.

"So what about you?" said Joyce, the wine glass teasing her lips, her pasta complete. "Must've been a bummer when your folks died."

"Total, complete, devastating bummer. I was just hanging around after they died, trying to move on but not wanting to let go. Stayed in the same house, but one day I got crazy and reno'd the kitchen. It cost me a fortune, but I didn't care, because I wanted to change something but I didn't want to leave. Never went into my parents' bedroom except to dust now and then, until the night Destiny got all naked and tried to coax me in. Seeing her in my parents' bed was a complete turn off, by the way."

"You're not like my dad then. He'd have banged her on top of my mom's coffin if he'd had half the chance. My shrink used to say I should give him a break, that maybe sex was his way of dealing with grief, but I say bullshit. He didn't have that much grief."

Bertrand wondered what look he had on his face, because she suddenly met his eye and froze.

"Sorry," she said. "On about my dad again." She took a drink of wine, but Bertrand kept his mouth shut, sensing that she wasn't finished. "My shrink also said it's had a negative effect on my ability to form relationships with men." She studied her empty pasta plate now, her wine glass still close to her lips, ready to fortify her nerve. "She said that until I move on, past my dad I mean, I'll never deeply bond with another man." She let the silence hang.

"Well you made friends with me and Jeff, and we're both men."

"Yeah I did. It felt right, didn't it? Like fate, like we were meant to be a team."

"We make a good team." Bertrand reached for the wine bottle, but as he held it up he discovered it was empty. "Oops. I think I've had enough."

Joyce drained her glass. "Me too. Let's retire to the bunker and get some sleep before you call Mr. Anti-Christ. I am deeply and completely bagged. But Bert, I haven't forgotten that you asked me out for Thanksgiving. I still intend to keep that date."

Bertrand smiled, delighted that she remembered. "Me too."

They left the paper plates and cups they had used in order to save time on doing dishes. Bertrand had ceased to worry about landfills full of garbage—full of bodies, yes, he worried about that, but not garbage.

"So is there really ventilation down here?" Joyce had gripped the pull bar on the bomb shelter's door, but waited for an answer before closing it.

"Yeah, Nolan had to cut through a foot or so of concrete to put in a connection to the furnace. The other bomb shelter builders had some little pipe going to the surface and a pump to run it, but Nolan wanted heat and wasn't worried about nuclear fall out."

Joyce shoved the door closed and shot the bolts. "Still seems pretty cold in here." She had her Uzi slung over her shoulder, but she took it off and hung it by the sling from one of Nolan's gun racks. "I'm so keeping that forever," she said before turning away from the gun.

Bertrand took off the holster and his Glock, wondering how much more he should take off before bed: his shirt? His jeans? It wasn't as warm in here as the rest of the house, granted, but it wasn't that cold. Perhaps that was Joyce's way of telling him to keep his clothes on. He fought to keep the look of disappointment off his face, knowing that alcohol often reduced the barrier between thought and expression.

"Well it is a bit of a tomb, but we've got the sleeping bags so we should be good." He sat on the left-hand couch, unzipping the sleeping bag so that he could use it as a quilt rather than squeezing inside. Joyce did the same, but to Bertrand's surprise she got up and moved behind the right-hand couch, shoving it toward Bertrand's, forcing him to lift his legs so that they wouldn't get crunched.

"What the—" He looked up, hopeful but confused as to why she was turning the two couches into a double bed.

Joyce's cheeks flamed red and she didn't meet his eyes, looking instead at her sleeping bag as she opened it up. "It'll be warmer if we're close together."

Bertrand nodded, trying to find words that would make this sound normal, like he didn't feel an erection rising in his jeans to press urgently for freedom. "Yeah. It'll be good if it gets cold."

Joyce reached for the pull string of the light and snapped it off, plunging them into a complete blackness. Now the world only existed in sounds and touch, for no light penetrated the concrete and steel.

Bertrand listened with growing hope and alarm. What should he do, just go to sleep? What did she want or expect of him? The zipper going down spurred Bertrand's imagination: she was undoing her jeans. Clothing slid to floor, and feet stepped over the back onto the right-hand couch—Joyce's couch. Old springs creaked as she slipped under her sleeping bag, already opened and ready for her.

"Good night, Bert," she said, and more creaking hinted that she'd turned on her side, her back to him judging by the sound of her breath as she sighed in relief to be going to sleep.

Bertrand lay back for a moment to swallow disappointment. What had he expected anyway, to get laid even though they lived in the middle of an apocalypse? But she had taken off her jeans, he was sure of that, and he didn't relish sleeping in his, especially with the erection that wouldn't die. He undid his belt, the buckle clinking to announce his actions. Joyce didn't say anything, so he unzipped them and slipped them down, tossing them off the end of the couch. Fuck it, he'd lose the shirt too, because he preferred sleeping in his underwear. He sat up and yanked the shirt over his head, tossing it in the direction of his jeans. Sure, she might see him in his boxers in the morning, but this had been his personal trainer. She knew his body better than any woman alive, the size of his love handles, the turn of his shoulders—she knew it all. It just didn't matter. He turned on his side, his back to Joyce, and let the exhaustion bury the arousal. He fell into a deep sleep.

---

The hand on his shoulder had been there for some time before the fog of sleep receded enough for Bertrand to be aware. The warmth proved the hand's persistent grip, and Bertrand spent a few moments wondering why he wasn't afraid of this grip until he remembered where he was: the bomb shelter. Joyce had turned in her sleep, and her breath exhaled onto his biceps. Somehow during the night, he'd rolled onto his back and she'd turned to snuggle against him, perhaps for warmth, although Bertrand didn't think the bomb shelter was that cold.

Joyce's hand moved, shifting on his shoulder, moving closer to his chest. Oh my God, she was waking up, cuddled up to him! Would she be angry? Would she blame him? But wait a minute: she had pushed the couches together; she must be the one who moved toward him, for he was still on his couch. She was the encroacher on his territory.

Of course he immediately pitched a tent. That would be embarrassing if there were any light, and it might be a problem if she expected him to get up and turn on the light, but a quick glance at his watched proved it was only midnight, hours before their appointment with Mr. Anti-Christ.

So for now he could just enjoy the closeness, the scent of her, which he loved even though it had been days since either had showered, had deodorized. The pheromones had free reign.

Her hand slid to the middle of his chest and into his thin chest hair, and Bertrand began to wonder if it was a controlled movement, or if her hand just wandered in her sleep. Every muscle froze, because he feared waking her, breaking the spell of her touch. For a moment he could pretend they were lovers.

Fantasy turned to reality when her thumb and forefinger found his right nipple and gently tugged and pulled. His breath escaped in a rush of surprise and excitement: that was not the wandering hand of someone half-asleep and unaware of her actions. The touch had been carefully designed to arouse. But Bertrand had no idea how to respond. Should he turn to her now and sweep her up in a kiss? Should he let his hands wander to her body? He stayed frozen, but now with indecision.

Joyce's hand did not stay frozen, but instead pressed flat to his chest and began to move in slow circles, descending over his belly and down to the band of his boxers, the destination terrifyingly obvious. She was about to explore his most personal anatomy.

Was he dreaming? Could something this incredible, this wonderful really be happening? Joyce's fingers delved under the elastic of the boxers, but the descent stopped there, her hand moving in slow circles again but not descending further. Was this as far as she intended to go? He wanted to grab her hand and shove it down onto himself, but that would be crude. How to let her know that he was okay with this action, that he was excited? Her hand was right underneath his erection, for God's sake.

Her fingers brushed his pubic hair and his breath again escaped in a rush. This must've been the signal she had been waiting for, because all coyness vanished and she took a firm grip on him, provoking another gasp. That was it! There was no more pretending they weren't making love.

He turned toward her, finding her forehead with his lips, her hip with his hand. Her face tipped toward him and they kissed with a passion and shamelessness that is easiest in complete black. They couldn't see each other's expressions even for a moment; they couldn't see each other's bodies. All contact was through touch and taste.

She wore panties and her shirt, so Bertrand had been right when he had guessed before sleep that she'd shucked her jeans. His hand slipped under her panties and around her buttock, pulling her close to him and pushing down her underwear.

Suddenly she was gone from him, releasing him and turning away, breaking free from his grasp. What the—? What had he done wrong? How had he offended her? But her sharp movements enlightened him and filled him with new hope. The creak of the couch suggested that she was raising her hips to remove her panties. Another movement in the dark told him that she'd sat up, and a rustle of clothing suggested she was removing her top, getting totally naked. If only he was right then that meant ... that meant his boxers needed to go. He shoved them down barely in time, for she turned to him and pushed him onto his back, rising up to straddle his hips. Did she know he was a virgin? Is that why she had taken control of their lovemaking? Her lips found his even as his erection brushed into her pubic hair, Joyce holding just high enough off him to prevent penetration.

Bertrand had to repress a surge, a near climax as her nipples brushed into his chest hair. She was topless! She was naked even though he could only see her by touch, and it was more exciting than seeing her breasts and cupping at them like a teenage boy. This was making love. Her hand took hold of him again and she rose up so that she could get over him, aiming his erection to near vertical. She pushed herself down onto him, working the tightness to slowly—excruciatingly slowly—get him inside her. Her lips never left his, but she began to gasp with each descent until she had him completely enveloped.

For a moment they both froze, locked together, joined as one with neither wanting to end the moment, but nature took over and Bertrand's hips thrust up of their own accord. The spell was broken, and they both moved urgently now, Joyce using her position to rise up as far as she could, Bertrand thrusting up to meet her as she descended. Their love-making was unpracticed but eager, their motions not always in sync at first, but becoming more rhythmic as they progressed, as their passion rose.

Bertrand couldn't hold back, couldn't wait any longer, but she cried out and rode him to their ends, both gasping and sweating until they settled, still locked together, still kissing. They drifted back to sleep in that embrace.

Bertrand did wake later, vaguely worried that they would be awkward with one another in the morning, but he pushed this thought away and slipped back to sleep. Surely there could be no consequences from something so great.

# 26

# MR. ANTI-CHRIST

The alarm on Bertrand's watch beeped out, demanding attention. His left arm was pinned, and it took him a moment to remember that it was Joyce—naked, warm Joyce—snuggled against him. He managed to reach over and turn off the alarm, hoping not to disturb her more than necessary, but she stirred.

"Is it time then?" asked her voice in the dark.

"Yeah, you can stay here and sleep if you want."

"The hell I will." She vanished from his side, the warmth lingering to remind him of how close she had been to his body. "If you're going to talk to Mr. Anti-Christ, I want to hear what this creep has to say."

The light snapped on, and in the sudden glare of the bare bulb Joyce stood fully naked, and Bertrand had to suppress the urge to pull her back down onto the couch. She was so beautiful. She looked down at him, the covers already tossed aside, his instant erection in plain sight, his body open to scrutiny, and for a moment her eyes widened and her expression softened, a smile teasing her lips.

"Maybe later." She turned away to search for her clothing.

Bertrand fervently hoped "later" would be soon.

He sat before Nolan's computer, careful to ensure that the wall behind him was the generic paneling of the basement, that there were no paintings or distinguishing features that someone might recognize. Joyce had agreed that she should stay out of sight. Bertrand was already known, was already a public figure and a target, but she could remain anonymous.

At precisely three a.m., Skype rang and Bertrand answered.

There sat the man who called himself Vlad the Scourge, the same man, 'the boss' they had met at Goth Knights. He still dressed in his anachronistic mix of modern and medieval, the black shirt now hidden by a black Kevlar vest, but the heavy cloak still wrapped his shoulders. Behind him an undressed wall of rock implied an underground hideout, but the lamp hanging to the right could have come from any modern lighting showroom.

"Greetings, greetings." Vlad's right eye still twitched. "It is so good of you to agree to speak to me. I have been assured that you have become quite famous. You have gone viral as they say."

"You could too, if you simply post a couple of YouTube videos explaining to everyone what you're doing."

"Ah, but you are already doing that so well. I suspect you will make more of these videos, but I can't promise the power will stay up. Electricity is what sustains your resistance, and so we must do without it for a time."

"Why do you hate people so much? Why all the killing?"

Vlad shook his head. "This should not concern you. Your desire should only be to save good men, God-fearing men, from the scourge that approaches, and this is why I have contacted you."

Joyce—sitting off to Bertrand's right and out of view of the camera— shifted with impatience.

Who was this guy, really? Bertrand couldn't keep the anger out of his voice. "It is my desire to save all men and women from this 'scourge' as you call it. Are you patient zero? Did this plague start with you?"

But Vlad again shook his head, keeping his calm even though Bertrand felt he'd hit a nerve. "I am God's Scourge. But as Noah was offered a chance to save himself and his followers from the flood, I offer you a chance to save yourself and your followers from the scourge. There is an island in the Caribbean called Barbados, and my followers have yet to reach it. It is warm. There are many good golf courses that could be converted to farms, the population has shrunk over the last few months because the tourism has collapsed, so you would be welcome. If you and your followers agree to leave Chicago, I will provide you a with plane and a daytime pilot who can fly you there very quickly."

"Why would you do this for us?"

"Because the world should have men of strong morals in it, and you can be their leader, their patriarch. You could write a new book of the bible to warn people away from wickedness and into piety."

"Come on. You're the most evil man I've ever met, already responsible for the deaths of thousands, and you speak of piety?"

Vlad leaned forward and as he clasped his hands. "Thousands? No. I am responsible now for the death of millions all over the world. I am the Scourge, and I am offering you the only way out of this apocalypse. You are a brave man and my admiration grew when I saw you leap from that truck and attack my command post. I considered converting you right there, but God spoke to me and told the time was not right. That is why I departed the command post from the other side and let you live."

"Crap, you were there, weren't you? You're the guy who fed on all the cops in that mobile home."

"This is not important now. May I arrange the plane for you? I know you will need time to gather those whom you deem fit to survive, who are men of God."

Joyce shook her head, but Bertrand was way ahead of her.

"No. I'll not abandon the people of Chicago. I will find you though, and this time I will bring an army. You're a sick twisted fuck. How can you brag about killing millions?" Bertrand wanted to draw his Glock and wave it at the camera, but it would be a useless and childish gesture, so he restrained his anger.

"Spoken like a true man of God. I offer you sanctuary, but you turn your back on it in order to save others. My first judgment of you is correct. You are above other men."

"I am not! If you so believe in God, why don't you pass some lead through your brain."

Vlad sat back in his chair. "Because suicide is a sin."

"And murder isn't? You're unbelievably twisted."

"I only take the godless, and they do not deserve life. I do have one other offer for you: join me. I can give you the gift of eternal life."

"Never. You'd make me into a serial killer, a ripper who could only live on blood."

Vlad turned to someone off screen. "You see? That is a holy man. He is offered eternal life, eternal safety and he chooses instead to fight for the righteous." Vlad turned back to Bertrand. "God instructed me to spare you last night, but I must now promise that if we meet, I fear he will not again intercede for you. I will be forced to convert you or kill you."

"And I promise that if we meet, you're toast. I won't be sparing my ammo."

"Farewell." Vlad raised a hand to wave.

"Fuck off asshole."

Vlad ignored the rudeness, instead turning to someone off screen and flicking down with one finger as if turning off an invisible light switch. There was an awkward moment for Bertrand, during which Vlad turned back to him and smiled serenely without speaking. Bertrand had just decided to again ask why Vlad was doing this, when the power failed, killing the computer and plunging Joyce and Bertrand into darkness.

# 27

# THE HERETIC

A knock at the door soon after sunrise disturbed Bertrand and Joyce from their morning coffee, which they had made using an old camp percolator pot on the barbecue on Nolan's back deck. Bertrand immediately drew his Glock, and Joyce quietly picked up her machine pistol, both quietly tiptoeing to the front door, but before Bertrand could even put his eye to the peep hole, Jeff shouted to them. "It's me guys. Don't shoot now."

Bertrand yanked open the door to find Jeff, his Ruger in a holster at his side as if ready for Wild-West gunfight. His face was smudged with dirt, and his jacket still had stuffing sticking out from the close pass of a bullet.

"Did you guys ever miss a party last night." He grinned and pushed his way into the house, slamming the door behind him and locking it. "Hey, do I smell coffee?"

"What happened." Bertrand pursued him into the dining room. "You look like hell."

"I'm actually good." Jeff plunked his backpack down on the table and unzipped it to pull out his silver laptop. "But I got some stuff I need to show you. That Bobs, dude, is she dynamite or what?"

Bertrand stepped back into the kitchen to grab a mug for Jeff while he booted his laptop. "I hope black is okay because we don't have any cream. I do have sugar though."

"Black and harsh is good." Jeff sat, and Joyce pulled up a chair so that she could see his screen.

"What happened?" she asked.

"Chaos. Thanks, Bert." Jeff accepted the mug and had a sip before he went on. "About a couple of hundred rippers came at us, but it wasn't like with the cops the night before, where there was some organization and all. They just charged for the front doors of the church, more like zombies but smarter and easier to kill. I don't think they were even supposed to be there, because a helicopter flew overtop a couple of times and a voice on a speaker kept shouting that this attack was not authorized and that they must withdraw."

"Not authorized?" said Bertrand. He and Joyce shared a glance, their conversation with Mr. Anti-Christ foremost on Bertrand's mind. "Then why did they attack? I assumed you stopped them."

"Not me—Bobs. Remember she talked about bulldozers? Yesterday while we were sweeping basements, she had Barry raze a bunch of houses close to the church. They trucked away the garbage up a few streets to block the way. I'll have to show you the easy way in. That's the kill zone at night. Barry left up houses like the one Emile and I were at last night, ground floor windows all bricked in and stuff. We're the little forts protecting the church and we're armed to the teeth, and a damn good thing too. The rippers came down the easy streets that aren't blocked, and Bobs ordered us by walkie to wait until they had pretty much reached the church doors, and then we opened fire."

"Holy crap," said Joyce. "So what went down?"

"They did. We're still picking up the bodies."

"Shit," said Bertrand. "And they ignored this helicopter telling them to stay away?"

"Yeah, a real military looking thing too, maybe a Black Hawk. For a minute I wondered if they were gonna fire on the crowd or on one of our block houses, but once we opened fire they bailed—I mean left, I don't mean jumped out."

"Wow." Bertrand had been standing by the window, but he sat heavily now. "We have no government if they're letting us get away with bulldozing houses and shooting hundreds."

"But the rippers must be starving." Joyce got up to refill her mug. "If they're ignoring orders from their own boss, if they're raiding a heavily fortified position—like, why aren't they going out into the suburbs and finding people who aren't prepared?"

Bertrand thought of the urban legends about piles of bodies in farm fields. "Could there be that many gone? Millions?" he asked. "Is it that bad?"

"Actually it's getting weirder by the minute." Jeff opened a browser. "I've got a bunch of news items cached that I found yesterday when the power was still up. Did you know Terry shot some footage of you fighting outside church? They put it up on YouTube and it went viral again. Then YouTube took it down, but way too late. It's everywhere."

A grainy image taken from midway up the church tower showed the riot police, the crowds and suddenly Bertrand's five-ton ramming the mobile command vehicle. The camera zoomed on the cop being attacked by the ripper with the knife and pulled back when Bertrand killed him. He was featured more than Joyce as the chief of police charged them, taking all those bullets to bring down. The name Bertrand of Chicago appeared in white print below a still capture of his face, and even Bertrand had to admit that with the anger in his eyes and the shotgun in his hands, he looked fierce. It was followed by a clip of his speech at St. Mike's when he shouted, "Our blood will be spilled, but not to feed the rippers!"

"Who put this up?" asked Joyce.

"One of Bobs' people."

"So she's like totally in charge there now?"

Jeff shrugged. "I kind of thought Father Alvarez was in charge, but he keeps referring everyone to her. She and her dad, they were military history buffs in a big way, and her dad was in the National Guard. But listen, you got to see more. Look at this."

Jeff showed them the *LA Times* website, which featured photo and video of long lines-ups to donate blood, with uniformed soldiers standing guard with M-16s. The headline stated: doing their part.

"Holy crap," said Joyce. "They've given up. They're just doing what they're told."

"Not everywhere." Jeff switched to a Texas blogger, who had footage and photos of soldiers fighting soldiers during the day through the streets of Dallas. The city looked more like Stalingrad than a modern city—many buildings smashed, their rubble strewn across the streets.

"What the hell?" said Bertrand.

"Civil war." Jeff clicked through more examples while he spoke. "I did the best I could yesterday to get a bigger picture of what's going on, but it looks like the west coast is under martial law, where people are forced to donate blood for the rippers. That's everything west of the Rockies. In the south, some states have called up their National Guard troops and seceded from the union because the federal government is riddled with rippers. Like, South Carolina says it right on their website, they're even using your word: rippers."

"Really?" Bertrand sat back, turning away from the destroyed buildings and shouting troops on Jeff's computer to look out the back window of Nolan's at a clear blue sky and singing birds.

"Oh yeah, and it gets weirder. This was Wikipedia yesterday morning, then later and then last night before the power crashed. See how the entries for ripper keep getting updated? There was an edit war going on, one side trying to change the definition of ripper to non-supernatural vampire. The other side was trying to change it back to just references to Jack the Ripper and that kind of stuff. The definition finally got locked out by an administrator, keeping the old definition."

"So they own Wikipedia?" Bertrand stood and walked over to the window. How long ago was it that Nolan had stood here when Bertrand and Joyce had run through his back yard? Three months ago? Nearly four. If they had known then how far the rippers had gone, would they have run for the hills like Barry had planned?

"Not just Wikipedia. They own Google," said Jeff. "Don't even bother searching for your name or ripper or even vampire anymore. They own Wikipedia, Facebook, Twitter and pretty much any ISP. They keep taking down blogs about rippers, even cached blogs like Nolan's old blog posts. They even took down your buddy Erics' website."

"Skype calls still go through, right?" Bertrand turned back to face Jeff and noted that despite his weariness, there was a light in Jeff's eyes. "You on something?"

"Uppers. Don't worry, Emile says I'll crash about noon and I'll be able to sleep till sunset. I was up all day yesterday with all this stuff and then I was up all night with the shooting. Hey, how'd you guys do here last night? Any action in this hood?"

Bertrand's ears and cheeks burned, and Joyce suddenly looked very hard at her mug of coffee, her cheeks as red as Bertrand's felt. Jeff didn't notice the awkwardness for a moment as he called up another website from his cache, but when neither of them replied, he looked up.

"Oh," he said, looking from Bertrand to Joyce. "Oh, my bad. Wrong question. I get it. Congratulations maybe? Right? Okay let's move on. No gunfire here anyway. So like Skype's still good when the power's up. I tell you they got the same problem we do when the power's down: communication. They need their cell phones and their Skype and stuff as much as we do. Problem is, I think even they're having trouble keeping the power up when they want it. I can't find anything from the east coast that's been updated in the last two weeks, which makes me think they lost power and never got it up again in, like, New York or D.C."

"I need to get a hold of Erics." Bertrand craved information and Erics had a wide network. "The next time the power comes back up I'll e-mail and skype him, because I don't even know where he lives."

"One of his captains is at the church sometimes—Marvin, Martin—something like. Father Alvarez isn't above taking their help, but he's not too keen on the Erics people being at his meetings and stuff. Maybe he thinks they're competition. But on that topic, you should see this: the pope has issued a fatwa on your ass."

"A fatwa?"

Jeff pulled up the website for the Vatican. "He doesn't call it that but he might as well. You've been excommunicated as a heretic, and he says you've started a cult to encourage people to drink blood."

"That liar!"

"That's the first thing people do when they're doing bad things: they publicly declare that you're doing whatever it is they're doing. But it gets better, or worse I guess I mean. He's declared the entire Archdiocese of Chicago apostate and excommunicated basically all of Illinois. He's also asking people to pray for the president—who like I said nobody seems to have heard from in the last couple of weeks—and to donate blood to help soldiers fighting insurrections all over the world."

Bertrand sat heavily. "Even the Vatican has been taken over by rippers?"

"As far as I can tell, it was taken over months ago and we just didn't know it. Europe's way ahead on all of this, and I think it's actually falling apart faster there because of it. From what I can glean from the few bloggers who still post, Europe's been without power for a month except for here and there."

"And I'm a heretic. Christ, I'm not even Catholic."

"Doesn't matter anymore. This just got a whole lot worse."

Bertrand looked from Joyce to Jeff. "We have to hunt down Mr. Anti-Christ. He's the head of all this, at least here in Chicago. We kill him and it'll be like chopping the head off the snake."

"Yeah." Joyce didn't look convinced. "That worked so well with bin Laden."

# 28

# APOCALYPSE SCENARIO

They reached the roadblock just west of the corner of Eugenie and Meyer, although Bertrand had trouble recognizing the neighborhood. The roadblock consisted of concrete road barriers, the kind that can only be moved with heavy equipment, so they abandoned Jeff's Xterra to walk the rest of the way. A half a dozen men and women with rifles and shotguns patrolled the barrier, but they waved Bertrand, Jeff and Joyce along with smiles, nods and one young man, barely out of his teens, even saluted.

The parking lot on the north side where Bertrand had smashed the command post had been emptied of the wreckage, although three Greyhound buses now lined up ready for a convoy. The south side of Eugenie east of Meyer was completely unrecognizable from yesterday morning. The nineteenth-century retail building—the ground floor windows bricked in with concrete blocks—still guarded the corner, but all the wooden post–Great Fire houses that had densely filled the block between Meyer and Cleveland were gone. Only chewed earth and some debris such as drywall or a few boards flattened to the ground remained to testify that, for over a century and a half, people had lived there. As a result, St. Michael's—on the east side of Cleveland—now had a clear field of fire to the west, and Bertrand now had a view of the church complex that hadn't existed since the Great Chicago Fire.

The lower windows to the church had been bricked in weeks ago, but now plywood covered the stained glass windows up to twice the height of a human. Two men on a cherry-picker worked to cover the windows higher up.

"Holy crap." Joyce stopped to take in the sight. "Barry doesn't kid around."

"Yeah." Jeff wiped his face with his hand, a weary look indicating that the uppers were wearing off. "He told me he had like four of those big excavators, some bulldozers, all kinds of front end loaders and a dozen or so big dump trucks going until sunset."

"Where did you say they took all the crap?" asked Bertrand.

Jeff pointed south. "It's piled on North Ave, to the west and the east, completely blocking the street and making it hell for anyone to get here, even on foot. It's like a mountain and it's treacherous to climb 'cause it's such a mess. They also piled it on most of the north–south streets, and he's still at it on the east side. Hear it?"

A thud reverberated through the earth, indicating that a machine with hydraulics hammered at a building, but the church blocked their view. Barry St. John himself, a white hardhat on his bald head, came around the corner of the church, heading for the stairs and the front door, when he saw them and changed direction.

"Bert, good to see you." He held out his hand to shake.

"You've been busy." Bertrand gestured to the empty ground to the west of the church. "Weren't the owners a bit pissed?"

Barry shook his head. "The ones that are still alive live in the church now, and we let them into their houses first to get out any food or clothes. That was only about five families. The rest of the houses were cleared by volunteers. Listen, I've been in touch with my people in Canada. Guess what? No one's manning the border during the day anymore. The gates are smashed and everything, so there's nothing stopping us from heading out except the highways, and I'm taking a bulldozer along for that. Word came back that the daytime police roadblocks are gone." He pointed to the buses.

"You're leaving." Bertrand couldn't help making it sound like an accusation.

"Yeah, about forty of us. We're going to pick up Martin's family along the way."

"I'll be sorry to see him go too," said Joyce.

Bertrand wondered if she was disappointed to lose the top guys from her Raiders. She didn't show it.

"Here's the thing," said Barry. "We were wondering if you guys wanted to come along."

"I can't just leave Chicago like that," said Bertrand, recalling the invitation from Vlad to abandon the city. "There're people in that church that need defending, and there's a real chance we'll see the National Guard coming at us or something like that. I mean, look at what we're doing." He waved at the empty expanse where the houses used to stand. "We don't have a permit for that, and I suspect the police department's still a bit sore at us for shooting up their guys and all."

"Oh Bert." Barry removed his hardhat and waved in the direction of the Willis Tower to the far south. "Where were you last night? Didn't you see the fires? I think about a quarter of the city burned. They've got a lot of angry neighborhoods to get through before they could ever get at us. People are congregating at churches all over the city."

"It's true, Bert," Jeff said. "There's just as big a crowd at St. James over near your old hood. They're bulldozing houses too."

"They bulldozed my house?" Bertrand resisted the urge to turn and run for Bissell Street. He'd always had it in his head that when things had settled down he would go back there and secure the place, maybe collect some photos of his parents to keep close.

"Relax, relax," said Jeff. "They didn't get that far down and they're working the east side of the church now, so you're okay for a couple of days."

"Point is," said Barry, "anyone who's still alive is going straight for the churches, the synagogues, the temples, the mosques—you name it—and they're setting themselves up as little defensive enclaves. It's funny how vampires start walking the streets and suddenly everybody finds the religion that they lost a generation ago.

We've actually got quite a population problem here." He gestured with his hardhat back at the church. "Father Alvarez has had to turn away hundreds, sending them on to Holy Name and Mount Carmel; there's even a group setting up shop at the archbishop's residence over on State."

Bertrand was about to push past Barry to head for the church, but he stopped. "Is the archbishop there?"

Barry shook his head. "Nope. Father Alvarez and about a dozen nuns went over to rescue what stuff they could, regalia, I don't know, but I think Alvarez figures he's going to have to find a new archbishop, maybe a new pope. You hear what's going on in Rome?"

"Jeff was telling me that I'm a heretic."

Barry laughed, a short bark without humor. "We all are. We're all wanted by the police, the feds, the pope—you name it—yet no one seems to be able to come and get us. Bert, it's completely falling apart. Think of my place up in Canada as a fall-back position. If things get too hot here, come and join me. No one knows it's there. It's not on any maps and there's only two roads in, and one of them goes over a bridge that would be easy to blow. It can hold about a thousand people and I've only got a couple of hundred so far." He pointed at the buses. "We're going in a convoy at dawn tomorrow, gonna drive all day and cross at International Falls. We'd be happy to have you guys along, and don't forget I've got power. You can keep making speeches from there as long as the Internet holds together."

Jeff yawned. "At this rate that'll be about two days. Look guys, I'm going to catch some rest in that block house." He pointed to a building just across the street from the church. "Keep me posted. Remember, we three should stick together, just like we have from the beginning."

Joyce stopped him with a call as he turned away. "Jeff, what do you think we should do?"

Jeff turned around, walking backwards now, one hand on the butt of his holstered Ruger. "I think Bert's right. I think we need to hunt down Mr. Anti-Christ and pass some lead through his brain, a lot of lead. I'm just out of ideas as to how find him."

Barry pointed at the buses. "Fall back with me if you need to, Bert."

Bertrand stood looking from the buses to the church. What to do? He was disoriented from his interrupted sleep, from the crazy pace of the last few weeks. Joyce answered for him.

"Draw us a map."

---

The inside of St. Mike's looked more like a refugee camp. While there weren't many people in the church now, their sleeping bags, stacks of luggage and hanging laundry all testified to the crowds that would return before nightfall. Bobs and Father Alvarez stood near the altar, looking to the right at the stained glass windows as more plywood went up, blocking out more light. The gloom of the church weighed on Bertrand's soul, as if all the light in the world were going out.

"There he is." Bobs pointed their way and headed down the aisle ahead of the priest. "Bert, we're gonna need you to do another broadcast tonight. We think they'll get the power up just after sunset so they can do their Twitter flash mob things, so we want to sneak the word in there while we can."

"Okay, sure. I want computer time then too, though, so that I can contact Erics."

Father Alvarez joined them. "We must be careful of this man, this Erics. I'm concerned that we know very little of him other than that he has started his own religion. False prophets can be very dangerous."

"True enough, but we need all the information we can get right now."

Bobs nodded agreement. "I've got good news there. One of my dad's old Illinois National Guard buddies is the colonel, and he's coming to meet us today, and guess what? He's a believer too. When the governor called up the guard last month he took them over to the Rock Island Arsenal and took it over. At first they thought the army would send regulars at them, but then everything fell apart, and it looks like the army's too busy fighting everywhere else."

"That's great news I guess. It means things aren't as organized at the top as I thought." Bertrand looked from one to the other, his hope welling. If they had the Illinois National Guard on their side, then everything changed.

"Good and bad." Bobs crossed her arms. "It's hard to kill an unorganized movement—just look at Afghanistan—Russians then us and still the fanatics are there."

"True, but when do we get to meet this colonel?"

"This afternoon. You're invited." She only pointed at Bertrand.

———

Colonel Webb of the Illinois National Guard looked as if he'd seen a few battles over the years. His gray hair was brush-cut short, his face weathered by sun and wind and yet he was as trim as a marathoner. His whole manner was that of a military man, but he also had the thoughtful frown of a scholar when listening to others, and a tendency to nod his head in understanding before they'd finished speaking.

He'd arrived at midday, dressed in camouflage and a flak jacket, riding with a convoy of five Stryker Assault Vehicles. Bobs had practically drooled over the eight-wheeled armored personnel carriers: "We could drive the rippers right out of Chicago with a dozen of those and take the Loop.

Bobs was obsessed with taking the Loop.

"Think about it," she had said to Bertrand. "We only need a wall on the south side, everywhere else we just pull up the draw bridges at night and the rippers would have to swim or use boats to get at us. Troops in water are an easy target."

Father Alvarez set them up in his conference room, but there was a glaring change: the painting of the current pope was gone, replaced with a painting of Cardinal George, the previous head of the Archdiocese of Chicago.

Bertrand had managed to get Joyce admitted to the meeting, and Barry was there, but many of the others belonged to Father Alvarez's new command structure, and most of them seemed to follow Bobs' lead.

Even her friend Terry was in attendance, but there wasn't a single white arm-band of the 1000 Souls.

Colonel Webb, after his introduction by Bobs, spoke with precision. "Let me start by saying what a fantastic accomplishment you have all achieved here." His voice had a slight southern drawl to it. "To have cleansed this neighborhood and fortified your position to withstand assault in such a short time is remarkable, and unlike anything I have seen elsewhere in the state. I will be recommending to all the people I will be speaking to in small towns and cities to do as you have done: find a focal point, shelter in it and fortify it."

"That's great." Bertrand fought to restrain his impatience. "It was really Bobs' doing, but of course we have a lot of concerns. First, can you give us some support if the Chicago P.D. comes after us again with arrest warrants?"

The colonel was already nodding. "The Chicago P.D. is no longer an effective force, as you proved the other night, so you have nothing to fear on that front. Their human numbers are far too devastated and have been plunging through desertions or conversions. As far as we can tell, city hall as a government simply no longer exists, because in the past three days there has been a seismic shift in this war. The most important one is that the rippers seem to be running out of food. The attack on your position last night was evidence of that and was by no means an isolated incident."

"Well that's good news." Yet Bertrand was uneasy. This colonel didn't sound like a man delivering good news.

"Yes, but we've taken prisoners during the last few weeks and held them for observation at Rock Island, and it looks like the parasites have a hibernation mode. The rippers can go weeks without feeding and still function before they slip into this comatose state and appear all but dead, until they sense a human near them, which brings them abruptly out of hibernation. I have regular doctors studying this, not scientists, so don't ask me how long they can stay in hibernation."

Bertrand's heart did sink now. "It could be years to hunt them all down and kill them."

The colonel nodded. "But the next two weeks are going to be the worst. That's why there's been so much wanton burning to find victims: they're desperate. I think the reason the Chicago P.D. is in crisis is that the ripper cops have been feeding against orders on their daytime brethren, whether they're part of the so-called Daylight Brigade or not. You folks are going to face a lot more fights like last night."

Bertrand couldn't contain himself. "Well are you going to send us help, then? Tell me you're not going to just abandon us to this fight."

The colonel met Bertrand's gaze across the table. "Sir, you've done great work getting the word out to people. But a very new danger has arisen. I still have access to several satellite surveillance systems, and it is my sad duty to tell you that a great catastrophe took place two days ago: Guangzhou in China, that's not far from Hong Kong, was hit by several nuclear weapons."

"Holy shit!" Joyce's expletive joined others around the table, who had all exploded with their own expressions of consternation.

Father Alvarez rose and held up his hands, palms out, to quiet the room. "Colonel Webb has little time, so we will pray for the dead later. Right now, please, continue." He sat.

"Thank you, Father." Colonel Webb looked around the room as he spoke. "Before you ask, no it wasn't one of ours and we don't know who did it, although our biggest concern is that it might have been the Chinese themselves in an attempt to destroy a region totally overrun with rippers. We just don't know. Now I know this will be a disappointment to you, but my first concern must be to secure America's stockpile of nuclear weapons."

"Can you even do that?" asked Bertrand. "Do you even know where they are?"

Webb was already nodding.

"I've been in touch with Colonel Stevens at Barksdale Air Force base in Louisiana. They've been under siege since last night, and he's been flying everything he can out to Minot Air Force Base in North Dakota. As far as I can tell, the rippers found out about the destruction of Guangzhou at the same time we did, and they've pushed all their daytime and nighttime troops at Barksdale." Webb looked around the room for emphasis. "Colonel Stevens believes they will fall within twenty-four hours, but has assured me that by then he will have either sent away or disabled every nuclear weapon on the base. He has also assured me that none of his troops will be taken alive."

"It's frigging Armageddon," said Joyce in the stunned silence that followed.

The colonel focused his attention of Joyce. "Not yet. Wisconsin and Milwaukee National Guards were called up too late and never formed up into their combat units, except for a few stragglers who've joined with us at Rock Island. However, the good news is that there are several National Guards that haven't gone over to the rippers, and I'm coordinating with them. Everything west of the Rockies has fallen, I admit, so we'll get no help from there. D.C. clearly went to the rippers first, and the only good news about that is things have gotten so bad that the Pentagon has stopped issuing commands for us to lay down our weapons and to open blood donor clinics. But we should not give up hope. If we can secure the nuclear arsenal, then we can be sure that hold-out cities like Chicago will not be nuked by the rippers or anyone else. That, ladies and gentlemen, is my top priority."

"Well how the hell do you think you're going to accomplish that?" asked Bertrand.

"I have to commit as many troops as I can to assisting the North Dakota National Guard in defending Minot. Whiteman in Kansas is evacuating the 509th bomb wing to there as well, so that we can benefit from consolidation. The 90th missile wing in Cheyenne are disabling their missiles and destroying their warheads, so that just leaves Minot and Malmstrom in Montana to defend, both within easy reach, and the Montana National Guard is mostly intact. The prairies are not seriously infested with rippers yet, although as the numbers of humans available for feeding on in places like Chicago gets smaller, we expect them to move out into the countryside."

"But what about ending this?" said Bertrand. "What about hunting down this guy, Vlad the Scourge, who claims to have started it all. The guy wants a frigging apocalypse on the scale of the great flood. If we could get him, then perhaps all these infections would end. He's the one who gave the rippers a quota to make more rippers every night. He's the one giving the orders."

"I cannot emphasize enough that my first concern is the nuclear arsenal. I admit he's a high-value target, should be taken out, but other than logistical support I can't help you there."

"What do you mean about logistical support."

The colonel and Bobs exchanged a glance. "I mean that I can provide you with some weapons and ammunition, and I think I know where he is, but it's a long way from Chicago."

"Where?" Bertrand sensed the monster, the superhero inside him rise up in anticipation.

"The night before last Minot tracked several helicopters outbound from Chicago. At first they were concerned that it was the beginning of an assault, but instead they stopped at four locations that we now believe must've been prearranged fuel depots. They carried straight on to a remote location in Montana called Cave Mountain."

"What the hell is there?"

Webb shrugged. "Nothing as far as we can tell, but we're thinking about the name, and the fact that there was a mining community back there back in the nineteenth century that's nothing but a ghost town now, and we're wondering if he's made some old mines or caves into a hideout. Perhaps he's worried about the nukes too."

Bertrand's heart leapt. "Yes! I spoke to him last night by Skype and he was definitely in a cave, like bare rock behind him, although it looked like he had a lot of comfort, like electricity and all."

"You spoke to him?" Webb leaned forward, clearly suspicious. "And what did you gentlemen chat about."

"He wanted me to become a ripper, and I told him to get lost. End of story. Are you sure he's there?"

The colonel shook his head. "I can't guarantee anything, but Minot intercepted a radio message last night and we heard the same one. It was to the Chicago P.D., ordering them to stop the assault of the rippers on your church until after four a.m. When was your Skype conference with him?"

"Three a.m. and he booked it."

"How?"

"He left a letter for me in the basement of my house. I seem to have impressed him with my speeches and my YouTube vids, the ones that get out anyway."

Bobs had been studying Bertrand very closely. "So you really want to go after him," she said.

"Well doesn't everyone in this room? Doesn't it make sense to cut the head off the snake? Colonel, shouldn't this be your biggest priority?"

But Webb was already shaking his head. "Satellite photos show armored columns from California moving up the coast to join others that are forming up in Oregon and Washington. They only travel at night and those are ripper states, so it is my belief that they are preparing for a drive on Minot and Malmstrom. Protecting those bases is key, and I will not waste my time going after one ripper hiding in a hole in a mountain."

"But he's the guy." Bertrand could hardly contain his frustration.

"He has also isolated himself for some reason. I tell you those nukes going off in China changed everything. Even if he's the commander of the rippers, he's placed himself in a location so remote that there wasn't cell phone communication from there even before the rippers. His only communication out is via satellite phone or radio, and after last night, Malmstrom started jamming his communications. As soon as they're able, they'll deal with his Black Hawks, but aviation fuel is becoming scarce for everyone. He's shut down for now. We'll deal with him later."

"How many people do you think he has there with him?" asked Bertrand.

"No more than a hundred."

"Then I'm going to round up everyone I can and I'm going after him."

The colonel was already shaking his head. "I won't be going with you, but like I said, I'll give you ammunition, a case or two of M67 grenades, that kind of thing. I have to reserve the heavier equipment for my boys."

"I'll go with you," said Bobs to Bertrand. "Let's talk."

# 29

# ARMY OF BERTRAND

Relief washed through Bertrand when Erics answered the Skype call.

"Greetings, Mr. Allan." Erics looked even older but still wore his purple three-piece suit. Behind him Bertrand could see evening light coming through a large window, and a prairie field of brown corn waved in the wind—corn that should've been harvested.

"Please, you can sure as hell call me, Bert. Your people made all the difference the night before last and I'm deeply in your debt."

Erics gave a toothy smile. "Did I not tell you that I understand the 1000 Souls? I sent you only Fighting Souls, Courageous Souls and Selfless Souls, and even a few Ruthless Souls."

"They did a hell of a job—"

"As. Did. You." Erics spoke each word as if they were separated by punctuation, pointing at Bertrand as he spoke with the cane. "You are a very dense soul, and this gives you great strength."

"Yeah, well I'm going to need it. Listen, I need your help again. We know where Vlad is, and we're going after him, but we won't be getting many people from St. Mike's to go with us. I was wondering if some of your people would be willing to go along."

"This, verily, is the most important task. Of course we will help you, as many of my people as I can contact. Also, it is no longer safe for my people to stay in Chicago. Murray tells me that Father Alvarez is distinctly hostile to my followers and is intolerant of our beliefs."

"He's probably just stressed about the pope and all."

Erics leaned forward, holding the polished cane between his hands for support. "I know his soul, and it is a dangerous soul for people who are not Catholic. Do not misunderstand me, he will do great things for Chicago, he will save the city if he can, but it would not do well for my followers to be near him once the current crisis has passed."

Bertrand shook his head. "He's a good man."

"I did not say he was a bad man, but good men can be dangerous to those they perceive as enemies, whether they are or not. It has been my plan to evacuate my followers from Chicago to come and join me here, but I will adjust this plan if it will mean the end of Vlad the Scourge, for he is the most dangerous soul: the Ruthless General. He is most ruthless, for he fights for his beliefs. He has ruled many times in history, always to the great detriment of humankind."

"I couldn't agree more."

"Now, tell me how I can aid you."

---

Bertrand drew his Glock and nodded to the door warden, a pudgy man with a revolver.

"Should be clear," said the man. "Bell tower says they can see a lot of fires to the north and west, but there's no activity anywhere near Old Town."

"Thanks." Bertrand turned to Joyce. "You ready?"

Joyce had her Uzi hanging from a sling on her shoulder, but she took it in hand.

"Should be a piece of cake. Let's go."

The door warden pushed open the heavy front door of the church, and Bertrand and Joyce rushed down the front steps in the dark. The streetlights were dead because of another power failure, but a generator hummed from the top of the building across the street, and a single floodlight fixed to a chimney bathed the street in front of St. Mike's with a harsh glare. They ran across the interlocking paving stone of the forecourt, past the white statue of St. Michael and straight for the front door of Emile's blockhouse. The door opened before they even reached the house, and Jeff, his Ruger drawn, held it open for them.

"I wonder where all the rippers are tonight?"

"West and north apparently." Bertrand headed through the door first at Joyce's wave, and once inside, Jeff slammed the door and bolted it.

"Emile's waiting upstairs," he said. "This way."

Jeff hurried up the stairs, the spring in his step proving him better rested this evening. The house smelled of kerosene lamps and candles, and as they made each turn of the narrow staircase, Bertrand caught glimpses of people, the light softening their skin and reflecting off the gunmetal of the weapons they carried. The house was very crowded, and no one was asleep. Many wore the white armbands of the 1000 Souls.

The top floor of the house had a computer in operation, obviously supplied with power from the generator above, which droned on, the white noise irritating to Bertrand only at first, because after a few minutes he ceased to notice it. But the room itself was lit with a single kerosene lamp turned low—apparently the generator's power supply was maxed out by the external lights and the computer. The furniture, except for a dresser and a dining-room table, must have been removed. The border of planes and trucks high on the wall suggested that this had once been a boy's bedroom.

Emile had given up all attempts at shaving, his black beard now thick and maturing. He had a wicked-looking rifle slung over his shoulder and a pair of binoculars in one hand as he stood by the window, looking north to columns of smoke that caught the moonlight and obscured the stars. Barry St. John stood beside him, his hard hat on the dresser, a beer in his hand and a sidearm holstered around his thick waist.

Emile looked over his shoulder. "Hey, Bert. Think we should go hunting?"

"I do, but not tonight, 'cause I've got bigger game. I want to get the guy who started all this."

"Mr. Anti-Christ? Is he nearby?" Jeff walked over to the window and borrowed the binoculars.

"No. Unfortunately he flew out yesterday, apparently as part of a squadron of Black Hawks, but some airbase in Montana tracked them to a mountain out there."

"Well they might as well be in Spain." Barry turned to a cooler and flipped open the lid to retrieve two beers, the sound of ice sloshing in water suggesting that he'd planned ahead for this refreshment while the power was on. He handed them to Joyce and Bertrand. "I'd be in my place in Canada by now, except every time one of my guys takes a drive up the Kennedy to get out of the city, they still find blockages set up by the rippers the night before to stop people from leaving, usually a pile of wrecked cars, and I mean a pile, like a crane would build. We've bulldozed a few clear, but the guys had to hole up for the night."

"We've got help that way," said Joyce, twisting open her beer. "The Illinois National Guard is planning a drive through to North Dakota to that airbase, and they'll let us tag along as far as Bismark, I mean that's where they'll head north and we keep going."

Jeff turned from the window and sat back against the sill. "How long is this drive?"

Bertrand sighed, knowing this weakness in his plan might provoke a negative response. "It's over a day—like a full day and night of driving."

"And we'd have to fight how many at the end?" Emile went to the cooler for a fresh beer.

"Over a hundred anyway," said Bertrand. "But here's the good news, Erics is giving this mission his thumbs-up, which means a lot of those people you've got downstairs will be willing to go. Better yet, Erics himself plans to meet with us somewhere along the way in Montana, city called Billings, and he promises he'll be going with us into the mountain."

"Into the mountain." Jeff took a big swallow of beer and gestured with the bottom of the bottle. "Sounds pretty grim there, Bert. What do you think we're going to find at this mountain? What's to stop him and his Black Hawks from flying back to Chicago tonight?"

"Hopefully his Black Hawks are toast by now. And I think he's run there for a reason. I mean we know he's been around Chicago for months, so why bail now?"

"The nukes," Joyce said. "Remember what Webb said about the nukes? Those nukes go off in China—"

"What the fuck?" Jeff stood up. "When did this happen?"

Joyce filled the others in and then went on. "Here's what I think: we know full spectrum sunlight kills the parasites. What about nuclear fallout? Why the hell did he run for a mountain the day after that explosion unless he was worried about fallout."

"From China?" Jeff's tone expressed his disbelief.

"From the U.S. The rippers have been attacking bases that have nukes. Maybe they're worried about a few being used here on cities like L.A. that have gone to the rippers."

Barry sat heavily on the cooler of beer. "Or maybe they're planning their own nuclear strike. Maybe Vlad the Scourge has run for the hills because he plans to really unleash his scourge. We know the guy's frigging genocidal."

Bertrand leaned back against the wall, suddenly weary and hopeless. He had always assumed the scourge was the ripper plague. He had never thought of nuclear destruction—that kind of Armageddon.

"Well," he said. "If that's the case, then we'd sure as hell better move fast. It'd be a total shit to secure Old Town only to have it blown from the face of the earth."

"Could be worse than that," said Barry. "Maybe you're too young, but you ever hear of the theory of nuclear winter? That was the big scare back in the eighties, when they figured out that if every nuke in the world was detonated at once it would put so much crap in the atmosphere that it would block out the sun and cause about ten years of winter with no growing season, maybe even trigger another ice age. If you want a scourge of biblical proportions, that would be it."

Jeff sat at the chair in front of the computer. "Maybe," he said. "But that means we'd have to fire the missiles at Russia and, like, China I guess, and they'd have to fire back. If things are as screwed up there as they are here, I don't see that happening."

"We can't take the chance." Bertrand tried to look more confident than he felt. "Colonel Webb says he's working to secure the nukes, and I think he's the right man for that job, but he's not going to rush all the way to the far side of Montana after one ripper, no matter how important. That leaves us."

Bertrand looked around the room. Jeff drummed his fingers in front of the keyboard, looking ready for action. Emile drank from his beer, but Bertrand remembered how good the man had been over the last few weeks, always ready for a fight. Joyce looked angry, but she always did when she was summoning up her courage.

"I'm going after this guy. Bobs is rounding up a bunch of her people to go along."

A white flare popped high over the city to the west, descending slowly, illuminating rooftops and streets, and throwing shadows into harsh contrast with light.

"What the hell is that all about?" Emile put the binoculars to his eyes to look below the flare.

"That's a detachment of the Illinois National Guard. They're clearing a route north up the 298 for their colonel with tanks and bulldozers. You'll be able to head for Canada in the morning, Barry."

Barry looked up from his cooler. "No, I think I'll head out with you, and I'll bring my crew with me. If this guy really is planning to pop nukes off, even just in Chicago, there'll be no hiding from the fallout in Canada. Most of my family's already up there, but I'm not going to run and hide if they're not safe. Alison can stay here at the church until I get back."

"'Course I'm coming," Emile didn't lower the binoculars. "Best fighting I did was beside you, Bert. I just can't sit around here while the world falls apart."

Bertrand looked to Jeff, who smiled and took a gulp of his beer. "I'm always up for a fight. Besides, I said the three of us should stick together."

"Great," said Joyce. "But we're going to have to work fast if we're going to leave at dawn. First problem, we're going to need some buses."

Barry gave a weary smile that had no mirth. "I happen to have some fueled and waiting."

Joyce smiled. "That's what we hoped."

# 30

# CIRCLE OF TWELVE

Winter would be a disaster. That became obvious to everyone on the Greyhound bus when they passed out of the suburbs and into the Prairies. Farm fields that should have been harvested were untouched, the corn withered and brown, the grain flattened by early snows that had melted in the seesaw of temperatures that is late autumn. But the true horror was the blackened fields, those that had been intentionally burned. Bertrand and Joyce sat in the front seats on the passenger side, their view out the windshield as good as the driver's.

The flat highway ran out before them, one of the Strykers that Bobs so coveted immediately in front, it's fifty-cal machine gun ready but unmanned in the cold wind. The three buses of Bertrand's little army followed the National Guard convoy in the relative safety of its wake.

"I guess we know why all those sunsets in October were so beautiful," said Joyce as they passed one of the blackened fields. "They were burning the harvest. They want people to starve."

"It's frigging evil," said Emile. In one of his many careers, he had spent time driving a bus, so he was their chauffeur. Bobs sat behind him with the gangly and eager Terry at her side. Bertrand had wondered if their relationship was sexual but didn't dare to ask. Maybe they were just friends. Maybe friends with benefits, sort of like he and Joyce.

"I think it's brilliant." Bobs stood up in the aisle to look through the front windshield, her blonde hair pulled back into a ponytail. "Not that it's good for us, but now we know why rippers are raiding grocery stores: they want to starve us into submission. This Vlad asshole sure knows what he's doing."

Emile glanced over his heavy shoulder at her and back to the highway. "Holy shit she's right. Why else would rippers care about food? They can't eat it."

"We need to make a plan for the winter." Bobs looked down at Bertrand. "And we'll need to think about the spring and how to farm the fields."

"Simple," said Bertrand. "We kill Vlad. We kill the rippers, and people will come back to the farms. There'll be money to be made."

"Gas will be a problem."

Bertrand fought down his frustration. Why did she have to be right? "We get power to refineries and they can operate. Aren't there millions of barrels in the country's strategic oil reserve? Besides, my biggest fear is that there won't be that many people to feed. How many have already died?"

Joyce shook her head. "No point in worrying about any of this until after tomorrow." She stood, pushing past Bertrand and heading for the washroom at the back of the bus. She had been frosty on the ride so far, shunning Bertrand's touch and staring out the window.

Bobs took her seat.

"So you're pretty famous now, what with all the speeches going viral. Even if the Internet totally tanks, pretty much everybody in Chicago knows who you are."

"Yeah, well I'd rather be an unknown computer geek than have to live through this disaster." But guilt tugged at Bertrand's soul. It wasn't true. He had been more alive in the last three months than he had been since the funeral of his parents. It had occurred to him that if the rippers hadn't happened, he would probably have just continued down his road of boredom and self-pity until he ended up a recluse like poor Needleman, the first ripper victim that Bertrand had known personally.

"You were made for this," said Bobs. "We're going to need a strong leader back in Chicago after this, one who can make tough decisions through the winter. Are you that guy? I know people would follow you."

"I don't want to run the world. Maybe an election or something, but like Joyce says, all that can wait."

Bobs shook her head and leaned in Bertrand's direction, putting one hand on his shoulder. "We're going to need a hero to get us through the winter, someone to inspire people. I've been pumping you up to every-body 'cause I think you're that guy. You make things happen, like this. Big things. And you don't run and hide."

Bertrand looked over, enjoying the touch of her hand and her admi-ration, but uncomfortable that Joyce might emerge from the washroom to see him communing so closely with this elfin twenty-year-old. Would she be jealous? "Funny, calling me a hero and all. That's what Erics called me, or at least he said I had part of the Dormant Hero soul. Weird concept, isn't it? I mean, thinking that someone else alive right now, seeing stuff right now, has part of your soul."

Bobs let go of Bertrand's shoulder and sat back to cross her arms under her small breasts and stare ahead at the Stryker. "It's bullshit. I took that asshole's test and he doesn't know anything, sure as hell not about me."

"What did it say?"

"Like I said, bullshit. Way off the mark."

"Well he's making this whole thing a lot more possible. When we link up with him and his people, we'll double our numbers if he's not exaggerating, and he says he'll fight right into the center of the frigging mountain with us."

Bobs looked over and rolled her eyes. "How can that doddering old fool be any good with a machine gun? The recoil would shove him back on his ass with the first shot. He may show up and all, but I guarantee that old fart won't be fighting."

The slam of the bathroom door prompted her to stand to let Joyce back her seat, but in the aisle, Bobs turned to Bertrand and spoke quickly as Joyce made her way up from the back of the bus. "Anyway, you need to think more about what your role is going to be in our new world order, because we're going to have one no matter what."

But as Joyce took her seat and settled down to snooze, Bertrand found he couldn't imagine anything beyond a battle at Cave Mountain.

―――――

Bertrand sensed a change, the bus slowing and turning, stopping and starting, but he was reluctant to open his eyes. The last 24 hours had provided an opportunity for sleep that most of them hadn't had in weeks, and as anxious as he was to get to the mountain before his quarry could run, Bertrand had found it easy to slip away into a world where he and Joyce lived in his house, a child in the baby room, a roast in the oven, his Glock on the bedside table.

That incongruity of the last image caused him to open his eyes. Jeff now drove while Emile snored several seats back. The midday sun bathed him in light that didn't reach deep into the bus. Ahead, a four-lane road led through a small city, and unlike other towns they had passed through, people lined the sidewalks here, many waving white flags with a black "1000" overtop of an infinite loop. They cheered as the bus passed, their numbers guiding the way to their rendezvous with Erics.

"Holy frig." Bertrand stood carefully, trying not to disturb Joyce's sleep, and moved to stand beside Jeff. "He wasn't kidding when he said that he controlled Billings. The whole city follows him."

Bobs lurched up and crowded the aisle so that she could look ahead through the windshield. "You should wave, Bert. Erics has been telling them you're their hero. Wave to them."

Bertrand began to wave. Did he look like Queen Elizabeth? How did she do it all those years? But Bobs wasn't satisfied, and she rummaged under Bertrand's bus seat, standing up with his Winchester. "Hold this up," she said. "Like this, by the slide."

She folded Bertrand's hand around the gun before he could protest, and he held it up as she indicated, making the gun the top of a T with his arm.

"Who the hell are you?" Joyce sat up to stare both at the crowds, Bertrand and lastly Bobs. "His publicist?"

"I've got an entire mountain to encircle." Bobs glared at Joyce. "Do you know how big those things are? Have you ever been out in the mountains? I need bodies. We're going to need to find all the exits from this mine if we're going to trap him in it, and since this thing was abandoned over a century ago they won't be easy to find."

"Since when are you the boss of this operation?"

"Since I'm the one who knows what the fuck I'm doing."

"Enough!" shouted Bertrand. "We're almost there. Corner of 28th and 2nd. See that weird white tent-like thing over the intersection: that's where he said we'd meet him."

The city was flat, but a sharp ridge rose on the horizon on the far side of town like a promise of more mountains to come. At the junction of two downtown roads just ahead, an artist's tribute to the mountains lofted above the intersection. Despite Bertrand's description of it being "tent-like," it was a permanent construction of white metal tubing rising from three street corners and sweeping up to the fourth like a smooth mountainside of white canvas that laced between the support structures. It looked unlikely to provide much shelter for the intersection in winter, since the panels made no attempt to form a perfect roof, but it was interesting in an artistic sense and brought a definite presence to the otherwise unremarkable street.

Crowds were held back by police barricades, but the men and women who patrolled them wore white headbands with the 1000 Souls logo in the center of their foreheads. In the middle of the intersection stood twelve very old people, eleven of them in white robes that billowed in the wind and would have fit well in a biblical movie, but the man on the far side of the circle, Erics, still wore his purple, pinstriped, three-piece suit. A red container of gasoline sat on the road in front of each person in the circle.

Jeff eased the bus to a halt and opened the door, by now everyone on board awake and gawking, many pushing into the aisle in anticipation of disembarking and stretching.

"Wait just a goddamn second," said Bertrand to no one in particular. "I don't like the feel of this, and what's with the gas cans."

"We're trapped." Joyce stood, forcing Bobs over in order to get close to Bertrand. "If we need to move these buses in a hurry we can only do it if we run over a bunch of people."

Jeff shook his head. "I think they're friendly, but I don't think we should all just go pouring off the bus."

"I'll go." Bobs started to push past Bertrand. "I want to talk to this asshole anyway."

"No way." Bertrand blocked her path. "I arranged his help and I'll go out."

"Not alone," said Jeff.

Several voices chorused agreement and offered help, but Bertrand turned to face the interior of the bus and put up his hands to quiet everyone. "Calm down. I'll just go and check things out with Jeff and Joyce. Everybody else stays on the bus for a minute. Emile, walkie back to Martin and Barry and tell them to keep their people on the buses for a couple of minutes."

Bobs started to argue but Bertrand shook his head. "Don't be offended, but I need a leader here in case everything goes sideways. Everybody's used to you shouting orders anyway, so just chill, okay?"

Bobs folded her arms but looked satisfied. "Okay. Until you get back on the bus, I'm in charge."

That wasn't what Bertrand meant, but he decided this was not the time to dicker about their fluid command structure. He headed down the stairs to a rock star's welcome. People shouted and cheered and pushed against wood barricades and the Erics pseudo-cops, who struggled to hold them back.

Bertrand started to approach the circle of twelve, embarrassed that he had forgotten to put the Winchester down before he got off the bus. Wearing a Glock and carrying a shotgun didn't seem appropriate when meeting the old man who had helped save St. Michael's Church.

Jeff—still wearing his Ruger in his holster—moved to Bertrand's left and Joyce to his right. Bertrand noted that she had brought her Uzi, slung over her shoulder by the strap. How did they look, all of them armed as if going to a gunfight instead of meeting with friends?

Erics put up both hands, palms out, to indicate that Bertrand should stop. If anything, the curious man looked more eccentric in person, his beard whiter and longer than the distorted Skype video had given the impression. His purple suit was more frayed than Bertrand had imagined, but it was clean and pressed, as if Erics had dropped out of the workforce in the eighties but kept the trappings. He supported himself with the elaborately carved wooden cane, which looked as if it may have started this new role as a piece of driftwood before an artist got to work. His disciples—the eleven others in the circle—were a mix of ethnic backgrounds. Some were black like Erics, several were white, at least one man was possibly middle-eastern and two were Asian. All were old, and all looked very determined, their jaws clenched, their eyes paying no attention to Bertrand or the crowd, instead looking into the center of the circle at a painted infinity symbol on the pavement.

When Erics spoke, it was immediately clear that he wore a microphone connected to a live public address system.

"The time of great trial has arrived."

The crowd fell perfectly silent. Oddly, the street behind the circle as far as the eye could see was empty of people, the Erics pseudo-cops holding the crowd away from it.

"We can't attack until tomorrow morning," called Bertrand. Why was Erics holding him back? Why weren't they meeting for a council of war, and why was Bertrand's heart beating so slowly and distinctly, heavy pounds that threatened chest pain? It reminded him very much of his panic attack in the road outside of Needleman's.

"What's this all about?" Joyce asked Bertrand. Her hand pressed her chest.

"You are the three," said Erics. "The three souls that always come together in times of need." He pointed to Bertrand. "The Dormant Hero."

The crowd suddenly roared its approval.

Erics put his hands out again, a gesture so similar to what Bertrand had used to quiet the people on the bus that he wondered if he was being mocked, but there was no slyness in the old man's face.

"For years, even generations, you go about life as an ordinary man, but in times of upheaval you rise up to lead and to fight and sometimes to die for the cause."

Bertrand didn't like the last part. To die for the cause? He fought to breathe normally. What was happening to him? Was it some kind of gas—hypnotism? Was he under attack?

Bertrand looked left to Jeff, whose forehead had broken out in a sweat in spite of the crisp fall air. He looked right to Joyce to see that her eyes were wide and that she had swung the Uzi down.

Erics pointed to her next. "The Angry Captain. A natural leader who charges at the front but languishes as a ruler."

"What the hell does that mean?" shouted Joyce over the cheers of the crowd.

Erics pointed to Jeff. "The Dependable Rogue, a soul who will reject positions of authority yet wields great influence in all events."

"I like a good drink too." Jeff turned to Bertrand. "Look, I'm suddenly not feeling well and you look pasty as hell. I think we should get back on the bus and book. Something's really weird."

"Your souls will need to be dense for the struggle in the mountain," said Erics. "Your souls must be the strongest they can possibly be, so we have gathered together four of each people who host portions of your souls. We share the same soul, Bertrand Allan. You and I."

He pointed at Bertrand and back to himself.

"I am too old to fight in the mountain with this host body, so my portion of the soul must join with your body, with your very dense portion of the Dormant Hero."

Now the crowd fell silent, breathless.

Erics voice softened and he sounded apologetic. "So that my soul portion does not dissipate to all the hosts of the Dormant Hero, it must be a sudden and violent and painful transfer. Our soul-portions must flee to your three bodies." He gave a pained smile. "This will be difficult for all of us."

Bertrand adjusted the shotgun in his hands, taking a hold of the pistol grip with his right and the slide with his left. "You're right, Jeff." Bertrand's voice carried far in the silence. "We need to get out of here. Let's just back up slowly."

Erics smiled again, and for a moment Bertrand saw a reflection of his fear, his chest pain. What was the nutbar doing? Now Bertrand was sure this man was a lunatic. Before he could back up, Erics dropped his cane, and he and his eleven followers suddenly bent over and picked up their red containers of gasoline.

"The 1000 live on!" called Erics, his voice booming over the crowd.

He upended the container and fluid gushed over him, soaking his suit and plastering his beard to his face and his chest—flattening his long white hair. The container wasn't even half-full, so this only took a few seconds.

"The 1000 live on!" shouted the other eleven, upending their plastic containers and soaking themselves. The stench of gasoline wafted through the air.

The eleven disciples blinked and wiped the gas from the eyes, but kept their focus on the infinity symbol in the center of the intersection. Erics, however, carefully drew a long barbecue lighter from his jacket pocket as if merely producing a fine cigar for a smoke. He looked straight across the circle to Bertrand. "Prepare yourself. I am coming to you now."

Bertrand's heart clenched, a tetanic contraction that could only be a heart attack. It robbed him of words, of actions and of hope.

Erics snapped the lighter. The fumes did the rest, bringing the tiny flame from the lighter to Erics' clothing and hair. A whoosh pushed heat across the circle in Bertrand's direction.

But while Erics cried out, his actions were controlled and prepared. He raised his flaming arms to form a T, the fingers extended to point to each of his disciples on either side. All eleven now raised their arms into the same T formation with military precision, as if they were graduates of some bizarre training. The flames at the end of Erics' fingertips leapt to the follower on either side, rushing around the circle to ignite all eleven followers until the circle of twelve burning humans was complete. It held for a full, prolonged heartbeat before it broke as people fell to twist and scream and burn. Only Erics still stood, and keeping his arms still stretched out, he brought his palms together in front, his fingertips now pointing straight at Bertrand.

Bertrand's heart let go, giving a heavy beat and another. He could breathe and move. And Erics was dying a horrible death. There were no burn units or paramedics that could save him or his followers. Bertrand suddenly knew that all he could do to help was to bring about a faster end to Erics' life.

He raised the Winchester and fired across the circle, hitting Erics in the chest and dropping him to the ground. Rage and fear and anger now flamed in Bertrand's chest. How dare this man put him in this position, make him a killer of humans? Bertrand stepped toward the circle, firing at the flailing and ruined people. Jeff's Ruger shot on his left and Joyce's Uzi fired three round bursts on his right as they advanced, the reek of burning flesh and hair now choking the square.

Brains and blood splattered the pavement, and part of the canvas awning above melted and fell, dangling over the street and twisting as the flames from Erics licked at the white material.

Bertrand stopped shooting and backed up in case more of the awning caught the flames, but it was over. The twelve lay dead, charred bundles and twisted lumps of flame scattered roughly in a circle on a pavement.

Someone in the crowd started shouting, "One thousand. One thousand."

Others picked up the chant until the whole crowd shouted it to the sky.

"We've got to get out of here," shouted Jeff.

But it was too late. The crowd charged.

# 31

# HORROR IN THE MOUNTAIN

B obs flew off the bus like an avenging angel—a dark angel—her AR-15 firing three round bursts at the crowd, dropping the people closest to Bertrand. Terry and Emile followed close behind, but just as they opened fire, a pudgy man who had been running at Bertrand with an outstretched hand shouted, "Stop! Stop! We love you!"

Screams and shouts of horror that the crowd had not expressed at the death of Erics and his disciples now sounded, and within seconds the tide turned, the crowd retreating, some helping wounded or dead friends, others like the pudgy man begging them to stop shooting.

"Hold your fire!" shouted Bertrand at the top of his lungs, pointing his shotgun into the air.

But with the crowd in full retreat, their backs to the shooters, the order was redundant. Bobs kept the rifle leveled at the pudgy man, but she held her fire, instead marching to put her barrel right in his face.

"What the fuck is wrong with you people!" she shouted.

"It's a misunderstanding," said the man, his voice high and squeaky, his hands raised in surrender. "People just wanted to touch you, to feel your souls getting denser. Listen, I'm the mayor of Billings—was the mayor of Billings. We just want to help any way we can."

"This is help?" Bertrand shouted, pointing with his shotgun at the burning corpses. He counted the other bodies, the people from the crowd shot by Bobs and Terry and Jeff and Joyce—and himself. Seven more dead.

"It's all right," said the mayor. "The 1000 live on."

Rage and fear are a dangerous mix. Bertrand wanted to shoot him. "Get. On. The. Bus," he said instead, again pointing with the shotgun.

---

Barry and Martin joined them on the front bus. They put the mayor in the first seat back and surrounded him so that they could all hear. His name was Ted Grimes, but in spite of the gritty name, he was effeminate for a balding, middle-aged man.

"Billings was lost months ago. I think the rippers raided into small cities like this before they hit you guys in Chicago, because all the news made it seem like everything was normal except for the real estate crash and the stock market. A lot of us hid out in the hills, and some tried to go over the mountains to the coast, but they came back saying there were roadblocks—border crossing type roadblocks right here in the U. S. of A. You couldn't go on unless you donated a pint of blood and signed a contract agreeing to do it every month."

"Every month?" said Joyce. "That can't be healthy. I get three months between donations."

The little man nodded. "Just when I'd decided to try heading for Grand Forks or Dakota, or maybe even Canada, Erics came with thousands of his people. They said they were making the way clear for you. That was just a couple of days ago. In one day they went basement to basement and pulled the rippers out into the sun, most of them shot dead first. It was glorious. They retook Billings, but there aren't many of us from the town left. There's a field to the east, and I seen the bodies: they're piled for acres, dumped there by dump trucks. They killed so many and they took so many away—west—I saw the trucks, people packed into them like cattle going to—"

Grimes broke down and sobbed.

"Pull it together, asshole," said Bobs. "I buried my parents and I'm not weeping every day."

"I lost my wife, three children and one grandchild," sobbed Grimes, looking up at Bobs in disbelief.

"Whoa! Whoa!" said Bertrand. "We'll add up the dead relative score later. Bobs, give the guy a break. Mr. Grimes, I'm sorry for your loss but you've got to bury your grief so that we can end this apocalypse now and begin to rebuild. So where are you with these Erics fanatics? Will they listen to you?"

"Yes. Erics said I contained a portion of the Jolly Leader and that they should trust me, but he said you and he are the same soul, so instructions and teachings from you are also from him. They believe you're him now. I kinda believe myself. Look what they've accomplished in Billings in just a couple of days. If only I'd known what was going on three months ago when people started disappearing, I could have got our own police to do something like go basement to basement, but by the time I became a believer the cops were all either rippers or dead."

"They go for the government and the cops first," Bertrand said. "It's not your fault, and I'm impressed they didn't get you."

"I spent the summer in the mountains camping." Grimes radiated shame. "I wasn't here for them, for my town, for my family. My wife and I ... since the kids left home things haven't worked out so well, see? She asked me to move out, so I went to our cabin out near Wind Mountain."

"Is that anywhere near Cave Mountain?"

Grimes looked up, surprised. "It's just up the road."

Bertrand turned to Joyce, who stood beside Bobs in the aisle. "We should aim to get to Grand Forks just before dawn in case the rippers own the town. Bobs, try and get a call through to Colonel Webb and ask him if we'll get any protection from Malmstrom."

"You won't." Grimes' voice had risen to a squeak. "The rippers took Grand Forks before they even took Billings. I found out the hard way trying to come back and barely got out of there alive, and only because I've got a four-wheel drive and I got the heck off the roads. I ended up coming through Helena, south of the Lewis and Clark Forest. It takes a couple of hours longer but it's a lot safer. Malmstrom's totally cut off and fighting with the rippers every night. During the day there's like this volunteer ripper army of cops and college kids and stuff that keep them bottled up. At first it didn't work so well, but I heard they're running out of jet fuel."

Jeff called from the driver's seat where he'd been keeping watch. "Bert, people are coming back."

Bertrand yanked Grimes to his feet. "You go out there and tell them that I'll speak to them soon, but in the meantime they're to keep the hell back from my buses."

Grimes hurried off the bus and Jeff closed the door.

"So we camp here for the night?" he asked, not looking like he thought it was a good idea.

Bertrand shook his head. "We can't keep this a surprise if we take too long to form. We should drive on asap, taking as many of the Erics people with us as we can, and get to the mountain before dawn. They won't expect us to arrive during the middle of the night."

"The Erics people?" Bobs looked outraged. "You still want to hook up with these lunatics after what that freakazoid just did?"

"Yes, yes, yes." Bertrand fought his frustration with the arguments. "You're the one who said we need to encircle an entire mountain. That means numbers, right?"

Bobs nodded. "Okay, you got me there."

Joyce spoke up. "But if we arrive in the middle of the night, rippers will be out and can see us coming. Buses are loud and we're going to need headlights."

"You just heard him: they've got daytime help. Once we start driving up that isolated mountain road—what's it called again?"

"Teton Canyon Road," said Jeff. "They could ambush us in the mountains and rain fire down on the buses. I don't like this."

"I thought it was open prairie until the last few miles." Bertrand turned so he could see Jeff. "Didn't you Google terrain it before we left?"

"I did, and it is. Wide open ground until the last few miles."

"Good, then we drive through the night and hold up a few miles back in open ground. At the crack of dawn we start up and drive in."

"How do we get the Erics people there?" asked Joyce.

"They got here just a couple of days ago, so they must have rides of some kind, maybe buses like ours to move that many people. We've got our generators and pumps, so we'll help them get fuel from gas stations on the way."

Joyce looked pensive. "Bert, what if we suck all the gas stations dry? How are we going to get back?"

"We'll worry about that tomorrow night."

Joyce nodded and pursed her lips together, and the bus went silent, because the unspoken hung in the air: *if there was a tomorrow night.*

---

The Erics people did have buses, and vans, and SUVs. Joyce organized them into a convoy, with Bertrand's buses following a dozen SUVs, followed by the buses of the Erics army, followed last by more SUVs that could run information to the front of the column if necessary.

Jeff drove the bus, relying on the GPS and going by Grimes' southern route that took them far from Grand Forks and Malmstrom Airbase. Emile squeezed up and down the bus making sure people had properly cleaned their firearms. No one slept.

Bertrand and Grimes sat together, and Joyce and Bobs knelt on the seats in front of them so that they could face back and plan.

"There's only one entrance to the old mine and it's pretty hard to find." Grimes had initially begged them to stay overnight in Billings, apparently afraid of the highway after sunset. Then he'd suggested he drive his own van, but Bobs had insisted he ride with them and Bertrand had agreed. Having someone who knew the mountain was better than he could have imagined.

"How did you find this mine if it's so hidden?" As Bobs spoke, her friend Terry stood behind her, busily clipping away at her long hair.

Bobs wanted short hair for the fight so that enemies would have less to grab if they got close.

"I was hunting up that way last year," said Grimes. "Lucky thing is it's not a shaft you can fall in but a drift. They found a vein of copper and they just followed it into the mountain, winding down and up and anywhere it took them. There's no railroad tracks or anything like that, because they just hauled the rock back with wagons and mules."

"So you've been in there." Bertrand could hardly contain his excitement. "How far in does it run? Are there caverns?"

Grimes shuddered and his voice rose an octave. "I didn't go far in there. It's real spooky, even with a good flashlight. Stuff got left behind, tools and stuff, and every corner I turned I expected to run into a body or something."

"But it's just got one entrance." Bobs said this with a tension that caused Bertrand to look over at her. Bobs' eyes had that ferocious look—that attack look Bertrand had come to know. What was she on about?

Grimes didn't know her and blathered on without sensing the danger. "Just one. It's going to be really hard for you guys to fight your way in, even in daylight."

"You're not one of the 1000 Souls." Bobs' eyes bored holes into Grimes' face, but still he was oblivious. "You even said yourself that they just showed up a couple of days ago. What brought you back to Billings, a city you said was controlled by the rippers? I'd have stayed in the mountains myself."

At last Grimes understood that this had become an interrogation, and his whole presence sharpened like a deer that hears an engine from around a curve on a highway.

"I was out of food!" It was a protestation of innocence.

"A hunter, in the mountains and you're out of food? You prefer to drive six hours into a ripper town and jostle elbows with the Daylight Brigade to clean out the grocery stores of canned food?"

"I'm not a really good hunter. I'm too fat to climb the hills these days."

Bertrand now smelled the rat and he admired Bobs' sense. He should have seen these inconsistencies.

"Anything else Bobs," Bertrand asked, because she had the look of a prosecutor who has yet to play the trump card.

"Terry." Bobs gave her friend, her lieutenant, a glance that spoke more than words could. He put down the scissors and started rummaging through a portable file folder while Bobs turned back to Grimes. "So you were up there all summer, right? Your cabin's near the road, right?"

Grimes definitely sensed his danger. "I'm not that close to the road, really not that close."

Terry pulled an eight-by-ten printout of a satellite photo from the folder and passed it to Bobs.

"These are sat photos provided to us by the Illinois National Guard. Show me on this photo where your cabin is." Bobs leaned over the seat and held out the photo but didn't let go.

Grimes hardly looked at it. "Oh, you can't see my place here because it's way under the trees."

"Bullshit!" Bobs' shout galvanized attention on the bus. "This whole area got logged out years ago. All that nice green we can see on the sat photo is new growth way less than a hundred years old, so they aren't big enough to hide a house."

"It's a really small cabin!" Grimes' voice had risen an octave.

"Is this your place right here? The one with the nice new metal roof?"

Grimes looked at the photo this time, but Bertrand noted that the man's fat fingers trembled as he reached for the paper. "Oh yup. I guess that is my place. It's just so nice and treed I figured that they were all above the house."

"Right by the road. So how come you didn't notice this big drill rig go by in July?"

Terry passed Bobs another satellite photo showing several vehicles at the base of Cave Mountain. She pointed to the yellow rectangle as she spoke. "Or how about all this waste rock that just appeared in August? Did you notice that?" She pointed to a scar through the green on the side of the mountain.

"I never go up there." Grimes' eyes were wide and his voice had managed to rise even higher.

"Not since you found the entrance to the cave."

"Like I said, it's spooky."

"And you never saw this cattle truck full of people go up the road?" She handed him another photo, and Terry began feeding one after the other that she passed on to Bertrand and Grimes.

"Or this one. Or this one. Or this one, you lying shit!"

"No! No! I just don't pay much attention to the road. I like music and I play it real loud when I'm lonely."

Bobs looked to Bertrand. "My folks had a cabin in Wisconsin, and I can tell you that if one truck—let alone dozens—went up the road during the summer we'd have noticed. This guy's in with the rippers."

"I am not!" Grimes shook his head wildly.

Terry calmly handed Bobs a .45 and she shoved the barrel against Grimes' left nostril, pushing his head back painfully.

"No, no, no! Please! It wasn't my fault. I can still help you."

Joyce took a hold of Bobs' gun arm and gently pulled it back, but when it was clear Joyce punched Grimes in the face with enough force to provoke a nosebleed.

"Jesus Christ!" Grimes pressed his fingers to his face, somewhat muffling his protest. "Why'd you have to do that?"

"Because you're leading us into a trap that's designed to kill us all," said Joyce.

"No!" But he saw the look on Joyce's face. "Okay, wait, wait!" He held up one hand to ward off another punch. "Okay. It is a trap, but if you guys would just give in and join with the rippers you could all live."

Terry passed Bobs another photo.

"Like these people?" She passed it to Bertrand.

It took him a minute to resolve the grainy image because it just looked like another scar on the side of the mountain like the pile of rock, but a human torso and legs stuck out from one side, and Bertrand sucked in his breath. "There's got to be hundreds."

Bobs handed another photo. "That was from last week," she said. "If you flip through these you can see it growing all summer. They didn't even bother to hide the bodies. They just dumped them out their back door."

"Please." Grimes still had one hand clamped over his nose, the blood leaking between his fingers, his voice nasal in tone. "I had no choice. I was in one of those trucks. You can't imagine it! They rounded us up like cattle right out of a city hall meeting. My own chief of police waving a gun in my face and telling me I'd been declared fodder. I didn't even know what that meant, and then they stuff us into the trucks and drive all night to Cave Mountain. Even in July that's a freezing ride and the only good about being packed that tight was that it helped us stay warm, but there was nowhere to go to the washroom or sit down and people were sick and then we got there."

He stopped weeping now, and someone from farther back in the bus passed him a box of Kleenex. He took a moment to stuff two of them into his nose to stop the bleeding, but hurried on when he saw the look on Joyce's face.

"They spilt us up and told the men, guys like me, that we could volunteer for the Daylight Brigade or die. You have to understand, if you're in the Daylight Brigade you get a lot of rewards like good food, pick of the women, booze and drugs." He saw the look on Joyce's face. "It's good for the women too, 'cause if they can get pregnant they don't get bled out. You just have to do your job during the day, and you get all that at night. And you get to live forever. If you get cancer or you get old they'll make you into a brid and the bugs'll cure you of anything. They can find and destroy cancer cells like crazy."

"Live? So that you can murder people." Bertrand's voice was low, but the rage was high.

"Wait, Bert." Joyce put out one hand to stop him from attacking Grimes. "We can use this. Tell us about Vlad. Why's he doing this?"

"Which Vlad?" Grimes looking genuinely puzzled.

"Vlad the Scourge, the frigging Anti-Christ himself."

But Bertrand had a different question. "What do you mean, which Vlad?"

"Don't you guys know?" Grimes looked to each in turn. "There's like a thousand or more all over the world. There's Vlad the Impaler, Vlad Tepes, Vlad the Angry. In India he goes by the name of some Hindu god, in China it's some ancient horror I don't even know what. You people have just got to join them. They're remaking the world."

Bertrand again resisted the urge to hit the pudgy little man. "Which one is at the mountain right now?"

"Vlad the Scourge. He's the guy for North America. Some say he's *the* guy and that the others are his disciples. God, you guys don't really know much, do you?"

"Educate me." Bertrand had to fight to keep his voice calm, his anger in check.

"One of them his the real Vlad, the Romanian prince that Count Dracula was based on, only he wasn't a count, see? He was a prince—he makes a big deal about that—and he fought the Turks like crazy. He's patient zero, the guy who started all this and spread the disease all over the world."

"Wasn't that like hundreds of years ago?" asked Bertrand. Could it really be true? If they defeated this guy would another fly over from Europe or China?

"I told you if you've got the bugs you live forever."

"This could all be bullshit," Joyce said. "We can't take this guy's word for anything."

"No." Bobs took back all the photos. "But there is one good thing. We've got him prisoner. Vlad must think we're sitting the night in Billings like this asshole begged us to, but we're on the way. Better yet he thinks when we do show up we'll do a frontal assault on his hideout, but from these photos I've picked out at least three different entrances. We'll hit them all at once. That is if you still think it's worth it to get this guy."

Bertrand thought of all the people who could die tomorrow, but then the image of the bodies in the satellite photo shoved that aside. "We should drag every ripper in the mine the hell out, and save any humans left, whether this is *the* Vlad or not."

Emile had joined them sometime during the interrogation. "All right! Let's kill them all!"

"Wait a minute," said Joyce. "What if there's another spy with the Erics people?"

Bertrand heaved a deep sigh. "We're just going to have to trust Erics' judgment. His people just got to Billings yesterday and he sent good people to us in Chicago."

Bobs rolled her eyes. "Great. I'm with ya, but I'm not happy about trusting the judgment of a guy who turned himself into a frigging torch."

Bertrand shrugged. "We don't have a choice."

# 32

# BATTLE OF THE MOUNTAIN

In the dark Bertrand went from bus to bus, and from van to SUV after they had halted on Teton Canyon Road. Flat plains spread around them, but not far ahead a heavy bulk thrust out of the earth to occlude the stars and prove the mountains close. The plains were brutally cold, well below zero, but the spectacle of stars forced Bertrand to stop in awe several times and stare up at the heavens. These were not stars dimmed by city lights. The topographic maps stated that they were at four thousand feet above sea level, so these stars were more spectacular than when viewed from Chicago even during the most widespread blackouts.

But a flush of pink on the eastern horizon kept Bertrand hurrying to organize his little army. Murray, the Erics captain that Bertrand had first met in Chicago, would lead the Erics people from Billings grouped with the Erics from Chicago. It was their job to encircle the base of the mountain to look for secret exits and to fight in through any they found. Barry St. John and Martin Morley, the former McDonald's manager, would lead Barry St. John's construction crew into the lower of the three entrances. Joyce would lead her Raiders, and Bertrand and

Jeff would go with her, sticking together as promised. Bobs would lead her army of St. Mike's volunteers, which included her die-hard loyalists from the community center. Bobs' people chose blue armbands, and Joyce's red. Barry's crew went with red bandanas.

"We keep in touch by walkie as much as we can," Bertrand said on each bus and at each smaller vehicle. "But remember that once inside the mountain the rock will probably block our reception. Be sure to leave rear guards along the way and runners to communicate with them."

Grimes they handcuffed in the back of the bus.

"If we fail I'm sure his ripper buds will find him tonight and ask him why he didn't warn them that we were coming a day early," said Bobs. "If not I'll deal with him."

Grimes looked terrified.

As soon as the first tip of the sun broke the horizon, they started the engines and drove for the canyon. The mountains lunged up from the plain ahead of them, the snow pink with the rising sun, the young conifers growing wherever the rock allowed. The road had hardly been paved up to this point, but as they took the north fork, it changed to gravel, but thankfully the dry air hadn't provided enough snow to block the road even this late in the fall, and for the most part there was no snow except on the mountains, whether due to sublimation or a warm spell Bertrand didn't know.

They kept a sharp eye up the hills for ambush by a Daylight Brigade as they entered the canyon; a stream on their left still bubbled along, ice free except for in a few still areas where beavers had dammed. On their right, the layers of fractured sedimentary rock rose at sharp angles, demonstrating the power of the earth's crust to heave up what was once flat.

"According to the map," said Jeff, standing beside Bertrand at the front of the bus while Emile drove. "That's Wind Mountain on our left. When we get around this corner we'll be looking at Cave Mountain."

Emile hauled over on the steering wheel as they made a sharp turn around the shoulder of a hill. Suddenly, less than a mile away, a strong mountain rose two thousand feet above the road. It had many shoulders, and its peaks had been worn down enough that several competed to be the highest part of the mountain, although one on the north side—the side farthest from them—looked a bit higher than the rest.

While most of the mountain had a thin forest of spruce, the southern face of gray rock was too steep and smooth to hold soil or trees. Near the bottom of the bare slope, the rock had fractured and a deep cavity showed the natural cave that gave the mountain its name.

Emile brought the bus to a fork in the road where a folksy wooden sign with snow white lettering declared:

**LEWIS AND CLARK**
***NATIONAL FOREST***
**RECREATION AREA**
**CAVE MOUNTAIN**
**DEPARTMENT OF AGRICULTURE**

"There's the scout." Bertrand pointed to a black SUV that powered toward them on the left fork, crossing a narrow Bailey-type bridge over the river. It flashed its headlights and performed a quick U-turn to lead them back across the bridge. They followed it through flat approaches to the mountain, snow and ice on either side of the road now as they passed through swampy areas and thin spruce, the few hardy deciduous trees bare of leaves.

A new road gouged its way to their right, climbing straight through trees ripped away by heavy equipment and tossed aside. The road leveled in a wide area, which had been made into a flat pad with the use of hundreds of tons of gravel. On one side, six helicopters sat smashed and burned, clearly destroyed where they had sat rather than while in the air. Several pieces of heavy construction equipment, including a bulldozer and a Bobcat skid-steer loader had been spared the air strike.

"It looks like Webb got a hold of either Malmstrom or Minot and closed Vlad's escape route." Bertrand pointed at the helicopters, hardly able contain his excitement. "This is just great."

The superhero inside him rejoiced. Bertrand had felt that heightened inner strength for so long since Needleman's that he had come to accept it as his normal self, but in the last day it had grown. Was it a psychosomatic reaction to seeing Erics die? Was he more powerful because he secretly believed Erics, or had his soul truly become denser?

Emile brought the bus to a halt and opened the door. Bertrand leapt from the bus.

People formed up quickly, easily over four-hundred souls all ready to risk everything. They were regular people. Some were teenagers. Some were middle-aged. They were all ready to die if they could just end this apocalypse and leave a normal world for others to repopulate.

Bertrand wanted to just run up the mountain trail that wound through the trees and rock, but Bobs hurried up and caught his arm.

"You have to say something to them, Bert. You have to inspire them."

"Time is everything." But even as he said this, he knew she was right.

He turned to the crowd, standing uphill from them so that they spread out below him. He could see every face. It irritated him for a moment that Terry stood in front with a video camera. They didn't need another YouTube video. This was it. He ignored the camera and summoned his courage. Inspire them. Why were they there?

"The worst evil in the world," he shouted, "is in that mountain." He pointed up the hill behind him. "I intend to go and get him, kill him, and drag him into the sun or burn his stinking corpse. I do this for my friends, in memory of my parents, for my city and for the world. Will you come with me so that we can take back our world from the rippers?"

Their shouts of "yes" broke the stillness of the morning, and shouts of "The 1000 live on!" were added by the crowd on the right with the white armbands.

"Our blood may be spilled today, but not to feed the rippers!"

More cheers rose to the sky.

"Let's go now and do what must be done!"

He turned and charged up the hill.

Cheers and pounding feet told Bertrand that the army followed him, and he thanked the sunlight that he could be sure the rippers wouldn't be able to shoot at them as they ran up the trail, but he kept a sharp eye for the Daylight Brigade. Surely they'd fire down on them now?

But as the thin mountain air slowed his charge and robbed his lungs of oxygen, no shots forced them to take cover. They could have been the only people for hundreds of miles.

Men and women started to pass Bertrand now, for even though he had lost a lot of weight in the last four months, he was far from ready to start running races.

"Hold back! Hold back!" he shouted. He wanted to be first into the mountain, the first to come to grips with the source of all the frustration and fear. This was why he had been born.

He needn't have worried. A square hole had been blasted into the rock as if a railroad company had begun work on a tunnel, the scoring showing that this was new work. Bobs led her people left, heading higher up the mountain for the natural cave. Bertrand ran into the mouth, but only a short way down the tunnel they found a concrete block wall with a heavy steel door. Several people, including Joyce and Jeff, had already stopped in front of it, turning to Bertrand to see what he'd say.

"First challenge. I should've known they'd block the way."

Joyce waved her arms at her troops. "Everybody get to the sides of the tunnel. I have help coming along." She turned to Bertrand. "While you were making your speech, I was talking to my scouts. Emile's bringing up that Bobcat, and he says it'll go through here no problem, but we're not going to knock on the front door until everyone's ready."

She adjusted the microphone of her walkie and spoke, but an engine—growing louder by the second—buried her words. The small front-end loader rolled into the cave on its four big tires, Emile in the protective cage. He stopped and waited for Joyce's signal.

"Come on. Everybody get against the walls," Joyce called, running up and down the tunnel to push people back. "We charge in pairs right behind the loader. Take that side, Bert." She pointed to the right where Jeff already waited. "You and I will lead."

Bertrand pressed against the gray rock, feeling oddly like they were rehearsing for a wedding procession with Jeff as his best man. He checked his Glock for the tenth time that day and put it back in the holster. He pumped a round into the breach of the Winchester, trembling with anticipation. The monster he'd wanted to attack against all odds at Goth Knights was here.

Joyce had one hand pressed to her walkie earpiece to hear, and Bertrand mimicked her so that he could listen in on his walkie.

"Barry here. I've got the cat lined up to smash our way in here. Let me know when to roll."

"Bobs here. My boys have put a whack of C4 on the door up here. Let us know when and we'll blow it."

Joyce looked across at Bertrand and he nodded.

"Go! Go! Go!" Joyce waved Emile forward even as she shouted into the walkie.

The Bobcat roared ahead, belching fumes and choking the tunnel with foul air. It slammed into the concrete block wall and pushed it and the steel door well into the next chamber.

"St. Mike's!" Bertrand had no clue where he got the idea to shout this, but even as the words left his lips he knew a lot of the people behind him would identify with that call. Back at St. Mike's were their families, their children and their hopes.

He charged through the gap, stumbling on fractured concrete blocks but righting himself in time to avoid tripping, his shotgun pointing the way. He gasped on fumes from the Bobcat even though Emile had shut it down as soon as he had cleared the wall.

Florescent lights on the ceiling, two four-foot bulbs, illuminated the little white-and-black machine through a haze of dust thrown up by their violent entrance, so Bertrand shut off the flashlight he had duct taped on top of the Winchester. He hurried past the machine, staying close to the rock wall. Farther along, another florescent light, the cheap kind that could be found in any hardware store, lit the next section of tunnel, which curved off to the left. Dark shapes clung to the walls near the curve, and even as Bertrand took aim, muzzle flashes from the enemy lit the tunnel with dazzling staccatos of light, creating a strobe-like effect.

Gunfire in a tunnel is loud. Gun reports from their enemy blasted Bertrand's eardrums, let alone the blasts from his shotgun. He should be afraid. Battle and death are what people fear, but he had never been so calm in his life, burying the exhilaration to aim and shoot at first one and then another ripper.

It didn't bother him that they looked ordinary, that one man reminded him of his high school librarian, another of his bartender. Rock chips and ricochets flew around the tunnel, nearly as dangerous as the bullets that whizzed past. First one and then another of the rippers dropped, others fled back down the tunnel.

Bertrand was aware that there was shouting in his walkie earpiece, but even with the volume turned to maximum he couldn't hear much of what was being said. He caught the words "heavy resistance" once, and another time he was sure he heard Bobs shout, "Fucking pussies!" He was vaguely aware of Joyce shouting across the tunnel, waving people forward as the rippers ran, but he was now in his own deafened world, the slow thud of his heartbeat the only thing proving to him that he wasn't a robot.

And the rage. There was a rage building that had nothing to do with Vlad or the rippers. It was a rage fed by his sense of abandonment. How dare his parents die? How dare God or fate damn him to loneliness? He should have had years more with them, their guidance, their help. Part of him knew this was trivial compared to the dangers of the day, and maybe that's why it surfaced now.

"Come on!" He waved people forward as he ran down the tunnel, seeking to avenge his parents' random fatality. Jeff outran him and stopped to crouch against the wall and fire.

Bertrand waited until Jeff was reloading and ran past him, rounding the curve to find many more rippers, but even before he could shoot, many discharged their weapons and turned to run. He tripped, saving his life as dozens of poorly aimed bullets went over his head, although one tore at the shoulder of his leather jacket, but even this near miss didn't provoke fear. He was invincible. He would destroy them all. He would find Vlad and drive a stake through his rotten heart.

The tunnel wound down into the bowels of the mountain, rippers waiting at each curve, at each bend, Bertrand deafer with each gunshot. They fired wildly at him, but Bertrand's calm side remembered Emile's admonishment.

"You can't carry infinite frigging ammo. Make your shots count. Don't just spray and pray." That was Emile's often-repeated prayer.

One ripper, an older man when he had changed, stepped out in the middle of the tunnel, so bold that as Bertrand's shot took the man in the chest and dropped him, he had to wonder whether the man was committing suicide.

"Count your shots," Emile had said. Somehow, despite the chaos, Bertrand had been counting. Five shotgun rounds. He could either draw the Glock and shoot with that or stop to reload, but he had no way to carry the shotgun. He should've thought of that, have made some kind of holster for it. With the barrel sawed short and the pistol grip, it would've been easy.

He stopped with his back to the rock, the gunfire from the rippers wild and over his head. Was it a trap? Were they just leading them in? He looked across at Joyce on the other side of the tunnel, who went down on one knee to drop the mag out of her Uzi and slam another home. He could see her shouting across the tunnel but heard her through the walkie rather than over the gunfire.

"Don't stop! Keep them running!"

He would make love to her again, and it wouldn't be rushed and urgent and in a basement. They would take their time and he would get to know her body.

Emile's heavy bulk rushed past, followed by Jeff's lanky figure.

Bertrand fed the shells into his Winchester. Perhaps a gun with a magazine would be better right now, but he had become comfortable with the weapon. In seconds he was in pursuit of the others, and when they stopped to reload Bertrand rushed past them.

A face peeking around a corner warned Bertrand of a new danger. An intersection. If they ran through this, the rippers could fire on them from one side or the other. This was why he had brought grenades. Bertrand stopped a couple of car-lengths short, firing at the pale face to make the ripper duck and hide.

He yanked the grenade from his jacket pocket and pulled the pin, looking across at Joyce who had also stopped and taken out a grenade, shouting into her walkie.

"Fire in the hole!" She nodded to him.

Bertrand tossed his grenade at an angle and down the intersection tunnel on Joyce's side, and she did the same on his side; the paths of the grenades crossed and they nearly collided. Bertrand made a flash note of that. Next intersection, they shouldn't throw at the same moment, because if the grenades had collided they would have dropped right in front of them. Instead they got lucky and the grenades bounced down the perpendicular tunnels as intended. He put his head down and covered his ears and closed his eyes.

The explosions were brilliant and deafening, even with his eyes closed and ears covered. He rose up and charged the intersection, but the explosions had thrown up rock dust that rose to create an impenetrable cloud. He breathed in the acrid scent, and it reminded him of the dust from a bag of pre-mixed cement that he and his father had poured into a wheelbarrow when doing renovations in the back yard. He had complained that day because his father had neglected to purchase particle masks, but now he took great lungfuls, letting the memory of that sunny afternoon help him stay calm. Who cared about lung disease now with bullets flying?

He was lost in the haze, running down the tunnel when shouting on the walkie penetrated his brain and gunfire behind him warned of a new threat.

"Bert! Bert! Are you alive?"

It was a dim voice even with the walkie volume turned to full, but it was Joyce's, and that's why it grabbed his attention.

"Yeah! It's me! Where the hell are you guys?" He looked back down the tunnel and saw muzzle flashes through the haze, a veritable smoke screen. "Stop! Stop! You're shooting at me!" He flung himself to the floor.

"No we aren't. Rippers came down the side tunnels after you ran through. We're pinned if we don't shoot, but we can't see you."

He should have turned right at the intersection and made sure Joyce's grenade had cleared that tunnel. Who knows what crevices or barriers the rippers might have had to hide behind? Now he couldn't fire back without risk of hitting his friends and they couldn't fire forward. Amateur's mistake.

"Then shoot!" shouted Bertrand. "I'm going around the next curve!"

He stayed flat on the floor and crawled forward through dust and sharp gravel, rounding the curve as bullets ripped over his head. He rose up to shoot, but no targets presented themselves. The tunnel was empty. He turned back, leaning out to look around the curve. He heard Joyce both through the walkie and the air. "Fire in the hole!"

He dropped to one knee and covered his ears. The explosion flashed and tore through the tunnel. Shouts and screams and more gunfire warned Bertrand that some rippers were retreating his way, and he was alone. He turned and ran farther on to find a bulge in the rock wall of the tunnel that offered some shielding. He took up his position aiming back down the tunnel. Men Bertrand didn't recognize ran around the corner. They had no red or white or blue armbands, no bandanas. Bertrand fired and a red hole appeared in the chest of one ripper and it dropped to the floor. Many others pressed to the tunnel walls and muzzle flashes lit up the dust.

Bertrand returned fire, causing some of them to run back into the cloud at the intersection. He wanted to pursue them but feared shooting at his comrades, so he used the respite to run farther along the tunnel looking for better cover. He needed to reload and breathe and figure out how he could rejoin his people without getting his head blown off.

"Bert!" shouted Joyce's dim voice in his earpiece. "Where are you?"

"Way beyond the intersection. Anyone you see up there is a ripper."

"We're trying to get to you but they keep coming at the intersection."

For the first time since the fight began, Bertrand heard Bobs' voice. "Bert? That you I hear? Where are you?"

"Separated from Joyce." Then a thought occurred to him. "Joyce, Bobs, can you guys hear each other?"

Two voices responded, "No," one stepping on and partially cutting off the other.

He was on the cusp, right between them, the curve cutting off the signals between the two companies and leaving Bertrand as the bridge.

"Joyce. Jeff. I'm around a sharp curve and there're no rippers here. I can hear Bobs so she must be down tunnel. I'm going to link up with her. Follow when you can."

291

"Don't die, Bert." It was Joyce's voice, and it thrilled Bertrand. Maybe she loved him as much as he loved her. Maybe that night in the bunker truly wasn't a one-of.

He turned and ran on alone, deeper into the heart of the mountain.

# 33

# THE MONSTER

The florescent lights became fewer and more spread out the deeper he went, the white electrical wire hanging between them like laundry lines. Bertrand ran on, Bobs' voice growing more distinct as he hurried down the tunnel. It continued to twist, convincing him that this was the original mine. The shoring now was a mix of nineteenth-century timber and modern steel jacks; the latter would provide little cover in firefight.

A shout ahead also came through the walkie.

"Bobs. I can hear you. I'm coming down a tunnel," Bertrand called back.

"You're going to land in a cavern. If you're coming down the tunnel I think you are, you'll see us across the way. I'll wave my flashlight at you 'cause there's not much light down here."

Bertrand was just wondering how much farther he'd have to run, his throat parched from rock dust and a lack of water. Another mistake. He should have carried a water bottle. Suddenly the rock walls disappeared and Bertrand found himself in an underwhelming cavern, the ceiling barely double his height. Fat pillars of rock had been left by miners to hold up the roof, and many modern jacks filled in other spaces to make it look more like a dark forest that a cavern. He switched on his light and flashed it around. If he were a ripper, this was where he would have made his stand, but no muzzle flashes replied to his light. Instead, about half a baseball field away, another flashlight waved at him.

As he crossed the cavern, the detritus of human habitation spoke of suffering and confinement. One area stank of defecation and urination—a makeshift latrine. In other places, clothing, mats and sleeping bags littered the floor. An empty pot sat on a camp stove, and mugs were lined up, running away from it like place-holders in a line for food.

When Bertrand reached Bobs, he wanted to hug her in relief but knew that would send all the wrong signals. She stood with her AR-15 slung over her shoulder, gray dust coating her face and clothes, sweat streaks running down her forehead and neck. A cluster of her followers and the ever-present Terry stood with her at a steel door.

"Bert. Great. Is Joyce close behind? We think we're going to have company in a minute. Come on in here and see."

She led the way through the door and suddenly they were in the twenty-first century. A bank of flat-screen monitors glowed on one wall, each showing a different security camera image: a sunny parking lot with their buses, the smashed helicopters in the background; a cloudy tunnel punctuated with muzzle flashes and men without armbands—rippers—fleeing a charge by Jeff and Joyce with Emile close behind; many rippers massing in a tunnel with one waving them forward; women and children pouring out a tunnel and into daylight, their clothing in rags and their skin stretched tight across their bones from starvation; a man sitting at a desk in a room looking at a laptop. He wore the cloak and the black leather, the mix of modern and medieval. Vlad the Scourge.

"That's the bastard." Bertrand pointed at the screen.

Vlad looked up from his computer and right at the camera—at them. He held up his gloved hand and crooked his finger to invite them to come in. He pointed to his left. Bertrand looked left and saw another steel door. He pointed to it and Vlad nodded.

"He's isolated," said Bobs. "Someone just needs to go in there and kill him."

Bertrand wanted to, but common sense prevailed. If Vlad was inviting him in, then it was a trap.

"We lock him in and deal with that first." Bertrand pointed to the screen that showed rippers moving along a tunnel. "And that. Where are they?

"The humans were here and I've got my people getting them out. I'll deal with the rippers, but I need you to kill Vlad."

"I'll wait for Jeff and Joyce. He's not going anywhere."

Bobs looked from Bertrand to the screen showing Vlad.

"Do you know what my mistake was at the community center, Bert?"

"Bobs, this is no time for—"

"I didn't plan how to motivate people beyond our escape. See, I motivated the whole neighborhood to band together there, and for a couple of weeks we were the safest place in the city, but then the rippers came in force."

"Bobs, you can tell me—"

"Let me fucking finish!" she shouted. "I motivated them to defend the center, even when guys twice my age were blubbering in the corner. I was the only one who believed we could not only get away but kill a bunch of rippers doing it too. I burned them alive and it felt great. But my fuck up was to have no plan for the next night. So there I was, stuck in the house with only Terry. I'd run around that day trying to convince people to move into a bunch of houses that could mutually defend each other, but most were trying to scatter out of the city, and so I figured out too late I would be isolated and alone."

Terry and the others had shifted at a subtle hand sign from Bobs.

"What's going on here?"

"You don't know how scared I was that night. I literally nearly shit myself because I was sure I was dead. Then you came charging in." Bobs backed up toward the exit, and now Terry and several others had their guns leveled at Bertrand.

"I saved you," said Bertrand. It was an accusation. "I saved your frigging life."

"Yes. And I need you to do it again."

"Bobs, we've won. Just wait for Joyce and the others to come up and we'll open this door and lob a hand grenade in and go in shooting. We could do it right now but I used mine up. You guys got any?"

"Bert, there's a long winter coming, and Father Alvarez showed me that religion can motivate people. They have to believe they're immortal in some way to hang together and fight. That's why religion doesn't work well in peacetime. People don't need it to give them courage to fight unless they've got cancer or something like that."

Bertrand pointed at the screen that showed Vlad. "We've won for God's sake. We kill this guy and everything goes back to normal."

"ARE YOU FUCKING KIDDING ME?" Bobs' scream pushed Bertrand back a step in surprise. "The population of the planet is probably one-quarter of what it was last Christmas, and by next spring it'll be a tenth, maybe even less. Right now there are millions of rippers just in America alone and they all need to feed—every fucking night. Millions more are going to die if they don't starve. Normal is over forever. I only came along on this stupid jaunt because I need to motivate people and for that I need a hero, preferably a martyr."

"What the—"

"I've built you into a bigger than life hero, Bert." Her eyes flashed. "I've made you a god, one that wouldn't give into the rippers like all the pussies in Washington and New York and on the west coast. We're going to have to fight their Daylight Brigades during the day too, you know. I've got a winter of starvation and civil war ahead of me."

"I'll be there. I promise we'll make this work. We've got all the Erics people—"

"I hate that shit. You know what he told me? I took his stupid test and it said I was the same soul as that evil freakazoid in there." She stabbed a finger at the screen where Vlad sat, patiently watching them. "He said I'm the Ruthless General—a general that would sacrifice anything to win. But that's not what I'm about. I just want to make sure that I'm never in the position I was that night that you rescued me, waiting for God to send a miracle. You were my miracle, Bert, but God helps those who help themselves. I won't be caught like that again. I'm not afraid to fight, but I'll never be trapped."

The monitor that featured the cavern showed flitting movement as rippers moved in. Bobs noted the movement. She put something down on the desk, but Bertrand was too busy studying her face to note what it was. All that was important now was to divert her from this course.

"Here comes the rippers into my trap," she said. "I'm going out to deal with them now. See my guys taking up positions? See Barry's guys coming down the tunnel behind the rippers. We've got them. Their only way out will be up toward Joyce's Raiders or up the tunnel after their slaves to the sun, and it's not even noon."

"Then lets lock him in and go mop up."

Bobs shook her head. "You go in there and kill that fuck or die trying, and if you try to come out this way Terry will shoot you, and I'll tell the world you died dragging Vlad into the sun. I need my martyr, Bert."

Gunfire sounded from the cavern. Terry opened the door and all of Bobs' young men backed out, their guns pointing at Bertrand. Bobs backed out last.

"Remember, Terry will be outside the door, and he'll blow your head off if you come out. Go and kill that monster for me. Be my hero just one more time. You know you want to face him."

She slammed the door.

On the monitor, Bertrand could see Terry and three others with blue armbands take up positions on either side of the door to the security room. Vlad looked up at him from the other monitor.

Bertrand could just wait. He could sit with his Winchester pointed at the door, with Vlad on the other side and wait for cooler and friendlier people to come within range of his walkie, but the truth was that Bertrand burned for revenge. He wasn't afraid of Vlad. He wanted him dead.

Bobs was right. He wanted to face Vlad the Scourge.

# 34

# THE SAINT

Bertrand raised his shotgun and put a hand on the doorknob, acutely aware that Vlad could see everything that he was doing. He checked over his shoulder at the monitor but it showed that Vlad sat patiently at his desk, looking up at the camera and thus out of the monitor.

Bertrand thought of hockey and decided a feint was in order. Attack was necessary. He had never felt so sure of anything in his life. Fear was buried. He had the gun.

He let go of the doorknob and turned in the little room to rush for the outer door as if he were running away to the door beyond which Terry lay in wait, but Bertrand turned at the last second back to Vlad's door, rushing in to open it with his Winchester raised and ready to shoot.

Vlad's room was much bigger. He actually sat at a desk on the far side with his back to Bertrand, something that hadn't occurred to him when looking at the monitor. In a flash, Bertrand took in the Ikea furniture that contrasted anachronistically with the rock walls.

He pulled the trigger, but just before the gun fired, a hand reached from beside the door and shoved the barrel in the air. A fist like iron took Bertrand in the side of his rib cage, shoving the wind from one lung even as the gun was ripped from his hand.

There had been another ripper who wasn't in view on the security camera.

How stupid could he have been to think Vlad was sitting there waiting to be shot?

Bertrand rolled on his side and looked up. The bartender from Goth Knights—Nicholas—was still dressed as if for the club, topless and showing off muscles and pecs and tattoos, his dog collar in place, although today it wasn't dragging a chain.

Bertrand sprawled on the floor, hitting his head on the rock, but he kept his senses and turned his Glock in the holster, pulling the trigger several times. Red holes bloomed in Nicholas's chest, and he fell back against the door. Bertrand rolled on the floor trying to yank the gun free so that he could turn it on Vlad but a fist grabbed a Bertrand by the hair and slammed his head on the floor twice, not with the force to kill, but to daze. Blood ran into his eyes, and for a moment his muscles wouldn't respond. He lay on the floor, his view of the room sideways, his left eye closest to the floor.

Nicholas sat against wall by the door.

"I'll be all right," he said, his eyes wide and frightened. "I can feel the healing, even in my heart I can feel them healing me."

Black boots and the hem of the cloak came between them, and Nicholas screamed. Suddenly the cloak moved aside to reveal a knife at Nicholas's throat and a gloved hand under his arm. Vlad dragged Nicholas across the floor to Bertrand and the knife bit deep, causing a geyser of blood to spray on Bertrand's face. A hand grabbed the back of Bertrand's neck and shoved his mouth over Nicholas's spewing artery.

Bertrand pushed back with his tongue in panic, desperate not to drink the blood, but his nose pressed so tightly against Nicholas's skin that he was suffocating. Instinct won out over his brain, and Bertrand gasped in a mouthful of blood. He tried to spit, to hold his breath, to fight to the end not to be made into a ripper. The world hazed, his vision blurred and he drew gulping choking breaths. As he passed out he shook with a fear like no other. He swallowed blood.

It started in his stomach, a buzzing as if someone had released a swarm of fluttering insects. He was aware that he had been dropped to the floor, that he was free to move, that he could search for his gun and shoot Vlad, but his body barely acknowledged his commands, allowing him only to flip onto his side and come face to face with Nicholas's dead eyes. The young man was exceptionally pale, his blood coating his naked chest.

The flutter in Bertrand's stomach—the vibration—radiated out to his heart, through his veins and arteries to his extremities. Panic was replaced with euphoria, a euphoria he fought. He didn't want to feel this good. He didn't want to go on this ride. He just wanted to be normal and live with Joyce in his home and rebuild his life and hear children laugh—many children.

An erection rose despite all efforts to focus on the rock, on the blood and the dead body, items that would usually induce flaccidness.

"NO!" he screamed, writhing and fighting not to feel pleasure from the parasites.

He tossed his head back, the ecstasy rising, his erection harder than ever before in his life, as if it would explode rather than ejaculate. Vlad sat in his chair, upside down now from Bertrand's contorted perspective. The ripper leaned forward, his hands clasped together as he studied Bertrand's change with great interest.

"NO!" He would not give in. But his fight was in vain, and he climaxed, a throbbing and pulsing that was like no other orgasm in his life.

"Fuck! No!"

From that moment he knew he had lost, that it was an impossible fight. There was no way to beat the parasites that now flooded through his body, reproducing at a fantastic rate, releasing drugs that could control him, take over even his sex drive, his ability to choose right from wrong.

"I can. I can."

He sat up, every vein and artery in his body pulsing, he shoved with his feet on the rock floor to back away from Nicholas's body, from Vlad. Bertrand felt the rock wall against his back and stopped, gasping for breath, fighting for control.

Vlad spoke, his weathered face creased with a puzzled frown.

"You can? You can what?"

Bertrand had to fight to speak, to use his own voice. "I can choose."

"Choose what?"

"I can choose not to kill. I can choose to die."

His hand went for his Glock, but Vlad moved faster, yanking the gun from the holster before Bertrand could turn it on himself and pull the trigger. Vlad returned to his seat and again studied Bertrand with deep interest.

"Truly, I have never seen anyone fight the union so well. You are a remarkable man and you will be an incredibly strong hybrid once the conversion is complete. I think I shall name you Vlad the Incredible. That is a name worthy of you, and men will cringe to hear your name."

"Why?" Bertrand's body numbed now, a buzz as if he had consumed a six pack of beer in a hurry. "Why are you doing this?"

"To you?"

"To humanity. To civilization. Why are you the Scourge?"

"Do you not listen to your own governments? You are destroying all that God created. For many years I thought I was too late, for I didn't understand nuclear weapons until far into the sixties, and then all I could do was move deep into Africa, hoping to be far from the fallout of nuclear war. I had failed to see far enough ahead, to understand that I'd been given this affliction by God so that I could be his vengeance. If a global nuclear war had occurred, the resulting radiation would surely have been lethal to me."

"But it didn't happen." Bertrand became aware of a hum that had nothing to do with his body—an engine hum, like a large motor, but muffled.

"It hasn't happened yet." Vlad held up one gloved finger, waving it at Bertrand as he lectured. "Your scientists have warned of dangerous population growth for years. It was time to dramatically reverse the trend."

"But they were wrong." Bertrand gasped for air in between sentences. "They said widespread famine by the year 2000, but they didn't know about better crop yields. India exports food for frig's sake."

"I have lived many centuries. War always comes from too many people. In time you will come to see my wisdom. Even now I have destroyed many nuclear weapons. When I am complete, they will be gone, and so will the science that allowed them to exist. I will make the planet once again into a green place."

"You're making it into a hell that will wipe humanity from the face of the earth."

"In time humans will cease to resist and will flock to my protection. We hybrids will care for you and restrict your growth. We will control all, and you will live simply as you once did, on farms that are worked with hands rather than machines. A little blood each month will be a cheap price to pay for safety and security."

"We'll be slaves."

"Not you. You will be a master."

Bertrand wanted to feel despair but some other drug had been released, a numbing drug, one that weighted on his arms and legs, but already a notion of hunger glowed in his stomach, and not a natural hunger.

"My friends will be here soon. They'll kill us both. I still win."

"Your friends will be busy for many hours yet, and I assure you that these doors are strong. I have also prepared a collapse in the cavern that will protect us. My good man, my new Vlad, I have been at war since I was born. Do you not understand that I would never allow myself to be trapped so? There is another exit." He pointed to a man-sized tunnel to the left of his desk, a tunnel that hadn't been in view of the security camera. "In a few hours when the sun has vanished, you and I will leave your friends to celebrate their victory of the day. Tonight we will bring them true war, and you will have your first feed."

Weariness pressed on Bertrand, not the exhaustion of life but of death, an exhaustion so complete that it could not be denied. Vlad nodded, clearly understanding and knowing the stages.

"When you wake you will be hungry." Vlad turned in his chair to face his computer. "Then you will be ready to accept your new self."

Bertrand resisted sleeping but it was impossible.

The hunger rose with a vengeance—a gnawing in his stomach that felt as if he were eating himself from the inside out. Bertrand sat up, the burning accelerating to radiate out to his whole body. Vlad still sat at his computer watching the security cameras, but he must have been aware of a change in Bertrand, for he swiveled the chair to again face him.

"You can feed on Nicholas first," he said gently. "It will not give you the true rewards of living blood, but there is enough there to quell the pain until nightfall, which is soon."

It was pain. As if the parasites had heard his words, the gnawing clenched and his stomach didn't just demand, it hurt with a vicious pain.

"Your army has been wonderful." Vlad clicked through security cameras, sitting aside so that Bertrand could see people celebrating and high-fiving. They controlled the mountain. Where was Joyce? Where was Jeff? Bertrand didn't want them to see him like this, a ravenous monster. He heard nothing through his walkie and looked down to see if it was on. The battery was dead.

"You have no choice now." Vlad pointed to Nicholas's body. "There is good blood still there. Use the knife to cut down to his heart. Your friends are coming back to the cavern so I will need to detonate my charges. Fear not, this room and my escape route are carefully reinforced. We will be safe."

Joyce would die. Bertrand knew she would come looking for him and thousands of tons of rock would be brought down on her head. His body was willing to respond to commands now and he crawled toward Nicholas.

Vlad gave a pained smile and turned away. "Even you must give in to the demands of the demons inside you. That is what I always believed possessed me until modern science spoke otherwise, yet what is a demon but something that takes you over and twists your will to its needs? And surely these parasites are an affliction from hell."

He turned his back on Bertrand and concentrated on the computer.

Bertrand—still on hands and knees—reached the corpse. It smelled wet and fresh and good ... if he could just dig in far enough to find blood, even coagulated, chewy blood.

But he could choose. He was strong. His soul was dense, denser than any soul in a millennia. He was sure. He was now a believer. Bertrand crawled around Nicholas, ignoring the demands on his stomach, a craving unlike anything he had ever known. Was this what a heroin addict felt? Was it worse? His arms and legs fought him, trying to turn him back to Nicholas but he continued toward the door and his Winchester. His hand closed around the pistol grip.

He turned to face Vlad, who still faced his desk.

Bertrand pulled the trigger and the gunshot slammed his ears. The shot went through the chair and shoved Vlad against the desk.

The ripper turned, his face a mixture of shock and admiration.

Bertrand pumped in another shotgun shell.

"You are brave." Vlad stood, a dark figure somehow taller and more powerful than his short stature should allow, a gory exit wound on his lower left abdomen. "But this changes—"

Bertrand fired again, hitting him in the chest. He racked the slide and fired again, catching his shoulder and again hitting him in the chest. He pumped the slide a final time but the gun clicked empty.

Vlad had fallen onto his back by his chair and stopped moving.

But Bertrand knew this wasn't over. This was a very old ripper, one the parasites could repair. He stood—debating how to finish this forever—but he was distracted by pounding on the outer door.

Bertrand hurried to the computer, resisting all desire to bend and suck the blood from Vlad's wounds. The security image showed Jeffery and Joyce leading a large armed group into the cavern. Barry and Martin already pounded on the outer door, their figures distorted by the wide angle. Vlad must've shot the bolts to lock the door while Bertrand was unconscious.

Bertrand's body fought every command, but he retained control through heroic effort. He went through the opening in the rock and found another room and the source of the engine noise. An industrial generator, large and yellow, roared away. Spare propane canisters, some only as big as barbecue tanks, were stacked near it. An exhaust tube ran up a tunnel that opened in the wall, one that Bertrand could access by a ladder, but was so narrow he would have to crawl on his hands and knees to pass through. The escape route. Bertrand climbed on the ladder and looked into the tunnel. It ran straight and steep, and a dim orange light far up burned his eyes. Sunlight.

He hurried back to the other room to find that Vlad hadn't moved. Cut his head off? Blow his brains out? He searched frantically for his Glock. More pounding on the outer door. Bertrand rushed to open the inner door and went into the cramped security room. He could see them all out there now. One monitor showed Bobs outside the mountain organizing the former slaves onto buses, the setting sun throwing long shadows across the gravel. He wanted to hate her, but if he hadn't gone in and confronted Vlad, they'd never have known about the escape tunnel. Vlad would have lived to fight another day.

When would the charges go off to bring down the cavern? There was no countdown anywhere. Had Vlad been lying? He doubted it, and he couldn't take the chance. He could open the door to tell them, but a demon owned him and it demanded blood. He didn't dare open the outer door that they pounded on, didn't dare get close to a possible source of food. He had to get them out.

A microphone on the desk gave him the answer. He pushed a button on it and spoke.

"Joyce. Jeff. Everybody." His voice came back to him through the door as a distinct boom, the voice of a god. "You've got to get out of there. It's a trap. There are charges on the pillars in the cavern that'll go off soon and make the ceiling collapse."

"Bert," shouted Joyce. "Are you in there? Bert, please open up."

Bertrand found himself unable to talk. He lusted for her in a way that was destructive, unnatural and evil. "I can't … I can't." He fought tears and focused on the crushing pain from his gut to steady his voice. "Joyce. I'm dead. Okay? I'm totally dead, but I've killed Vlad. All that's left to do is burn our bodies to purge the parasites."

Joyce flew into a rage, hammering at the door and screaming.

Bertrand couldn't help it. He went and pressed his ear to the door to feel the pounding of her hands, the closest he would ever come again to her touch. The pounding stopped.

He went back to the microphone and saw Jeff and Barry holding Joyce back from the door.

He keyed the microphone. "You know I love you, but I can't be with you now. I'm really sorry that I'll miss our Thanksgiving date, but you have to get out of here before the charges go off. Please go."

Jeff called out. "You sure there's nothing we can do? Dude, be straight with us. Are you ripper?"

"Vlad forced blood into my mouth. I've gone through the change. I'm dead. Please, go. Barry, please take everyone to your fortress in Canada. This is going to get much worse before it gets better. Go quickly. There's nothing more you can do here and there are going to be explosions. You have to get out. I'm going to detonate a propane canister in here to burn Vlad." Bertrand found talking exhausting. He found everything exhausting except for his desire to open that door and attack. He was so hungry.

"I'll never murder for blood!" he screamed, more to his stomach than his friends. "RUN! Get out of the mountain. I'm done."

He turned away but a lump on the desk caught his attention. The hand grenade sat there like an invitation, one he hadn't noticed before. That must be what Bobs had put down. If only he had paid attention, had noticed it before, he would have opened the door to Vlad's room and tossed it in first. It could have saved him.

A thought occurred to Bertrand: could the sun save him now? Could it burn the parasites from his body without killing him? How many were in his bloodstream at this moment, and would their mass deaths cause a stroke?

It was a faint hope but he clung to it. He watched his friends run from the cavern, and it ripped his heart that Joyce wept. So she did love him. It was a wonderful and terrible revelation, but it gave him strength. He took the grenade and walked into the inner room to find Vlad sitting up and blinking at him.

"The demons will heal." It was a guttural whisper.

Bertrand fought with his desires and walked into the generator room. He grabbed a barbecue propane tank and dragged it back into Vlad's room. The ripper clearly couldn't move yet and watched with helpless interest.

"You would go to Hell?" he whispered, his strength clearly not coming back very quickly.

"I am in hell." Bertrand opened the valve on the tank and let the propane gas flow.

"Burning is a horrible way for a hybrid to die." Vlad still did not look afraid, but his fragility gave Bertrand strength.

The mountain shook with explosions. Bertrand looked up at the computer in fear. The camera showed falling rock in the cavern before the camera was destroyed and the screen went to static. Did Joyce get out on time?

"All the scriptures say that those who kill themselves will go to Hell." Vlad's voice was a bit firmer. "I believed you to be a holy man."

"I'm not killing myself. You did."

He held up the grenade so that Vlad could see it.

"So I go to meet God," said Vlad. He raised one hand. "Farewell."

"Fuck you."

Bertrand headed for the generator room and the escape tunnel, climbing the ladder quickly and squeezing into the tunnel. He found he could just get enough bend in his knees and elbows to crawl up the tunnel. It was a struggle, and the last orange light of the sun burned his eyes but he kept going, consuming the pain, paying for misjudging Bobs, for thinking he could save the world that he had known.

A shuffle behind caught his attention and he looked down between his legs. A head blocked some of the light from the generator room. Vlad was coming after him.

Bertrand looked up toward the sun and said his goodbye.

He pulled the pin on the grenade and rolled it down the steep slope of the tunnel. The stench of propane told him what would happen next, but still he turned and made one last desperate attempt to climb.

The explosion slammed his ears and the fire baked his feet.

He screamed and climbed, the pain in his legs an agony he couldn't endure.

But he didn't die. He continued to climb. Part of the little tunnel collapsed, and he had to squeeze past rock that was unforgiving. If he hadn't lost so much weight over the summer he would've been trapped there for eternity.

The air freshened, and at last he spilled out of the hole and sprawled on the mountainside, his whole body trembling with reaction as the final orange rays seared into his brain. It was the last time Bertrand would ever see the sun, and it vanished before it could cleanse.

# 35

# BARRY'S TOWER

Summer brought thunderstorms that swept in from the west and poured rain on to Barry St. John's tower in the woods, deep in Canada. Summer also brought new life. Joyce gave birth the same way she fought, with focus and anger and short sharp commands to those around her: "Water. Let go of me. Now! Here comes the baby now!"

There was a doctor at the tower, but she was short on anesthetic and was not a surgeon, so she didn't dare a cesarean when one wasn't required.

Weeks later, during the oppressive heat that fed a new thunderstorm, Jeff found Joyce a room on the third floor where the windows could open, and he fixed bars on the outside to ensure rippers couldn't get in to attack, although there had been few this way since the daytime raids Barry had led on the nearby town of Atherly during the spring, dragging them from the basements into the sun. Their detachment of Bertrand's Army now lived here, but Bobs had taken her people back to Chicago. The Erics had dissolved to go and preach their new religion far and wide.

Joyce nursed her daughter as the lightning flashed, the lights of the room off so that they could drift to sleep together, but Joyce was restless tonight, so she sat propped up in her bed and watched the lightning strike closer with each bolt, illuminating the clouds that swept in on them.

She drifted in and out of sleep. A flash silhouetted a human figure, a ripper that clung to the bars of the window, and Joyce opened her mouth to scream for Jeff. Her hand sought the Uzi on the bedside table, but her daughter nursed on, unaware of her mother's panic.

"It's me, Bert." The hoarse voice did sound like Bertrand. It had an alien quality to it, as if the vocal chords were no longer used to functioning, yet something struck to the core of Joyce's heart. This was her dead hero.

"Bert! Jesus Christ you scared me. Go to the door and Jeff'll let you in. I'll call him." But she knew this was not going to happen as much as she wanted him to be alive.

"Is she mine?"

Joyce nodded and wept. "Yes. I named her Margaret after my mother. Bert, I wish you could see her. She's so beautiful."

"Like her mother." But the voice held no emotion.

"Bert. Is it really you?"

"It's me. You won't see me again, but I'll be around. I'll watch over you, and I'll watch over her and her children. I'll be your holy ghost."

There was an edge of madness.

"Isn't there anything we can do?"

A slam of lightning outlined a skeletal frame. It was not the chubby Bertrand she had first met at the gym, but an emaciated Bertrand.

"Live. Never give into the rippers. Never be their slaves."

"Never." Joyce wanted to say more, to tell him how much she loved him, but a flash of lightning showed that he was gone.

She wept and nursed and slipped into sleep. In the morning, Jeff told her it must've been a nightmare, but Joyce knew the truth, and she never stopped looking out for him at night whenever the weather was warm and restless.

Bertrand headed south down the highway, making for the bridge over the Mattagami River gorge on his way to Chicago. He'd searched far and wide around St. John's tower, but the rippers had been eradicated. Joyce would be safe for the summer and the winter. He needed sustenance, and the only food he allowed himself was the blood of rippers. It was a starvation diet, for most of the blood was useless to him, but it dimmed the pain in his belly. Chicago still had a lot of rippers in its far-flung suburbs, so he would spend the winter there, cleansing his city. If his house still stood—his parents' house—he would live in the basement during the day. He was the monster now, but not for humans to fear. Just rippers.

He was not afraid to go home.

# ACKNOWLEDGEMENTS

I must thank so many people, but my first writing instructors made everything else happen: Dr. Margaret Docker, Associate Professor at University of Manitoba, and Melanie Fogel, former editor of *Storyteller Magazine*, who both patiently schooled this semi-literate physics graduate in grammar and other writing essentials. I would also like to thank the many people who gave their time to this novel: Mark Alliksaar, a technical instructor and cliché checker; Mark Downie, who guided the storyline; Rebecca M. Senese, beta reader extraordinaire and fellow writer; all of *The Fledglings Writers Group*, for years of work, especially Karen Danyluk, who has the copy editor eye and devoted time to proof the published versions of the 1000 Souls series; Matt A. Baker, a careful editor; Michael Custode, for great artwork on the original cover of *The Book of Bertrand* and for other cover treatments and evocative graphics; Barry Currey, for the awesome cover of this edition; Pectopah Productions, for financial backing and support; and most of all to my wife, Susan Docker, for insisting that we move ahead without fear or compromise.

### Special Thanks to You

Most importantly, thank you for reading this book. To paraphrase Tolkien, I wrote a book that I would enjoy reading myself. It delights me that you read to the end and onto these acknowledgements. I'm flattered and awed. I hope you were as engaged as my characters, and that for a brief while you were transported to a more dangerous but less complicated world.

I would love to hear from you. Visit me at **beyondtheslushpile. com** or send an email to **mike@michaelandremcpherson.com**. I'm on Facebook (Michael Andre McPherson) and Twitter @mcpherson_ mike. If I've moved you to prose, please write a quick review. Tell your friends, tell your family, make a point of bringing up the book in casual conversation. You get the idea.

Thanks so much - the 1000 live on!

### BUT WAIT! THERE'S MORE!

Keep going for a sneak peak of what's coming next.

**GENERATION APOCALYPSE**
by Michael Andre McPherson
**Book Two of** *1000 Souls*
pectopahbooks.com
**Published 2012**

# PROLOGUE

He had just turned ten when the world ended. At first it was fun, because some of the teachers stopped showing up at school. The principal, tall and angry, kept stuffing the students into the gym to watch movies, promising each day that the next would be normal. Instead, fewer and fewer of Tevy's friends came to school, and one day neither did the principal.

In the evenings, his parents spoke in anxious whispers, careful to ensure he didn't overhear, but one word often leaked out: *rippers*. He heard their neighbor, old Mr. Costa, say to his dad that there were rumors of murders happening all over Chicago, but for some reason it was never on the news. "They don't want us to know," Mr. Costa said, pointing his cane south in the general direction of city hall.

One morning his parents didn't go to work, and they kept him home, letting him play *Call of Duty* when the power was up. That was another big change: the power failing, the lights going dark, sometimes for hours on end.

One day he helped his dad board up the ground-floor windows.

"Is there a hurricane coming?" he asked, passing his dad another screw.

"Not the windy kind," his father replied.

Nights became very scary. Sometimes he heard screams and run-ning feet on the sidewalk outside, and one night Mr. Costa's house burned down, with all kinds of people standing on his lawn but none helping. Tevy's mother pulled him from the window and covered his eyes. He wanted to scream because he was afraid, but his mother whis-pered in his ear, "Don't let them hear you. We have to pretend we're not here, baby. Please don't cry. We must be silent."

Silence. He had learned that lesson well.

The next night, the world did end. The rippers came for them.

The shouting frightened him beyond all reason, and he hugged his mother with all his strength. They called out rude suggestions with foul language and promised to hurt them all if they didn't come out. He wanted to obey their commands, believing their lies, but his father knew better.

"Stay in the closet," he whispered as he shoved Tevy back amongst the shoes and the coats. "It's like hide-and-seek, but you mustn't lose. Do you understand me?"

The intensity of his father's actions, the fear in his eyes, and the plead-ing of his words warned Tevy not to argue. He had always known that his parents loved him, but from that day forward, he understood that loving parents lay down their lives for their children. Like his parents.

The last time he saw them alive, his mother was loading a revolver and his father was holding a hunting rifle. His mother blew him a hur-ried kiss. The closet door closed. Then came the shouting and breaking glass, and a whoosh accompanied by a wave of hot air and the stench of gasoline. Guns fired and his mother screamed curses at someone, foul language he had never before heard her use.

He wanted to leave the closet, but he remembered his father's last words. He wanted to scream, but he remembered his mother telling him how silence could save his life. He clamped his hand over his mouth and wept, but he didn't scream. He didn't make a sound.

But the dull roar told him that fire, or the choking smoke, would soon kill him. He had to leave the closet. Suddenly, there was a lot more gunfire and a lot more screaming, but not from his parents. Then his mother spoke her last words. "My son!" she shouted. "In the closet! Please—" Her voice choked off wetly. It wasn't a normal sound.

The closet door yanked open, letting in a billowing cloud of gray that stung his eyes and made him choke. A strange man on his hands and knees reached for him. Had there been a halo around his head?

"Come on!" He grabbed Tevy's arm and yanked him from the closet. "I'm here to save you."

Tevy climbed onto the man's back as directed and hung on around his neck as the house cracked and groaned from the flames. They spilled out onto the front porch, and the man stood, scooping Tevy into his arms and running from the house. It was the first time Tevy had seen dead bodies—real dead bodies, not like his grandfather in the coffin at the funeral home. These bodies had chunks of their skulls missing or bloody holes in their chests. They were splayed at strange angles and had nightmare-inducing expressions on their faces—gaping mouths and bloody teeth.

"We've got to get him to St. Mike's," said a woman with a machine gun. "What about his parents?"

The man, his savior, shook his head.

The woman turned, stared off into the distance for a moment, then shot one of the corpses on the lawn in rage.

Tevy understood. The world as he knew it had ended forever. But he remembered to be silent, so he bit his tongue as he wept and buried his face in the man's shoulder, breathing in the stink of a sweating saint.

———

Kayla had worried about homesickness when she showed up at Atherley College, but by the second week she was more concerned about where she could buy a gun. Her roommate, Ashley, had gone missing, and there was talk of a serial killer hunting around the campus. The police said they shouldn't worry, that Ashley had probably just succumbed to the strain of college and headed down south to live on the streets of Toronto or maybe even Chicago.

Neither Kayla nor the other girls in their student residence believed that for a second, and they all found it disconcerting that the police were downplaying Ashley's disappearance.

"Frigging cops have no clue," Rachel said. She was in her third year and a lot older than Kayla, who wouldn't turn eighteen until December. "Last time a girl was assaulted was in my first year, and they practically locked us all down for a month until they caught the asshole. This time they tell us to go about our business as usual? I got this." She showed them all the Taser her dad had sent. "Get some protection girls, and I'm not talking about condoms."

But Kayla's parents were committed pacifists, even though Sioux Lookout, the little town where they lived, made a lot of money from tourist hunting and fishing. The town was so far north that the only way to go farther was by plane, and she already missed the sound of those little aircraft taking off early every morning to fly campers up to the high lakes. She considered dropping out and going home, but her mom suggested she stay at the college.

"Something's going on in town," she said on the phone. "There've been a lot of house fires. Your father and I are thinking of taking Kevin and heading down to a hotel in Thunder Bay for a few days."

That frightened Kayla. Why would they take her little brother and abandon the family home just because an arsonist was loose in town? What about their teaching jobs? The news reports didn't mention the problems in Sioux Lookout, but they didn't mention Ashley's disappearance either.

Kayla found Rachel in the common area reading a textbook, her dark hair tied back in a tight ponytail.

"I need to buy a gun," said Kayla.

Rachel looked up from the book, and her expression showed approval rather than surprise. "That's pretty much impossible to do legally now." She slapped the book closed.

"I don't care about legally. It's my body and no one's gonna take me without a fight."

"My dad knows a guy." Rachel stood and stretched. In another time—a month ago—Kayla might have thought Rachel needed to lose a few pounds, but that seemed so irrelevant and petty now. "Dad's decided I need an upgrade from the Taser. He's getting me a Glock. If you want, I can get you one too."

Kayla did want, but her weekly allowance from Mom and Dad hadn't been deposited into her bank account yet. "How much?"

Rachel smiled. "Don't worry. You can pay in installments. We're doing it for a few other girls too. Dad says we need to be our own police force here, watch out for each other."

And they did. No one went anywhere without an armed partner, but it turned out this serial killer wasn't just interested in women. Boys started to disappear, and even a few professors. The college president responded by going on a rant about absenteeism. By mid-October, rumors began to circulate about a cult of serial killers. Some guy down in Chicago was all over the Internet talking about rippers—blood drinkers. He said you couldn't believe what you see on the news, and Kayla fervently agreed. Her parents had found Thunder Bay just as dangerous as Sioux Lookout.

"It seems like a house burns down every night," said her mother in a quick phone call. "We've decided we're better off at home, and things seemed to have quieted down since the band council took over policing from the OPP."

When Kayla's physics professor didn't turn up one day, she decided to go home. Teaching assistants now taught half of her classes anyway, and they seemed as lost as everyone else as to why the campus was in a state of crisis unnoticed by the administration.

But she was too late.

She managed to hitch a ride in a rusting Jeep Cherokee that took her all the way to Sioux Lookout. The driver was young, Ojibwa, and cute. He told her his name was Ted, but she was pretty sure that was just the name he used with non–First Nations.

He was twenty and chatty, his jeans snug fitting and his muscles lean. He'd been out west working on the oil sands projects, but things had gotten weird and his grandmother had asked him to come home.

"The farmers," he said about his journey thus far. "They're burning the fields out in the Prairies instead of harvesting—some kind of protest, the newspapers say. Don't know much but it seems stupid to me."

He continued to say, "Don't know much," several times during the two-hour ride, but Kayla began to believe he knew quite a bit, and she was really glad he was there when they pulled up in front of the burnt shell of her childhood home.

He let her cry for a while on the front lawn, and his hand on her shoulder was a comfort. Her knees were getting wet in the fresh snow as she let the tension of the last few weeks pour out. She was detached, almost watching herself cry. She couldn't stop.

"Sorry," he said finally. "You should come to the rez with me. Gran said I had to be there before sunset. She said that was really important."

Kayla considered saying it was okay, that she just wanted to be a here a bit longer, that she'd stay at the Sunset Motel, but she was angry. Someone was going to pay for this, and she had to be alive to deliver that punishment.

She went with him to the little bungalow in the woods, and his grandmother had clucked and shouted at him and reached high to cuff his head, but she reluctantly let Kayla stay the night on the frayed couch.

The next morning, Kayla helped Gran with the dishes while Ted went off to a band-council meeting. If Gran spoke English, she didn't use it with Kayla. Ted came back with a grim expression.

"We got to go. Most are going."

"Where?"

"Most are heading up north, flying to the high lakes, away from... people."

Had he been going to say white people? He looked embarrassed, guilty.

"I can't go there."

He nodded his agreement. A long chat broke out in Ojibwa between Gran and Ted. It rose to shouting, but never aggressive, just both trying to be heard over the other, both used to talking this way.

"I can take you back to the college," he said finally. A four-hour round trip for him.

"I can't ask you to do that. If I could just get a ride into town, I'll get the bus tomorrow." Every Monday morning a bus headed down to

Atherley with people who spent the week working there or at the pulp mill in Dryden.

"There won't be a bus." He turned and began zipping up her pack for her.

"Well, I'll hitch a ride then. Don't worry, I can take care of myself."

But she didn't feel that way. Had her parents gone back to Thunder Bay? She'd checked her phone about a hundred times during the night, calling her mother, texting her little brother, but there had been no replies. In her heart she knew there was only one reason that little brat hadn't texted her back with some amusing or snarky message, or a least an excited 140 character tweet about the house fire. He had always loved trying to fit his sentences into exactly 140 characters.

"It's not safe to hitch a ride." Ted opened the door, letting cold air into the little house. "There are people in the day who work for them—for the rippers."

And Kayla knew the world had changed forever. They were talking about them, the serial killers that slashed throats and drank blood, the ones that guy in Chicago, Bertrand Allan, kept talking about in his YouTube broadcasts. The rippers were humans that had changed, that had millions of strange cell-sized parasites in their blood and their organs, parasites that only allowed them to digest blood. No other food could sustain rippers.

"Thanks," she said to Ted. "Really, I don't know how I can thank you."

They rode in silence back to the college, the trees frosted with fresh snow, the road unplowed. Ted's Jeep had four-wheel drive, but he rarely used it because it sucked too much gas. "A lotta gas stations closed. It's hard to come by."

She tried to give him every bit of cash in her wallet even though he had refused and even seemed insulted.

"You'll need gas," she said. "Please, you probably saved my life."

He took it in the end, perhaps just to get her to stop. "It's probably worthless paper anyway," he said before he sped away, clearly anxious to get back to his grandmother before sunset.

Kayla found the dorm in a panic, girls crying and packing.

"What's going on?" she said to Rachel, who wasn't crying but was stuffing a pack with clothing.

"We're getting the hell out of here." Rachel suddenly stopped and looked up. "Hey, I thought you'd gone home."

Kayla didn't want to appear weak, but it was too much. She shook her head and bit her lip, unable to speak but successfully fighting back the tears—until Rachel swept her up in a hug.

"Oh, baby. It's okay. It's okay," Rachel said over and over as Kayla wept. "We've got a place to go, a safe place."

"Where?" Kayla pushed back from the hug and wiped her cheeks.

"It's a new student residence about a mile from here, but it's built like a fort. I don't know why but everybody already calls it 'The Keep.' The contractor who built it is sending a bus over for anyone who wants to join him—and they've got a lot of guns."

"Good." Kayla pulled out her Glock and looked at it for a moment, sensing the new life that was before her. "I'd like an upgrade to a machine gun."

---

**Read it now.** Visit pectopahbooks.com to find the most convenient way to buy.

# *1000 SOULS*: THE SERIES

Book One
**SACRIFICE the LIVING**
*The End is Now*
Published: 2011

Book Two
**GENERATION APOCALYPSE**
*No One Dies of Old Age*
Published: 2012

Book Three
**HERETICS FALL**
*Hell Hath No Fury*
Published: 2014

Book Four
**VAMPIRE ROAD**
*Journey Home*
Published: 2011

Book Five
**JACKY'S WAR** (Working Title)
Anticipated Release Date: 2015


**Buy the books, connect with the author and sign up for exclusive bonus offers:** pectopahbooks.com.

---

**What soul do you host?** Find out at 1000souls.com.

# ABOUT THE AUTHOR

Michael Andre McPherson earned a bachelor's degree in physics from the University of Toronto, but soon found his true love of writing after a trip to Afghanistan.

Working in the film industry for more than ten years, McPherson's assignments ranged from production managing low-budget independent films to camera assisting on Hollywood blockbusters. He has since left the film industry and now co-owns a multimedia software development company.

McPherson's short stories have been published in *Storyteller Magazine* and have won various awards in the Bloody Words Mystery Convention's short story writing contest. His story "Working with Psychos" won first prize in the 2006 Great Canadian Story contest, while he placed third in the James Patrick Baen Memorial writing contest for another short story, "Acclimatization." He is currently hard at work on his 1000 Souls series.

McPherson lives in Toronto with his wife and three children.

www.ingramcontent.com/pod-product-compliance
Lightning Source LLC
Chambersburg PA
CBHW030016180626
46810CB00001B/63